One Night of Passion

ELIZABETH BOYLE

One Night of Passion

An Avon Romantic Treasure

AVON BOOKS
An Imprint of HarperCollinsPublishers

AVON BOOKS
An Imprint of HarperCollins*Publishers*
10 East 53rd Street
New York, New York 10022-5299

To my good friend and fellow author,
Jaclyn Reding
Always there to lend a sympathetic ear
and to prop me up when all seems lost.
She is what good friends are all about.

Danvers Hall
1818

There are not many who are tossed out of the ton amid scandal and ruin and then return to find themselves fêted and rewarded. Such has been my misfortune.

Since my restoration to Society's good graces, I have received entreaty after entreaty to recount my perilous adventures.

In fairness, I must confess, I have given my eager audiences a well-told tale, full of duplicity and danger, of great follies and foes overcome. And to every one of them I have lied.

For my story is, and always was, a love story.

If I were to tell the truth, I would regale them with the heroic deeds of my impossible, formidable Georgie, my dearest and enchanting Cyprian, and how in one night of passion she stole my heart, and in the process saved a nation.

Colin, Baron Danvers

Chapter 1

London
1799

"**G**iven the evidence and the documentation offered to this court, I have no other choice,
Captain Danvers, than to see you relieved of all duties
and obligations in His Majesty's Navy." With those
words said, the Lord High Admiral brought his gavel
down on the court bar. The responding thump, like the
last clap of a hammer on a coffin nail, was followed by
stunned silence.

After all, the packed hearing room at the Admiralty
had just witnessed the end of one of the navy's most
brilliant careers, some said one that rivaled even Nelson's.

Few doubted they would ever again see such a pre-
cipitous and fatal descent in their lifetime.

There wasn't a man in the room, officer or jack tar,

who wasn't saying a prayer of thanksgiving that it wasn't his hide being flayed, his livelihood sinking to the bottom of the icy Atlantic.

But then again, most of the men in the room held their posts as men bound by the honor and code of the sea, the written and unwritten edicts that Captain Colin Danvers had flagrantly violated. No one disputed the damning evidence of his treason and duplicity. Not even Nelson, the captain's staunch supporter and mentor all these years, had offered to attest to the man's innocence and character given the irrefutable facts.

So the future that had once shone like the North Star for Captain Danvers now looked as bleak and murky as a Thames fog.

Cashiered out of the navy.

Forfeiture of all his prize money—a sum that had made him the envy of his peers.

It was a moment worthy of silence.

As for the man himself, Captain Danvers stood before the Admiralty Board, his back ramrod straight, his shoulders squared like a taut reef bar. And despite the fact that he'd just been cast out, he faced his judges with the same indomitable spirit that had been his undoing.

"Is that all, my lords?" he had the audacity to ask.

The Lord High Admiral blustered, his whiskers shaking in anger. "Consider yourself lucky you aren't hanging from a yardarm, you insolent pup."

Several heads nodded in agreement. Truly, if it had been any other man, he would have found himself swinging before the day was out. But lofty familial connections had kept that prospect at bay.

Danvers, treasonous bastard that he was, had recently inherited his father's barony. And if that wasn't enough, the captain's maternal grandfather was none other than the Duke of Setchfield, a man few people dared cross.

No, the Admiralty couldn't hang Captain Danvers, but the punishment they'd enacted was just as effective.

They'd taken the man from the sea. From Society. From a life among his peers. A life about to be spent, some said, landlocked in a hell of disdain and scorn.

In the back of the hearing room, a pipe whistled the end of the session, and the trio of judges rose in unison.

Danvers bowed to them, making an elegant and noble show of it. Then, as if he had just been handed the command of the entire fleet, he turned smoothly on one heel and, with his head held high, began the long march out of the room. The crowd melted apart, leaving him a lonely aisle. He walked past the downcast glances, the whispered observations, and, by many, the cut direct as they turned their backs to him.

Yet as he made his departure, it was as if he didn't see any of it.

Damned, it was observed by an old captain hours later at one of the officers' clubs, *if the bastard didn't walk out of there smiling like the devil himself.*

Georgiana Escott stood before the door to her uncle's private dining room, girding herself for the confrontation that was about to take place. The letter clenched in her hand, outlining the latest indignity to be heaped upon her by her uncaring relation, was the final straw in a lifetime of enduring her uncle's disinterest and parsimony.

If only Mrs. Taft hadn't died, she thought. Then Georgie and her sister, Kit, would still be safely ensconced in the lady's Penzance home where their uncle had deposited them for fostering eleven years earlier after their parents' deaths.

Uncle Phineas had wanted nothing to do with his orphaned nieces then, so why should he go to all this fuss now?

Really, Georgie decided, if there was blame to place for this debacle, it was entirely the vicar's fault.

If the righteous man hadn't been so scandalized at the idea of Georgie and Kit remaining in Mrs. Taft's small cottage after the lady's untimely death and taken it upon himself to write to their uncle, she would not be in this position.

Then again, if the vicar had known the truth about Mrs. Taft's past, he and his wife probably wouldn't have called on the lady at all and counted her as one of his "finest" parishioners.

Oh, bother the interference of men. Georgie paced in front of the dining room doors. *They just go about arranging women's lives without so much as a by your leave.*

Well, she wasn't going to stand for it.

And certainly not this, she thought, clenching the letter in her hand even tighter. Marriage to a man four times her age! A man reputed to be the worst reprobate in all of England!

Luckily for Georgie, Lady Finch, an old family friend, had written her detailing the wild rumors circulating the gossipy *ton* regarding her impending betrothal to Lord Harris. Knowing Uncle Phineas, Georgie had little doubt that he probably would have informed her of her nuptials with just enough time to dress for the ceremony.

Especially considering that her intended bridegroom had already buried nine wives.

Georgie had no intention of being the tenth. Why, even that horrid old sot Henry the Eighth had had the good sense to go and die after six.

She straightened her shoulders and her resolve, and proceeded into the dining room without knocking.

Better to beard the lion in his den, Mrs. Taft had always said. But then she'd also added that surprise and cunning were essential tools in any lady's repertoire when dealing with the deadliest of all beasts—men.

And beastly was a perfect description of Uncle Phineas.

"Uncle, I must speak to you," she said, leaving him sputtering over his soup at her untimely interruption.

"What the devil do you want?" Phineas Escott, Viscount Brockett, demanded once he'd finally regained his composure.

Georgie stood her ground. "What is this news that I am to be wed?"

Her uncle shot an angry glance in his wife's direction.

Lady Brockett shook her head, her fat sausage curls bounding this way and that in alarm and denial. "I said nothing to the girl, Phineas. Not one word."

"Aunt Verena had nothing to do with this, Uncle." Georgie wasn't overly fond of her all-too-selfish aunt, but she wasn't going to let the woman bear the brunt of her husband's displeasure. "I received this letter not an hour ago from Lady Finch. She states she has it on good authority that I am to be wed."

"How did you get your hands on that?" he demanded. "I gave orders for her letters to be—" He stopped short of admitting that he had been intercepting the girls' private correspondence, so instead he turned the blame back to her. "A thief, that's what I've got for a niece. A Seven Dials pickpocket under my roof."

"Uncle, never mind Lady Finch," Georgie said, not wanting to admit how she had obtained the letter. "I will have an answer. Am I to be wed?"

Lord Brockett huffed and sputtered, and then wiping his chin in a great display of impatience said, "Yes. And I'll brook none of your saucy tongue on the matter. The papers were signed this afternoon, and the only thing left is for the banns to be read."

Georgie's entire body shook with anger and the desire to give her uncle a lashing the likes of which he had probably never heard, though most likely deserved. However, she clung to her resolve and held herself steady with every ounce of mettle she possessed. "Is Lady Finch correct that my intended is Lord Harris?"

Again Uncle Phineas's accusing glare spun toward his wife.

The curls bobbed and danced in denial once again. "I haven't breathed a word of it to anyone, my dear," Aunt Verena said. "I swear it."

He looked anything but convinced as he took a sip of his wine, his hard gaze swinging back to Georgie. "You should consider yourself a lucky girl," he told her. "You'll be a countess. Which is far above what the likes of you deserves, if you ask me."

"I don't give a fig about becoming a countess," she

replied. "Not if it means marrying some infirm rotter, old enough to be my great-grandfather."

"Bah!" Uncle Phineas shot her a glance that said he considered her the stupidest girl alive. "Don't you see that this is to your advantage? Harris is old, I'll grant you that, but he has no children and several fine estates that are not entailed. It will all be yours once he turns up his toes. And he'll as likely die before the year is out, either from some ailment or another, or go aloft to get away from that scold's tongue of yours."

He laughed, a rude guffaw of a noise that only made Georgie clench her teeth tighter to restrain herself from knocking him over the head with the nearest silver salver.

"I'll not marry him, Uncle. I will not." Georgie took a deep breath. "According to Lady Finch, he'll demand . . . demand . . ." She had never understood Society's strict need to mince words, and she certainly wasn't going to now. Not when there was so much at stake. "Oh bother," she said. "Demand an examination before we are to be wed."

Uncle Phineas's buggy eyes blinked several times, obviously trying to ignore what she was hemming and hawing about.

So Georgie spelled it out. "An examination of my person by his physician to determine if I'm a virgin."

This forthright outburst sent her aunt swooning in her chair, while Uncle Phineas turned a stormy shade of red at the declaration of such an unmentionably private matter.

"Have you no decency, girl?" He took a fortifying swallow of his wine. "Though what should I expect, raised as you were by that disreputable harridan."

"A woman you hired, Uncle," Georgie pointed out. "And paid a pittance for the privilege."

"Bah," he said, casting aside her comment with an indignant flutter of his napkin. "You'll marry Harris, and I'll hear not another word on the matter. Now get back to your room and leave us to finish our dinner in peace."

Georgie held her ground. "How could you approve of such a man? Worse yet, this horrid examination?"

"The Harrises have always demanded that their brides be virgins, and the current earl is a little more particular than most." Uncle Phineas took another gulp of wine. "Apparently, the last Lady Harris wasn't as pure as her family assured him. So this time he isn't taking any chances. He demanded that verification be part of the betrothal agreement. And that's that. I'll not hear another word of it. His physician will be here on the morrow, so there is nothing you can do about it. You'll submit to this . . . this . . . this *examination*," he finally sputtered out, "if I have to have every footman in the house hold you down."

Tomorrow? So soon?

Georgie's knees quaked, her stomach turning over. She thought she might get sick, right there and then on Aunt Verena's best Turkish carpet. Not that it wouldn't be poetic, but it certainly wouldn't help her case. So she steadied her nerves and tried to think.

She and Kit could run away. Flee town.

How? They had no money, no family to shelter them, nowhere to go. At least not anywhere that Uncle Phineas wouldn't find them.

Georgie shook her head. "How can you do this to me, your own niece?"

Before Uncle Phineas could reply, Aunt Verena stepped in. "This isn't your uncle's doing, Georgette. Your guardian found the arrangements highly favorable. All your uncle did was to do you the favor of finding a willing marriage partner."

"My guardian?" Georgie stared at her easily befuddled aunt, who had yet to remember either her or Kit's name once in all these years. "Whatever do you mean? Uncle Phineas is my guardian."

"Verena, enough," Lord Brockett hissed under his breath.

"I won't have her speaking ill of you, my dear," Aunt Verena retorted. "She might as well know who is truly answerable for this. While your Uncle Phineas has had all the responsibility and heartache of caring for you and Katherine—"

"Kathleen," Georgie corrected.

"Oh, yes, yes. Kathleen, if you must. But that doesn't change the fact that your uncle and I, your dearest and only relations, have seen fit to oversee your welfare since your parents' deaths, while your legal guardian, that dreadful Lord Danvers, hasn't cared two whits about you ungrateful girls," the woman said before her husband could muzzle her.

Dearest relations? That was stretching matters a bit far.

Uncle Phineas and Aunt Verena had packed the girls off for fostering in Penzance three days after their parents had been laid to rest. And not once in the eleven years that followed had there been so much as a visit or even a letter hinting at such "concern" from their only relations.

No, concern had been the sole domain of Mrs. Taft

and her seafaring husband, Captain Taft. They had looked out for the girls with all the concern and, yes, love that their relations would never have thought necessary.

Georgie looked from her uncle to her aunt and then back to her uncle. "Is this true?" she asked him. "Is this Lord Danvers my legal guardian?"

Her uncle's nose twitched, while his brow furrowed into one dark line. "Yes," he finally admitted. "Your father left what money there was and your guardianship to Lord Danvers's care. But make no mistake about it, I have borne the full brunt of your expenses. Your guardian has done little but approve a few meager expenditures and fob off his responsibilities on me." He huffed a few times and then tossed his napkin down on the table.

Oh, the devil take all, Georgie thought. Not only did she have Uncle Phineas directing her life, but now she also had some unknown and obviously uncaring guardian making her life miserable.

Didn't any of these men have better things to do?

"Then I demand an audience with Lord Danvers," she said. "I'll tell him what I've told you. I won't marry Lord Harris."

"Lord Danvers hasn't time to listen to the complaints of a self-serving chit. The documents are all signed and the announcements will be made in the papers day after tomorrow."

"Surely this Lord Danvers can't be so heartless as to marry me off without seeking my counsel?"

"Your counsel? Why would he want that?" Uncle Phineas shook his head in the same contemptuous way he did when Aunt Verena complained about the servants pilfering the good sherry or her inability to find a milliner who understood her difficulties in finding the perfect hat for her head. "Consult a woman about marriage. What utter nonsense!"

Georgie glanced over at the salver again, but restrained herself. "Hardly so, if I am the one who has to bear the indignity of this examination, let alone share a bed with a man who is rumored to carry the pox."

"*The pox*," Aunt Verena gasped, as if just saying the words would be her undoing. She began to swoon in earnest, her head lolling one way, then the other, her yellow curls dancing like daffodils in a spring breeze, her breath coming in big wheezy huffs. "My salts! My vinaigrette!"

Lord Brockett reached over and patted his wife's hand. "Steady there, old girl."

"Such vulgarity," Aunt Verena managed to gasp. "And at dinner, no less."

"Now see what you've done, you faithless chit," Uncle Phineas said, turning his attention back to Georgie. "I can see my money was ill-spent on your upbringing. If that worthless Taft woman weren't dead, I'd insist on getting every shilling back. Why, you sound like a Penzance doxy, not a decent miss about to become a countess." He picked up his wineglass, then frowned when he discovered it empty, so he reached for the decanter. "Now off with you, baggage. I would like to finish my meal in peace."

Georgie leaned over the table and moved the decanter out of his grasp. She met his angry stare with a stubborn one of her own. He could say all he wanted about Mrs. Taft, for certainly she hadn't been the best choice to teach the girls to be ladies. But right now,

Georgie was thankful that she had learned other lessons from the worldly woman—like how to stand up for herself.

"Uncle, if you have no say in this marriage matter, then I will discuss it with Lord Danvers. Summon him here. Tonight if you must."

He waved her off. "Impossible. The man is tied up with his own problems. And most likely has fled town by now. He was convicted of treason this morning, or so says the *Times*." He shoved the newspaper lying beside his plate toward her. "You ought to consider yourself lucky that I had some say in this, or there is no telling who you would be engaged to right now."

"A traitor?" She glanced down at the headline and saw only too clearly that on this, her uncle was being honest. *Treason*. Her guardian had been convicted of treason. Other words from the long, detailed article leapt out at her.

Dishonorable. Cowardly. Appalling.

What had her father been thinking in leaving his children's guardianship to such a man?

For the first time in her life, Georgie found herself wishing that her uncle *was* her guardian. And as much as it graveled her to admit it, she needed his assistance.

Desperately.

Why, she'd even cater to him if she must, for the specter of some old, smelly man taking her to his bed was enough to restrain her temper over the situation.

"Uncle, you did promise me a Season," she said, edging the wine decanter a little closer to him, like a tempting bribe. "Let me have it so I can at least try to gain a better offer. 'Tis only three months' time."

"A Season? For you?" Uncle Phineas shook his head.

"Out of the question. Good money out the door on that one. Your sister mayhap, for she'll fetch a fine fortune with some help from your Aunt Verena. But you? Hardly." He laughed, and his merriment stung even if it held some measure of truth.

At one and twenty, she was a little old to be venturing into the Marriage Mart, and she'd be the first to admit she wasn't the delicate and cultured miss preferred by the men of the *ton*.

She was too tall, too rounded of figure to be called lithe or petite. And far too headstrong ever to keep her opinions strictly on such safe subjects as the weather or her favorite flavor of ices at Gunter's. Especially when her favorite topics were Italian art and innovations in navigation.

Still, it didn't hurt to try. There had to be some man out there who would take her off her uncle's hands. She cast aside the last remaining shreds of her pride and resorted to begging.

"Surely, Uncle, even you can spare me the consideration of a Season, and if not for me, then out of respect for my father's memory."

The moment she said the words, she knew she'd gone too far, for Uncle Phineas's face went a mottled shade almost as ruddy as the wine in the decanter.

"Bloody consideration? I've gone and found you a husband worth twenty thousand a year, and you throw it back at me like some spoiled Bath miss. And how dare you call on your father's memory as if he were some saint. Bah! He made his choice when he took your mother to wife. French trash, that one. And did he listen to his family or friends? No! Well, he learned his lesson the hard way when she murdered him, and I'll not see this family disgraced again with a runaway marriage or some equally grievous scandal." He leaned across the table and shook a finger at her. "Listen very carefully to me, gel, and don't even think of brooking another word on the matter. You'll marry Harris and you'll be well pleased in the bargain." His finger went from waggling in warning to pointing at the door.

For a moment, Georgie considered all the things she could say, all the arguments she could offer, but she knew they would be useless.

There was only one thing left to do.

Take matters into her own hands.

As the door to the dining room slammed shut, Verena shook her head and let loose a long-suffering sigh of exasperation. "What a burden children are. Aren't you glad we never had any?" She paused for a moment and took a recuperative sip of her wine, her gaze still resting on the spot where Georgiana had reduced their pleasant dinner to such a terrible scene.

The girl was nothing but an uncontrollable hoyden—why, it was a miracle Phineas had found her a husband at all considering her ill manners and questionable breeding.

Questionable breeding.

That notion gave Verena a terrible start. What if the girl wasn't a . . .

"Have you considered, my dear," she began, struggling to find the right words to broach such a delicate subject, "that your niece may not pass Lord Harris's exacting standards?"

Brockett nodded. "Of course. That Taft woman was

a disreputable hag—albeit a cheaply had one. So I have no doubts that she let the chit run wild. Lord knows what trouble the gel found around the docks of Penzance. Why, that nosy vicar said she went down there daily to watch the ships come and go."

At this Verena's eyes widened with horror.

Young ladies near docks? Dear Lord, what kind of men had their Georgette been in contact with?

Oh, they might as well start packing for the country now.

For as Phineas had explained it, they were to receive Georgie's dowry for allowing her the privilege of becoming Lady Harris. Lord Harris's havey-cavey reputation amongst the *ton*, coupled with his history of losing wives under highly suspect conditions, was enough to make his attentions toward any marriageable miss unacceptable—earl or no. Even the well-to-do *cits* about town, who'd all but give up their fortunes to see one of their daughters become a countess, were unwilling to go that far to advance themselves socially.

In truth, Lord Harris was beyond the pale.

Yet for the Brocketts he appeared like a saving angel. With their bills and accounts having gone unpaid for several years now, and threats of foreclosure surrounding them, they needed Georgie's dowry badly.

Money that should have been theirs to begin with, or so Phineas had claimed. Money from Phineas's mother's dower holdings that had been willed to his younger brother, Franklin, and then to Georgiana and Kathleen, passing over Phineas and Verena completely.

Oh, life was so unfair at times, Verena thought. That two such awful girls should be so rich, when their relations had pockets to let.

Luckily for them, Lord Harris hadn't been concerned at all about Georgie's fortune—all he had wanted was another bride to hopefully get with child.

And a virgin one at that.

That point troubled Verena more than she cared to admit. For if Georgie wasn't as innocent as they had promised Lord Harris, then the money would not be forthcoming.

And where would that leave them? Run out of the city? Forced into disgrace?

The very thought left Verena feeling ill. She reached once again for her ever-present bottle of vinaigrette.

"What if she doesn't pass? What will you do?" she asked Phineas, tears threatening to spill down her cheeks.

Her husband leaned back in his chair and wiped at his greasy chin. "Then I will give the old goat the younger one for a wife. She's a frightful piece of baggage, but far too young to have gotten herself into *that* kind of trouble." He smiled at his wife, and reached over to pat her plump fingers. "Never fear, Verena, one way or another, one of those girls will be Lady Harris before the month is out, and you and I'll not have to fret any longer."

Georgie came barreling out of the dining room and nearly tripped over her thirteen-year-old sister, Kathleen, who was kneeling at the closed door.

"Kit!" she whispered, not wanting her aunt and uncle to discover her sister eavesdropping. It would only add to their always growing list of the sisters' unpardonable sins.

She caught her young sibling by the arm and pulled

her away from the dining room and toward the stairs. "How many times have I told you listening at doors is going to get you into trouble!"

Ignoring her sister's admonishment, Kit shook herself free and launched right into the situation at hand. "What are you going to do, Georgie? You can't marry that awful man!"

"I don't know," she confessed. Then she glanced away from Kit's worried expression, and hurried up the stairs to their attic refuge in the long-unused Brockett nursery.

"Uncle can't do this to you. It isn't fair," Kit complained, following hot on her heels.

"There doesn't seem to be much choice in it," she told her as they entered the room. *At least not right this minute.* Georgie closed the door behind them and let out a long, desperate sigh.

Pacing across the threadbare carpet, she tried to think of some way out of this despicable betrothal. But what could she do in so short a time? And what would she do in the morning when Lord Harris's personal physician arrived?

Georgie's stomach lurched anew, so she settled down onto the shabby window seat, hugging her trembling legs to her chest. Lady Finch's letter, still clutched in her hand, fluttered to the floor.

Kit followed and flounced down on the carpet near Georgie, taking up the dropped correspondence and smoothing out the wrinkled pages. "What reason did Uncle Phineas give? I couldn't hear everything." She smiled sheepishly at her admission, but offered no apologies for her behavior. "Surely he can't mean to force you into this—even if he is our guardian, he is still family. And family wouldn't do that to one another, would they?"

At this Georgie laughed, a weak and bitter noise. She turned and gazed into Kit's earnest and fearful gaze. "Family may not, but our relations have never considered us such. As it is, the problem lies in the fact that Uncle Phineas isn't our real guardian. Aunt Verena let slip that Father left the legal responsibilities of our care to a Lord Danvers. Apparently this marriage is his idea."

"Lord Danvers? Who is he?"

Georgie shook her head. "I haven't the least notion. Tonight was the first time I've ever heard of him."

"Do you think Mrs. Taft knew of this?"

"No," Georgie said. "Of that I'm certain." Mrs. Taft might have been deficient in many ways as a foster parent, but if she had known that someone other than Uncle Phineas had held the purse strings, she would have moved heaven and earth to see that "her girls" had been allowed the privileges and tutelage that other young ladies of their rank were afforded. Money had always been scarce in the Taft household, as the captain was often away on long voyages, and any extra money he did bring home was usually invested back into his ship.

No, there was no way that Mrs. Taft had been aware of this Lord Danvers.

But now that Georgie was, and once she'd undone her engagement, she'd find this scurrilous man and see to it that he never presumed to order her life in such a high-handed manner again.

Or Kit's either.

"You can't let this happen," her sister said, looking

up from Lady Finch's letter. "You just can't. We could go to this Lord Danvers and appeal to his sense of honor."

"I doubt he knows what the word means," Georgie told her. "Apparently, he was court-martialed today by the Admiralty. Obviously, dishonorable conduct is second nature to the man."

Kit frowned. "Oh, that was what was being said about someone being a traitor. I thought you were referring to Uncle Phineas."

Georgie smiled. "That goes without saying."

They both laughed.

Kit took Georgie's hand and gave it a squeeze. "You'll just have to find this Lord Danvers and convince him of the error of his ways. Look how well you've done with me. I hardly ever eavesdrop now."

Georgie's gaze rolled upward. If only eavesdropping were Kit's lone sin. She also had a penchant for stealing, but thankfully today her talents had resulted in the retrieval of Lady Finch's letter from Uncle Phineas's desk before he could toss it away, as she suspected he'd done with several other of the dear lady's missives.

"Rest assured, I plan on finding this rogue, and when I'm done with him, he shall possess a full understanding of the meaning of honor and duty. But first I have to find a way to stop this engagement."

Kit perked up. "Lady Finch mentions an examination," she said, pointing to the paragraphs in which the horrified lady had informed Georgie of Lord Harris's legendary and nearly fanatical insistence that his brides be virgins. "She says Lord Harris will only have you if you can be 'verified as unbreached and untouched.' " Her sister paused, glancing back over the words one more time, a puzzled look on her face.

"You shouldn't be reading that," Georgie snapped, snatching the overly informative pages away from her all-too-curious sister.

Kit smirked and grabbed the pages back before Georgie could stop her. "Well, what if you were? Touched, that is. You know, ruined." Her eyes sparkled with a devious blaze. "Lady Finch says quite clearly that Lord Harris will only marry you if you are free from such a blemish of reputation. If all you have to do, Georgie, is ruin yourself, then what are you waiting for?"

"Kathleen Oriana Escott, you shouldn't even know about such things, let alone suggest that your own sister engage in them," Georgie said, trying to use her most severe tone, though in the back of her mind she chastised herself for not thinking of it first.

Kit got up from the floor and curled up into the opposite corner of the window seat. "Aren't you already ruined, as it is? That's what Aunt Verena said when you went out walking by yourself that one morning."

"No, unfortunately I don't think a solitary walk in the park will be enough."

"You'd have thought you'd been touched by half the men in London by the fuss Aunt Verena kicked up. And just for going for a walk." Kit sighed. "I wish we were still in Penzance."

"So do I." Their uncle's house was so very different from the sunny and comfortable cottage where Mrs. Taft had made a home for them, Georgie sat back in the seat, laying her cheek against the cold windowpane. The chill ran all the way to her soul.

For even if it was possible to become ruined in one night, it would preclude her from ever having the kind of life she'd hoped one day to find.

For in her heart of hearts, she'd always dreamt that eventually she'd find her own small piece of love. That she might feel the same windswept thrill she got from watching the grand ships sail out of Penzance into brilliant sunsets, bound for exotic lands and adventures that she could only imagine.

And imagine she had. For when Captain Taft was in port, he'd given the girls free rein on his ship. During those precious weeks, Georgie would indulge her dreams by "sailing" his ship, the *Sybaris*, to a myriad of exotic countries.

Her imaginings were only fed further by the captain's exaggerated tales of adventure, while his rough-and-tumble crew had taken the orphaned girls to their hearts, spoiling them like a bevy of indulgent uncles. From them, Georgie and Kit gained an education in knots and lines, in sea lore, in climbing to dizzying heights atop the mainmast, until they both put many a man to shame with their rare talents.

And at night, when the stars twinkled above in a glittering array, Georgie had cast up just as many wishes that one day she'd find a man who'd indulge her dreams of adventure and faraway places—this improbable knight would take her far away from England, as well as from the poverty and obscurity that ruled her life.

On the deck of that foreign-bound ship, her admirer would gaze at her with rapt attention, he'd love her for who she was, not for the maidenhead she possessed.

As her parents had loved each other.

Her uncle could make all the ugly accusations he wanted about her parents. But she knew the truth—they had loved each other deeply, and their tragic deaths had been the result of treachery . . . but not from each other.

Whenever she thought of that horrible night her parents had died, she forced herself to remember her sweet mother tucking her into bed, cooing a soft, soothing prayer in French, her father standing in the doorway of the nursery, dressed in his greatcoat and holding a lantern.

But the rest of her memories from that fateful eve, Georgie kept locked tight in her heart, for she feared them more than this impending threat of marriage.

And like her parents, it seemed so was she about to lose herself in the duplicity of others.

If only they had lived. Then she would have had her Season like other girls.

Oh, to have a Season in London. Not that she ever would now, but it was a nice dream. To have one chance to gracefully enter an elegant ballroom . . . to look about the refined crowd and have her gaze meet that of a roguish, devilishly handsome man, and *just know*.

Just know that he is the one who will understand all her secrets. All her desires. All her hopes.

"Why is it impossible for you to get ruined?" Kit was asking, breaking into Georgie's wistful musings. "You aren't so bad-looking that you'd scare away one of those horrid rakes Lady Finch warned you about in her last letter."

Georgie sighed. "How many times do I have to tell you not to read other people's correspondence?"

"You wouldn't have those letters if I didn't pinch them from Uncle Phineas's study," Kit grumbled.

She had Georgie there. For how could she truly complain when Kit's larceny had revealed her impending and unwanted betrothal?

"Still, it seems to me," Kit was saying, "that the best solution is for you to ruin yourself."

"I don't see how, Kit," she told her. "Lord Harris's physician is coming in the morning. It would be impossible to find a likely man on such short notice. We haven't been allowed out even for social calls, let alone the type of ball or assembly where I might be able to find a willing candidate."

That seemed to quell Kit's enthusiasm, at least for a few moments. Then suddenly her sister sat up. "What about this ball? The one Lady Finch talks about here?" she said, holding up the last page.

"The Cyprian's Ball?" Georgie sputtered, this time taking away the letter for good.

"Yes, that's the one." Kit nodded, already off the window seat and dancing into the middle of the room. "It's perfect. And according to Lady Finch, it's tonight. You could be ruined inside of an hour, or however long it takes, and be back before you were missed. Why, from the sound of it, every man in town will be there, and I am sure that includes all the ones who are adept at despoiling young women."

While Georgie spent the next five minutes lecturing Kit on all the reasons it was beyond the pale even to consider such a notion, inside her breast her heart hammered with the possibility that London's most notorious bacchanal offered.

The Cyprian's Ball.

It was a crazy, impossible notion. Lady Finch had only mentioned it as a warning to Georgie not to allow herself to be led astray, or she could end up one of the wretched and lowly unmentionable women who attended such scandalous affairs.

And yet, that fate was the only thing that could possibly save Georgie from marrying this horrible man.

For a wild moment, Georgie considered Kit's suggestion, then just as quickly shook it off.

No, she couldn't do it. She couldn't consider it.

And yet . . .

"You could sneak out the back," Kit was saying, her hand on her chin as she laid out the possible means of escape. "That is, once Cook passes out from the Madeira she steals from Uncle's cellar. But once she's snoring, you can easily take the backstairs, then slip out the garden gate—it's never locked according to the scullery maid, because Uncle lost the keys years ago and doesn't think anyone knows." Kit's gaze rolled heavenward as if to say that their uncle was the stupidest man alive. "From there," she said, continuing her plans, "you could go directly to the corner by the park and hail a hackney. No one will ever know you've gone."

"Kit!" Georgie said, trying again to sound severe. Really, she should be shocked that her young sister could so easily come up with such an elaborate plan or have such knowledge of their uncle's household after only three weeks of living under his roof. "Where do you get such notions? How do you know such things?"

Her sister had the audacity to look affronted. "I listen. And I ask questions. And if you weren't always sitting around with your nose buried in a book, or gazing at that atlas of yours, you'd hear what the maids talk about. This house is very ill-run. Quite slipshod. Apparently the staff has been stealing Uncle Phineas and Aunt Verena blind for years." Kit dismissed that revelation with a careless wave of her hand. Then she glanced at the old clock that ticked loudly, and somewhat inconsistently, on the mantel. "We'll have to wait until after eleven, for according to the parlor maids, it takes Cook at least three or four glasses to get good and truly foxed."

With that Kit grinned, and Georgie couldn't help feeling her sister's infectious spirit prodding her into this impetuous and dangerous notion.

Ruination. Why, the very idea sent shivers down her spine.

If anything, since she wasn't going to get her Season, wasn't going to get her dreams of love and adventure, she might as well live one night, dancing at the edge of Society, throwing herself into the arms of impropriety.

Dancing. Oh dear, she'd need dancing slippers. And so much more.

Georgie looked down at her own sensibly shod feet and frowned. Up from her frayed hemline rose the same poorly fashioned plain poplin gown she'd been wearing for nearly four years, which she'd recently died black in honor of Mrs. Taft, who'd been like a mother to them, and deserved to be mourned as such. Georgie knew that draped as she was in an ill-fitting, poorly dyed gown, she would hardly fit in with a roomful of elegantly attired Cyprians.

She'd look like someone's poor maid, not a beauty for the taking.

"I have nothing to wear," she said, interrupting Kit's ongoing litany of how they could borrow enough coins from their aunt's hidden pin money to pay for the cab fare and the possible need to bribe one of the footmen.

At this stumbling block, Kit finally paused, yet only to take a breath. "Oh, dash it and bother," she said, flouncing back down on the window seat. "Too bad Aunt Verena's twice your size, for she has more than enough vulgar gowns to dress all the fallen women in London. If only we knew some of those ladies, for I hear they have gowns to spare, though I haven't the vaguest notion why they should possess them, when we wear nothing but cheap poplin and worsted."

If only we knew some of those ladies . . .

Georgie took a speculative glance at her sister. Oh, but they had.

Mrs. Taft.

Their foster mother had spent ten years as one of the highest paid ladies in Marseilles before she'd met her English husband, Captain Taft, and he'd impulsively married her, plucking her from her less-than-respectable past. They had loved each other dearly until the day two years past when the *Sybaris* had returned to Penzance with the terrible news that the captain had been lost in a ferocious storm.

The Tafts' happiness had spilled over onto the sisters, for the couple had treated them as beloved offspring rather than foster children to be endured for the extra income they provided.

And while Mrs. Taft might not have known the latest dance steps or how to do tatted lace, she did have an intimate understanding of men, one she'd considered her duty to pass on to Georgie.

Your mother, God bless her soul, should be the one to tell you this, she'd said. *But with her gone, you'll have to make do with my experience. Not that it will hurt to know more than most, for it is in a woman's experienced arms that a man is at his weakest.*

And that hadn't been the extent of Mrs. Taft's gift. She'd also let the girls dress up in her collection of elegant and scandalous gowns, leftovers from her ruinous past.

While they were now decidedly out of fashion, they were French-made and well done at that—just the right mix of elegance and coquetry. For Mrs. Taft hadn't been just any dockside dove, but a lady highly coveted, whose time and services commanded a lofty price, as evidenced by the rich silk drouguet fabric and delicate embroidery the gowns boasted.

And any of them would fit Georgie. At least for a night.

"Oh well, it was a good idea," Kit was saying.

"And it still is," she told her sister, bounding across the room and pushing aside her bed, to reveal her battered trunk. Throwing open the lid, Georgie dug through her own meager possessions to the gowns she hadn't dared think she would ever wear. Immediately, she plucked out her favorite, a gown of changeable silk, the color shimmering from a rich, royal purple to hints of blue.

"Mrs. Taft's gowns!" Kit whispered, her hand reaching out to reverently touch the Holland lace on the sleeves. "Oh, I thought they were lost."

Georgie ran her hand over the collection of expensive silks and laces.

"Will you do it?" Kit whispered.

Georgie considered all that lay before her, weighing her choices one more time. *Do I dare?*

Life as the tenth Lady Harris, or ruination?

Then she glanced back at her trunk full of treasures. It was all there to tempt her, the gowns, Mrs. Taft's revelations about men, and Kit's seemingly foolproof plan—as if finally the Fates were telling her to take her life into her own hands.

Georgie nodded, shaking out the gown of changeable silk and casting it a critical eye.

"Try it on," Kit urged. "I think that gown will make even you look pretty."

Georgie took no offense at her sister's blunt assessment of her looks and charms. She was too tall to begin with—towering over most men who she met. Her height and size almost made her movements far too bold for current tastes, wherein petite, reticent ladies were considered fashionable.

Looking down at the almost magical dress in her hands, Georgie thought the color might become her. And even if her hair was an indifferent shade of honey and her skin still too sun-kissed, perhaps the gown was eye-catching enough to tempt a man to her side.

She hoped she could find one she didn't loom over and who wouldn't ask her to dance before he took her to his bed . . .

Truly, her lack of skills in dancing, Georgie mused, should probably be the least of her worries.

Kit continued to dig through the trunk. "Before you

put it on, you'll need this." She pulled out a linen corset, the once white ties now yellowed with age.

Georgie grimaced, but she knew she'd never fit into Mrs. Taft's gown without some help.

Tugging it on, Georgie found the ingenious under-garment was hardly the torture suit that English ladies wore, but designed for comfort, with a soft cotton lin-ing and not a hint of whalebone.

Kit caught hold of the strings in back and gave them a rueful tug. "Too tight?"

Georgie shook her head, amazed at the transforma-tion the undergarment wrought.

Suddenly her waist became more defined, and what it had done to her chest was nothing less than a won-drous miracle. She actually had a figure.

Kit rose up on her tiptoes and threw the gown over Georgie's head. As the silk fell in a soft rustle around her, Kit let out a tiny gasp.

"What's wrong?" Georgie asked.

"Oh, come and look." Kit led her by the hand to the long narrow mirror in the corner. "You're a regular princess."

The low-cut bodice revealed just enough of her breasts to tempt a man to come closer. The sleeves were a gauzy, filmy silk, scandalously short, revealing bare limbs that were barely hidden by the rich, delicate lace gloves that went with the ensemble.

A wide satin ribbon wound around her waist and tied in the back in a large bow, the ends trailing in a flutter nearly to the ground, and begging to be undone. The skirt fell in a wide circle to a cutwork hem that danced and swayed as one moved, and hinted at well-trimmed calves and silken-clad legs beneath.

There was no doubt, this was a gown made to attract the eye of a man.

"I only need one more thing," Georgie said, returning to the trunk and digging around in it, muttering to herself as she tossed the contents out around her.

Where were they? The shoes she remembered.

Then she spied them. White satin, they were covered in beautiful silk embroidery, echoing the decorations along the hem of her gown. She slipped them onto her feet, but to her dismay they didn't fit.

"You'll never get by in those, Georgie," Kit said, eyeing the heels. "Why, you'll trip and break your neck before you make it downstairs."

Georgie shot her sister a quelling glance. Kit's assessment might be true, for even Georgie would admit she wasn't the most graceful belle, but she was going to wear these shoes, for they were the most beautiful things she had ever seen. She took a couple of handkerchiefs and stuffed them inside so her feet would fit better.

Kit held her breath as Georgie tucked her toes once again into the shoes and rose trembling and teetering onto their heeled heights.

Looking into the mirror, she took a deep breath and realized the first part of her transformation was complete, now she had only to find a way to the ball . . .

And a man willing to take her to his bed.

"Now for your hair," Kit said, happily setting to work, making suggestions and helping with the rest of Georgie's transformation.

In an hour, their work was complete and they had successfully navigated their way through the darkened house to the kitchen door.

"Go upstairs," Georgie told her. "And bar the nursery shut. Don't let anyone in, unless you absolutely have to." Not that anyone ever came to check on them.

Kit nodded and glanced anxiously out into the night. "Georgie, do you know what it means to be ruined?" Suddenly her oh-so-worldly sister sounded like the innocent thirteen-year-old that she should be.

Georgie's cheeks flamed with warmth, despite the cool night air of the garden, and she was thankful for the darkness hiding her embarrassment.

"I think so, Kit. Enough to see me free of this Lord Harris."

Chapter 2

"**I** will not marry you, Lord Danvers. Not now or ever." Lady Diana Fordham, the esteemed and all-too-respectable daughter of the Earl of Lamden, put down her dainty foot with the same resolute finality of an innkeeper about to toss out a pair of unruly patrons. She pointed toward the door. "Now, if you and your cousin would be so kind as to leave—"

Colin, Baron Danvers, formerly Captain Danvers of His Majesty's Royal Navy, stared at the outraged woman before him. Where was the sweet-faced and soft-spoken miss he remembered courting and asking to marry him?

The Earl of Lamden stood behind his daughter, his usually jovial features set in hard lines. He had yet to say a word, but that was probably because his once sweet-spoken daughter had found the tongue of a fish-wife and was giving Colin a dressing-down that not even the earl could top.

"I said, my lord, you can leave," she repeated. "I will not marry you!" She thrust out her hand and opened her fingers to reveal the ring he had given her three years earlier, along with a miniature of himself that he'd had done for her at her request. "Take it," she told him. "I'll have no reminders of *you* around here. None!"

Behind him, his cousin, the Marquis of Templeton, whom he'd brought along to stand up for him, let out a low and very inappropriate whistle.

Diana shot a furious glare in that direction.

Temple was duly stifled, though knowing him as Colin did, Colin could well imagine what his imprudent cousin was thinking and how long he would be able to keep it to himself.

"Lord Danvers, why would you think that I would still want to marry you?" Lady Diana shuddered, the ribbons on her perfectly fashionable gown swaying about in a fluttering chorus of dismay. "My father chose you because you were a gentleman, a respected one. And now I see that we were both deceived, wickedly so. If you think I will be dragged into your exile of disgrace, you are sadly mistaken." She turned from him and sniffed into her handkerchief.

The Earl of Lamden drew his arms around his daughter and glared over her blond head at him.

"Lady Diana, Lord Lamden, there has been a mistake," Colin began. "If you would both just trust that this is not—"

"Trust?!" Lamden sputtered, his muttonchop whiskers quivering. "I don't trust blackguards. Especially cowardly ones. And a coward is what you are. Don't try to deny it. The accounts in the papers are quite detailed."

Diana glanced up from her misery, the furious expression glaring through her tear-stained features seeming to say she agreed completely with her father's assessment of the situation.

Colin took a deep breath. Certainly Lamden and his daughter didn't believe . . .

Yet their outraged faces told him exactly what they thought. They accepted as gospel every one of the treasonous charges that had been leveled against him.

"My lord, my lady, if you would but consider my family connections, my previous record with the Admiralty, my honorable intentions in this matter . . ." He leaned forward, holding out his hand to Lady Diana. "Then you would see that we can be wed as planned."

She shrank away from his outstretched fingers as if they were dripping with plague.

"Harrumph," Lord Lamden snorted, stepping in front of his daughter, shielding her from Colin's advance. "Marry you? I'd rather she marry that wastrel cousin of yours. No offense meant, Templeton."

"None taken, sir," Temple told him. "But really I don't see any reason to cast Danvers here into the briars. So he's a bit done in. But I'm sure he's got a good explanation for why he turned coward."

"A bit done in?" Lamden blasted. "Temple, you're a cockeyed idiot. Done in? You act as if he's got a few gambling debts. He's no better than his rapscallion father. I should never have listened to your grandfather's assurances that he wasn't infected by the Danverses' poor bloodlines. Your cousin is a traitor to the King and our country. He's brought disgrace to himself, to your family, and worst of all, to this house."

At this Lady Diana offered another appropriate

sniff—though she hardly had the mien of the humiliated innocent her father made her out to be. The murderous gleam in her eyes said that she was sorely disappointed the Admiralty hadn't seen fit to hang Colin from the nearest yardarm.

Why, the furious chit looked more than willing to tie the noose with her own tidy, unblemished hands.

"Now, I ask you to leave before I've a mind to call you out," the furious man demanded, pointing at the entryway where the aged Lamden butler had already pulled the great oaken door open.

"Now that should prove truly entertaining," Temple muttered under his breath. Both Colin and Lamden glared at him, though it did little to stifle his levity.

"Do you mind?" Colin shot over his shoulder at his cousin.

Temple grinned, this time at Lady Diana. "No, not at all."

She frowned back and then returned her glare to Colin. "I have no need to listen any further to your lies. Good day to you and good riddance." She turned to leave, but then spun back around. Reaching out, she took Colin's hand, dropping the emerald and pearl engagement ring into his palm, along with the miniature. Without another word, she turned on one heel and marched up the stairs.

"Away with ye, Danvers," Lamden said, his Scottish heritage coming to the forefront in the angry burr tingeing his threats, "before I do call you out. The Admiralty may be afraid of your grandfather's lofty connections, but I'd have no qualms seeing you consigned to a cold grave. The Lamden name is as old as the

Setchfields', older I'd dare say, and certainly not to be sullied by the likes of cowardly dogs."

Colin flinched. He'd never been called a coward before, and he didn't like it overly much. But this was a situation of his own making and he could hardly call out Lamden for an insult that to most would seem deserved.

So instead of demanding satisfaction, he bowed low to the elderly gentleman and said, "My apologies, sir. I meant no insult on your good name. Please give my regrets to Lady Diana." He paused for a moment, glancing up the stairwell where his betrothed had fled. "That is, when she is of a mind to listen."

Lamden snorted. "That'll be a cold day."

Temple added his bow, to which Lamden snorted yet again and made an impatient wave to send them on their way. So Colin and Temple took their hats and cloaks from the Lamden butler, and left.

They weren't even halfway down the front steps when Temple said, "Demmed waste of a good heiress, that."

Colin shot his cousin an annoyed glance. He hadn't been marrying Lady Diana for her money—for despite what the papers, the London gossips, and the Admiralty had declared, he actually still had plenty of money.

Only Temple—perpetually short of funds, despite the fact that he was heir to their grandfather, the Duke of Setchfield's heir—would think first of Diana's money.

"Why don't you marry her?" he suggested.

"Marry Diana?" Temple laughed with what Colin

thought was a tad too much irony. "Grandfather would in alt, but you heard Lamden, the old boy would never hear of it. He certainly doesn't want the likes of me, someone who spends too much time off shooting in Scotland or gadding about at house parties, marrying his precious daughter."

"Tell him the truth. Tell him what you are really doing when you are off 'shooting' in Scotland."

Temple cocked a single brow. "Why don't you tell him what you are up to with this trumped-up court-martial? You would no more disobey a direct order and leave a battle than I would be caught mucking about in some cold Scottish bog shooting at some demmed bird." He paused and motioned at the closed and probably barred door of the Lamden town house. "Go on, tell him the truth. And when you get done with him, would you mind enlightening me?"

Colin knew he shouldn't be surprised that his cousin would see past Nelson's grand deception. If anyone knew a thing or two about deceiving the *ton*, it was Temple. And though he knew he could trust his cousin with the truth, he was compelled to silence on the matter.

There was too much at stake. And so he said nothing.

"I thought as much," Temple said, nodding in knowing agreement. He glanced over his shoulder, back up at Lamden's four-story colonnaded home. "Still, a pity one of us didn't get her. Diana is a rare gem. Always has been."

Temple stepped off the curb to wave down his driver, Elton, who was waiting in the mews. Colin paused, glancing back over his shoulder, still shocked by his betrothed's abrupt refusal.

To his surprise, he found Lady Diana peering down from a window, her eyes ablaze with a fiery passion that he had never before seen light her features. She hardly looked the heartbroken, ruined *parti*.

But then again, her gaze wasn't on him. It was drilling into the back of his cousin's wine-colored jacket.

Colin swallowed what was left of his pride.

Egads. Diana had never loved him.

The realization hit him harder than he cared to admit, and at the same time, it made perfect sense. Her easy acquiescence to delay their wedding all these years. Her vehement refusal to marry him today.

His court-martial had only been an excuse. She'd cried off because she didn't love him.

He didn't know why it suddenly mattered that she should have loved him. It wasn't as if he'd been in love with her.

But witness now to Diana's intensity, her ability to shine with such fire, he knew that a wife should love her husband.

And by the same token, a man should love his bride.

Unequivocally, and without restraint.

"Are you going to stand there like a forlorn pup all night?" Temple asked. "First a court-martial, then an afternoon wasted securing a special license the bride so kindly tossed back into your face. Come along with me, for I hate to see your day finish in utter failure."

Colin glanced at his grinning cousin and sighed. Only Temple could make light of such a disastrous turn of events. Deciding against another look up at Lady Diana, Colin climbed in and Elton started off.

Temple leaned back on the leather squabs and sighed. "What a sad lot we are. All dressed up and our evening completely empty." He fiddled with his elegantly tied cravat, while glancing out the window. "Let me think . . . I know there was something happening tonight. What was it?"

"Save yourself the trouble," Colin told him. "I'm hardly in the mood for one of your debaucheries."

Temple sat up straight. "Debauchery! Oh, that's it. The perfect way to salve your broken heart."

Colin shook his head. "I'd hardly say I'm suffering from all that."

"Oh, you can't fool me. You were always too serious by half," Temple chided. "If I know you, you had the next twenty years all planned out. Diana would produce your heir within the year, and a spare two years hence. When you were at sea, she could reside safely out in that manor house your father left you in Devonshire. And when you finally tired of fighting the French and living on weevil-ridden rations, you'd come home to be lord and master of your peaceful household, without any thought of love or passion or fun."

"Fun?" Colin said. "Who said marriage is supposed to be fun?"

"Well, it damned well should be if it means settling down and all," Temple grumbled.

"I'll have you know that marriage is a matter of duty and honor." At least that was what he had thought until a few moments ago when he'd seen that look of longing in Lady Diana's eyes.

Now he wasn't too sure.

"Have it your way," Temple said, leaning back in his seat and crossing his long legs out in front of him. "Since your evening has been cleared of your previous engagement, literally, that is." He chuckled at his own pun, while Colin did his best not to groan. "I have the perfect event for us to attend. Consider it your first lesson in disreputable behavior. If you are going to be a scoundrel—which is why, I may assume, you were run out the gangplank or tossed overboard, or whatever you naval fellows say—you might as well gain your lessons from an expert."

Temple tapped on the roof to get his driver's attention. After he gave Elton directions, he sat back down.

Colin shook his head. "I'm in no mood for gambling and drinking tonight. Besides, I can use the time well enough to see to other matters."

Temple eyed him. "Other matters, eh? And so soon. Could you by chance mean a new ship?"

Glancing out the window, Colin did his best to ignore his cousin's perceptive inquiries.

His cousin continued unabashedly. "My, how interesting that you've secured a position so quickly. Now who on earth would hire *you* to captain a ship?"

"Easy there," Colin warned. "Just leave off on your speculations. 'Tis better for all concerned."

"Must be something rather urgent," Temple mused, a grin pulling at his lips, "if you are fleeing town so soon. And probably on the morning tide, if I were to guess. And mind you, I'm only guessing."

Colin shot him an irritated glance. He actually planned to sail in two days—on the morning tide—but he wasn't going to tell his cousin that.

"You can't turn down the offer of just one drink,"

Temple said, applying the same wheedling tone he'd used when they'd been school lads together and Temple had devised some novel sort of mischief. "Besides, you'll never make a proper bastard if you continue to live by duty and honor alone. And you do want the world to think you are one, don't you?"

Colin shook his head. "You aren't going to let me be, are you?"

His cousin grinned. "No, I consider it my sacred duty to be the one who introduces you to your new existence. Come now, I'm just proposing one small drink. A toast, let's say, to your unnamed ventures."

Colin knew well enough that one drink with Temple was asking for trouble. But then again, he'd spent most of the day up to his neck in problems, so what was one more in a long list?

Besides, Temple might be right, he didn't know much about living outside Society. The ordered regulations of naval life that had guided him since he'd set sail as a midshipman at the age of thirteen no longer applied.

If he was to do what needed to be done, he'd have to convince the world he was the traitor and scoundrel the Admiralty had declared him to be.

He held up a single finger. "Just one drink."

"That's the spirit," his cousin declared. "I've a grand evening in mind."

Colin wanted to groan. This was how it always started with Temple—and quickly got out of hand. He'd probably wake up in a fortnight only to find himself in Ireland, without his wallet and any recollection how he had spent the last fourteen days other than the evidence his pounding headache would provide.

Still, he had one advantage that might hinder Temple's enthusiasm and plans.

"Considering the greeting I just received at Lamden's," he told him, "I doubt I'll have much of a reception at your club."

Temple's grin spread across his face. "As if I ever do! But forget White's. I have a better place in mind. Have you ever heard of the Cyprian's Ball?" When Colin shook his head, his cousin's smile widened even further. "I thought not. Too much time at sea and not enough living the good life here in town. The Cyprian's Ball is just the place to mend a broken heart."

Colin wasn't about to comment on the state of his heart. Especially since he could hardly describe it as "broken."

In truth, Lady Diana had done him a favor by jilting him. She'd set him free. As free as Nelson had by casting him out of the navy.

So instead, he said, "A ball, you say? I'm hardly in the mood for dancing and debutantes."

"Who said anything about dancing?" Temple replied with a hearty laugh.

Colin should have known that any assembly highly recommended by his rakish cousin would be anything but respectable.

The Cyprian's Ball was no exception.

The great room overflowed with the city's highest-paid mistresses, courtesans, and ladies of questionable repute—and milling merrily through this ignoble milieu were the crème de la crème of the *ton*'s randiest males—all eagerly seeking a new conquest.

If there was ever a place to begin working on his

new reputation as a disreputable bounder, Colin had found the right spot and the best of company.

Given the notoriety of the ball and the infamous crowd gathered there, few guests caused much of a stir, if any. But when Colin arrived, a groundswell of stunned silence rolled through the room.

By the time Temple arrived on the steps beside him, all eyes were turned in their direction, a wave of whispers already rising to a dull roar.

"Court-martialed."

"Terribly rich . . . at least before."

"Should be hanging in front of the Admiralty."

"Bloody coward. Can't believe he'd show his face."

Colin ignored the commentary. Given Lady Diana's reception, he supposed he couldn't expect anything less. Most of the men in the crowd, those in uniform especially, gave him the cut direct. The majority of the ladies regarded him with scant interest, his less than rosy financial state more of a concern to their mercenary interests than his social ruin.

"See," Temple said, waving at several of the groups of ladies as if they were old friends. Finally, one older lady, far past her first bloom, and probably past her second and third, waved back. "There's someone who hasn't heard of your disgrace. Or your lack of funds."

"Temple, I don't think—" Colin turned to leave, but his cousin caught him by the shoulder.

"Oh no, you don't," he said. "You promised. One drink. And I mean to see that you keep your word."

Colin glanced over the room packed cheek to jowl with lightskirts and Paphians. A table on the far side looked to be serving some sort of brew. "I don't think the refreshments are why one comes here. Besides, it will take an hour, maybe more, to reach our cups."

"You noticed that?" Temple said, lifting his lorgnette to his eyes and gauging the distance for himself. "But you see, that is the beauty of seeking our one drink here. In addition to a cup of the weakest punch in town, on your way to claim it, you may just find a woman who steals your heart at first glance."

"Don't be ridiculous," Colin told him. "Remember? I'm the one who wants a *wife*. A sensible lady of good breeding. Not one of these high-flyers."

"If that's what you wanted, that should have ruled out Lady Diana to begin with," Temple mused. "Such manners! I always suspected she possessed a shrew's tongue under all those tight lacings. No one can be that proper."

Ignoring his cousin, Colin continued, "When you come into Grandfather's title, you'll understand the obligations of family and the need for marriage."

Temple regarded him with a mix of skepticism, as if that type of dour responsibility would never rest on his shoulders.

But Colin knew it all too well—ever since his father had died in a carriage accident the previous year, leaving Colin the barony and all the rights and responsibilities it held.

And though his younger brother Robert stood to inherit behind him, he was an irresponsible young rapscallion, hardly capable of taking on the Danvers' estates and obligations. Robert was heading into the army for the sole reason that there wasn't a school or university left in England that would accept him. He'd shown a fondness for munitions that had blown up portions of the dean's house at his most recent alma mater, and then there had been the incident at his previous school involving a monument to Oliver Cromwell and a small canon.

Unfortunately, Colin's half-brothers Orlando and Raphael, twins from his father's second marriage, to the daughter of a Spanish grandee, weren't much better. Raphael's antics had all the earmarkings of rendering Robert's exploits amateurish. Luckily, Colin had been able to secure the pair a place in a school that was willing to take them on the grounds that neither lad shared Robert's well-known interest in explosives.

No, Colin needed a wife, a gentle lady who could help him oversee his brothers' upbringing and add a stamp of respectability to the family name that it had long been lacking.

Oh, his father had been respected in diplomatic circles, where the previous Lord Danvers had spent forty years working for British interests. But in the narrow world of the *ton*, he'd always been regarded as a bit of an oddity—with his far-reaching travels and Spanish-born second wife—and therefore not quite up to snuff.

Colin had hoped that marriage to the sensible and esteemed Lady Diana would bring him the one thing the Danvers men never seemed able to attain: a normal life.

His father had eloped with his mother, Lady Susannah Devinn, the daughter of the Duke of Setchfield. Scandal had surrounded their marriage from the moment they'd dashed to Gretna Green until fourteen years later when the still spirited and independent Susannah had died of a fever following the birth of a daughter. The poor babe had followed her mother into a cold grave in Westphalia, where the Danvers family had been living and gathering information for the Foreign Office.

No, Colin certainly wasn't about to follow in the shoes of his globe-hopping, spy-chasing father. It wasn't in his nature.

At least so he'd thought until six months ago, New Year's Eve, after a dinner party with Nelson and all his captains. Hours into a celebration spent toasting the upcoming year and the victories they would share, the admiral had taken Colin aside and revealed evidence of a viper in their midst.

It was then that Nelson had asked Colin to become unfettered from the constraints of his uniform, to cut himself loose from naval regulations and codes of conduct, to become a social outcast.

So freed, Nelson believed that Colin would be able to find the turncoat nestled within the admiral's inner circle—a man selling secrets to the French and undermining British supremacy at sea.

For who better to be viewed as a likely partner than a man with a grudge, a man without connections, a man who had supposedly just lost a considerable fortune?

They hoped to lure out the turncoat, dangling Colin as a possible ally, someone with inside knowledge, who would very likely take French gold without the honorable burdens that plagued a true and loyal officer of His Majesty's Navy.

And though he'd readily agreed to the resulting disgrace, he hadn't foreseen the rippling effects that would wipe away his relationships with his friends . . . his family . . . his betrothed. If he grieved for the loss of Lady Diana, it was mostly for the likely embarrassment he'd caused her. He only hoped their broken engagement wouldn't be a detriment to her future happiness.

"Now," Temple was saying, "watch and learn from an expert on what it means to be a dishonorable scoundrel. And try to remember—you are bad *ton* now."

As his cousin waded into the crowded room, maneuvering through the ignoble assemblage with practiced ease, Colin knew he didn't belong there.

His practical nature took over, for he had a ship to supply and a crew to finalize, and all before he sailed in two days' time. He hardly needed to be looking for a mistress. Besides, there were still some hours left to the evening, so perhaps he could start looking over the reports he'd been sent by Nelson before calling it a night.

As he turned to make his escape before Temple came back with a pair of likelies on his arm, he found himself nearly bowled over by a tall dervish in purple silk.

"Oh!" she gasped as he tried to catch his balance, his hand mistakenly cupping a breast, his other grappling around the curve of her lush hip.

"Unhand me, you oaf!" she ordered, her heel landing solidly atop his newly polished boot.

Whether it was a mistake or intentional, Colin couldn't tell. Gritting his teeth through the pain, he pulled his foot free before it sustained any permanent damage, then planted himself on the marble floor as if he were standing on a pitching deck. But the lady still teetered and wavered over the edge of the stairs, so he hauled her into his arms to save her from plunging into a heap of silk below.

She trembled for a few more seconds, then finally came to rest in his embrace.

In all the years he'd been betrothed to Lady Diana, he'd only gone so far as to kiss her properly gloved hand, but in a matter of seconds he felt as if he knew the lady he held intimately—how her body curved to fit his, the fullness of her breasts against his chest, the length of her willowy limbs wound around his with a strange familiarity, like they had been lovers for years.

So as the whirl of purple silk and lace began to stop fluttering, he looked down expecting to find just another glittery member of the demimonde, yet to his surprise, he discovered he was holding the oddest-looking Cyprian he'd ever seen.

Instead of the perfectly coiffed hair and array of paste jewels one associated with ladies of her profession, her blond hair was piled atop her head in a mêlée of hoydenish curls, barely held together with a handful of plain tortoiseshell pins. Her features bore no paint or artifice so commonly used by the incognitas and soiled doves; instead, her cheeks were rosy with the natural pink of embarrassment.

Oh, her dress was obviously that of a lady of easy virtue—the neckline was far too low to be considered respectable, while the hemline rose too high to be modest. The lace and silk allowed tantalizing hints of the wares beneath—long limbs, soft, luscious skin, and curves that no lady of the *ton* would ever dare bare so brazenly in public.

No, what made her such an oddity was that while all

the pampered felines around her primped and moved with sensual precision and calculated poise, this lady was as graceful and engaging as an alley cat in lace.

She swiped her tangled web of hair out of her face with one hand, while the other made a none-too-elegant sweep at her coiffure with a couple of negligent pats, brushing the wayward strands this way and that.

When she finally just resorted to tossing her hair back off her brow, he saw her eyes—and through them, he could have sworn he saw down to her very soul.

They were the most earnest, fathomless brown he had ever seen, wide and deep, like a sable night. He was caught by some secret they seemed to hold, an innocence that he didn't believe could exist—not here amongst London's most jaded.

Innocence?

What was he thinking? An innocent at this gathering was about as likely as Lady Diana putting in an appearance.

"Are you well, sir?" she asked, shaking her arms and rattling at his grasp on her.

It was then that he realized he still held her . . . not that he minded having her so close.

For as they'd become entangled, her perfume had encircled them with a soft, subtle hint of flowers. Violets, he thought. Hardly the usual thick, annoying cloud of eau de cologne or lily of the valley favored by London's fallen ladies.

The scent enticed one to come closer and inhale deeply of its fresh bounty.

Perhaps that was why he didn't just set this chit

aside and leave . . . No, he suspected his hesitation sprang from something that ran far deeper than just her beguiling perfume. For in that heartbeat of a moment, when he'd looked into her guileless eyes, something inside him thrummed to life.

Like a prevailing wind, it swept over his senses, whispering and prodding him to take advantage of the rare opportunity standing before him like a newly discovered Spanish treasure.

Colin had felt this way on several occasions, mostly at sea while engaged in battle when he'd spy an opportunity to take advantage of an enemy's weakness, breaking ranks to seize the Fates with his own hands.

It was a reckless, dangerous temptation, but one he knew from experience wouldn't disappoint him if he gave in to its siren invitation.

He need only trust its whispering call and step out of his usual cautious and conventional self.

And right now, for whatever reasons, his instincts were prodding him toward this odd, tempting armful, bringing to mind Temple's earlier prediction.

Some nonsense about finding a woman who steals your heart at first glance . . .

It was just that, nonsense, he told himself. *Utterly ridiculous . . .*

Obviously tired of waiting for him to release her, she shook herself free, and with more strength than he would give a lady credit for. Straightening out her gown with one hand, she sighed over the state of it, then tugged her lacy shawl back into place over her bare shoulders.

"Oh, I have hurt you," she said, before giving herself

one last unladylike shake, sending more of her hair tumbling into disarray. "I'm so sorry. I fear I'll find my death in these demmed shoes. If not, apparently, the death of someone else."

She held out her foot, giving Colin a fair view of a high-heeled shoe, but an even better view of a well-trimmed calf enveloped in silk stockings. Glancing down at the footprint atop his boot, she blushed even more. "I didn't break your foot, did I?"

Colin laughed, despite the fact that he had little to no feeling in his toes. "No, I think I'll recover in a fortnight or so. But 'tis hard to believe such lovely shoes could be so treacherous."

She laughed in return, a sort of forced gaiety rising to her lips. He suspected she did it only out of sympathy for his poor attempt at humor.

And even more so, he found himself wondering what her laughter would sound like when it was allowed the freedom of spontaneity. He suspected this lady laughed with a rich joy capable of infecting all who heard it.

He didn't know why, but he also thought that it had been a long time since she had laughed. Genuinely, wonderfully laughed.

"I mean to say . . ." he began, trying to think of what witty comment Temple might use to secure the lady's attention, and at the same time wondering why he was trying so hard . . . "Well, what I meant to say is that I fear it isn't my foot that is mortally wounded, dear lady, but my heart."

At his exaggerated compliment, she laughed, this time a little too hard.

"And you find that funny?" he asked, a bit piqued to find his chivalry taken as a source of humor.

Her hand went to her lips, stifling the remaining giggles threatening to spill out. Then she glanced up, unabashedly staring, as if she were looking at him for the first time, and weighing some great decision— something that he alone could answer for her.

Yet whatever remedies she sought, he obviously didn't suit, for she sighed again, her gaze dismissing him in a blink of sooty lashes, then drifting over his shoulder toward the crowded ballroom, searching for someone.

Someone else.

Colin didn't like the realization that for some reason he'd come up lacking in her estimation. And for the life of him, it bothered him more than he cared to admit.

What the devil was wrong with him? His fiancée had cried off not an hour earlier and he was more irritated about an odd little Cyprian passing him over.

He glanced across the room to see if he could follow her gaze, but the blinding crush of people offered no answers. "Are you looking for someone?"

"Actually I am. A blackguard to be specific," she said, her blunt answer leaving him open-mouthed.

"A what?" he sputtered.

"A blackguard. You know, a rake. A regular at these affairs."

That accounted for every man in the room, Colin estimated, with the exception of himself. "Anyone specific?"

"Oh no," she said. "Any rake will do. Just so long as he is amoral and experienced. But I must be on my way, as I haven't much time." She started toward the steps again, then paused, glancing over her shoulder at him. "Do you know anyone who might be available?"

It had been a while since he had been to London, but he didn't remember the ladies of the demimonde being quite that blunt.

Especially this minx. She wasn't wasting a moment.

"Well, I would say I have a certain reputation," he offered, trying to remember what Temple had said. He was bad *ton*. Beyond the pale. A terrible bounder. Colin considered scowling at her a bit, but figured that might be a bit over the top.

She pursed her lips and eyed him critically. "Are you sure? You seem a bit too honorable for what I have in mind."

Too honorable, indeed. She needn't sound so terribly disappointed at such a notion.

Mayhap he should have scowled.

"Let me assure you," he said, recalling Lady Diana's blistering assessment of his character, "I have it on good authority that I don't possess an iota of honor."

She considered him once again, and this time offered him a conciliatory smile.

If you think so, her skepticism seemed to say.

"Weren't you about to leave?" she said, more as a suggestion than a question.

"No," he lied. "I was waiting for someone as well." That wasn't entirely an untruth—he was supposed to be waiting for Temple, who he now hoped was completely trapped in the crush.

Again she regarded him with an air of disbelief.

"Perhaps we can search for our parties together?" he

said, offering his arm. He didn't know what possessed him to make the suggestion, but for some reason the idea of her venturing into this room of predators tugged at his honor.

The same honor he wasn't supposed to possess.

"How very kind of you," she said, in the proper tones of a Bath miss accepting a dance at Almack's, her fingers lightly coming to rest on his sleeve. "Perhaps you can offer me an introduction. I fear I don't know a soul here."

Her odd request, made with the manners and tone befitting a debutante, rattled at Colin's better sense. As did her unwitting confession that she didn't know anyone at the ball.

Who the devil was this woman?

She certainly wasn't some chit in her first Season— she was too old to be trotting about the Marriage Mart. Looking at her, he gauged her to be at least twenty. Besides, no decent lady would be seen at such an assemblage unmasked and unescorted.

As they moved into the crowd, she walked with her head held high, her gaze constantly taking in her surroundings with the elegance of grace befitting a countess.

Perhaps she was the by-blow of some nobleman who'd afforded his ill-gotten issue an education in hopes she'd be able to gain suitable employment.

Gauging from her curious mix of manners and morals, Colin decided, she'd hardly make a modest lady's companion, not with her flair for salty language.

And she was certainly unfit for a governess, her

questionable morals aside. It was her full figure and wayward halo of curls that cast her out of that profession.

No lady in her right mind would hire such a temptation into her household.

"May I inquire why are you in search of such a man?" he asked. "Most ladies of . . . of your . . ."

"Of my profession?" she offered.

"Yes, your profession, prefer someone a little more . . ." He tried to think of a polite way to put it.

"More what?" she asked, pressing the point.

"Plump in the pockets," he finally offered. "You know, financially secure, over someone inclined to reckless abandon."

"Tonight I prefer *reckless*," she confided, her eyes alight with mischief and a trembling mystique.

The way she said the word—*reckless*—ignited his imagination. Suddenly his mind filled with images of tangled sheets, her limbs entwined with his, their bodies pressed together for a night of unforgettable passion.

He broke his gaze away from the bewitching enticement of hers.

What the devil was he thinking?

He was Colin Danvers, the sensible member of his family, the honor-bound eldest son. The man who put duty and obligation first. Always.

Still, he found the urge to tell her *I'm reckless* very tempting, for his thoughts were filled with the notion of catching her up in his arms, carting her off somewhere private, and showing her just how reckless two people could be.

Then again, the only thing stopping him from opening his mouth was the overwhelming suspicion that she'd laugh again, and he didn't think rejection twice in one night would be overly good for his new reputation as the *ton*'s leading ne'er-do-well.

Chapter 3

Georgie couldn't believe her terrible luck. Of all the men in the room, she had to fall prey to the nicest one of the lot.

Certainly he had the look of a man who refused to follow the conventions of society—his hair, unlike the current fashions for pomades and styling, fell in a wayward manner past his collar. Thick, dark, and glossy, it was as black as a raven's wing she'd once found on the beach.

His green eyes held an intensity that made her feel as if few things escaped his sharp gaze. He also possessed a rugged quality about him, unlike the pampered and paunchy fellows prancing about the ballroom beyond. She suspected he wasn't a man who spent his days in the mindless pursuit of the perfectly tied cravat—evidence that she'd become only too intimately aware of while trapped in his arms, for his body was solid and muscled.

Even his face lent a rakish discord to him—his hawkish features marking him with a resolute stamp, especially the deep cleft in his chin and the narrow scar running from one corner of his mouth down to his square jaw.

He was everything a rake should be but for one important thing: intent.

He practically smelled of decency. For in all his handsome trappings, Georgie could sense a cloak of honor intrinsically wrapped around him as if it were woven into the velvet of his dark coat, as blinding white as his shirt and cravat.

It wasn't anything he had said or done, but it was just something she knew. Oh, how could this have happened?

And yet . . . she wished with all her heart he was the one. *Her rake.*

Even when she'd told him what she sought to find this night, a man capable of reckless abandon, he'd replied with a polite jest.

Why couldn't he have taken her hint and tossed her over his shoulder, stolen her away to his disreputable bachelor rooms, and taken her virginity with all the impunity of a highwayman?

Unfortunately, her handsome, tempting rake was a knight in shining armor, offering to escort her around the room as she imagined one might if he were returning her to her chaperone after a dance at Almack's.

Almack's indeed!

Oh, the irony of her situation didn't escape her. All her life she'd wanted a handsome, elegant, noble man, and here, of all places, she'd found him and couldn't get rid of him. And she was certain of one other thing: She'd never find her despoiler with this man nearby.

So how did one get rid of a nice gentleman?

Lady Finch never offered advice on that subject since most ladies wouldn't let a man with those desirable qualities out of their satin clutches, not even if their lives depended on it.

Georgie chewed on her lip and considered her options as they continued to parade past rake after eligible rake. Perhaps she could tell her escort she had a headache. Or she could pretend to twist her ankle . . .

No, she dismissed both of those ideas. He'd probably feel it was his duty to seek medical assistance for her.

She let out a long, hopeless sigh.

"See any likely candidates?" He nodded at a pair of middle-aged men ahead of them. "What about one of those fellows?"

Georgie winced. The man in the primrose-yellow silk jacket and mulberry waistcoat was far too paunchy. The man to his right had the look of a dissolute, all right, but his vice was obviously of a different chord, for he swayed to and fro, cup in hand, already foxed though the hour was still early.

"No, and *definitely not*."

He smiled in agreement and continued escorting her through the crush.

If she was going to be ruined, she wanted it to be at least memorable . . . with a man who was handsome and passionate, and full of life . . .

Not these poor examples . . . She hadn't realized that most of the men in the *ton* were more akin to her Uncle Phineas than the man on her arm.

Oh, if only for tonight, she thought, slanting a glance up at him, *he could be my rake.*

When she'd tripped into his arms and their bodies had tumbled together, she'd never known such a thrill, such a sudden rush of desire.

Despite the fact that she was an innocent, in that moment she knew what it meant to want a man . . . to yearn for his bare skin against hers, to feel his hands cup her breasts in more than just a mistaken brush of fate . . . and to let her body meld to his in a heated, torrid rush.

Even now, with her hand resting on his sleeve, the tempting warmth beneath his jacket worked its way through her kidskin gloves, leaving her fingers tingling.

He paused for another couple to pass before them. "Do you mind telling me how you expect me to make an introduction if I don't know your name?"

Her name?

"Oh bother, I quite overlooked that I'd need a name," she muttered half under her breath.

"Overlooked the need for a name?" he repeated.

Georgie cursed, this time silently. Not only was her duly-appointed champion handsome, but his hearing was as sharp as his wit.

"Now isn't that interesting," he was saying. "Let me guess, avoiding creditors?"

"Certainly not!" she said.

He scratched his chin, his fingers stopping at the deep cleft there.

Georgie wished she dared to touch that same spot. Run her fingers along his jawline, following the thin scar until it came to rest on his lips.

He smiled at her, and the movement broke into her

reverie, which was straying dangerously into imagining what it would be like to kiss him.

Georgie, stop it, she told herself. *You need a rake, not a suitor.*

"Oh, come now," he was saying. "Don't you have a name?" He smiled again, one that curved his mouth into a kissable dream. "Why would a lady want to hide her identity? Let me see . . . Perhaps an old lover you wish to avoid?"

"Something like that," she demurred. *My future husband, to be exact.*

He reached out and took her hand. "Your name is safe with me. I'm leaving town in two days' time and won't have a chance to tell a living soul your secrets."

He was leaving town? Georgie thought she should be thrilled that it was unlikely she'd see him again, but she wasn't.

Especially with him holding her hand, his fingers entwined with hers, creating a feeling so intimate, she could barely breathe, let alone get out the one thing he wanted to hear.

Her name.

"Come now, what is it?" he repeated. "I can't keep thinking of you as my deadly shod Cyprian."

Before she could laugh, a voice called out of the crowd, "Georgie! Georgie, what the devil are you doing here?"

She immediately froze. Oh, this was disastrous. How could she have been discovered? And here, of all places?

She swung around, ready to be denounced and hauled home in disgrace, but to her surprise and relief, a pair of drunk and raucous Corinthians were shaking hands and continuing their loud greetings.

"Georgie, my good man! How the devil are you?" one said to the other.

She let out a sigh, and then turned to find her companion studying her intently, one brow cocked quizzically.

Her face must have shown every bit of fear and dismay that she'd just been caught.

"Georgie?" he asked. "Is that your name? A rather unusual one for a Cyprian, don't you think? Aren't French names more popular over such a patriotic moniker?"

"'Tis an old nickname," she said, still glancing around.

"It fits," he told her. "Much better than Yvette or Celeste. Do you mind if I call you Georgie?"

She shook her head. "No, not at all."

"Good, then we have that settled. And I am Colin, Lord—"

His introduction came to a sudden halt when their path was suddenly blocked by a trio of men, all in naval uniforms.

Oh, these three might be wearing the gold-trimmed and decorated uniforms of officers, but the voracious and hungry light in their eyes told her they were no different from the rabble of shore-hungry common sailors who flooded the docks of Penzance with every incoming tide.

Instinctively she stepped closer to Colin.

Colin. She liked the sound of it as well as the security of standing in his shadow.

"What do you want, Brummit?" Colin asked the large man who'd come forward.

"To see you swing like a dog," the man said, the

drab on his arm laughing in a shrill, high-pitched titter, her sagging jowls wavering with the movement.

Georgie understood now why Lady Finch had warned her about the hard life of a fallen lady. The pair with these gentlemen looked as if they had traveled every ruined mile on their hands and knees.

"I'm sorry to disappoint you, Captain," Colin said. "But I had other plans."

The second one stepped forward. He was the short-est of the three, but Georgie thought just as deadly from his beady gaze and taut stance. Like a terrier searching out a rat.

"So the ever perfect and sanctimonious *Romulus* still thinks he's better than us. But I suppose we must pity you since *this* is all you can afford now," he said with an insolent sneer toward Georgie.

Whatever she was, Georgie was of no mind to be re-ferred to as *this*, as if she were some sort of refuse rot-ting in the gutter. She started forward, about to open her mouth and speak her mind, when she felt Colin's hand, the one covering hers, tighten, warning her to stand down.

This isn't your fight.

"Leave her out of this, Paskims," Colin told him, in a tone that dared them to challenge his authority. And even better than his defense came a slight caress of his thumb over her hand, which she knew, knew with all her heart, meant that he didn't see her in such a tawdry light.

Paskims continued, "I say, how dare you show your cowardly face in public, *Romulus*. As if you still ruled the seas."

The others chuckled.

Romulus. She realized what once had been a nickname of honor was now being bandied about like an insult. But why? And what had Colin done to deserve such vehement animosity?

"Don't you have anything to say, Remus?" Colin nodded to the third man, who held back from his friends.

"To the likes of you?" The man sniffed. "Just that I agree with Paskims. You've certainly come down in your choice of companions. There was a time when you were too good for such common trash."

The other two laughed.

And the one called Remus wasn't done. "Perhaps I'll start calling on Lady Diana. I hear she's no longer engaged."

At the mention of this Lady Diana, Colin immediately dropped her hand.

"Go ahead and try," he said. "Lamden wouldn't let you cross his threshold. Not unless you've finally and miraculously made captain, *Commander* Hinchcliffe."

Hinchcliffe colored to a shade reminiscent of Uncle Phineas's favorite port.

If anything, Georgie gauged there was an even greater animosity between the two of them—not unlike their namesakes.

Romulus and Remus.

She doubted any of these gentlemen, Colin included, would believe that she had any knowledge of classical literature, but she actually knew the story quite well.

In one of his illicit trips to France, Captain Taft had given passage to a group of émigrés, including a classics tutor from Paris. The man had repaid his fare by spending the winter teaching the Escott sisters Greek and Latin, before he'd gone on to seek a position in London.

Romulus and Remus. Brothers who founded an empire and ended up at each other's throats—until one of them died.

Hinchcliffe edged a bit closer to Colin, his chest puffed out. "You aren't fit company for *decent* ladies." He shot another withering glance in her direction, his nose pinched so tightly, Georgie wondered if he could breathe. "So where did you find this poor excuse for a whore?" he asked. "I'm surprised you can afford her—that is, unless the rumors of you accepting French gold over the years are true."

Colin had held himself in check long enough. He could tolerate all the insults they wanted to sling at him. After all, if he were on the other side of the fence looking at a brother officer who'd been court-martialed without a proper hanging, he might be tossing a few insults himself.

But he wasn't about to let them hurl their animosity at the lady on his arm. Whatever she might be, she didn't deserve to bear their insults.

But even as he surged forward, fist balled into a solid hammer, a hand caught his shoulder and reined him back in.

"There you are, Cousin. I was starting to fear you'd ducked out on me."

Temple. Colin had almost forgotten that he'd come with his illustrious cousin.

"You'll not believe the trio of ladies I just met." Temple's assessing gaze swept over Georgie in a quick flash, and from the slight uplift of his brow, Colin could tell his cousin found her an oddity as well.

And not in an intriguing way.

"Templeton," Paskims said. "Stay out of this."

Temple smiled at the three. "What have we here? A party without me? How rude."

Hinchcliffe snorted. "Templeton, you're a perfect fool. Be on your way, if you know what's good for you."

Colin's cousin struck the perfect Corinthian pose, lorgnette in one hand, his other on his hip. "A perfect fool, you say? You should try it, Hinchcliffe. Foolishness would be a tremendous step up for you and your colleagues. You never know, you might find the change refreshing."

Paskims and Brummit shot looks at Hinchcliffe, and Colin knew the three of them were weighing whether to issue a challenge, or just haul Temple outside and beat the daylights out of him.

With a slight shake of his head, Hinchcliffe made it clear that they were to hold their positions. And the pair did.

Not that it surprised Colin; while the three outwardly worked like a pack, Hinchcliffe was their undisputed leader, though lower in rank.

"This isn't the time or place," he said, his gaze still on Colin. "But soon, Romulus. Very soon, we shall meet and finish what you started."

They moved off, much as they had arrived, taking their ill wind with them.

Beside him, Georgie let out a loud sigh. "I may have been mistaken about you, sir. You do appear to have a certain reputation," she said, glancing back at the departing trio. When she turned and looked up at him, it was with something akin to admiration and . . . interest.

While earlier he'd tried his best to convince this Cyprian, who was quite possibly out of her mind, that he was a rake, now . . . now he knew only too well he wasn't the man for her. Nor was any other man in this room right for her.

The drabs on Brummit's and Paskims's arms had shown him only too clearly how much his fresh-faced little Cyprian did not belong here. The last thing he wanted was to see Georgie's bloom turned into the sad and sallow look of an aging lightskirt.

While he knew that, as a cad and a bounder, he shouldn't care, he did.

"Why, it sounds like you're barely received," she was saying, her excitement scarcely concealed. "So if you're available for the evening, I think you'll do quite nicely."

Quite nicely?

Colin sputtered, trying to come up with a reply. He'd been propositioned by women before, usually with flirtatious glances, mayhap a note passed by a servant, even a slippered foot sliding up his leg under a dining table.

But never in his life had he been told by a lady that he might "do quite nicely."

Temple didn't bother trying to conceal his laughter. He burst out in a loud guffaw, bending over and clutching at his bottle-green waistcoat.

"Did I say something wrong?" Georgie asked. "Or was it my inglorious entrance that has you frightened?

Truly, once I am out of these demmed shoes, I promise I'm not so cowhanded." She blushed again and held out her foot, the flash of silk stockings pushing aside his bothersome notions of honor or innocence. "Well, at least not most of the time," she added hastily.

His cousin glanced first down at her foot and then back up at his cousin, before breaking into new gales of laughter.

"Temple!" Colin took him by the arm and gave him a good shove. "Leave be. This isn't what you think."

Temple held up one hand and said, "Let me give you two some privacy. You obviously have much to talk about." After he had backed a few steps away, he could still be heard chortling away, *"Quite nicely."*

Colin cringed. Knowing Temple he'd never hear the last of that one.

Without hesitating, he reached out and caught his little Cyprian by the hand and started towing her toward the door.

"Are we leaving?" she asked. Her eyes sparkled with hope. And invitation.

Oh no, he realized too late. *She thinks I am going to accept her offer.*

"No, I'm taking you home," he said. "You don't belong here."

His gaze once again swept over the gaudy ladies who made up the assemblage and saw by comparison the sparkle in Georgie's eyes and the fresh glow of her silken, unpowdered skin.

Most definitely out of place.

For if he wasn't a rake, then she was certainly no Cyprian.

Not even if her body was ripe and lush . . . Her way-

ward hair promising to spill seductively over a pil-
low . . . Her dress enticing a man both to view treasures
so well exposed and to desire nothing more than to explore the real bounty hidden beneath its shimmering
silk . . .

Colin's blood thrummed to life again. It brought
with it that cursed whispering need to claim her as his
own.

"In fact, I know you don't belong here," he said, this
time more to himself than for her benefit. "I mean to
see you safely home."

"Take me home?" she whispered. "But I thought . . ."

"Yes, I know exactly what you thought, but I am not
the man you seek."

Her glance, both furious and full of denial, said otherwise.

"Let me take you home. What you'll find here will
not bring you happiness."

"I never said I was looking for happiness, I was
only—" she started to blurt out. Whatever she was going to say, she stopped, her shoulders straightening
and her lips drawing a serious line of dismay across
her rosy face. "If that is your decision, then I fear, sir, I
shall look for companionship elsewhere." She started
to flounce away.

Colin caught her just before she stumbled anew on
her high-heeled shoes. "Have you any idea of the danger you could find here? Of the nature of men?"

She plucked herself free. "I'm well aware of the nature of men. *I wouldn't be here if I wasn't.*"

Her sardonic tone pricked his conscience. She
wasn't here because she wanted to be—she was here
because someone had forced this situation upon her.

He cursed the devil who had driven her to this place. What had the brute been thinking to compel someone like Georgie to such straits?

She must have seen his concern, because she added, "I can take care of myself, thank you very much. Please, go join your cousin, so I can get on with my business." She crossed her arms over her chest, her toe tapping as she waited for him to leave.

They stared at each other in stubborn silence, neither willing to concede their position. Despite his resolve not to fall prey to her appealing offer, Colin still felt the lure of temptation dangling before him.

She was a handful, a foolish handful. And the most unusual woman he'd ever met.

Still, what could he do? Cart her out of the room and demand she stop practicing her trade? He was sailing in two days' time. Then he'd be gone and she'd be . . . be back seeking carte blanche from another man.

He took one last look into her dark eyes. "Don't do anything you'll regret tonight, Georgie."

"I wouldn't have anything to regret if you were willing to . . . to . . ."

As her words trailed off, Colin spied something more behind her angry words.

Fear and desperation.

She looked as if she was about to say something, tell him the truth of the mystery and sadness behind her gaze, but Temple was coughing and sputtering away in a false maneuver to gain Colin's attention.

Colin let him choke.

"You should see to your cousin before he falls prey to a fit of apoplexy," she said, pulling her hand free from his. "Men of his age can hardly afford to allow such an ailment to go unchecked." With that she turned and dashed into the crush like a packet ship under full sail.

"My age?!" Temple exclaimed as he returned to Colin's side. "What the devil did the chit mean by that?"

"That you are an incorrigible old devil," he told him, giving him a couple of well-meant and hard blows to the back.

"What's that for?" Temple asked, stepping out of reach, and immediately setting to work to straighten his elegant evening jacket and ruffled cravat. "Dash it all, I just saved you from the worst-dressed, plainest little wren in the entire room. As well as a thrashing from your former shipmates."

Colin shrugged off his cousin's defense. "I found her quite refreshing. As for those three," Colin said, glancing over to where Paskims, Hinchcliffe, and Brummit stood entertaining their companions with a vast array of lies about their daring and exploits, "I could have taken care of them."

Temple made a rude noise in the back of his throat. "Another lesson in being beyond the pale—you will be considered a likely candidate for a thrashing or a duel by every greenling, stripling, and newcomer to town looking to cast himself as a dangerous fellow. Don't let yourself be dragged into a futile search for their manhood."

Colin nodded, but he was only half listening, his gaze locked on Georgie as she sauntered along the edge of the crowd, her gaze flitting from man to man as she renewed her search for her "rake."

"Let her go," his cousin said quietly.

"Uh, what?" Colin said.

"I said, let the chit go. You can't shoulder her burdens, not when you have so much to do before you." Temple paused, his distant gaze moving over the wayward crowd, as if he too sought his own lost Cyprian. "When one endeavors to save a nation, to serve his King, one sometimes must look past one's own desires."

Colin did his best to ignore his cousin's advice.

"You cannot help her," Temple told him, experience and concern lacing every word. "For you cannot protect her once you leave. You already know that. Just remember your task at hand, whatever it may be." A smile curved his lips. "And if you care to enlighten me as to its nature, mayhap I can help you."

Glancing over at his cousin, Colin laughed. "No. Don't even think about trying to wheedle details out of me."

Temple shrugged, then glanced one last time in Georgie's direction. "If you are going to be regarded by society with a critical eye, your other lesson is to avoid poor helpless little country girls. Why, that dress alone marks her as a castoff." Temple caught Colin by the arm and turned him away from Georgie, steering him instead toward some tables that had been set up in the corner for gambling.

"When did you become such an expert in women's fashion?" Colin asked, craning his neck so he could keep his gaze locked on her.

He shouldn't care, he shouldn't be spending tonight worrying about one wayward Cyprian. Temple was right. He did have greater concerns weighing on his shoulders.

And yet . . .

"I've always had an intense interest in women's fashions, mostly in how to remove them." Temple laughed and continued to propel Colin farther from her. "Actually, a keen sense of current fashion is the mark of someone who has little sense and too much time on his hands." He shrugged. "I do have my own appearances to keep up, and being a fashion wastrel is one of them." He fluffed his hand over his own oner- ously tied cravat and perfectly cut coat. "Your charity case is wearing a French gown at least twenty years out of fashion. Something that well made that hasn't been redone ten times over means she didn't buy it from some rag dealer in Petticoat Lane.

"Therefore, I would surmise that she inherited it— which means she is either following in the household trade or the family is in dun territory and she is their only way out." Temple shuddered. "To think she is the family salvation. Lord have mercy on the lot of them. They'll starve before that poor wren makes enough to keep the creditors at bay."

Colin shook his head. "And you got all that in one quick glance?"

"Yes." Temple shrugged. "Years of experience. Years of observation and experience."

He didn't quite agree with Temple. There was more to Georgie's story than such a simplistic explanation.

Colin glanced again in her direction, but the crowd was now too thick to find her. "So, based on your years of experience, what will happen to her?"

Temple shook his head. "Better that you don't know. Just try to remember her clumsy manners and cherish the bruise on your foot."

He did a double take and stared at his cousin. "How did you know about my foot?"

"The large, telling print atop your boot."

Georgie had restrained herself from looking about the room for Colin for a good hour, but she could no longer resist and searched the crowd high and low until she spied him and his cousin engaged in conversation with a pair of gorgeous Cyprians.

Real Cyprians, she thought, glancing down at her own gown, the one she'd thought so lovely when she'd pulled it from her trunk. Now she realized how hopelessly out of date it truly was. Against the fine, sleek gowns of the ladies around her, their hair and jewels so perfectly arranged, and their faces made more enticing with touches of kohl and rouge, it was obvious she didn't belong here.

How right Colin had been to point that out. And how foolish she was to think a man that handsome would find her intriguing enough to take her to his bed. Not that she'd done anything to recommend herself to him.

She cringed to remember.

Demmed. She'd said *demmed* not once, but twice. No wonder he'd told her she didn't belong there. Cursing like some rough sailor, she probably seemed more fit for strolling about the docks.

And if it wasn't her wayward tongue, then most likely her foot tromping had been enough to frighten him off.

Still, she wouldn't have minded so terribly much being bedded by him.

If only he had found her enticing as well. She thought she'd caught him glancing at her, his green eyes glowing with a hot passion that said he knew exactly what she looked like without her dress on—and how to get her out of it—but she was probably just kidding herself.

For despite his reassurances that he was a terrible rake, Georgie knew that whatever transgressions had earmarked him as a scoundrel and brought out the animosity of those officers, it was undeserved.

Well, almost.

When he hadn't let go of her for such a long time while they stood entangled at the top of the stairs, she'd have sworn she felt sparks running between them—as if their bodies already knew how well they fit together.

Yet it hadn't been enough to keep him.

She glanced at the ladies around her, some fluttering fans with the grace of butterflies, catching a man's attentions with their artful movements, others able to entertain their admirers with their witty remarks.

Georgie cursed silently again. What did she know about flirtation? What did she know about any of the arts of luring a man?

Little to nothing.

That humbling insight was only made worse by the realization that now she'd have to search in earnest . . . or give up and go home. As she glanced at the rather desolate collection of men in the room, the latter option became very appealing. Colin was the handsomest man among them, though his cousin ran a close second.

The rest of the crowd carried such a foul air of debauchery about them that they made the idea of marriage to Lord Harris almost palatable.

That was until the crowd parted a bit and two gentleman started sauntering in her direction.

And one of them she knew. *Uncle Phineas!*

Egads, she thought, ducking behind a potted palm and peering out between the fronds. *What is he doing here? And who could he be with?*

Then it struck her who she was staring at. *Her betrothed.* Lord Harris.

Who else could it be, given the looks of distaste and the wide berth the ladies were giving him?

Georgie thought she was going to be sick.

Her intended was a tall man, his face and limbs emaciated and yellowed. His scraggly shock of white hair was combed over in one direction so as to conceal his bald head. The attempt failed miserably.

He walked with a cane, which he used to poke at ladies who strayed within his reach. And when one of them squawked in dismay at being prodded in the bottom with the gold tip, he cackled and laughed until he wheezed like a blacksmith's bellows. "Come along, wench," he offered the offended woman. "I'll give you a poke with something that'll have you more than squealing."

The woman turned her nose in the air and stomped off, amid laughter from the men in the area and Lord Harris's raspy guffaws.

Georgie bit back the bile rising in her throat. This was her guardian's idea of a good husband?

Oh, wait until I get my hands around your neck, Lord Danvers, she thought, plotting his demise in a hundred different torturous manners. If anything, seeing her intended buoyed her resolve to find a rake, but also imparted a new urgency to her search—she must find someone with all due haste and depart before Uncle Phineas spotted her.

Stepping out from her hiding spot, she started to move in the opposite direction when suddenly her path was blocked by none other than Colin's three adversaries.

She didn't have a chance to escape them, for they had her outmaneuvered, each man taking a point like a well-trained squadron.

"Hello there, pigeon," the one called Brummit said. "We saw you cast off our old friend and decided to see if you were interested in some real sport tonight."

Paskims shot the man a dark glance, but when he turned to her, he was all smiles.

"Please ignore my friend's lack of manners." He caught up her hand and drew it to his lips before she could stop him. "We really weren't properly introduced. The name is Paskims. Captain Paskims, my dearest lady. And I think by the end of the evening you can rest assured you will find my company most compelling." With a waggle of his brows, or with what she suspected he attempted to pass off as charm, he tried pulling her closer.

She plucked her hand back, hiding it in the folds of her skirt. Later she'd scrub it clean with lye soap, but right now she only wanted to back away from his advances.

But they'd planned their attack well, for only too quickly, Georgie found herself pinned to the wall.

Commander Hinchcliffe swept the other two aside. His brown hair held a burnished glow of copper in the twinkling light of the candles overhead. He exuded an overall power and strength in his wide shoulders, as if he dared anyone to challenge his authority.

And of the three of them, Georgie knew without a doubt, this man, the one Colin had called Remus, was the most dangerous.

"Commander Hinchcliffe, at your service, madame. It is lovely to make your acquaintance this evening," he said, bowing curtly, but not reaching out to take her hand as Paskims had.

For that Georgie was thankful. His voice, even in just those few words, sent ripples of fear through her.

This was a man who would not be denied.

And she had no doubt what he wanted, as his assessing gaze swept over her with the calculated coldness of a northern breeze.

Whether or not he liked what he saw appeared to matter little.

And in that moment she wished that Mrs. Taft hadn't been so honest in her description of what happens between a man and a woman—for the thought of any of these men touching her thusly was enough to make Georgie's skin crawl.

Sometimes knowledge wasn't the blessing that most claimed it to be.

"There seems to be some mistake," she said as brightly as she could muster. "I see someone over there I was supposed to meet." She tried to brazen her way through their line, but they held fast, tightening their ranks with practiced ease.

"Oh, not so fast, pigeon," Brummit said, blocking her escape with his outstretched arm. "Whatever else you've been offered tonight, it can't begin to compare with what we've got in mind." He smirked at his friends. "And if it's the price that's the problem, we've just come into our shares and are in a generous mood. That is, if you don't make this difficult for us."

His tone suggested that he hoped she would.

"Truly, I am engaged elsewhere, sirs," she said. "It has been a pleasure to meet you." Georgie tipped her head and tried to duck under Brummit's arm.

But Commander Hinchcliffe was too fast for her. He caught her quickly and efficiently, hauling her back into their circle.

"Now that wasn't very polite," he said. "But telling." He glanced at his companions. "We'll have to stay sharp tonight, gentlemen. She's a quick one."

While Georgie had grown up with the rare and less refined tutelage of Mrs. Taft, the wharf and docks of Penzance had also been her schoolhouse. And as she'd gotten older, she'd learned to keep out of the way of men like these.

For what they had in mind, she suspected, wasn't just a simple bedding. And that notion kindled a bundle of fears that reached all the way down to her toes.

She took a fevered glance around the room, trying to discern if Colin was anywhere in sight—though why she thought he'd come to her rescue she couldn't fathom. Though it hardly mattered, for even if he was inclined to rescue her, he was nowhere to be seen.

Panic rose within her. What if he'd left with that other woman? The real Cyprian. The gorgeous redhead with all the airs and manners of a duchess?

Oh, why hadn't she just given in to his offer to take her home? She'd let her foolish, stupid pride get in the way of her better judgment.

And then, when she was about to give up all hope, she spied Colin standing on the stairs near the doorway looking in her direction. He was about to leave and was taking one last survey of the room.

And indeed the redhead stood not too far away, watching Colin from behind her fluttering, lacy fan while expertly chatting away with Temple.

Georgie swiped at a wayward tear.

Please come back, she prayed. *I was a fool not to listen to you.*

But it was too late. He'd turned his back and rejoined his party.

Temple frowned as yet another high-flyer flounced out of their way as they crossed the crowded the ballroom. "Dammit, Colin. That's the fourth batch of likelies you've scared off. Will you quit telling them you have no money?"

"Well, neither do you," Colin pointed out. On the ride over to the assembly hall, Temple had confided that he had had another falling out with their grandfather. The duke disapproved of Temple's pursuits and regularly made his displeasure known by cutting off his young heir's allowance.

"Yes, well, it is only a temporary financial setback," Temple assured him. He cocked an assessing glance in

Colin's direction. "You didn't have to give up all your money, did you?"

"All of it," Colin lied. He knew better than to let his cousin know that he had even a farthing. Temple could charm and wheedle coins out of the hands of a beggar. And besides, he would, as always, be back in their grandfather's good graces within a fortnight. "You'll just have to do without tonight."

Temple glanced once again after the lady. "That foolish chit practically begged me to set her up in new lodgings just last month. I thought for sure—"

"That she'd be ignorant enough not to have heard of my troubles, and therefore be an easy conquest?"

His cousin laughed. "I suppose so. Dash it all, even in my worst scrapes, I haven't had this effect on the fair sex. Especially not *these* ladies." Pausing for a moment, Temple tapped his chin with his lorgnette. "I wonder if I should try getting myself tried for treason? If only to get the packs of marriage-bent mamas off my back. You know, it might be just the trick to keep me free this Season."

"I wouldn't recommend it," Colin advised. "At least once I leave you'll have a chance at some company tonight."

"You are right there," Temple agreed. "Still, I don't like the idea of you going home—alone. Not on what was supposed to be your wedding night. Bad luck, I'm sure of that. I'll tell you what," he said. "You go stand over there—near that potted thing—and hide back a bit. Let me see if I can straighten everything out with that bit of muslin. I'll tell her you were recently held captive in a seraglio and escaped with some lessons that would surprise even her jaded tastes."

Colin laughed. "Don't go to any bother. It probably would be better if I just left."

Clucking at this notion, Temple shook his head. "That's the old Danvers talking again. And if I remember correctly, we buried him on the way over. There must be some likely bit of muslin, a rare incognita, an extraordinary vestal who could tempt that heart of yours to do something other than beat wildly over a well-trimmed sail. And not that gel you keep glancing about to find again. She'll be the ruin of you. She has that look about her."

Colin shot him a glance worthy of his grandfather's most withering stare, but it only made his irrepressible cousin laugh as he strolled toward the redhead and her companion.

He should have known his cousin wouldn't give up until he'd found Colin a worthy match. Temple's cure for anything that ailed one was the balm of a good woman. But not this time. Colin was ready to call it a night. He had much to do before he sailed, and there seemed no point in lolling about . . .

Except to find Georgie once again . . .

Nonchalantly he let his gaze sweep over the room, until his search came to an abrupt halt. There she stood, far across the room, her back to the wall and encircled by none other than Hinchcliffe, Paskims, and Brummit.

It was obvious from her fearful stance and the wide-eyed horror lighting her eyes that she was in over her head.

And drowning.

While it might seem the three officers were just trying to charm her, Colin knew the trio had more in mind than some "good sport."

They'd probably singled her out for the sole reason that she'd been with him earlier.

Yet even as he was about to take that first step, the honorable one that would be his natural reaction, he stopped himself, Temple's gloomy advice ringing in his ears.

. . . One sometimes must look past one's own desires.

Mayhap Temple was right. Lord knows his cousin had been at this devilish business long enough.

Colin tried to remind himself that he had a new reputation to maintain—that of a selfish, reckless bastard. He could ill-afford to become the noble knight in shining armor right now, particularly over one Cyprian . . . and especially in front of those three.

So he took a deep breath and turned his back on her. *His impossible, maddening, and enticing Georgie.*

With a resolute heart he started for the door, but halfway there he made the mistake of looking back.

For there, on the flushed pink of her cheek, sparkled a great tear. Glowing like a beacon, it beckoned to him, and him alone.

Colin cursed. Cursed himself. Cursed his wretched honor. Cursed his responsibilities.

For there was nothing else he could do now . . .

Chapter 4

What had she been thinking, coming to such a place? Georgie cursed herself for once again tossing the anchor over with the rope wrapped around her foot, as Captain Taft would have said.

If only she could just figure out how to get away from these three and then find a way to leave without Uncle Phineas catching her, she'd never, ever do anything this foolish, this reckless again.

"Gentlemen, I'm afraid there's been a mistake," a deep, rich voice said, the tone harboring an edge that would tolerate no resistance. "This lady is with me."

Colin.

Slowly, Georgie turned her head and discovered that perhaps she'd made her vow a little prematurely. For she found herself staring into the wide, solid chest of the one man in the room who her made feel wickedly reckless.

Her gaze moved over his rich velvet coat, his straight, timbered shoulders, up past the carved jawline marred by that thin scar. She couldn't help wondering what had caused it, and if she would ever know the secrets that seemed such a part of this mercurial man.

"What do you want, Romulus?" Hinchcliffe sneered. "I thought we were well rid of you and that cork-brained cousin of yours."

Georgie wondered at the man's nerve. From where she stood, eyeing the grim, dangerous set of Colin's mouth, along with the rest of his hard and unforgiving features, she couldn't fathom why the three just didn't up and leave.

In truth, he frightened her a bit, and he was on her side.

Even his eyes seemed to burn with a disregard for danger. The shade of green, like the fast-shifting tidal waters near Penzance, warned of the hazardous mood boiling beneath his exterior.

"I told you," he said. "This lady is with me." It wasn't just a statement, but an order, given without any thought that it would be contradicted or disobeyed.

Suddenly she envisioned him standing on the deck of a mighty frigate, uniformed and in full command. Everything about him spoke of undisputed authority—his proud stance, his commanding tones, and the challenge and determination alight in those eyes.

This was a man who was up against three imposing adversaries and apparently didn't seem to find the situation all that daunting—a Sir Walter Raleigh and

Charlemagne all in one. He had leapt to her rescue and he barely even knew her.

In addition, her heart clamored that perhaps he could also save her from her other niggling problem . . .

Perhaps she was putting the cart before the horse on that one, but she could hope. And it didn't stop her from edging herself closer to his imposing side, declaring her choice without another thought.

"Yes, I'm with him," she told her tormenters. "My apologies, my lord," she said, glancing once again up and over her shoulder at her knight errant. "I became lost in the crush and had trouble finding my way back to you."

"No, my dear," he said, taking her hand and putting it on his sleeve in a possessive and protective declaration. "The apologies are all mine. *I shouldn't have let you go in the first place.* But I've remedied that by coming to fetch you."

If just the mere touch of his hand, his suggestive words, sent her heart galloping, she dared to wonder what it would be like to have him touch her elsewhere . . .

"Shove off, Romulus," Paskims said, his piggy eyes growing even narrower, while his face started to flame in anger. "Why risk what little reputation you have left, when everyone in this room knows you should have spent this afternoon dancing on air for what you did?"

A slight smile turned on Colin's face. "So quick to see me hang, eh, Paskims? I really don't relish spending my afterlife awaiting you in Hades. Besides, given the way you like to falsify your logbooks, I'm quite sure you'll beat me to those black gates long before I end up under the hatches."

If it was possible, Paskims' face mottled to an even deeper shade of red. "I should kill you right now for that insult."

Colin appeared nonplussed. "I doubt you'd dare. For you know as well as I do it would be pistols for two and breakfast for one. And I do like my breakfast on time."

That sent Paskims surging forward, until that is, Hinchcliffe stopped him with a firm grip on the man's shoulder.

Georgie edged behind her protector. She'd seen officers like Paskims in Penzance—loose cannons, Mrs. Taft had called them—craven and cruel in their anger.

"See here, you poltroon," Brummit said, stepping into the fray. "The gel is ours for the night and you'll not be stealing anything more that you don't deserve. Not now, not ever again."

"I most certainly am not yours!" Georgie said over Colin's shoulder, emboldened by his reassuring presence. "Besides, what did this gentleman ever steal from you? The only thing I see that you could possibly possess is a penchant for cowardice."

So much for my promise not to stray into recklessness, she thought, the moment the hasty words escaped her lips.

Brummit's hand balled into a fist. "You rag-mannered bitch. I'll not listen to your saucy tongue for another minute," he said, stepping toward her, but only too quickly finding her champion in his path.

Georgie aimed a look of pure delight at the terrier-sized brute. "Go ahead," she said, nudging Colin forward, "give him what he deserves."

He shot a perturbed glare over his shoulder. "You aren't helping."

She glanced back and once again realized that it was, after all, three against one. "Oh, I suppose not."

"You can't think you're going to win this, can you?" Brummit asked Colin. "Just hand her over and you won't have to suffer any further humiliations. It's not like any of these birds would want you. Especially once they learn you're done in. Ruined. From what I hear, not even your grandfather is acknowledging you."

The shoulders before her stiffened once again, drawing their taut line even straighter.

Meanwhile, Brummit hadn't finished his telling disclosures. Leering at Georgie, he said, "What say you, my sweet? Perhaps he doesn't look so appealing now that you know the truth. Your prig there hasn't two crowns to rub together." His broad, bandy chest puffed up all that much more. "Now we three, we've prize money galore. Taken enough Frog ships in the last few months to keep you in silks and velvets for months."

"Or out of them," Paskims added, winking at her, his bushy eyebrows waggling about again like a pair a black moths.

Georgie shuddered, for even the thought of any of these men divested of his uniform was enough to send her running to her uncle's side to beg him to marry her off to Lord Harris without any further ado.

"Stand aside, Romulus," Brummit repeated. "This girl is ours."

Her protector turned slightly toward her. "What say you?"

"If you don't mind, I'd rather go with you."

"So be it," he said, with an imprudent, perilous light glowing in his eyes.

Dear Lord, what had she just agreed to?

Georgie had never considered herself overly sensible, but for half a heartbeat she wished she were more like other young ladies and was safely home stitching some bit of frippery. Then Colin's hand once again closed over hers and squeezed it, and suddenly Georgie was very glad she wasn't like other misses.

For they hadn't the chance to feel his touch.

"Gentlemen, you heard the lady, she is going with me," Colin said.

He turned to leave, and when he did, Paskims struck out in a flash, catching Georgie's free arm and yanking her out of the shelter of Colin's shadow. Even as the man plucked her away, Colin moved to strike him, but failed as the other two officers caught him by the arms and wrestled him away from her.

"Damn both your hides," he roared. "You'll not do this to me or the lady." He struggled back and forth, but Brummit and Hinchcliffe had him firmly clamped in their grips.

Paskims laughed, taunting Colin by making a great show of drawing Georgie close, his rummy breath bringing tears to her eyes. "Stop wasting your time, *Romulus*. Just because you wanted to debauch the little bitch first. You always were a selfish bastard. Don't worry, we'll leave something for you." He tugged Georgie into his arms. "Come here and see what you turned down, you bothersome little—" Then he used a name so bad that several of the rougher ladies around them who'd stopped to watch this tableau play out gasped in shock.

It wasn't that Georgie hadn't heard the phrase before, but it had never been thrown at her and she found she didn't like it one bit. And if that wasn't bad enough, out of the corner of her eye she spied Uncle Phineas barging through the crowd, his greedy gaze set on the growing knot of people who were gathering around them. Unfortunately the crowd was placing loud wagers as to the outcome, and she knew Uncle Phineas could never resist an opportunity to gamble.

Georgie didn't have a moment to lose.

Paskims shook her hard, rattling her attention back to the situation at hand. "Didn't you hear me, gel? I want a kiss, you little—"

Unwilling to wait around and find out whether the man had the bad taste to repeat his ugly slur, she balled up her hand, reeled back from Paskims, who was even then trying to lower his filthy mouth to hers, and planted her fist squarely into his nose with every ounce of strength she possessed.

Now Georgie hadn't grown up around the docks of Penzance without the occasional tussle, much to Mrs. Taft's despair, but the boys of the town only tangled with Georgiana Escott once before they learned their lesson.

Paskims learned his too late.

He instantly released her, leaving her teetering on her high-heeled shoes. His eyes opened wide in shock as he wheeled around like a spinning top on its final turns, before falling backward.

"My nose! My nose!" he wailed in a high-pitched nasal screech. "She broke my nose."

Georgie leaned over to survey the damage she'd wrought. "It's not broken." Why, it was barely bleeding.

"Get up," she dared him, shaking her fist before him. "And I'll give you another. Mind you, this time I'll make sure I break that demmed beak of yours."

Paskims stayed decidedly ensconced on the floor, complaining and wailing over his supposedly life-threatening condition.

Hinchcliffe charged forward. "I'll teach you to lay a hand on your betters, gel."

Before he could reach her, Temple stepped in front of him, appearing from out of nowhere in the crowd and blocking Hinchcliffe's progress.

Georgie watched the fast-moving emotions flitting across Temple's face. Shock at her quick dispatch of Paskims, then the barest hint of laughter at the man's continued ravings, and finally a line of outrage and determination so very similar to the one Colin still wore.

And then suddenly all those hints of heroism were gone and in their stead were all the trappings of a masher.

"Air! Air!" Temple cried. "I cannot stand the sight of blood. I must have air!" He wavered and faltered, latching heavily onto the unsuspecting Hinchcliffe, effectively pulling him out of Georgie's way.

"Get off of me, Templeton," Hinchcliffe complained, trying unsuccessfully to push him away. "Leave me be, you dandified idiot."

"Oh dear God," Temple wailed, pointing down at Paskims. "That man is bleeding on my best evening shoes! A valet, a tailor, a shoemaker, I do say, anyone come quickly! I need help!"

Just then there was a thwack and a loud gasp, and Georgie watched as Brummit went sailing past her, holding his gut and gasping for air.

Colin was once again at her side. He shook out his fist and then held a hand out to her. "If you want to leave, come with me now."

One look into his fathomless green eyes, and Georgie only too willingly reached out and let him pluck her from the chaos erupting around them.

He plotted a quick course through the crowded room, while behind them, Brummit, Paskims, and Hinchcliffe struggled to find their feet, shouting complaints and making calls for help from their uniformed brethren scattered about the room.

Georgie swiped a few stray locks out of her face, only to find Uncle Phineas standing in the path before them.

Colin shoved him out of the way, sending him floundering into the crowd, his pudgy arms waving about like a pair of windmills.

She made the mistake of looking back to see if he was hurt, and his livid gaze met hers.

"What the—?!" he called out.

Yet before their pursuers could overtake them or Uncle Phineas could regain his footing, Georgie found herself towed out the front doors, down the steps, tripping and spilling along as she tried her best to keep up with Colin's unrelenting pace.

Once they gained the street, Georgie felt her heart sink. Even if they were to find a carriage, it would essentially be trapped in the press of vehicles. There was nowhere for them to go, no means of escape.

Colin swore under his breath, looking this way and that, as if weighing his choices. Then he dashed straight into the confusion of curricles, cabriolets, and elegant barouches.

Drivers shouted curses at them as they set horses to prancing and tossing their heads in their traces.

Georgie stumbled once or twice in her wretched shoes, the high heels and ill fit a serious detriment to flight—but then again, she hadn't planned on creating a scene that would have an angry mob nipping at her hemline as she fled the ball.

Halfway across the street, Colin snatched a dark blanket from a carriage seat, throwing it over Georgie's shoulders like a shawl. The driver started down from his perch, shouting out a protest, until he spied Colin.

"To the corner, Elton," he said. "And we'll meet you there . . . in good time."

"Yes, milord," the driver replied, scrambling to pick up his reins, and shouting complaints to the other carriages blocking his path.

They set off anew, Georgie shrouded in the smelly horse blanket. So much for her dreams of the ermine-trimmed cape she'd once seen in a fashion magazine. Still, she didn't complain, for the dark wool covered her telltale dress, and from the shouts behind them, their followers had not let the crush of vehicles or the prospect of picking their way through a dark, horse-littered thoroughfare lessen their zeal.

"Your driver doesn't find this unusual?" she asked, wondering if Colin was in the regular habit of dashing about with disreputable women, and an angry mob hot on his heels.

"He's not my driver," Colin tossed over his shoulder. "He's Temple's man. And if you knew my cousin, you wouldn't consider our predicament unusual in the least."

Once across the street, Colin continued down the block until they came to an alley.

He darted down the narrow way, dodging the refuse blocking their pathway.

To her dismay, she stumbled, this time landing in a heap on the dirty cobbles. He turned around and plucked her up from the ground with barely a pause.

"My shoe," she cried out, realizing she'd lost one of her shoes the moment her stocking-clad foot touched the cold ground. "My shoe fell off." She turned to go back.

"Forget it," he told her tersely, catching her once again by the hand and making for the lamplight at the end of the alley.

"But it's my shoe!" she complained, the dirty alley soiling her only pair of silk stockings.

"I'll buy you a shopful of new ones tomorrow."

"I don't want a shopful, I want *my* shoe." Georgie pulled to a stop again. "Besides, according to those men back there, you haven't any money."

"I have enough," he told her. "Unless you prefer they give you the blunt for it."

As if to prove Colin's point, Hinchcliffe cried out from the entranceway from which they'd come, "There they are."

"Do you want to go back now?" Colin asked, once again towing her along.

"No," she muttered reluctantly, mourning the loss of Mrs. Taft's beautiful shoe. At least, she told herself, she still had one of them.

They went across another street and down another alley. When Georgie thought she couldn't run another step, he suddenly came up short, plunging her straight into his back.

It was like hitting a wall of muscle.

"In here," he whispered, pulling her into a darkened doorway.

He gathered the blanket around them, hiding them in the shadows, while their pursuers passed by.

Georgie's hand lay on his chest to steady herself, her trembling legs threatening to give out. As she leaned closer to him, let his body envelop hers, she suddenly understood Lady Finch's warnings about rakish young men.

For standing in this darkened doorway, pressed against Colin's all-too-masculine body, Georgie sympathized wholeheartedly with the young ladies who let themselves be led astray.

Right now, she wanted nothing more than to sink into his arms, lay her head on his chest. To feel him pull her hairpins free and whisper tempting offers into her ear while he continued to undress her.

In a blinding flash, the temptation of passions unknown blazed a path from her heart to her quaking knees, and Georgie knew she would never be the same again.

Even after Hinchcliffe and his partners were gone, Colin remained poised and ready, his body protectively covering hers.

She certainly wasn't going to stray from his shielding warmth. Certainly not from the man who seemed destined to be her savior—in more ways than one, if she had any say in the matter.

Hazarding a glance up at him, she found him staring at her.

Georgie didn't know what she had expected to find there, but it wasn't this . . . this mischievous, fiery light glowing in his eyes . . . a devil-may-care smile on his lips . . . his body tense and ready, alight in a fierce energy.

Why, he was enjoying himself! And as much as she shouldn't admit it, so was she—from the heat of his body enveloping hers, to his arm wound protectively around her. Even the reckless tattoo of his heartbeat beneath her fingertips hammered away as if to awaken some wild creature inside her.

Her rake. Her dangerous, tempting rake.

"I think we've eluded them," she whispered, her mouth suddenly gone dry.

He nodded, his gaze locked on her lips.

Ruin me, she wanted to urge him. *Take me back to your rooms and make me a fallen woman.*

His mouth moved closer to hers, his head tipped slightly, his gaze dark and penetrating. Georgie thought all her prayers were about to be answered.

She closed her eyes and parted her lips, just as she'd seen in an old painting, and waited.

And waited. And waited.

Her lashes fluttered open. What the devil was wrong with him now?

There on his face passed an odd look. Georgie knew it was a harbinger of bad news, and it was, for he stepped away from her abruptly, leaving her shivering in the cold draft of his wake.

"Come along," he muttered, turning on one heel and stalking up to the end of the alley.

Disappointed and cursing her continued bad luck with this man, Georgie trailed after him, the cool night air chilling her fevered skin. Whatever was wrong with her?

He had wanted to kiss her—of that she was positive. So why hadn't he done it?

Damn his moral fortitude, she thought. *He's probably still of an opinion that he is taking me home.*

Not if she had anything to say about it.

She caught up with Colin at the corner, where he was cautiously surveying the street beyond.

What she needed was a way to breach his noble intentions, to undermine his solid principles.

For she'd seen that spark of rakish delight in his eyes and knew that the thread of ruination was at hand.

It only needed a little unraveling.

Suddenly there was a shout once again from down the street. "Got you trapped now, Romulus," Hinchcliffe cried out.

When she glanced in the other direction, she spied Brummit and Paskims steering a single-minded course in their direction.

They were trapped. Not that it seemed to occur to Colin.

He was off and running, hauling Georgie along at a reckless clip straight for Hinchcliffe. She wanted to tell him to stop, but then she spied his intent.

Lord Templeton's carriage was careening around the corner behind Hinchcliffe, a grinning Elton driving the horses straight at the unwitting man.

Colin barreled along faster and faster, towing Georgie, her feet pedaling almost in the air to keep up with him.

Hinchcliffe stood in their path, his broad chest puffed out, his eyes narrow and mean.

Colin barely even paused. His arm shot out as they passed the man, hitting him squarely in the chest and knocking the commander on his backside and out of Elton's fierce path.

Right on their heels, Brummit and Paskims were nipping like terriers, and Colin shouted at Elton, "Keep moving."

Elton nodded and whipped up his reins. Even as the carriage started to lurch forward, Colin caught the door and yanked it open.

He swooped his other arm around Georgie's waist and pulled her tumbling within.

They crashed in a heap on the floor of the opulent carriage, with Colin calling out a hasty set of instructions. The driver snapped the whip and had the horses dashing away even before Colin finished speaking.

They sped straight for Brummit and Paskims, the two men diving out of their path, their shouts lost in the frantic clippity-clop of the horses and the creaking springs of the carriage.

Georgie found her voluminous skirts tangled with Colin's long legs, and as she tried to steady herself against the wild rocking of the carriage, one hand came to rest on the muscled length of his thigh, the other wound around his shoulders.

He too caught hold of her, his arms closing in around her waist, giving her the solid anchorage she sought. His hand came to rest under her breast, his fingers brushing along her bodice, sending shivers down her spine. For a moment she lay still in his arms, her heart hammering, her body atingle at the new sensations his intimate touch evoked. Catching her breath, she tipped her head back so she was face-to-face with him—this complete stranger, and yet so very familiar.

There in those deep green eyes glowed the same tempting light she'd spied in the alley.

This time she wasn't going to give that fire a chance to extinguish. Instead, she intended to fan it until it blazed a life of its own.

And so she pulled herself even closer to him, until her lips met his in an impetuous, passionate kiss.

Chapter 5

True to Aunt Verena's worries about young ladies loitering about the docks of Penzance, Georgie had been kissed before, but those had been hastily snatched affairs from wayward boys who hadn't heard the warnings about her right hook.

But this time she had no intention of sending this man toppling backward for his impertinence.

No, she *wanted* this man to kiss her and keep kissing her.

And best of all, his mouth vanquished any opinions she might have held about his honorable nature before their lips touched.

He pulled her closer, impatiently gathering her in his arms, as if possession by his lips was not enough.

She understood his hunger, for the same need had commandeered her very soul.

His tongue edged across her lips, and her mouth

opened to welcome him. He groaned, a deep and primal growl, as he teased and taunted her to tangle with him, their tongues caressing each other. If she hadn't been indecently sprawled across him on the floor of the carriage, she knew her knees would have buckled in the wake of the molten fire growing in her belly. It made her insides quiver; it made parts of her positively melt.

Drowning . . . she was drowning.

And if his kiss could evoke this kind of response, she wondered what would happen when they . . .

Made love . . .

Admittedly, he'd turned down her offer earlier, but now things had changed. He had changed.

He'd come back for her.

And in the alley, when she'd looked up into his eyes, she would have sworn she'd spied more than just lust alight there.

He desired her. Wanted her with the same breathless passion now threatening to consume her.

The very idea sent her arching toward him, her breasts pressing against him, her hips swaying over his breeches. There she felt the hardness that would be her undoing, her salvation.

Yet this man was no longer just the means to solving her most immediate problem; he was offering possibilities of which she had only dreamt.

For one night, this man would love her, cherish her, and give her enough memories to last a lifetime. Memories to keep her warm when Uncle Phineas cast her out on the streets and she was consigned to a life of servitude.

His strong, steady hands, hands that had pulled her

close, had gathered her into his warm embrace, now caressed her. His fingers twined in her hair, stroked her cheek, and slid down over her bare shoulder. She shivered as his heated touch grazed her bodice. His fingers dipped inside the neckline of her gown, tenderly exploring her breasts.

And from his sigh and groan, for once she didn't mind that they were hardly the voluptuous shape that Kit seemed to be sprouting.

As he reverently caressed them, his thumb rolling over nipple until it rose to a hardened peak, she sensed that he found them irresistible, perfect under his passionate tutelage.

His lips pulled away from hers, leaving her gasping for air, lost without the warmth of his mouth, the teasing of his tongue to guide her. But his lips soon found a new refuge as he placed a blazing kiss over the peak of her nipple. She sucked in a deep, shocked breath, her entire body blazing to life with a new fire as the rough surface of his tongue lapped over her.

A deep breathy sigh slipped from her lips, as a languid need spread through her veins.

She arched back, allowing him total access to her, wondering at her own brazenness as she curled her fingers into his dark hair and held his head to her breast.

How could she ask him, nay, beg him to give her the answer to the ragged, trembling need that was overtaking her? How could she find a way to convince him to free her body from the entangled sensations that offered a whispered promise of something . . . of something she didn't quite understand.

Yet her body seemed to recognize it, her hips swaying and rocking as if they knew the truth of what was to come.

But Georgie's rising desire tumbled abruptly back to earth as the carriage lurched to a stop.

The jolt broke them apart, breathless and panting. Colin stared at her, his eyes wide and blinking, as if he were seeing her for the first time. Seeing something in her that he just couldn't fathom.

And as in those magical moments in the alley, Georgie felt their world shifting beneath them once again, changing the rules, changing them.

"Milord," the coachman called down from his perch. After a few polite moments, he repeated it again. "Milord?"

Colin shook his head, like someone being reluctantly awakened. "Yes, Elton," he replied, his voice as ragged as her own breathing.

"Beg pardon," the driver said, "but is there anywhere in particular you want me to go? These town horses don't take to a good run. Would ye be wantin' to go to yer room near the Square or to Bridwick House?"

Georgie watched an odd play of emotions cross Colin's face; his brow furrowed, and whatever passions had claimed him before were suddenly lost.

Bridwick House. The very words startled him to attention, as if reminding him of some other obligation, some other errand of honor she was keeping him from.

"Not *Bridwick*, Elton," he said. "Not there."

He said it with such vehemence, it left her wondering what problems resided at this house.

Suddenly, she thought of something that had never occurred to her. Perhaps he didn't want to go to his apartments or to this Bridwick House because he kept a mistress ensconced there.

Or, even worse, a wife.

Lady Diana . . .

The name rocketed out of her memory. Hinchcliffe or Brummit or one of those mullet-heads had taunted Colin about a Lady Diana.

. . . Perhaps I'll start calling on Lady Diana. I hear she's no longer engaged . . .

Georgie would bet her remaining shoe that this Lady Diana was somehow connected to Bridwick House, and she was just as certain this other woman wasn't his wife. A fiancée, perhaps.

Truly, what should she care if Colin was married or betrothed and seeking companionship elsewhere? Men were free to keep mistresses or spend their evenings with ladies of the demimonde.

But for some reason, she didn't want to think that this man would. There was just such an air of knight errant about him.

And right now, her knight was offering her a small smile, an apology of sorts, that filled her once again with dread.

He reached over, and for a moment Georgie thought he was going to renew his kiss, but to her dismay, he gathered her up and deposited her on the well-appointed leather seat. Instead of joining her there on the cozy cushions, he took the opposite bench and pulled the trap door to the roof open even further.

"We are taking the lady to her residence." When he turned back to Georgie, he was once again the proper gentleman, the rogue seducer gone in an instant. "Where do you live?"

"Aren't we going to your home? Your driver mentioned a house or your rooms . . . either would do fine."

Hadn't Lady Finch explicitly warned her never to go to a man's private rooms? And for that reason alone she knew his lodgings were exactly where she wanted to be.

Besides, it was no longer for the sole purpose of ending her unwanted betrothal; now there was another problem to contend with . . . the erratic pounding of her heart . . . the begging need this man had awakened in her with his tempestuous kiss and his daring touch.

"I don't think my rooms would be appropriate, Georgie. Not now."

"What about that Bridwick House the driver mentioned?" she asked impulsively.

"The only place you are going tonight is back to your own house. To your own bed."

He didn't want to spend the evening with her? This was an unmitigated disaster! And after his more than enthusiastic kiss, she had thought she'd found the answer to her dilemma.

"Did I do something wrong?" she asked.

Colin heard the question and nearly flinched at the underlying accusation there.

She hadn't done anything wrong . . . in fact, she'd done everything right.

Too right.

"No," he told her. "It's just that it's growing late, and I have some important business to attend to in the morning."

Like trying to repair my broken betrothal, he thought,

using the very proper image of Lady Diana as an excuse to get himself out from under this odd little Cyprian's spell.

But Diana isn't coming back, a devilish voice whispered in his ear.

That wasn't entirely true, despite Lady Diana's vehement declaration that she no longer wanted to marry him. And the fact that he was no longer sure about his choice of bride was irrelevant.

Colin knew only too well that once all the misunderstandings about his court-martial were cleared up, their families would move heaven and earth to see the breach between them mended—meaning he couldn't in all honorable intent consider his betrothal over.

Then again . . .

Dash it all, he was starting to doubt even the inevitability of a reconciliation.

This was all Temple's fault. He was the one who'd cast doubts into what Colin had always held as undisputable beliefs—his marriage should be a meeting of good breeding and political gain, not "fun."

And if Temple had thrown a tangled line into his straight and well-trimmed notions about love and marital obligations, Georgie had stirred them into a whirlpool of contradictions.

Just as he'd told Temple, he and Lady Diana were a perfect match, a choice marriage between a titled gentleman and a lady of quality.

And Georgie? She was certainly no lady—the facer she'd planted on Paskims's nose proved that. Not that the bastard hadn't deserved it after the foul name he'd called her.

But still, Colin thought, he should be shocked by her bossy manners, forward attentions, and ability to land a flush hit better than most men.

He should be appalled and repelled by such shocking behavior.

But instead he was intrigued.

Why, he hadn't had so much fun at a London social event . . . well, ever. Dashing out of the Cyprian's Ball, her hand tucked in his, the room erupting into chaos around them, their enemies hot on their heels, the sparkle of mischief in her eyes teasing him, had been . . . exhilarating.

And damn it all, if the chit hadn't enjoyed every minute of it as well.

The old Colin, as Temple had called him, would have been worried about appearances, trying to do the right thing, and certainly never would have caused a row at a ball that was sure to end up being the most oft-repeated *on dit* for the upcoming Season and beyond.

He'd like to blame his newfound notoriety all on Georgie. But perhaps it had been brewing all this time. Perhaps Lamden had been right—deep down Colin was a true Danvers. Like his scandal-driven father, like his rapscallion brothers. Of course, his father's ill-gained reputation had taken two runaway marriages and nearly thirty years of travel and deception for the Foreign Office to attain its less than sterling luster.

And all it had taken to open Colin's own Pandora's box of mischief, to turn his world upside down and inside out, had been the introduction of one beautiful little troublemaker, and a few hours at the Cyprian's Ball.

Glancing over at her, he rephrased that thought.

One all too tempting enchantress.

If only he hadn't kissed her. But somehow in the tangle of dashing into the carriage and Elton's rather hasty departure they'd been thrown together, and the rest . . . well, the rest was inescapable.

He tried telling himself he'd only returned to her side to save her from a bad situation. To make sure she was delivered back home where she belonged.

He certainly had not intended to kiss her, any more than he could consider the tempting offer so obviously sparkling in her hauntingly dark and mysterious eyes.

No, he couldn't. No, he shouldn't. *Absolutely not.*

That, Temple would probably say, with a doleful shake of his head and a couple of taps of his lorgnette, *was the old Colin talking*.

And what if Colin accepted her proposition? He didn't know if he dared, for he suspected it might come at a higher price than just mere coins.

"Where do you live?" he asked, determined to follow his best intentions and see the lady home safe. "Elton will see you taken there without any further delays."

"What?" she sputtered, scrambling up in her seat, her tousled hair falling about her shoulders in a honeyed array of willful curls. "You can't do that to me. Not now!" Her outrage flared with the same passion as her kiss, her body arching toward him, her breasts rising and falling with her ragged breath.

In an instant, he hardened, remembering all too well the way she'd trembled and moved with him on the floor of the carriage. The silk of her skin, the curve of her delicious breasts . . .

Ignore the breasts, he told himself. *Forget the feel of them under your fingers.*

Honor, duty, King and country, he reminded himself. He had a mission to undertake. Yes, that was it, remember his mission.

"You'll not take me home," she was repeating.

"I most certainly will." Colin took a deep breath. He'd never met such a stubborn chit. And troublesome . . . and rag-mannered . . . and all too desirable . . . He shook that last notion aside. "I apologize if my earlier lapse in manners gave you the wrong impression, but you are going home."

"I am not going home. I went to quite a bit of trouble to go to this ball," she said, her impetuous temper heating every word, the same anger he'd witnessed as she'd urged him to give Brummit the thrashing the cad deserved.

Now he was on the receiving end. Colin squirmed in his seat, unused to being the subject of a lady's ire.

Lady Diana's outrage had been shocking enough, but her ill-temper hardly held a candle to a furious Georgie.

She leaned forward, tapping a gloved finger against his chest. "I will remind you that it was you who picked me out for the evening. Now you'll do your part and take me to your rooms." She crossed her arms over her chest and stared straight ahead, as if daring him to do otherwise.

"I did not," he shot back, feeling his own temper getting the better of him. He'd been taught never to argue with a lady, but Georgie was another matter. He had a feeling she'd actually like a good row. "I did not pick you out."

"I disagree. You came back and claimed me for the

night." She set her shoulders in a defiant line. "I have witnesses."

"Witnesses?" he sputtered.

"Yes. Captain Hinchcliffe, Captain Brummit, and Captain Paskims."

"Commander Hinchcliffe," he corrected.

"Aha!" she said. "So you agree. They were witnesses to your declaration."

"It was hardly a declaration," he said. "More of an offer to save your lovely hide."

This seemed to take her aback, and a feminine softness rounded her harsher points. "You think I'm lovely?"

"That is beside the point." *Lovely, yes. And gorgeous and tempting, as a matter of fact.*

"Not to me." Her lashes fluttered over her dark eyes, and she shot him a glance that sent his blood rising once again.

Colin shook his head, trying to clear his befuddled senses. How had this gotten so out of hand? From his telling her she was going home to his telling her she was lovely?

He suspected this astounding minx could talk a pickpocket out of his best purse, spin circles around the Inn's best solicitors.

Colin sat back in his seat and stared at the wry set of her mouth—as if she supposed she'd won.

Presumptuous baggage! He was of a mind to have Elton stop the carriage and dump her out where they stood—no matter the surroundings.

He'd wager she could take care of herself in the middle of Seven Dials.

And yet, he possessed a sneaking admiration for her direct and forward stance. There was something utterly refreshing about a lady who saw the situation in such black and white terms, and made no attempts to keep them to herself. No, from this hoyden, there were none of the usual carefully chosen words or pretty phrases meant to please a gentleman.

So unlike Lady Diana . . .

He didn't know why he was making such a comparison, or why it mattered. But it did matter. He couldn't see Georgie marrying a man she did not love, or choosing the obligations of Society and tradition to rule over her heart, as Lady Diana would have if fate hadn't intervened for them. And for that, he admired the little spitfire. At least he did until she began badgering him anew.

"You are determined to ruin everything, I can see that now," she was saying. "And if that is the way it is to be, then take me back to the ball."

"Take you back?" he said, saying the words only to see if he'd heard her correctly.

And to his complete dismay and irritation, he had.

"Yes. Take me back," she said, her mouth setting once again in the unmistakable line of defiance.

"You would go back to those men? To Hinchcliffe and Brummit and Paskims?" He shook his head. "They are not the type you want to be spending your time with."

"They were exactly the kind I was looking for," she told him. "Now, if you don't mind, *I* have business to complete." This time she rapped on the roof of the carriage. "Stop this blasted carriage at once. Stop it, I say."

Given the lady's commanding tone, Elton responded like any good servant and pulled the reins back, bringing the horses to a halt. She leaned over, flung the door open, and started out with a determined step.

"Oh no, you don't," he told her, catching her by the waist and hauling her none-so-gently back into her seat. "I didn't risk my neck so you could go frolicking back into that lion's den. Now tell me where you live."

He issued his words in the same tone of command that would have marshaled a shipload of sailors and marines into seeing his orders obeyed.

Not Georgie. Instead, she appeared ready to lead a mutiny. A successful one.

"I cannot return home. Not yet. Not until I've . . . until I've . . ." Her cheeks flushed and her gaze darted away from his as her words came to a faltering halt.

Whatever was wrong with the chit? He was offering her a chance for an evening away from her profession, away from her livelihood.

Then suddenly he understood. Why it hadn't struck him before; he could have kicked himself.

She wasn't mad that he was refusing her charms. She was angry over her lost income.

Not that she would have seen much more than a few farthings from Hinchcliffe, Paskims, or Brummit, despite all their boasts of prize money.

The trio had a history of parsimony when it came to ladies of her profession. And worse . . .

He looked up and found that Georgie's stubborn features were melting into a near panic.

"Now will you just leave me be," she pleaded. "I've

only a few hours left before . . . before . . ." Tears threatened to spill down her cheeks.

Egads, the gel should be on the stage instead of the Haymarket trade, he thought. She was the most convincing wronged innocent he'd ever seen.

This display might be just a Cyprian's trick, her way of extracting a higher price by feigning a measure of innocence she likely didn't possess, but it worked damned well in tugging at his heart.

After all, this was her occupation. While she had claimed earlier that she wasn't interested in the usual compensation a Cyprian demanded, he hadn't believed her then and he didn't now.

Not completely.

For he couldn't shake his suspicions that there were other reasons that had brought Georgie to the Cyprian's Ball. Ones far more compelling than a new frock or a string of sparkly baubles.

Perhaps Temple was right, and she was working to save her family from ruin, or some other noble cause.

"Oh, so that is how it is." He leaned back in his seat. "I understand." And while he may appreciate her indignation, he certainly wasn't going to let it sway him into allowing her to return to the ball.

Not so long as the devil's own trio lurked about there.

"You can come with me," he told her, before he could stop himself.

"With you?" she asked, one brow arching upward.

She needn't sound so incredulous.

"And what is wrong with me? Contrary to what those bounders you are so taken with said, I still have enough blunt to pay my debts. And I suppose I do owe you for what you've lost tonight."

I haven't lost anything yet, he thought he heard her mutter under her breath.

She sighed and took a deep breath, as if she were using her utmost patience not to knock him over the head. "You think you owe me money?"

"Yes," he said. "Your fee for the night. I believe I've left you without your evening's earnings."

"Oh yes, my earnings," she said, catching onto the subject as if he'd thrown her a rope. "Yes, I suppose you did." Then she stuck her stockinged foot into his lap and wiggled it. "And my shoe. As I recall, you promised me a shopful."

"I did not," he said.

The delicate brow arched again. The one that warned him not to quibble the point, she was right.

"You only lost one shoe," he said, doing his best to ignore the heel of her foot rubbing against his thigh, the way her dress fell back to reveal the trim line of her calf.

"But it was my best one," she replied, bringing the remaining shoe up to rest on his other leg as if to present her evidence.

Point well taken, he thought, as his less than honorable intentions started to get the best of him again.

What he needed to do was get her the coins she required and get her home.

Then he could get on with his life and forget this entire evening.

He could almost hear Temple's smug chuckle at that notion. *You never know where you'll find love*, his cousin had jested. *Once you see her, you'll be enchanted for life.*

Love at first sight.

Since when did he lend Temple's wit and wisdom on women any credence?

His answer came in a glance at the strange Cyprian seated across the carriage—those tea-brown eyes, which seemed to see right through his bluff and bluster; her wistful glances, full of anticipation and a hunger not unlike the one sending his blood racing.

Eyes? He was getting poetic about a woman's eyes?

What bothered him more was that for the life of him, try as he might, he couldn't say with any measure of certainty what color eyes Lady Diana had, while in less than a few hours Georgie's fair features were imprinted on his soul.

In an instant he understood why his ruined engagement wasn't the complete loss he suspected it would be for someone who was truly in love.

Earlier in the day, words like those hadn't meant anything more to him than something poets made up and romantics eulogized endlessly.

And now?

He didn't know what he believed.

Of one thing he was certain, if he was to regain control of his bewildered senses, he needed to put as much distance between himself and this tempting little armful as he could.

"How much do you need?" he asked. "I'll pay you what you require and take you home."

Georgie wanted to grind her teeth in frustration. He was going to just give her coins and send her on her way?

Of all the rakes and cads in London, out of a room of

ne'er-do-wells and bounders, she had to find a man whose kisses conveyed so much promise yet his honor held sway.

This would never do!

Georgie shot him a sidelong glance and found that he too was watching her.

She had no idea what one charged for an evening, so she named the first ridiculously high amount that came to mind. An amount she doubted he had on hand, and one that would ensure they had to return to his rooms.

He coughed and sputtered. "For that price, miss, you'd have to be a virgin." Then he laughed as if such a notion was a fine jest.

But I—she almost said, stopping herself just in time. Instead she tried to join in and offered a small laugh of her own.

Colin was shaking his head. "Listen, even if I had such an amount, I certainly wouldn't hand it over just to see you safe."

"I won't tell you anything for a penny less," she declared stubbornly.

Georgie suspected this man was not contradicted often, for each time she naysayed his orders, he got this vexed look of disbelief on his face, as if he hadn't heard her correctly.

So she repeated herself.

"I can't go home without the full amount," she said. If he could use his honor as a defense against her charms, then perhaps she could use it to find a way around his noblesse.

And then another lesson from her classics tutor

came to mind. The story of Troy and a wooden horse. If she remembered her Greek mythology correctly, all she had to do was get into his house under some pretext, and then she would have him at her mercy . . . At least that was the theory.

"Half," he countered.

"Half?" She tried to sound both insulted and outraged. This was after all her body they were haggling over, and she didn't like the idea of letting herself go cheaply like a stale loaf of bread.

"Half," he repeated. "Or I take you to the magistrate and let him find you a home."

She sucked in a deep, outraged breath. *The magistrate?* He wouldn't dare.

Georgie glanced over at the hard, unreasonable tilt to his brows, the steady line of his jaw, and realized he would. So she nodded her head in agreement.

He reached for the trap and opened it. "I've changed my mind, Elton. Please take us to Bridwick House and then we will be seeing the lady directly home."

"Aye, milord," Elton said.

Bridwick House. Georgie's gaze wrenched back up toward Colin. "It's rather late," she offered. "Won't our arrival disturb your mother, your family . . . your wife?"

She held her breath as she waited for his answer.

"*We* won't be disturbing anyone, for you will remain in the carriage." After the longest few moments of her life, Colin finally added, "And I am not married."

She resisted grinning.

They traveled along for some time before the carriage rolled to a stop in front of a comfortable and fashionable house. The entire block had an air of respectability and gentility that Uncle Phineas's and Aunt Verena's barely fashionable neighborhood lacked.

Georgie doubted many Cyprians saw the inside of these houses.

Colin was out of the carriage in an instant, and as Georgie started to follow him, he said, "Oh no. You stay right where you are."

"But—" she started to protest.

"No." He jerked his thumb at the house next door. There was a candle still burning in one of the first-floor windows. "The magistrate's residence. And it looks like he's still awake."

Georgie sank back into her seat, letting him think she was defeated.

Oh, but she wasn't. She hadn't come this far, gotten this close, to let Colin's better judgment get in the way of her losing her virginity.

He said something in a low voice to Elton and then was up the steps in a thrice.

Georgie tapped her one shoe impatiently, counting slowly to fifty before she leapt out of the carriage and started up the steps in a great hurry.

"Oh no, you don't, miss," the driver said, hopping down from his perch and following hot on her heels.

She turned around and smiled as sweetly as she could. "I have to use the necessary."

Elton's gaze rolled upward. "You can wait. So get back in like his lordship told you."

Georgie hopped up and down a bit. "Please, sir. I fear I cannot wait much longer."

The man remained unconvinced, and pointed a finger back at the open door of the carriage.

Apparently, deception was not going to work on the worldly Elton. So that left only the direct approach. She yanked open her reticule and fished out nearly every coin she had.

Offering them to him, she said, "Is this enough for you to just leave?"

"Madame!" he said. His tone implied that she'd insulted him. But as she started to return her meager offering to her purse, he coughed a couple of times. "Well, now, I suppose this might make a good story for Lord Templeton."

Georgie latched onto that notion like a coconspirator. "Oh yes, Lord Templeton will find it an excellent lark that you left me here with his cousin."

"That he will," Elton said, grinning, his gnarled hand scooping up the coins. In a flash, he jumped back up on his seat and clucked at his nags. "Have a nice evening, ma'am," he called out as the carriage rolled away.

"I plan on it," she whispered after him.

She made her way up the stairs slowly, teetering on her one shoe.

She got to the doorway about the same time Colin came bolting down the main staircase.

He stood in front of her, blocking her entrance, looking over her shoulder, out into the empty street. The crunch of the wheels and the clip-clop of hooves were now only faint echoes.

A low growl rumbled in his chest, but his frustration and anger didn't frighten Georgie.

"What the devil did you do?" he demanded.

"What you should have done," she replied, sailing past him and into the house. "Now you owe me for the driver as well."

Chapter 6

Colin couldn't believe the utter nerve. Why, she'd probably bribed Elton to leave and now she wanted compensation for her transgressions. Of all the audacity. Of all the nerve.

And yet it didn't surprise him. The woman seemed to know no bounds. Really, he should blame Temple for this entire debacle. Given that his cousin was always in arrears, especially on his servants' salaries, Elton had probably been more than happy to take her offering. And now Temple's perpetual lack of funds had left Colin with a handful of trouble.

Even worse, as she sailed through the very proper and decent doorway of Bridwick House, he couldn't shake the overwhelming feeling that something about this scene was very right.

That she *should* be the one crossing this threshold.

After all, it was supposed to be his wedding night.

His grandfather had given him Bridwick House as a wedding present, and the efficient staff was nowhere in sight, obviously wanting to give the bridal couple their privacy.

The only evidence of the Setchfield servants was a brace of candles glowing on a side table.

Georgie wandered about the foyer, staring a bit wide-eyed at the glittering arrangement of fancy furniture, as well as the grim and forbidding paintings of Setchfield descendants that disappeared into the darkness of the stairway.

Instead of being properly awed, she seemed more bemused. "This is *your* house?"

"Not for long," he said. Colin doubted his grandfather would feel obligated to let him keep it now that he had disgraced the family with his court-martial and lost the connection to Lady Diana.

"Because of . . . of what . . . what those men said about you?"

"Yes, something along those lines," Colin said, not of a mind to go into the details. If she thought he had gambling debts, that was just fine with him. But he took some comfort in the fact that she didn't seem to know who he was . . .

Why that suddenly mattered he couldn't fathom.

"Well, if you have to give up this house, you should at least take some memories with you." She moved closer to him, her eyes alight once again with her irresistible offer for a night of reckless passion.

Colin's imagination gave way to any number of memories he could have about Bridwick House . . . mostly of her naked in his bedchamber upstairs.

"Where are the servants?" she asked, her fingers

trailing along the edge of the silver salver on the table.

"Gone for the night."

She cast a sidelong glance over her shoulder. *How convenient,* it seemed to say.

The stillness and solitude of the house were broken by the hypnotic sashay and rustle of her skirt. Her funny, hip-hopping stroll around the foyer, he assumed, was her attempt at a graceful turn. And yet he was mesmerized.

As she moved, the fabric of her dress shimmered in the candlelight, rippling like a restless sea about her lithe body. The undulating and caressing waves of the sea.

When he'd been a brand-new midshipman, barely thirteen at the time, there had been an old grizzled sailor on the ship who'd taught him much of the sea's lore, including tales of mermaids—those wild, hoydenish sirens of the waves. He'd almost convinced Colin that they truly existed . . . And after all those years, now Colin suddenly believed.

Georgie was like one of those fey, wild creatures who the old sailor told him would magically appear one day—if only he looked hard enough—a gift from the Fates to a lonely sailor. A prize to catch hold of and never let go.

So when she swept toward him this time, his fingers caught her arm, the bare part between the lacy edge of her gown and the top of her long white gloves. He couldn't remember ever touching anything so tempting, so silken in all his life.

Around him, the rare and intriguing scent of her perfume once again teased his nose. He took a deep breath and let it out.

"Who are you?" he asked, wondering if she were truly real.

She glanced up through her tangled curls. "Yours. Yours for tonight."

He brushed her hair aside and looked once again into her eyes. Somehow he knew he could drown in their sable depths.

For as he tipped his head down to claim her offer, to throw himself over into her mysterious seas for tonight, he knew he wanted her . . . wanted her . . .

Always.

The startling realization wrenched him back. Always?

That wasn't possible. Not after a few hours.

No more possible, he told himself, than mermaids.

He set her aside, putting enough distance between them to let the chill of the room cool his ardor.

"Here, let me fetch a light," he said, catching up the brace of candles. "The one I took with me blew out, so I was coming downstairs to get another when I heard the carriage leaving."

He sent her a significant glance about that mystery and the brazen chit grinned back.

Colin started for the stairway, and then realized if he took the light, he'd leave her in darkness. Besides, he didn't feel right about leaving her alone. "Come along then."

She cast him a sidelong glance and a sly smile.

He wagged a finger at her. "Oh, don't get any ideas. You're coming along so you don't get into any more trouble."

She nodded in agreement, but he had a feeling it wasn't to anything he'd just said.

They climbed the stairs slowly, Georgie limping along on one shoe.

Colin stopped at the first landing. "Why don't you take that blasted thing off? You'll fall and break your neck hobbling along like that."

She clung to the rail and pushed her foot out from beneath the hem of her gown. "Will you do it?"

Colin glanced down at the soft silk of her stocking, the gentle curve of her calf, and knew there was no way he was going to take a closer look. He had a good idea of the temptation that lay hidden beneath her hemline.

"No, thanks." He started up the stairs again and then paused once more. "You do realize that we are here to fetch your money and then we are leaving. Immediately."

"*Of course.*"

Her tone implied otherwise.

Once they reached the first floor, Colin marched determinedly down the hall.

Into the study. Open the sea chest. Count out her coins. Leave.

He repeated his course of action with each step. *Into the study. Open the sea chest. Count out her coins. Leave.*

It was such a simple, straightforward plan. How could it fail?

Well, he did have to factor Georgie into his course. That, he suspected, was as predictable as sailing into a gale wind.

He got to his study and knelt before his sea chest, which sat on the floor, packed and ready for his voyage. He had hated the thought of leaving so soon after his marriage, but he'd been able to secure a good ship far more quickly than he and Nelson had thought possible, and therefore he needed to be off as soon as the vessel was ready to sail.

From behind him, he heard Georgie's deep intake of breath when she entered the room. He assumed that she was most likely awed by the rich luxury of their surroundings.

It was by all accounts a glorious room, decorated with gilt chairs, rich wall hangings, a large and rare Japanese vase on the mantel, and other valuable oddities about the room.

But none of these treasures were what drew the lady's attention.

To his utter amazement, it was his sea chest.

"So you are a sailor," she said, kneeling beside him. She quickly stripped off her gloves so her bare fingers could trace the nailed pattern on top. All the splendor of the room seemed to pale before her as she reverently touched his simple and utilitarian sea chest. "Oh, I should have known."

Was it his mistake or did he hear a bit of awe in her voice?

"Coming or going?" she asked.

"Leaving. I have a new ship and I sail soon."

She let out a small sigh of envy. "I'd love to go to sea."

"It's not that wonderful." He felt like a rotter having to prick at what was obviously a treasured desire. Besides, he was also lying. Being aboard his ship, feeling the deck moving beneath his feet, the salty air stinging his eyes and filling his lungs . . . it *was* the heaven he saw burning in her eyes.

"I know it's not likely. But just to be able to go . . ." She stared down at the sea chest, as if it held all her dreams and desires, and when she looked back up at him, there was something in her gaze that said he was the man to give them to her.

No, I'm not, he wanted to tell her. Instead, he got down to business and thrust the key into the lock, turning it, the tumblers rumbling as they fell into place until the lock snapped open.

It also seemed to snap her out of her pining spell. She sat back on her heels and let him sort his belongings in peace. At least for a few moments.

"Where are you bound for?"

"Naples." Colin winced as the word tumbled out. He'd refused to give Temple any hint regarding his upcoming voyage and to this woman, this stranger, he divulged his plans without even thinking.

"Really?" She sighed again before rushing on. "I've always wanted to see Vesuvius. My father told me all kinds of stories about it. Have you seen it? Does it really smoke and rumble still?"

He glanced back over his shoulder at her. "Your father traveled?"

"Oh yes." Her eyes were aglow at the very thought. "Actually, my parents went there together, on their wedding trip, and—" She faltered, then her mouth snapped shut as if she'd just revealed state secrets. She made a great show of smoothing her skirts, as if everything was normal.

Colin considered her unwitting disclosure as he dug around in his trunk. Her parents took a wedding trip to Naples?

Oh yes, he thought, most Cyprians had parents who went to Italy on their wedding trip. That certainly ruled out his theory that she was some nobleman's by-blow.

So who the devil was she?

His fingers wrapped around the leather bag that held his personal money and he pulled it out of the chest. Quickly, he counted out the amount they'd agreed upon. "Here."

She regarded the coins with a mixture of curiosity and dismay. Her hesitation prompted him to take her hand and pour them into her palm, closing her fingers over them and holding her hand closed tight.

"Take it," he urged her.

She shook her head. "You don't understand. That's not—"

"Not enough?" he ventured. "It probably isn't. But unfortunately it's all I can spare at the moment."

She was staring down at her hand, his fingers still closed over hers. And when she glanced up, there lay a path of tears on her cheeks. They glistened and sparkled in the firelight, beckoning him to wipe them away, to wipe away the cause of her misery.

"What is it, Georgie?"

"I can't accept your money. Not without . . . without . . ." She wavered over her confession, her cheeks deepening to a rosy hue.

He smiled at her. "Without earning it?"

To his surprise, this notion brightened her features. "Yes. I can't accept your money without . . . well, you know."

Colin laughed. "My sweet little Cyprian, if you can't say the words, how do you expect to accomplish the deed?"

Even as he issued his challenge, he realized he'd just

provoked her to test his floundering limits. To push his studiously held restraint until it gave way to her unnerving charms.

She began a transformation from tentative Paphian to enchanting seductress, one which left Colin's heart hammering in his chest, his mouth gaping.

"Who needs words," she said.

Georgie knew she had but this one last chance to entice Colin into her arms. Staring down at the floor, she relished the warmth of his fingers wrapped around hers. The disarming heat flooded her veins, brought back the tremors he'd awakened in her in that reckless moment in the carriage when they'd kissed, when his touch had explored her body in wild abandon.

If only she could get him to kiss her one more time, to push his desire over and beyond his infuriatingly noble intentions, tear down his teetering wall of reserve, which she suspected was being held in check by nothing but bluff.

He wanted her.

Of that she was sure.

Oh, she might never have been with a man before. Never been held in a pair of sturdy, muscled arms before, but she *knew*, knew with an innate understanding that resonated from her heart that he desired her as madly and passionately as she wanted him.

This night was no longer a game of chance in which to carelessly wager and deliberately lose her virginity—no, it was her chance for one haunting night of passion that would be her legacy. The memories of having been loved and cherished and pleasured would warm her cold life when it returned to the inevitable ashes and cinders of her dull existence courtesy of a furious Uncle Phineas, and that accursed Lord Danvers.

So casting aside the images of her weary future, she held tightly to the night before her.

Slowly she glanced up at Colin. She let out the breath she'd been holding in a long, slow sigh. One of her curls had fallen across her brow, so she reached up to push it aside.

His entire body stilled, his gaze following her movements with a raw hunger, like a cat watching an unwitting bird on the hedge. She sensed the power of his strength, the intensity of the need behind his muscular frame, taut and waiting for her next move.

Unlike the bird in hedgerow, she flew closer to the hunter.

"Why do you want to send me away?" she whispered.

"I must," he told her. While his words said one thing, his tone implied an entirely different inclination.

She shook her head, to tell him it was a foolish idea, but one of her blasted curls fell back over her face. About to rake it back in place with her fingers, she had a better idea.

She pulled her hand free from his grasp, letting his gold and silver coins tumble and plunk to the carpet like fat drops of rain. Then she caught his hand and guided his fingers through her hair, letting them fall prey to the entangled snare of her willful strands.

With his hand trapped, she edged closer to him, letting her cheek nuzzle the inside of his wrist, her lips briefly touching his warm skin. Then she tipped back her head, so she looked directly into his hungry gaze and let her mouth fall open ever so slightly in an unquestionable invitation.

Kiss me, she silently beseeched him. *Kiss me again.*

The battle waging behind his green-eyed gaze looked to be as tempestuous as any he'd likely waged at sea, fierce and nobly fought.

But she hated to be the bearer of bad news.

He wasn't going to win this one. Not unless victory meant making love to her.

Colin let out a groan, one so earthy and primitive that it almost frightened her, and when the last ragged sigh left his lips, his mouth swooped down and covered hers.

Now it was her turn to surrender.

His tongue teased her lips open further, only to sweep past them and continue to wage his own form of warfare.

Taunting, tasting, and devouring her.

She sank against him, from a rush of passion and a sense of relief. But as her body thrummed to life, tightening first in her gut and then running down to the heat between her thighs, a rush of alarm assailed her.

As much as she had sought this out, she never realized that it would be like this—so alive, so exhilarating.

So passionate.

She couldn't stop now, her body would rebel, her senses defy any urge toward flight from this heady, daunting course. Instead, she clung to him, her hands plucking and plying the buttons of his jacket open, pulling it over his broad shoulders and tossing it with glee to the floor so she could begin her virgin explorations of a man's body.

His waistcoat quickly followed.

Now seeing him in his shirtsleeves, she paused, overwhelmed at the idea of touching his bare flesh, but her fingers seemed to be of another mind, for they roamed at will over his crisp linen shirt.

She reveled in the solid wall of his body—where beneath her fingertips his chest rose and fell in a discordant, ragged rush, his heart hammering and pounding in a wild tattoo.

Encouraged and enlivened by her first forays, she strayed further afield to the thick cords of his back, the narrow line down to his hips. Her hands pulled him closer, until their bodies met and merged.

In that telling moment when they touched, she discovered the true power a man could possess—hard and solid, his manhood pulsed beneath his breeches, as if it too beseeched her to free it from his clothing.

Colin continued to kiss her, his hands combing her hair, plucking her wayward pins out of their arrangement, letting them fall to the floor in a pitter-patter as they hit the coins scattered there.

When her curls finally fell free, they tumbled down over her bare shoulders like a shawl of silk. Obviously content with the havoc he'd unleashed with her hair, his hands wandered restlessly, searching for more prey, running over the neckline of her bodice as if in reconnaissance, looking for any place where he could breach the silk gown's embroidered defenses.

And when his fingers paused over the exposed swell of her breasts and began to draw back, she gasped, her lashes fluttering open.

Oh dear, no. The conflict in his eyes said he was once again weighing his reckless decision to take her into his arms.

Reaching for his fingers, she brought them back to her breast.

"Do that again," she urged him. "Please."

A lazy smile traced its way over his lips, and he indulged her—but this time his fingers dipped inside her gown until they found the hardened nub of her nipple and rolled lazily over its sensitive tip.

"Like that?" he whispered into her ear.

"Oh yes," she sputtered in relief, as his lips nibbled her earlobe, tickled her neck, and then trailed down the same emblazoned path his fingers had taken.

Her head tipped back, her shoulders arching, her chest rising up to meet his touch, to let his lips taste her warm skin. His hand had untied her bodice and it was now open to his all-too-welcome invasion.

And when his lips closed over her hardened nipple, his tongue laving over the pebbled flesh, he awakened desires in her that she never would have believed possible.

Georgie's knees quaked and she teetered on her one remaining shoe.

Colin didn't say a word, just grinned and then swept her up and carried to the settee near the fireplace. He laid her down, letting her recline back on the rich, soft fabric, warm from the red embers glowing in the hearth. The fire, along with the candles Colin had brought up, cast them in a soft circle of light.

"Don't you want to go to the bed?" she said, nodding toward the darkened bedchamber beyond.

"No," he said, without glancing in that direction. "I want to be able to see you."

Georgie opened her mouth to protest, but then realized that she wanted to be able to see him as well. To see his face, to watch his reactions so she could please him as he was pleasuring her.

With each passing touch and kiss, she wanted him never to forget this night.

He knelt before her and ever so skillfully undid the rest of her bodice, pushing it off her shoulders, pulling her arms free, one at a time.

Georgie was of no mind to resist, rather her need was feeding a growing impatience for him, and to her relief, his fingers began untying the strings that held her skirt on. When it came free, he grinned, pulling the thick silk down over her legs, and tossing it over his shoulder so it too landed in the growing pile of clothes and coins and promises of a passionate night . . . which was now only a shift, corset, stockings, and her sole remaining shoe away from perfection.

"I can't believe you made me leave my shoe behind," she teased, wiggling the toes of her shoeless foot.

"Less to remove now," he said, unlacing the lonely shoe, and throwing it over his shoulder. It landed with a thud, but she couldn't see where in the dim light.

He untied her garters, then rolled her stockings down one at a time, his gaze never leaving hers. The filmy, delicate leggings too found their way somewhere into the pile of discarded clothing.

Colin's fingers trailed up her legs without any sign of stopping anywhere decent. While her first reaction was to close her knees tight against him, she tentatively opened her thighs, for his touch was so tempting that she couldn't resist his explorations.

Besides, that so very private place had grown hot

and wet, aching with the desire to be touched and stroked.

And when his head dipped down and his lips followed the heady path of his fingers, her mouth opened in a wide O of amazement.

Ever so gently, he parted the flesh between her thighs.

She started to quake, rising up in alarm at the shocking sensation.

"You'll like this, Georgie," he murmured. "Believe me."

Her hips swayed to their own cadence, one her entire body seemed to recognize. As much as she had known that Colin wanted to make love to her, now she knew that what he was doing was going to bring her immense pleasure.

His tongue teased her, sending ribbons of pleasure unwinding in a wild jumble. His fingers parted her even further, and this time she had no hesitation over his exploration.

She wanted his eager kiss to continue to fan the fires building inside her—and she hoped he knew how to extinguish them.

Again and again, his tongue dipped and laved over her, and with each swipe of its rough surface, her hips rose and fell to meet him.

Suddenly the fevered pitch in her body became a discordant blur.

"Oh please," she managed to whisper. *Please don't let this ever end.*

Yet she knew it was about to, for her body was coiling tighter and tighter. Her heart raced, and her breathing, well, she could barely catch her breath as she gasped and searched for air.

And still he persisted—unrelentingly. His kiss continued even as he slid a finger inside her. This only added to her blinding need for his touch, her need to be filled.

"Where are you?" he whispered up at her.

"Lost," she told him. "I'm utterly lost."

"Aye, Georgie, so am I." Colin grinned, as her hips swayed and bucked, searching for the heated pleasure that had been so abruptly wrenched away. "Let me help you."

This time, his tongue washed over her in slow, deliberate strokes. He tormented her already beleaguered senses and brought them once again back to that stormy, windswept precipice. She was rising this time at a dangerous, dizzying pace, one he seemed to anticipate before she did.

She must stop him, she had to before she fell.

Fell into darkness, fell into oblivion.

Her fingers wound into his hair, stroking his neck, clutching and holding him fast, as she searched for something solid on which to cling—someone to catch her when she toppled from this quickly escalating spiral upward. Then her world exploded, awash in wave after wave of pleasure.

"Oh please, yes," she gasped.

And even as she plunged headlong into the bliss of unchecked passion, he caught her.

Just as she'd always known he would.

Colin watched her find her release, the surprised and shocked moue on her lips, her lashes fluttering in surrender, her hands pulling at him.

He continued to kiss her, propelling her through her abandon, until she was gasping for air.

"Oh help me," she was saying. "I'm falling."

He gathered her up in his arms, kissing her lips, whispering encouragement into her ears, stroking her still trembling and responsive body through even more restless waves.

Finally she sagged against him, her head resting on his chest.

Then he felt something he'd never felt with a woman.

That she trusted him. Georgie trusted him utterly and completely.

But she shouldn't. She couldn't.

Though a notion worthy of striking terror in his heart, instead it filled him with a boundless sense of peace.

She trusted him.

Ignoring his own raging need, he cradled her closer. "I should take you home."

He should have taken her home to begin with. Before she'd issued her challenge.

Who needs words . . .

Certainly not Georgie. And he supposed he didn't either.

Words would have gotten in the way, and for once in his life he had wanted to feel. Just feel.

And Georgie was so touchable. So willing . . . so perfect.

"That was amazing," she whispered. Her fingers ran absently over his chest, as if her limbs had grown heavy. "I didn't know it was possible. Not like that."

"Then I'm glad I could give you something to remember."

"I doubt I'll ever forget *that*," she said so emphatically that he laughed. "What's so funny?" She scrambled up and looked him squarely in the eye, her unforgiving honesty demanding answers.

"It isn't," he told her, tweaking her nose. "It's just *you*."

She didn't ask what he meant, a sly smile turning her lips. She nestled even closer to him, her bare legs curling into his lap, her arms winding around him. "I'm glad the servants are all out, though it is odd that they are *all* gone. It is almost as if you planned on having such an evening." She looked up at him, her eyes sparkling. "I thought you said you hadn't come to the ball seeking companionship. But I fear you've been found out."

"It isn't like that," he managed to say, suddenly realizing he hadn't given much thought to his forgotten bride in the last hour.

Not even a passing moment of regret.

And even as he tried to summon up Diana's features in his mind's eye, as he tried to put the image of her petite form in his arms, imagine her curled up to him, he couldn't see it. Couldn't imagine that she would have cried out with such reckless abandon as she found her release.

No, she would have come to his bed out of duty . . . an idea he now found more repulsive than he would have thought possible.

He'd never be able to take another woman to his bed, not unless . . .

He shook his head, unwilling to finish that thought.

Unless she was just like his willful Cyprian.

She hadn't cringed at the sight of his work-callused hands. She'd touched them reverently, just as she'd touched his battered sea chest.

None of the treasures in the house impressed her or held her in their rich thrall, nor the money he'd offered her, now scattered on the floor like crumbs for the birds in Hyde Park.

No, she'd found joy in the parts of him that most in the *ton* would have snubbed or misunderstood.

So who was this woman who loved the sea? Who longed for the sights that still brought gooseflesh to his arms even now, after all these years of sailing?

Georgie touched and understood a part of him that no one else ever had. And he wondered if anyone ever would.

Glancing over at his packed sea chest, he felt a twinge of regret at the sight of it.

He didn't want to leave. For the first time in his life, he didn't want to sail away.

And in that moment, he truly understood what the poets and troubadours went to so much trouble to try to explain.

He understood the unexplainable.

In his arms, she continued to ramble on, talking about their encounter with an openness he found refreshing.

"... and I fear I would have died of embarrassment if someone was to come in to tend the fire, or had heard me and come to investigate." She glanced up at him. "Was I too loud? I think I was rather loud."

"No, you were just right."

She let out a long, relieved sigh. "Good. It was

tremendous and I wanted you to know. I didn't think I could manage a round of applause, for truly you deserved a standing ovation, so I just called out. I didn't realize how loud it was until I said your name." She finally paused and took another breath. "I would hate to think I was so loud that I woke the neighbors. Especially the magistrate."

Colin laughed again. "I believe all the neighbors are old and hard of hearing so you may make as much noise as you want. And if we wake the magistrate, I'll pay the fine quite happily."

"We, milord?" She wiggled her brows at him, her own quirky attempt at suggestive flirtation. "It would be my honor to make you call out in the night—and see you in dun territory, for I fear your fine will be rather hefty." Her hand slid down his chest, past his waistband to the hardness still raging with need.

Her fingers stroked and teased him, and he forgot any thought that this was some innocent miss, for her touch was bold and sure.

"I . . . I . . ." he started to say, but his words trailed off as she found the buttons on his breeches and began prying them open, one by one.

He tried to protest, but her lips came up and silenced his mouth. Her saucy, outspoken tongue challenged him to keep up with her. And as their mouths tangled and danced, her fingers were quickly working to release the round oval locks that held him prisoner.

When the last one opened, she murmured against his lips. "Now, milord, let us see who awakens the poor magistrate."

Her hand wrapped around his manhood, easing it free of his breeches and welcoming it with a reverent stroke of her fingers.

He groaned. "You wicked chit."

"Oh, I plan on being terribly wicked," she said. "If that is what you want."

She nearly unmanned him, his need clambering free of the fragile restraint he thought he could maintain.

He wanted her more than he had ever wanted a woman before.

She infected his senses, left him breathless. And suddenly it wasn't enough—he wanted her in his bed. He wanted her beneath him. He wouldn't stand for anything less than seeing her once again restless and ragged with need, begging for him to follow her into oblivion.

A growl rumbled in his chest.

"Come with me." His words were hardly a request. And before she could respond (or argue, knowing Georgie), he swept her into his arms and carried her from the study.

He kicked the adjoining door to the bedroom wide open with his booted foot. Storming through the portal, he set a straight course for the large bed that took up most of the room.

His hot blood and need for passion clashed with the calm, understated elegance of their surroundings. He had instructed the servants to have his bedchamber be as comfortable and welcoming as possible for his virginal bride.

Several vases overflowing with hothouse roses were set about the room, scenting the air with their rich perfume. A single candle burned in the holder near the bed, its meager light to afford the bride some modesty. The bedsheets and thick comforter had been turned down, awaiting a timid bride and a patient groom.

With one hand, he wrenched the carefully done bed apart and tossed the woman in his arms into the middle of the rumpled sheets.

She laughed with glee, her arms opening to him, calling for him to join her. That she wanted him, craved him as much as he desired to join with her, filled him with a reckless sense of daring.

Reckless. She'd said she wanted a reckless night.

So did he.

She was struggling up from the chaos he'd created, crawling to the edge of the bed, her hands eager to get ahold of him. She plucked and pulled at his shirt, until he yanked it off, mindless of the tearing threads. His boots came off in the same heedless manner. And even as his last boot came free, her hands were already tugging his breeches down over his hips.

Her shift followed, coming off in a flurry of muslin.

When it came to her corset, his fingers fumbled over the tied cords that held her body imprisoned.

"Damn this wretched thing," he muttered.

"Oh, let me," she said with the same impatience, pushing aside his hands, and quickly freeing the knot he'd managed to make. With that undone, Colin caught either side of the garment and ripped away the aged and frayed silk lacing.

Instead of being shocked by his force, she purred in triumph to be free from its confinement. She fell back onto the bed, naked and welcoming.

"Come to me," she said, holding out her arms. "Love me, Colin. Love me for the rest of this night."

He was atop her in an instant, his mouth covering hers. She kissed him back, her hunger once again challenging him.

"Oh yes," she said, encouraging him. "Love me, Colin."

His hand went down to her apex again. This time he was only going to tease the fires, before he filled her with his manhood.

She reached to touch him as well, her fingers enslaving him, stroking and rubbing the glistening wet head.

Long-limbed, her legs wrapped with his, her thigh rubbing against his hip, her body swaying already, calling to him to come dance with her, to tame her endless need.

She shifted beneath him, guiding him toward her.

He needed no further encouragement. While he wanted to bury himself in her, dive into her with one triumphant stroke, something held him back—made him use the only bit of restraint Colin could still claim.

Slowly he eased himself inside, sliding a bit deeper with each stroke. Beneath him, her impatience was waging war with his restrained pace.

Her hands grasped at his hips, bidding him to go deeper, pushing and pulling at him, urging him to match the frantic pace her hips had found.

"Take me," she pleaded. "Don't stop. Don't stop for *anything*."

Recklessly, he let go and filled her.

And even as he did so, he felt something stop him. A barrier undeniably breached and irretrievably broken.

Colin stopped, his eyes springing open and staring down at the woman in his arms.

A virgin? His Cyprian was a virgin?

Impossible.

He swore he saw something of a grimace on her face, before she once again moved restlessly beneath him.

"What are you waiting for?" she whispered, her lips and teeth nipping at his shoulder, her hands pulling his hips toward her, her body rising to meet his. She was not about to let him break the magical cadence that had been drawing them both closer to fulfillment. "I want you so much. I need you so much."

He began to move again, and she murmured in approval, her body happily rocking to meet his. The moment passed so quickly, he told himself he was imagining things.

A virgin at the Cyprian's Ball? Unlikely.

And yet he'd swear . . .

Whatever he'd discovered, it quickly faded from his mind, as he found himself gazing down at her, the warmth of her body heating his, the soft scent of her perfume invading his soul, an unthinkable notion started to take root in the back of his mind.

How can you let her go when you've fallen in . . .

Colin pulled her closer and let himself fall into the unbelievable.

Georgie had sensed his hesitation when he'd come to her virginal barrier. Thankfully, Mrs. Taft had told her to expect some measure of discomfort when it was breached and it had hurt, but only for a moment.

Now . . . it was pure bliss.

Even though that had been her only goal of this

night—to find herself breached and ruined—now she wanted so much more. She wanted him to find the same release she'd had under his skillful touch. She wanted him to remember this night, and never to forget her.

Somehow she knew he wouldn't—for this hasty, wild passion between them had bound them inexplicably together, entwined their hearts.

Now as he moved inside her, he carried her back to that same place he'd taken her before, and this time she didn't hesitate to follow, knowing the heavenly reward of that heady climb to the top.

The fire blazing between them carried them upward and onward, together.

She heard him groan and cry out, loud and triumphant, just as she had done earlier, and even as his ragged breathing whispered hot encouragement in her ear, she too joined him in that breathless freedom.

Colin rained kisses down on her soft lips, her damp forehead, on the tops of her shoulders. He hauled her closer to him, so that their bodies continued to be but one. He didn't want to let go; he didn't want this night to end.

Ever.

Suddenly her boisterous ways, her outspoken nature, her reckless manners were no longer such oddities—they were something he would always need. All his old ideas of womanhood fell to the wayside, for they had been what was expected—to find a respectable, biddable miss and marry her. Have a family and live his life finding passion somewhere other than in his own bed, in his own home.

Just as he'd never thought his career would find him outside his beloved navy, a world of order and regulations, of duty and unquestionable honor—now he found that he no longer wanted the kind of woman he'd thought so essential to his well-being.

As Georgie nestled against him, a sly smile tugging at her lips, her eyes closed and her features smugly content, he found himself wondering what she liked for breakfast, tea or chocolate? Why did she love the sea? Where had she come from? And a myriad of other questions that would take a lifetime to ask, answer, and explore.

For if there was anything he knew for sure now, it was that he wanted her. This impossible woman.

Wanted her for a lifetime.

The daunting, exhilarating notion left his mouth dry and his heart pounding.

Dear God, in just one night, he'd fallen in love.

He tugged her closer. What could he do? He had only two days before he must sail, and he didn't know when he'd be back.

His mind raced with options, including taking her with him, but that was impossible, as much as he suspected she'd leap at the chance to sail away—sail anywhere. Yet his mission was too dangerous—and she was too distracting.

At this, he smiled. A delightful distraction she'd be, but where he was sailing, he couldn't afford to be diverted.

While officially all his property and money had been seized by the court, he still held a small manor house in the Lake District that was free and clear.

He could send her there, along with an income to ensure that she didn't want for anything.

But what if he didn't return? Then what would happen to her? And what if there was a child?

There was only one choice. He'd have to marry her. It was the only thing he could do. Besides being the honorable thing to do, it was also the right thing to do.

But how? And on such short notice?

Then he remembered the special license in his jacket pocket. It hadn't held the name of the bride, for it had been dashed off by the archbishop upon the request of Nelson. Somehow in Nelson's correspondence Lady Diana's name had been left out, so the archbishop had added a note that the bride's name could be entered by the officiating clergy.

Colin grinned. He'd marry her. He'd haul her down to the local parish and marry her at first light. And if the vicar balked at the unusual request, he'd take a page from her book and bribe the proper and upright man.

Dammit, he'd do it right now, but he doubted the vicar would be all that amenable to being awakened at two in the morning.

No, there were more pleasant ways to pass the hours, on this his wedding night.

Georgie jolted awake as she did most mornings, her body drenched in sweat, her nostrils filled with the stench of smoke from the fires that always haunted her dreams.

No, please don't shoot . . . The desperate words died away before she had a chance to cry out.

It always took her a disoriented moment or so to awaken and this morning her confusion was only compounded by the fact that her surroundings were completely unfamiliar.

The panic she usually was able to shake off suddenly gripped her tighter as beside her, someone stirred.

She sat up in alarm. She wasn't in her own bed. And she was far from the quiet and safe shelter of Mrs. Taft's cottage, or even the noisy and pretentious halls of Uncle Phineas's and Aunt Verena's house.

She was . . . with *Colin*.

Her cheeks grew hot, her body quaked with memories, ones still so fresh and new she had a hard time believing they belonged to her.

Then she remembered why she had come to this place.

Oh dear goodness. The examination! Lord Harris's physician would be arriving at Uncle Phineas's in a few hours, and Georgie still needed to find her way home.

Panic nearly sent her catapulting out of the bed, but she held herself in check. If she wasn't careful, she'd wake him, and that was the last thing she wanted to happen.

He might insist on seeing her home.

Might?

She smiled to herself. Her knight, her hero would insist. No, she had to leave, and quickly, before the servants stirred.

But before she fled, she paused for a moment and memorized every bit of him. The dark cast of his hair, the cleft in his chin, the line of his jaw now shadowed with a dark beard hiding the thin scar there.

They'd made love twice; no, she remembered, three times. And with each passing instance, she'd fallen more and more in love with him.

Reluctance to leave kept her nestled in the warmth of his body, in the refuge of his bed. How she wanted to reach out and touch him, but even that, she knew, was too much of a risk.

Ever so carefully, she slipped from the bed. The morning had yet to break over the horizon, so the room was still cast in shadows, the candle long ago gutted out. She felt around the floor and found her torn corset and shift.

Tiptoeing from the room, Georgie made a silent retreat to the adjoining study where the rest of her garments lay scattered. She groped around and found her remaining clothes, but not her shoe.

Wretched, accursed thing, she thought. *Where the devil could it be?*

Back in the bedroom, she heard Colin tossing about, the sheets rustling as he rolled to and fro. She held her breath and waited until he stilled again and his breathing resumed its even cadence.

Taking one last look around, she realized her shoe was nowhere to be found—and considering she had already lost the other one, there seemed no point in continuing to search for its mate. Instead she discovered a pair of men's slippers that had been set out near the fireplace, probably by some thoughtful member of the staff. When she stuffed the two halves of her corset into the toes, the added fabric made them fit her feet—somewhat—well enough so that she needn't pad her way through the morning chill barefoot.

Casting one last look at Colin's sleeping form, she restrained herself from rushing to his side and kissing his brow in farewell.

Instead she blew an airy kiss in his direction and left without another glance back, tears stealing down her cheeks.

Chapter 7

Naples, Italy
One year later

Colin rowed silently ashore with only the vaguest bit of moonlight to guide his course. The lack of visibility didn't bother him, for he'd made this trip twice before in the last twelve months, all with the same precautions to ensure that no one saw him.

As he pulled the small rowboat ashore beneath the British Ambassador's palatial residence, he cursed under his breath.

Sir William Hamilton's house glowed like a beacon, illuminated with hundreds of candles and brimming with guests, their laughter and voices spilling out of the villa's open windows and graceful balconies.

Hardly the perfect time to make his secretive report, but Nelson's message had said to come at once, so he had no choice but to attempt to slip into the villa unnoticed.

Before he continued, Colin took a glance back past the boats nestled in the harbor. He continued scanning the water, searching to see if he could spot his ship, the *Sybaris*, moored just beyond the mouth.

Even though he knew exactly where she lay at anchor, he couldn't see her. He'd given orders to run without lights and to maintain strict silence, so as to avoid being detected, and it appeared his precautions were working.

By morning, he and the *Sybaris* would be well away from Naples and no one would know they'd been there.

He didn't want anyone reporting back that his ship had been spotted so close to Nelson—they needed to maintain the illusion that Colin was still on the wrong side of His Majesty's Navy.

He climbed up the hillside and into Sir William's statue-laden garden. As he picked his way through the classically laid-out landscaping, he realized that since his last visit, the British Ambassador had added several more pieces to his prized collection of Roman antiquities.

Just as he was about to step out onto the pathway, the distinct, bright laughter of a woman filled the garden, diverting his attention. Colin knew he was about to be discovered by Sir William's other *pièce de résistance*, Lady Hamilton.

"Come along, my dear," she was saying brightly. "You must join my party now that my wretched Lord Nelson has decided to work all evening on his dispatches. I will be quite desolate without some good company."

"I must beg off, my lady," her companion demurred. "I have to be getting back to my lodgings."

He couldn't quite see the stranger with the ambassador's wife, since she walked on the other side of Lady Hamilton, but her voice sent his heart pounding.

His earlier concerns forgotten, he leaned dangerously out into the path, searching for any clue that would reveal this mysterious woman's identity—the color of her hair, the way she tipped her head, the way she moved.

He found himself peering through the half-light of the garden, trying to discern her face, straining to hear more of her voice.

It's not her, he chided himself. *It can't be.*

His Cyprian. His Georgie.

In the twelve months since that unforgettable, passionate night, he had dreamt of nothing but Georgie. She might have stolen out of his bed, but not out of his heart.

When he'd awoken and found her gone, he'd been devastated. Especially when he'd pulled back the sheets and discovered the truth of the matter.

The stain that had been her virginity.

She had been an innocent, and he'd ruined her. The only other evidence of her arrival in his life had been her forgotten shoe, which one of the servants had found later in the day discarded where it had been aimlessly tossed—up on one of the bookshelves.

He'd immediately enlisted Temple's help and the two of them had scoured the city, using his cousin's connections to find the little Cyprian, but to no avail. And in the end, Colin had sailed down the Thames without knowing what had become of her.

So as the two women breezed past him, their heads tipped together like chattering schoolgirls, he refrained from leaping out like a madman and yanking off the straw hat which hid the woman's features.

Yet there was something so familiar about her.

"Georgie," he whispered into the night.

The lady stopped and turned, glancing back in his direction.

"Is there something wrong?" Lady Hamilton asked.

"Nothing," the other lady murmured, before she rejoined Lady Hamilton. "I just thought I heard someone."

Lady Hamilton laughed. "I fear you've been spending too much time skulking about ruins if you are hearing voices in Sir William's statue garden. We must keep you here in Naples until you're fully recovered and used to the company of the living."

The lady laughed and shook her head. "Your civilizing influence will have to wait, for we go north tomorrow to see a Roman temple that is reputed to be the finest in the area."

"Old piles of stones!" Lady Hamilton complained, "I'll never understand their appeal when the sights and charms of Naples are ever so much more delightful."

Both women laughed and then said their good-byes. Lady Hamilton continued gaily into the house, while her friend paused for a moment looking over the garden before taking a side path around the house toward the street.

Colin remained in his hiding spot until the garden once again was still.

He shook his head. He was certainly going insane when he started seeing Georgie in the bored wives of English antiquity hunters.

"You're a bird-witted fool, Colin Danvers," he told himself softly. Stealing through the remaining garden, he climbed the trellis that ran to the balcony of the room set aside for Nelson's use as a study in the Hamiltons' palatial Neapolitan home.

Once Colin had made his secretive arrival into Nelson's rooms, a solitary figure stepped from the shadows of the villa. Glancing once at the balcony, the silhouette froze momentarily, before reentering Sir William's house and rejoining the party that would most likely continue until dawn.

Later that evening, long after the candles in Lord Nelson's study had burned low from the passing hours, there was a knock at his door.

"My lord," called out Lady Hamilton from beyond the locked door. "The gaming is about to begin. Will you join us?"

"In a moment, my lady," Horatio, Viscount Nelson replied, returning to the balcony where he'd been standing in the shadows watching Lord Danvers make his escape.

It was with a heavy heart that he watched his friend leave.

Danvers was one of his best captains—and as it turned out, an exceptional intelligence officer. The information he'd been collecting in the last year had aided British efforts on more than one occasion, and yet he'd been unable to find the one thing they absolutely needed to discover.

The identity of the traitor in their midst.

Then as Colin slipped over the wall, the one thing that Nelson had feared and half hoped wouldn't happen did.

A second figure stepped out from behind a statue and began a furtive chase after Danvers. But the man wasn't as cunning as Danvers, for he walked near enough to one of the garden's torches for Nelson to see the color of his coat.

An English naval uniform.

So it was true. He was being betrayed by one of his own. It pained him more than the loss of his arm at Santa Cruz.

But who? There were at least five English ships in port, and perhaps fifty officers in total in Naples who could be wearing that uniform.

There was nothing left to do but let his trap catch this accursed spy.

It was just too bad he had to use Danvers to lure the man and his French friends out into the open.

He only hoped Colin was wily enough to escape their enemies, who now would most certainly be alerted to his activities and likely have a full accounting of his current orders.

And if Colin wasn't clever enough . . .

Nelson didn't want to consider what he had just done. By not telling Danvers that his secret mission had been discovered by their enemies, Nelson was literally feeding him to the sharks.

It had not been an easy decision, but with the French descending down Italy's boot like voracious wolves, a necessary one.

At the door, Lady Hamilton continued to knock impatiently. "My lord, are you well? I shall send for your manservant and your physician immediately if you do not open this door."

Nelson shook his head, fighting the urge to call Danvers back, to signal the *Sybaris* into shore and call an end to this charade.

But he couldn't.

This was war, and they must uncover who on Nelson's staff was selling secrets to the French.

And right now, Captain Danvers was Nelson's biggest secret . . . and best weapon.

"I'll have a key brought if you do not open this door," Lady Hamilton called out.

Nelson smiled at the country accent tweaking the lady's words. It always came out when Emma was vexed or excited. He made his way over to the door, limping from the injuries plaguing his leg, and twisted the latch open.

"Who are you closeted away with?" Lady Hamilton demanded as she sailed into the room, glancing left and right in a bold search for a rival.

"No one," he replied. "I'm all alone."

"You're a charming man, Horatio," she said, "but a poor liar."

"If I told you it was a matter of state, would you leave it at that?"

The lady placed one of her delicate hands on his cheek and stroked his face. "No. For you work too hard, my love. You must rest if you are to regain your strength."

"There is too much to do for England."

"England will survive this night without your safe-keeping," she whispered, as she moved into his ready embrace. "Especially when there is much you could do for me."

Nelson welcomed her concern and her love. This

was his Emma, his dearest girl. She gave him a much needed respite from the heavy duties and responsibilities that weighed on his heart.

Like Lord Danvers.

"Come downstairs and enjoy some company," she said, drawing back a bit and smiling up at him. "These secret meetings drain your vigor."

"Why do you think I've been having a secret meeting?"

She glanced about the room. "Your chair is turned to that one over there," she said, pointing at the other chair in the room. "And if you were doing your regular paperwork, as you profess, you would have Mr. Tyson up here to assist you. As it is, you insisted on being left alone, undisturbed. I must conclude you had a private meeting to attend." She eyed him carefully. "And sorry business it was, for you look as if you have just consigned someone to the dog."

"The cat," he corrected.

"Oh, yes, that horrid thing. What was it, fifty lashes or a hundred?"

"Nothing like that, my lady," he told her, leaving the room and following her down to the party.

Far worse, he thought. *I have sent my friend out to die at the hands of a traitor.*

The village of Volturno, Italy
A fortnight later

Clinging to the worn sheets, Georgie writhed and tossed in her sleep. Someone was arguing in the distance, their words unintelligible, but their voices so familiar.

She shifted again, trying to discern what they were saying.

I'm going, Brigette. I must. I promised her I would be there tonight. If I'm not there . . .

Papa, no! Georgie tried to cry out. Her feet pedaled against the footboards of the inn's bed, trying to catch up with the departing figure, lost in the darkness of her nightmare, quickly consumed by the hiss of flames.

Somewhere in the blackness, the crack of a pistol brought Georgie awake. The bed linens were soaked in sweat, her hands wound around them so tightly, her knuckles glowed white.

"Georgie?" Kit called out, scrambling up from her smaller bed across the spacious room. "I thought I heard—"

More shots finished her sister's speculations.

Georgie sat bolt upright. The shot she'd heard hadn't been part of her nightmare, but a harbinger of what was about to arrive in their midst.

The French. The rumors of their coming were no longer just the stuff of idle gossip.

"Get dressed," she told her sister. "We need to leave. Now."

Cautiously, she approached the balcony off their room, not daring to venture out onto it, but edging the door open enough to take a look.

The moonless, rainy night afforded little in the way of views, though beyond the inn and in the distance, Georgie spied the red flicker of torches moving through the streets and the higher flames of fires that were consuming anything the French could find to burn.

And the mayhem was getting closer with each passing moment.

Damn their hides, she thought. Even worse, they were coming in from the south, cutting off any hope of them slipping back down the coast to Naples.

What was it Mrs. Taft always said? *Out of the frying pan . . .*

Here they had fled England in the wake of the physician's discovery that she wasn't a virgin, and her uncle's decision to wed Kit to Lord Harris in her stead, and now they were in all likelihood about to find themselves at the mercy of the French.

Better them than Uncle Phineas and Lord Danvers, Georgie thought wryly. Still, if only Italy could have remained the haven that they had found it to be . . .

At least they'd had a few months of peace. It had been the first time in over a year when Georgie hadn't felt hunted and haunted.

It had started back in London once Georgie had realized the full extent of her predicament. She had even gone back to Bridwick House to see if word could be sent to Colin about her condition. But the house had been shuttered tight, and her knocks and inquiries at both the front door and servants' entrance had gone unanswered.

Oh, Colin, she had prayed on more than one occasion. *Please come and find me. See us away from this wretched disaster.* But as far as she knew, he'd sailed off on some unknown ship and she would never see him again.

Yet her prayers hadn't gone unanswered, only in an entirely different manner than she'd ever thought possible.

Late one afternoon when their uncle and aunt were out making preparations for Kit's wedding, a solicitor had called. He had come regarding Mrs. Taft's will. Apparently the good lady had left her entire estate to the girls. The small, slight man had pushed his spectacles up on his nose and apologized profusely for taking so long to get the funds and properties in order, but he'd had some difficulties finding a buyer for the *Sybaris*, Captain Taft's ship.

But recently he had completed the sale, and the money was awaiting them in the bank—the solicitor just needed to know what arrangements they wanted to make with their inheritance. Hardly a fortune, but for Georgie's and Kit's needs, it was more than enough. Mrs. Taft's will even provided that Georgie be allowed the discretion of managing the money for Kit and herself, though the solicitor said he thought it best to ignore such a foolish notion and simply turn the care of their inheritance over to their uncle.

Georgie did her best not to laugh in the man's face. Turn over this heaven-sent sum to Uncle Phineas? She might as well toss it all in the Thames and be done with it.

Instead, she thanked the man for his concern, fetched Kit, and quickly packed whatever belongings they could carry. They departed the Escott town house in all due haste, with the rather shocked solicitor in tow.

Their first stop was at the bank. Even as the clerk counted out their traveling expenses and the banker drafted a letter of credit for one "Mrs. Bridwick," Georgie fashioned their best avenue of escape. If they fled north to Scotland, west to the wilds of Wales, or even to Ireland, their uncle would follow.

No, the only thing left to them was to flee Britain outright. Since the war with France had torn apart most of the Continent, it left only Italy as a safe place for them to seek refuge—with new names and new identities that would hide them from Uncle Phineas and their guardian, Lord Danvers, until Kit reached her majority.

There would be no more unsolicited marriages for either of them, Georgie vowed.

And from the bank they had gone to the docks and taken the first vessel heading down the Thames.

A ship, as chance would have it, headed for Naples. Standing on the deck, the wind blowing through her tangled curls, Georgie had wrapped her hands protectively over her stomach and hoped that mayhap, somehow, she'd find Colin again.

And this time, she wouldn't be so likely to flee from his bed. She only hoped he would be as happy to see her.

A chill wind from the open door wrenched Georgie back to her current problem even as more shots rang out. She hastily began dressing, pulling on her gown and boots.

Her gaze turned to the sea, almost in longing, for it was their only hope of escape. But there wasn't time to find a ship or even a boatman to take them away. She even considered stealing one of the numerous overturned fishing boats on the beach, but knew she and Kit alone could never drag one of them down to the water's edge.

Yet as she turned back to the room, she swore she saw a flicker of light in the bay. Like a lamp suddenly lit, then just as quickly extinguished. She moved closer to the balcony and peered into the darkness, trying to discern anything outside, but between the dark and the steady rain that had begun to fall sometime during the night, she couldn't see a thing.

In her desperation, she must have been imagining it.

Kit was already dressed, and was struggling to get a boot over her foot. "Sir William said the French troops wouldn't dare come this far south."

"Apparently he was wrong," Georgie replied, wishing they had heeded the advice of his wife, Lady Hamilton, and stayed in Naples. But Kit had wanted to sketch the ruins outside this tiny seaside hamlet, and Georgie had reluctantly agreed to the side trip. Besides, she'd needed some rest from the hectic social whirl of Lady Hamilton. The ambassador's wife had been unduly kind to them since their arrival in Naples, helping them find lodgings, introducing them around. Georgie suspected the lady knew her story of a deceased husband was a fiction, but akin to scandal herself, Lady Hamilton had deftly ignored the deficiencies in Georgie's tale and gathered the two girls into her social circle.

As more shots rang out, this time followed by shouts and the warning chimes of the church bells, Georgie finished dressing, all the while trying to come up with an escape plan.

As they both donned dark cloaks, Georgie went to the nightstand and retrieved the only possession of her father's that she still had—his pistol. Tucking it in a pocket inside her cloak, she sent up a little prayer of thanks to Captain Taft. The man had seen past her delicate sex to teach her how to use it. Even more so, she was thankful that last night she had taken the precaution of priming and loading it.

Her hands were shaking so badly, she didn't know if she could manage it now. She also hoped that she didn't have to fire the tricky piece. Shooting at harmless targets was one thing . . . at another person—that was an entirely different matter.

Kit stood by the door, her valise in one hand and her drawing pad and tool bag in the other.

"I'm ready," she whispered.

Padding across the room, Georgie reached into the basket next to her bed and found it empty.

"Where's—" she started to ask.

"In your satchel." Kit grinned. "It seemed the best way."

Georgie nodded in agreement, tucking the bag under her arm, her cloak swirling around her and the satchel like the protective wing of a bird.

She swept past her sister and into the hallway. Carefully they made their way down the darkened staircase of the inn and into the common room. Usually a sleepy place, with quiet patrons enjoying dishes of *orecchiette* and eggplant, politely sampling glasses of the local vintage, the room had erupted into chaos as the guests were trying to determine what was happening or how to escape.

"Monsignor Artimino, have the boy fetch my horses!" demanded an imperious English marquis who had made it known to all the guests in the past week that he was far too important to pay any of them heed. "I have connections with the King of England," he was saying, though no one was really listening, "and he'll hear of this if I am not well taken care of."

Georgie doubted the invading French army cared a whit and a half about his lordship's association to the English crown, other than to add his head to the pile of other noble necks they had shaved with Madame Guillotine.

The years of Terror were mostly over, but that hadn't stopped the French forces, remnants of the early Revolutionary armies, from keeping their guillotines sharp. Especially now that they were invading other countries under the skillful direction of their latest leader, a Corsican by the name of Bonaparte.

The marquis and his fatuous complaints were unceremoniously elbowed aside by the matronly, heavyset widow who had arrived three days earlier. "Monsignor, I must have the maid pack our bags immediately," she said, her daughters ringed around her like frightened chicks. "I will not stay one minute longer if I am to be awakened by ruffians at all hours."

As more shots erupted, one of the daughters squeaked in fright, while the eldest one dropped in a dead faint.

Georgie had no time for any of their antics, but she did need help finding a way out of this mess. She glanced around the room looking for the inn's other guest.

Mr. Pymm.

At first she had thought she had met him before, for he seemed vaguely familiar—almost like a haunting figure out of one of her odd nightmares. But how could that be? For according to the innkeeper, Pymm was an ailing gentleman from York, and Georgie had never been further north than London. The garrulous innkeeper had also informed her that Pymm had sought the sunshine of Italy for his health and to further his studies of antiquities—though they had yet to see Mr. Pymm at any of the picturesque settings around the town.

Instead, each morning the man set out in a donkey cart, with a driver-cum-interpreter who looked more like a bandit than a guide, and the pair weren't seen again until late in the evening, whereupon Mr. Pymm would limp into the inn, cane in hand. When pressed to join the company, he would profess to be too tired to visit, and retire immediately to his room.

Two nights earlier, the English widow had been complaining of megrims, her laments keeping everyone awake until the wee hours when Mr. Pymm had finally come to her aid. Apparently, he was a physician of some renown and offered a potion that had not only silenced the lady, but left her sleeping until well into the next day, when she'd declared Mr. Pymm a miracle worker to one and all.

At the time, Georgie had wondered why, if he were truly such a fine physician, he hadn't healed himself? But she had given it no further thought until now, as she spied the mysterious and supposedly ailing Mr. Pymm spryly darting down the hallway toward the kitchens.

She never knew why she did it, but at the sight of his retreating figure moving at a breakneck speed, Georgie just knew she'd found her way out of Volturno and out of harm's way.

Catching Kit by the arm, she dragged her sister past the others and into the empty kitchen.

If Mr. Pymm had a way out of this mess, which Georgie would have bet her best garters he did, they were going with him.

The door to the rear garden stood wide open, and Georgie didn't hesitate. She barreled out into the darkness and the pouring rain. Just ahead lay a small path down to the beach. There she spied the bobbing light of a small tin lantern sputtering and flickering in the rain and wind.

Why would he be going to the beach? Unless . . .

Then Georgie remembered. *The light offshore.*

It hadn't been her imagination. A ship. And running without lights, suggesting that its arrival wasn't just a lucky coincidence.

An ailing antiquities scholar, indeed! Their Mr. Pymm was involved in some havey-cavey business, but what it was, Georgie didn't care. Since he was obviously fleeing the French, she deduced his loyalties weren't set in that direction. And so as long as he wasn't dealing in supplying Englishwomen to Persian harems, she didn't care where his interests lay.

In the village, the shouts and din of alarm grew closer. The church bells now rang with a frantic peal, punctuated only by screams and wails from the villagers of the little town as they were rousted from their beds by their belligerent invaders.

"Which way?" Kit asked, peering out from beneath her now dripping hood.

"To the beach." Georgie nodded ahead of them. "See that light? That's Mr. Pymm. Apparently he has friends awaiting him. And I intend to see that we join them." She continued forth, down the side of the cliff, trying her best to recall the path they had taken a few days earlier. Of course, that had been in the morning when the sun had been high above and the sea had beckoned Georgie with its dancing, flashing waves.

Now in the darkness, they stumbled and bumped into each other as they felt their way along the rain-slickened path, following Mr. Pymm's meager light as it danced ahead of them.

Then Georgie heard it—a sound as familiar as her

own voice—the sound of oars straining in their locks, and the grinding of wood as it met the rocky beach.

A longboat!

She didn't need to see it to know it was there.

"Did you hear that?" Kit whispered, having spent nearly as much time as Georgie playing aboard Captain Taft's ship, as well as at the docks near their Penzance home. "A boat. I swear I heard it."

"Oh aye, Kit," she said softly. "I heard it too. They must be up near the boulders, at the end of the beach." The night was so pitch-black, coupled with the rain, she could barely see her hand before her face. At least they had Pymm's lantern to follow like a tiny, sputtering beacon.

"What if they won't fetch us away?"

Georgie put her hand on the butt of the pistol tucked inside her cloak. "They'll take us, never fear. They'll have no choice." They'd reached the end of the rocky trail, for their slippers were now sinking into sand.

She held Kit fast for a moment, since Mr. Pymm had stopped as well.

He stood some distance ahead of them, swinging the light back and forth, and then up and down.

Obviously he hadn't heard the longboat's arrival as they had. But then again, over the crash of the waves and the falling rain, it wouldn't be something she'd expect just anyone to be able to discern.

"I thought Mr. Pymm was a gentleman," Kit said. "Why, he's acting like Mr. Waterby out to escape the excise men."

Georgie smiled at the reference to their Penzance neighbor who'd been well-known about the area as a smuggler. "And there is his reason," she said, as some-one near the boulders stepped out with a light in hand and made the same signal back.

Mr. Pymm's shoulders heaved up and down in what must have been a great sigh of relief before he darted up the beach like a sandpiper, bobbing and weaving amongst the waves which rushed up to meet the sand.

They really didn't need to follow his lamp any fur-ther; his cursing and complaining were enough to guide them. Apparently Mr. Pymm didn't like getting his boots and breeches wet, but Georgie considered that a small inconvenience if it meant he wasn't about to get his neck shaved by the French.

And with that sobering thought in mind and Kit still in tow, Georgie continued her flight after him.

They caught up with the mysterious Englishman just as he was struggling to throw a leg over the side of a boat. The craft was manned by four rough-looking sailors, two of them at the oars and the other two strug-gling to keep the boat from being sucked back out into the surf. They all wore dark oilskin coats and wide hats, leaving them nearly invisible in the dark night.

Smugglers. Just like Mr. Waterby and his crew, Georgie thought. At this point she didn't care what cargo they chose to carry outside the law, as long as it could include a few paying passengers.

"Wait, please wait," Georgie said, coming to an abrupt halt as a large looming figure stepped forth.

"What the hell did you bring along, Pymm?" The man's voice boomed above the din of the stormy waves and the pelting rain. In his hand, he still held a sputtering lamp, the other held one of the longboat's ropes. "I was only told to fetch you."

Georgie faltered for a second—the man's command-ing voice rippled through her memory, sending ghostly reminders up and down her spine.

To fetch you . . . She shook the echoing words away. For the imposing tone had belonged to only one man. Colin.

She twisted her head to get a better view of this stranger, but the pitch-black night and driving rain made it impossible to discern his features. Even the poor lamp he held offered no hint of the man hidden in the darkness.

Meanwhile, Mr. Pymm was twisting around, and at the sight of the sisters he nearly fell out of the boat.

"This is not my doing, Captain." He shot an angry glance at Georgie. "Whatever are you and your sister doing here, madame?"

"What does it look like, sir?" she replied, settling her bag carefully into the bobbing craft, and helping Kit climb aboard. "Escaping, much like you."

"Escaping what?" the man with the lantern asked, directing his question at Mr. Pymm and ignoring her.

Again his voice rippled down her spine, leaving it tingling with memories. Georgie chided herself. As if this rude rogue could be Colin!

"The French, sir," Mr. Pymm told him. "An entire regiment of them, I'd say."

"The French?" the captain said, spitting the words out more like a curse than question.

"Yes, the French," Georgie repeated for him. "And if you don't mind, we'd prefer to be off with you and Mr. Pymm before they discover us. I assume you have some sort of ship out there." She swung her arm out to-ward the surf and darkness.

"Now see here," he said, holding his lamp aloft, offering her a hint of the rough contours of his face. And there in the solid line of his jaw was a cleft in his chin. However, any resemblance to Colin ended with the less than honorable outburst that followed.

"What we're doing here is none of your business. Now be off with you," he said, waving his hand at them as if they were some bothersome flotsam fouling his lines.

His manners set Georgie's teeth on edge. "You'd leave us here? Defenseless Englishwomen at the mercy of the French? How dare you!"

"Defenseless? Bah!" he scoffed. "Listen here, I'm not in the business of rescuing women, nor is this longboat big enough for two more passengers. So get your sister out, or I'll toss her to the fish."

Once Georgie shook free of his grasp, she immediately drew out her pistol. She put the muzzle up against his chest and shouted over the storm and waves, "You toss her out and I'll make sure there is room enough for us by leaving your carcass here for the French to pick apart."

He stiffened for an instant, but then in a quick sweep of his arm, he sent the pistol flying from her hand and into the tossing sea.

It was only then that she met his angry glance, and realized she was face-to-face with the one man she'd thought she'd never see again.

The man who had saved her in London. The man who'd loved her so thoroughly. The man who'd left behind more than the memories of his touch.

Colin. She had dreamt of this moment, prayed for this moment, and now all she wanted to do was flee.

But she had no choice—once again she was at his mercy, once again she needed him to rescue her from the ill fates that seemed to follow her.

But what the devil was he doing here—in Italy? And in the dead of night rescuing the mysterious Mr. Pymm?

Her questions only reminded her of how little she knew about the man she'd fallen in love with that long-ago passionate night.

Obviously he hadn't seen her face, for he still continued on, ranting and raving about her high-handed tactics.

"Madame, you have no idea who I am or what you are getting yourself into—"

"I wouldn't be so sure," she said, whirling around and making for the longboat once again, drawing her hood deeper around her face and wondering what he would say when he learned the truth.

Colin did a double take. After his last trip into Naples, he'd thought he'd talked himself out of seeing his Cyprian in every woman he met. Yet for an instant, he thought he'd seen Georgie's face looking up at him from beneath that bedraggled and dripping cloak.

Besides, he also swore he was hearing things, for it seemed that her valise, the one stowed between her sister's feet, was wailing like a baby.

A baby? Now he truly was headed around the bend.

"Christ sakes, what have you got in there?" he asked, pointing at the valise.

"Why, my belongings, you ninny," the woman said, blustering past him and patting the bag as if to make sure it was well secured. Then she turned back to him, her hands on her hips. "You can toss away my pistol, but you're still taking us, whether you like it or not."

To his utter disbelief, the pushy bit of baggage waded into the cold water with a determined stride, hitching her skirt up in the process, revealing a pair of matronly boots attached to sensibly clad legs bound up in a gray wool.

But in his mind, the boots became a pair of embroidered slippers, her stockings, shimmering silk . . .

Limbs that wound around his as he covered her with his body . . . silken thighs that he had parted so eagerly . . . the woman urging him on, challenging him, telling him what she wanted . . .

His body hardened at the memories, so Colin took a deep, mind-clearing breath of the bracing air.

He considered dunking his head under the waves and letting the cold water bring him to his senses. Instead, he took another deep breath and started after her.

The hell if he was going to let this chit commandeer his longboat.

It would serve her right to be left behind for the French. And probably save the English a passel of trouble, for he suspected she'd bedevil her captors into an unconditional surrender.

"Now listen here—" he began, fully intending to catch her by her round hips and toss her back into the sea where all good harpies belonged.

But the ping of a bullet ricocheting against the rocks stopped him. He whirled around to discover that Pymm and this interloper hadn't been exaggerating.

The French had arrived in Volturno.

And they weren't wasting any time trying to hazard a path down to the beach. Already they had set up fir-

ing lines along the cliff and were raining a barrage of
bullets down on them, the deadly lead whizzing past,
spitting up sand and splashing into the water.

Colin immediately flung both lanterns, his and
Pymm's, into the sea, dashing out their telltale lights.

But it was too late to hide their position, for the cliffs
behind them, where once there had been darkness,
were now suddenly illuminated with torches and the
silhouettes of dozens of men. Considering the impor-
tance of the information Mr. Pymm supposedly carried, he wouldn't put it past the French to send an
entire bloody regiment after the man.

And since they'd discovered their meeting place, it
would only be a matter of time before they spotted his
ship, and the rest of the French forces in the area would
be alerted as to the presence of the *Sybaris*.

He cursed again, this time loud enough to be heard
over the waves and wind.

"Away, sir," Mr. Pymm squawked. "We must be
away this instant."

Colin couldn't agree more. "It seems you brought
friends with you, madame," he told the bothersome
woman between him and his longboat.

"I brought them?" She uttered a curse that would
put a blush on the cheeks of a Kingston whore.

"Yes, you!" he said, edging closer to her, his finger
waggling under her dripping-wet nose. "Your caterwauling has probably woken up the entire Italian
coastline."

A wave of cold water washed between them, soaking them both to their waists, but it did nothing to cool
either of their tempers.

"Why, you blithering fool! Those lamps probably

alerted every last one of them." She whirled around and without so much as a by-your-leave, she hopped into the boat and took up one of the empty oars.

"Are you coming or not?" she had the audacity to ask, as if the boat was suddenly hers to command.

Having finally found the trailhead that led to the beach, the French troops were swarming down the path. He should toss her, her sister, and their baggage out onto the beach and not look back.

Lord knew the heartache he'd found the last time he'd come to the rescue of a lady in distress—he'd spent the last year waking up from restless dreams, his thoughts possessed by haunting, tempting images of an enchantress beckoning him to find her, to love her once again.

Yet he could see Georgie doing much the same as this lady. With the French at her heels, he imagined his little Cyprian would be putting up the same dash and vinegar that she'd shown Paskims, Brummit, and Hinchcliffe at the ball.

At least, he told himself, he didn't have to worry about becoming infatuated with this lady, for she hadn't any of Georgie's charms. Georgie might have been a bit impetuous and headstrong, but this woman was a regular harridan.

And where the devil was her husband?

He should be saving her sorry hide, not leaving the unwanted task to strangers.

Then again, Colin reasoned, if he had such a wife, he'd be sorely tempted to leave her behind for the French as well.

"Captain," she was shouting. "Are you staying or are you coming with us?"

Colin grit his teeth. Damn his wretched honor, he could no more leave this troublesome pair behind than he could ignore the bullets whizzing around him. He nodded to the other crewman who still held the boat in the churning surf, and they pressed their shoulders into the sturdy craft, and heaved it back into the wild and restless sea.

As the first receding wave started to capture them, they scrambled in, each taking an oar. Colin found himself in the seat next to his unwanted passenger, and he grabbed the end of the long oar she held and added his strength to hers.

He was shocked to find that she knew what the devil she was doing, and she had the muscles to guide the heavy oar through the turbulent seas. Over and over, they pulled and lifted and pulled the oar again through the water, making their escape even as the French troops raced across the beach.

The troops continued to fire at them, but the darkness and the rolling surf quickly consumed them, giving the French little to aim at other than their own vanity that they still may yet succeed and capture the longboat.

"Good job, Captain," Mr. Pymm called out. "We've escaped them."

If Colin felt any of the man's relief, it was short-lived, for the troops on the beach began sending up rockets. The whizzing missiles illuminated the night, leaving streaming ribbons of light in their wake.

"Put your shoulders into it, men," Colin cried out. "Make for the *Sybaris* like your life depended on it."

Beside him, the lady's hooded head swung around. "What did you say?"

"We're going to my ship. The *Sybaris*."

"The *Sybaris*," she repeated, the name falling off her tongue like an old friend.

In that moment, a rocket exploded overhead, illuminating her features ever so briefly. He saw the determined curve of her chin, the turn of her generous lips, and a pair of dark eyes that took his breath away.

Georgie. And yet, not Georgie.

He glanced back at her, but she'd turned her head to her sister, the girl grinning like a fool.

"The *Sybaris*," she said again, with a shake of her head as if she couldn't believe it.

Perhaps she'd heard of them, he thought. Not by choice, his reputation as a pirate and worse was widely known about the Mediterranean.

But she hardly seemed concerned. More like in alt.

Before he could spare another glance in her direction, the longboat bounced into the side of his ship.

"Get up the sides, lads," he shouted to his men. "Tell them to rig a swing and be quick about it."

"We haven't time for such nonsense," the woman said, tossing the long strap of her satchel over her shoulder. As she clung to the bag as if it contained her very life, Colin thought he heard an odd wailing again.

He shook his head. Considering the rain, those infernal French rockets, and her complaining, it was lucky he could hear at all.

Once again caught woolgathering, he looked up to find that she'd given her sister a hand up onto one of the ropes trailing over the side of the ship. Before he could shout a warning or tell her to stop, the girl, despite her slight figure and frail appearance, began scaling up the side of the *Sybaris* with the ease and speed of one of his best hands.

"Now if you don't mind," the lady said, bustling past him in the pitching longboat, her movements matching the shifting waves beneath her as if she were one with the water and the small craft. Her agility and skill belied her sex, for she caught hold of the fluttering rope ladder and swung her leg and body over the side, beginning to climb as if she'd been at sea all her life.

He stared open-mouthed at the sight of it, wondering what this she-devil would do next—demand to share command of his ship?

Overhead, a new volley of French rockets screamed their arrival like a bevy of hell-bent banshees. The rockets' belligerent shrieks brought his attention swiftly back to the business at hand.

One of his crewmen was still in the boat, as was a green-looking Pymm.

"Up with you, sir," Colin told him, catching one of the loose ropes and shoving it into the man's unwilling grasp. "'Tis this or you'll have to swim for it."

The rockets overhead burst into a flash of lights, once again illuminating the *Sybaris*. The girl had made it up and over the rail, while the lady was about halfway up.

"What the devil are they doing, Captain?" Pymm shouted over the waves and the banshee peal of a new volley of rockets.

She glanced down at them, this time her dark gaze filled with disdain for Pymm.

"How can you not know, sir? They are signaling." She nodded over his shoulder.

Colin turned his head, and much to his consternation discovered a well-lit French ship-of-the-line rounding the point. It didn't take but a second for him to assess the danger. At three gun decks high, and most likely carrying a complement of sharpshooters strung through her lines, she was capable of blowing them out of the water.

And the *Sybaris* was still at anchor. Could his luck run any worse?

The sight of the formidable vessel sent Pymm's reluctance to the bottom in a heartbeat. With a muttered complaint about field assignments, he started crawling and scrambling up the side like a crab crossing hot sand.

Colin followed suit, shouting orders to the remaining crewman who was still trying to secure the pitching longboat.

"Cut it loose," he shouted at him. "We haven't any time."

When he reached the deck, he began barking orders to make sail, for every moment they sat here, the French ship and its ninety-four guns drew nearer. The lamps were all still dark, for they'd been sailing without lights to prevent detection, so the deck was pitch black—not that it had done them much good. They'd be able to sail more quickly with some lights, but that would also pinpoint their position. He just hoped the crew could move swiftly in this blasted darkness.

"Mr. Livett!" Colin bellowed. The ship's master dashed forward. "We have additional guests," he told the man. "Get these women off my deck and see that they are secured below."

"Aye, aye, Captain Danvers."

The lady spun around, clutching her valise to her

chest. "Captain Danvers?" she asked. "Did you say, Captain *Danvers*?"

"Yes, madame. Captain Colin Danvers, at your service," he replied.

Your reluctant service, he wanted to add, wondering what the chit had to complain about now—that he change his name to suit her needs, or was she going to stage a takeover of his ship much as she'd done to his longboat?

"Captain Danvers?" she repeated. "Are you any relation to Lord Danvers?"

"Yes. I am Lord Danvers."

She shook her shrouded head and backed away from him, from Mr. Livett. "No. No, it cannot be."

"Yes. Now if you don't mind—" he began saying, reaching out to take her by the elbow and propel her into Mr. Livett's care.

She drew back from him, pulling her sister behind her, as if she had just discovered they were captive on a plague ship and he was the lead leper. "Are you certain? Baron Danvers and Captain Colin Danvers?"

"Yes, I am quite certain as to who I am," he said. "Now, I insist that you—"

"Take us back!" she demanded. "Take us back to shore immediately."

Colin shook his head, wondering if his ears weren't still playing tricks on him. "Take you back? Madame, have you gone mad?" He shook his head. "No, don't bother to answer that, I already know." Turning to Mr. Livett, he said. "Get them below. Now!"

The lady held her ground. "I will not stay on this ship. I will not be subjected to your tyranny. Take us ashore immediately."

Colin had heard enough. He stalked over to her and stood toe-to-toe with the lady. He couldn't really discern her features in the stormy blackness swirling about them, but in a flash from one of the rockets, he found himself pinned by her angry gaze. A pair of dark eyes caught and mystified him. And then just as quickly the shadows returned and he could barely see anything of her tall figure. But one thing was for certain, he'd stared into those eyes before; he knew he had.

"Listen here," he sputtered. "I've got a French first-rate about to turn this ship into third-rate kindling. There isn't time to indulge this foolishness. Now do as you are told and get below."

"I will not. I'll not stay here another minute. Just give me the longboat. I'd rather take my chances with the waves and the French."

"The only way you're getting off this boat is by swimming, so why don't we start with this." He leaned over and picked up her satchel, which was heavier and bulkier than what he assumed a lady's belongings might weigh.

Then again, he wasn't an expert on what ladies carried in their traveling bags. Not that he was going to find out, for as far as he was concerned the lady and her sister could bloody well go to the French . . . or to hell for that matter.

Without hesitating, he stalked toward the railing, fully intending to heave the damn thing overboard.

"No!" she screamed, shoving past Mr. Livett, sending the poor man sprawling on the deck. She caught hold of Colin's arm just as he was about to give her valise the heave-ho. "Are you insane?"

With that, she did the one thing he would have expected from only one other woman.

She doubled up her fist and planted it squarely between his eyes, sending him pitching toward the rail.

No lady planted a facer like that. Except . . .

"Georgie," he gasped, sinking to his knees as stars burst before his eyes. Beneath his hands, the satchel shifted under his grasp.

Damn well moved on its own.

There weren't just undergarments in the thing, but something alive.

He shook away the remnants of her punch and yanked the bag open—only to find a red-faced, screaming baby wailing away inside.

A babe? He'd almost thrown a baby overboard. The air rushed from his lungs as if she'd added a direct hit to his gut.

Overhead, another volley of French rockets erupted, illuminating the decks of the *Sybaris* like Vauxhall Gardens.

The baby paused in its laments and stared in wonder at the grand lights overhead before bursting once again into tears.

"Give her to me," she said, pushing him aside and reaching inside to cradle the child in her protective embrace.

"Georgie," he whispered again, this time reaching out to cup the face he'd longed with all his heart to see.

Yet instead of rushing to his arms, she backed away from his touch, her eyes wary, her features set in hard, unforgiving lines.

"Aye, Colin. 'Tis me."

Chapter 8

Hours later, Colin took one last look through his spyglass and felt satisfied that they'd been able to escape the French. All around them, the sea was clear and blue. The fleet and speedy *Sybaris* had once again eluded capture.

At least for now.

So why wasn't he elated? Because he couldn't shake the feeling that the French ship's sudden appearance in Volturno, on this night of all nights, wasn't mere happenstance. Nor their raid on the sleepy little village just a coincidence.

His three encounters with French patrols in the last fortnight suggested otherwise.

Tonight had been a trap. And that could only mean someone had betrayed him.

Betrayed. The very idea gnawed at his gut.

In addition to that, he had another problem . . . the lady belowdecks.

Georgie. His impossible, unpredictable Georgie.

And yet not. The woman who had regarded him with such hatred, such vehement animosity, bore little or no resemblance to the woman he remembered passionately joining him in his bed. Her unfathomable coldness had kept him from sweeping her up in his arms and declaring his love for her.

Well, that and the French bearing down on his stern.

Now that he'd taken care of that minor problem, he thought with some chagrin, he'd solve whatever problems existed between them and then see that she never left his side, ever again.

Not that he blamed her for her anger or the punch she'd thrown—that he'd nearly tossed her baby into the water was enough to make him sink to his knees and beg for forgiveness. But there was more to her fury than just his temper getting the better of him . . .

The moment he'd gazed into her eyes, fell into their mysterious sable depths, he'd seen that something had gone utterly wrong for her, for them, in the last twelve months. For the life of him he couldn't figure out what it was.

Other than that she'd had a child.

A baby! Colin's heart swelled. Though he knew next to nothing about children, he'd counted the months and had a pretty good reckoning the babe was his. It had to be—with that shock of Danvers dark hair, it would be hard to believe it wasn't his.

His daughter. That in itself filled him with incredible joy and awestruck fear.

"Should we hold this course, Cap'n?" Livett asked, his question pulling Colin back to his immediate problems. "Or are we to go to Naples as that peevish lubber Pymm has been askin'?"

"Hold this course," Colin said. There was no point in going to Naples, since Nelson was no longer there. He'd been unexpectedly recalled home, and was well and gone from that place by now. Though he doubted such information was common knowledge as yet. "Anything else, Mr. Livett?"

"Aye, Cap'n," the ship's master said. "It's the lad. He's been down in the stores again."

Colin closed his eyes and counted to ten. Rafe!

His twelve-year-old half-brother, Raphael Danvers, had snuck aboard the *Sybaris* before they had sailed from London. He'd come out of hiding three days into their voyage, having declared that the school Colin had found for him was a waste of time, and that he wanted to learn about life firsthand. In the ensuing months, he'd tangled lines, caught the ship on fire twice, and nearly drowned after a fall from the head.

The devil himself would have been more welcome aboard.

"Where is he now, Mr. Livett?" Colin would deal with his brother after he'd seen Georgie.

"Can't rightly say. He's gone and disappeared since . . . since . . ." The man hemmed and hawed.

"Out with it," Colin said. "He's my problem, not yours."

"He went and drank up a bunch of rum. He's three sheets to the wind." Mr. Livett glanced up into the lines. "At least he hasn't tried to climb topside this time."

A hand on either side of his forehead, Colin wondered what he had done to deserve such a brother. Why couldn't Rafe be more like his twin, Orlando? Orlando, who was probably right now reciting Latin verbs and excelling at the top of his class.

Not stealing rum and tossing up his dinner to the fish.

"See if anyone can find him before he gets himself in a worse scrape," Colin said, "then throw him in one of the lockers—one without any liquor or rations—and I'll see to him as soon as I can."

With that, Colin proceeded below. With each step, he pushed Rafe's escapades further and further from his mind, while his heart started hammering with excitement. Still cold and wet from the storm that had worked to blow them away from their pursuers, Colin didn't care.

There was only one thing that mattered to him right now.

Georgie.

Whatever was troubling her, whatever he'd done to anger her so, he'd fix it. He'd be her true knight errant, ready to vanquish the demons tormenting her. He'd shelter her from harm, offer her his name, give their child—

"Captain, may I speak with you?" Mr. Pymm poked his head out of the quarters he'd been given, then waved Colin into the crowded compartment that at best was no more than a glorified closet.

"I think you'll find my cabin more amenable to a discussion, sir," Colin told him, motioning down the corridor.

Mr. Pymm snorted. "Mayhap a few hours ago, but

that blasted woman has taken over your quarters. She's gone and turned it into a regular nursery."

"And that surprises you?" he asked. "Given her arrival in our midst, I'm amazed she hasn't organized a mutiny yet. And since you mentioned it, I was just about to go have a discussion with her."

"Before you confront the lady, Captain, we need to talk. I must get word to Nelson. As soon as possible."

Colin eyed him closely. "Why?" Although he trusted Pymm—given the man's longstanding association with his father, along with a few comments he'd heard Temple make—he still held anyone connected to Nelson as suspect. Besides, his only orders had been sketchy directions to pick up a Foreign Office agent on the beach near Volturno before the French overtook the village. He'd been shocked to arrive and discover that his passenger was none other than the infamous Mr. Pymm.

Whatever the matter, it must be very dire indeed to draw Mr. Pymm out of his comfortable London office and into the field once again.

"What is so urgent?" he asked.

"These," Pymm said, drawing Colin into the cramped quarters and closing the door. The man held up a packet of letters. When Colin reached for them, Pymm pulled them back. "Don't bother, sir. They are in code."

"But you know what they say?"

Pymm shook his head. "No. Not exactly. That's why I have to get to Nelson first, then London immediately afterward." He fastidiously tucked the packet back into his jacket. "Lord Sutton will be able to confirm my suspicions."

Colin remembered his father marveling at Lord Sutton's skill at unraveling coded messages, no matter the language or difficulty. Yet even the use of the Foreign Office's legendary linguist didn't explain Pymm's suspicions.

"If you don't know what they say, how do you know these are so demmed important?" he asked.

Pymm's beetle brows furrowed. He crossed his arms over his chest, apparently unused to having to justify himself.

Colin waited him out.

"Oh, if you must know, the agent who carried these offered some hints as to their contents before he met with an unfortunate accident," Pymm said.

Colin knew enough of Pymm's reputation to know that the courier's "accident" hadn't been a happy one. But most likely a telling one.

"What did this man say before his 'accident'?"

"That we were too late to stop him. He'd already completed his mission, and was on his way back to Paris." Pymm shook his head. "That is why we must get to Nelson."

Colin felt as if he were dealing with his brother— another master in subterfuge. "Why Nelson?" he asked again in growing frustration.

"Because these documents are from *Mandeville*." Pymm all but spat the name out.

"And Mandeville is . . . ?"

Pymm's eyes widened. "You don't know? Your father never mentioned him?"

Colin shook his head.

"My good man, he's a French agent who's operated in England for years. There are reports about him going back to Queen Anne's time."

"Impossible. Why, that's nearly a hundred years ago," Colin said. "It can't be the same man."

Pymm shrugged. "Possibly not. But then again, Mandeville is like no other agent. Some say he's a ghost. There one minute, gone the next. I almost had him once. But I was too late. All I found in his wake were my best agents, dead. Murdered. I've been chasing him ever since." Then Pymm's voice turned so deadly, so full of fierce intent, that Colin felt the chill of it run down his spine. "And when I find him, he'll pay."

"So what has this Mandeville to do with Nelson?" Colin asked.

"The man I obtained these documents from boasted that Mandeville's orders are quite explicit." Pymm paused for a moment. "See that Nelson doesn't trouble the French ever again."

Colin's mouth went dry. "The French intend to have Nelson murdered?"

Pymm's grim features tightened as he nodded. "Yes. That is what I believe these documents will confirm."

"Why would the French risk putting all that in documents anyone could read?"

Pymm sneered. "New regime. Apparently Mandeville hasn't been paid in recent years and wanted their agreement in writing." Pymm's mouth moved in something that approximated a smile. "It certainly makes my job easier when no one trusts each other."

Colin's thoughts were still fixed on Nelson. "When? How? Whom do they intend to send?" It would be impossible to warn Nelson now—he had a good week's head start and had mentioned he might go overland

with the Hamiltons, rather than by sea. He wouldn't
have any notion where to start looking.

"But I have to warn him," he muttered more to himself. He looked up at Pymm, a burning resolve warm-
ing his chilled heart. "I have to know how this is going
to be done."

The man shook his head. "Knowing Mandeville and
his methods, he probably already has someone in
place. Someone close to Nelson and willing to betray
him."

Colin's gaze shot up. "That would mean—"

"Yes, the man you have been attempting to uncover," Pymm commented.

"How do you—" Colin stopped his question.
"Never mind. My father always said you could testify
as to what color drawers the King wore on any given
day."

Pymm shrugged, as if such intelligence were mere
child's play. "And you have his flair for blustering into
situations you are ill-prepared and ill-equipped to handle. If Mandeville is behind this, I would recommend
you leave this to me."

"I will not," Colin shot back. "It sounds to me like
you could use some assistance if it's taken you this
long to capture one man." He crossed his arms over his
chest.

"As if you are any good to me now," Pymm said.
"They obviously know all about you."

"So you noticed that tonight was most likely a
trap?"

"That you've surmised the obvious gives me vol-
umes of comfort," the indignant man replied. "And

here I thought Nelson was crazy to send you out to gather his intelligence. Still, you may prove useful yet."

Colin chose to ignore the man's jibes. Pymm was, after all, according to his father, the greatest spy who had ever lived. "When I get my hands around this bastard's neck, they won't need a hangman. I'll go up and change course immediately."

Pymm reached out once again and stopped him. "Have you considered, Captain, that Mandeville's agent may be on this ship?"

"On the *Sybaris*?" Colin laughed. "I handpicked every man aboard. I trust them with my life, and I wouldn't hesitate to trust them with Nelson's welfare."

"I wasn't talking about your crew, I meant your passengers."

"I've no other passengers on this ship. That was until tonight, until we picked you up. You and . . ." Colin's words trailed off as suddenly all his earlier speculations and questions took form into an unthinkable answer.

Georgie.

Pymm let go of his arm. "You see my point."

"Impossible. Mandeville's agent a woman? It's impossible."

Not Georgie. It couldn't be her. Suddenly, it wasn't just Colin's sodden clothes that were giving him the chills. "Are you telling me you suspect a woman, a young girl, and a baby of being part of all this?"

"Women are capable of deeds as foul as any man." Pymm shuddered. "In my business, I never credit that myth concerning feminine delicacy. Especially when they go about unsupervised. When they aren't properly kept, they become quite unpredictable." He nodded toward Colin's cabin. "As for that widow and her child, the babe could well be a foundling brought along to complete her guise. As for Mrs. Bridwick's sister, why, there was a Dutch agent who liked to use midgets to—"

"Bridwick?" Colin asked. "Did you say Bridwick?"

"Aye. Mrs. Bridwick." Pymm eyed him. "You know her, don't you?"

Colin nodded. "Yes. We met about a year ago in London."

"And Mr. Bridwick?"

At that, Colin made a small, tight laugh. At least he knew the answer to one of his questions; Georgie wasn't married. Instead, she'd taken the name of his house as her own. "There is no Bridwick."

"And you say you met her in London? Under what circumstances? Who introduced you?"

Colin stepped back from the man's sudden inquisition, bumping into the closed door behind him. "No one introduced us. We met by chance at . . . at a ball."

"By chance? No such thing," Pymm declared. "She must be the link. Sent to London to determine your plans and then returned to Naples to ingratiate herself into Nelson's company." The man rubbed his hands together. "Now all that is left is to interrogate, I mean, um, *question* the lady and determine who she really is."

Pymm started for the door, but this time Colin stopped him.

"There will be no interrogations or questioning of the lady until you offer me solid proof."

"Proof?" the man asked. "Of course I have no solid proof. That is what the interrogation will provide."

Colin shook his head.

Pymm threw up his hands and paced around his small cabin. "Fine. Then consider this." He held up one finger. "She appeared in Volturno the same day Mandeville's courier passed through." He smiled and held up a second finger. "I overheard her telling one of the other guests at the inn that she had come there at the suggestion of Lady Hamilton, who thought they might find the area perfect for sketching. Apparently, Mrs. Bridwick had spent the last few months in Naples, where she and Lady Hamilton had become friends. Close friends." Pymm paused. "I don't think I need to tell you that anyone within Lady Hamilton's circle has direct access to Lord Nelson."

Colin did his best to keep his features neutral. It had been Georgie he'd seen in Naples with Lady Hamilton. But he wasn't about to tell Pymm that and give the man more fuel for his witch hunt, nor did he believe she was the traitor they sought.

She couldn't be. Yet . . . he had met Georgie right after his court-martial and before he'd sailed. Suddenly his mind ran wild—her unrelenting desire to gain access to his apartments, her interest in his sailing trunk and where he was heading. Her almost calculated seduction . . . he'd certainly had questions about her that night, for nothing about her had rung true, and now . . .

"Any more reasons on which to base your conjectures?" he asked. He wasn't about to hand Pymm his case, not until Colin had a chance to gain the truth from the lady herself.

"Theory. A provable, irrefutable theory," Pymm argued. The man pursed his lips, then finally a third finger came up. "She knew enough to follow me to the beach."

"Good Lord, Pymm, she already pointed out your problem with that one. With those bloody lamps you insisted we use and your cursing, you all but took her hand and led the way."

"Well, it was dark and I detest field assignments," he muttered in his defense. He scratched his chin, his devious mind plucking and discarding facts, until suddenly he brightened. "The evidence is on your face."

"My face?"

"Yes, Captain. Have you looked in a mirror? Why, she blackened your eye like a first-rate pugilist." His eyes widened at that notion. "She might not even be a woman, but a man in disguise. Oh, leave it to the French to send a man posing as a—"

Colin laughed, halting any more of Pymm's fantastical speculations. "Rest assured, Mrs. Bridwick is a woman. Of that I have no doubts."

Mr. Pymm's eyes widened.

If Colin didn't know better, he'd say the man was scandalized.

"Oh, this is most irregular," the man finally sputtered. "Highly so."

Ignoring him, Colin said, "Yes, well, that matter aside, I don't see that you have any proof of her guilt." Even as Pymm opened his mouth to protest, Colin held up a hand to stave him off. "And until you can offer me evidence, hard evidence, there will be no interrogations of"—he started to say *Georgie* but caught himself— "this Mrs. Bridwick."

"This is what comes of associating with women," Mr. Pymm said in a ruffled manner. "The lady is certainly hiding something, and I see no reason for cosseting."

Colin smiled. "While I concede the lady has her secrets, I disagree she's a French agent. And I mean to prove your assumptions wrong."

Given Mr. Pymm's reputation as a renegade agent, one who often operated outside the regular course of business and who liked to give his superiors at the Foreign Office a "hell of a time," as Colin's father used to say, he wasn't about to risk the chance of Mr. Pymm taking matters into his own hands.

A good head taller than Pymm, Colin towered over the man and used his most menacing tones, the ones that had made him the scourge of the Mediterranean. "Hear me well, sir. *I* will get to the bottom of this, but by my own means, not yours. That means no poisons, no powders, no extortion, and especially *no accidents.*"

"Harrumph," Pymm replied, his skepticism written all over his features. But one good sign—he took a step or two out of Colin's shadow, smoothing his coat and straightening his spectacles before he spoke again.

"We'll use your methods," he conceded with a decided sniff. "For the time being. But eventually you'll see I'm right. I just hope it isn't too late." He held up the packet of papers again. "In the meantime, I want these documents secured and guarded. Day and night. I'll not take the chance that her midget is a cutthroat and thief, and have them stolen right from under my nose."

Shaking his head, Colin could see that he was going to have his work cut out for him, both getting to the bottom of Georgie's mysteries and keeping her out of Mr. Pymm's path. "There is a hidden compartment in my cabin. Your papers will be safe there."

Pymm's mouth drew into a tight line. "Oh, that will

never do. Not as long as you allow her to share your bed."

"The lady is not sharing my bed," Colin told him. *Not yet.* "I'll see her moved to other quarters. I assure you, no one on the ship knows about the compartment but you and I. It is the most secure place aboard. Will that satisfy you?"

"I suppose it must. But mark my words, Captain Danvers," Pymm said, shaking his finger under Colin's nose. "That woman is trouble. Trouble, I say."

With that theory, Colin couldn't argue.

Georgie turned at the sound of the cabin door opening.

"Sssh," she whispered, pointing at the small bundle atop Colin's bunk. "I've finally gotten her to sleep. She was quite restless after being tossed about." Even as she said the words, she regretted her choice of phrasing.

Tossed about.

Colin blanched. "If I had known she was—" he said, his words stumbling over one another.

Georgie shook her head. "I know you wouldn't have done it on purpose. Let us forget it happened. I know I'd like to." She edger closer to her daughter.

He nodded in thanks and began to close the distance between them.

As he stepped into the circle of light offered by the lamp overhead, Georgie's heart sang with recognition. While her body longed for him, ached to melt into his embrace, she took a deep breath and tried to remain calm and objective.

She couldn't believe the truth that still stung like the storm's icy spray: her Colin was also Baron Danvers. Her legal guardian. The selfsame man whose machinations she'd fled London to escape.

The irony that she'd landed back into his unwitting care didn't escape her.

Yet, looking at him, she found it hard to believe he was her guardian, for she'd always envisioned Lord Danvers as a selfish old fool cut from the same cloth as Uncle Phineas. Still, how could a man who wasn't more than a couple of years older than she be her guardian? None of it made any sense. Colin Danvers remained as much a mystery today as he had a year ago.

Even then, at the Cyprian's Ball, he'd stood out as different. Oh, his fashionable coat and buff trousers had marked him as a gentleman that night, but there had been something altogether different about his manners. She'd even thought him too honorable for her plans.

Despite the fact that he wore the plain clothes of a sailor, he was so much more than a mere man of the sea. Whatever he wore, Colin Danvers persisted in puzzling her.

Gentleman or rake? Merchantman or pirate?

Though right now it hardly mattered what disguise he chose to cloak himself in—he was dripping wet from the rain, and forming puddles around his feet.

"You're soaked," she said, trying not to sound concerned. She hardly cared if Lord Danvers caught his death from a chill. But suddenly this sodden man appeared more Colin than cretin. "Get out of those clothes at once, Captain."

At this he grinned. "Still rather to the point, aren't you?"

Georgie felt her cheeks grow hot. "That isn't what I meant. It's just that you are—"

Now it was his turn to stave off the explanations. "I was only teasing." He shrugged his coat off to reveal he was indeed soaked through—his white shirt clinging to his chest and arms.

Clearly, Colin had changed in a year. He'd grown leaner, his face lined with concerns she wanted to reach up and brush away. His face and hands were deeply tanned from long hours in the brilliant Mediterranean sunshine.

If it was possible, his body seemed even more virile than it had the night of the ball—hardened by long hours of toil and work aboard his ship.

Without so much as a care, he stripped off the wet shirt and grabbed a length of toweling from one of the pegs, dragging it through his hair and swiping it across his bare torso.

She could almost feel the planes the cloth traveled over—for she'd trailed her hands across him time and again in her dreams. As the memories started to warm her insides, Georgie looked away, embarrassed at the direction of her wayward thoughts.

This was Lord Danvers, she reminded herself. *Not Colin.*

Colin was gone. Lost to her for always. And yet . . . She stole another quick glance at the man before her.

He was combing back his wet, tousled hair with his fingers. It was still as dark as a raven's wing, and just as unruly. Picking up a length of leather cording, he tied it out of his way, taking on an appearance more mercantile than piratical.

Georgie wondered what it would be like to yank the cord loose and set the ruthless rake free once again . . .

Hadn't he done the same to her? Plucking her hairpins from her hair, letting her unruly curls fall about her shoulders, transforming her from an old maid to a wanton.

Colin, she wanted to whisper. *How I have longed to find you. How I have longed to return to your embrace.*

She glanced up into his eyes and realized he was watching her. A keen, burning fire blazed there. Suddenly, she felt stripped bare, as if he could read her thoughts and knew she still desired him.

The heat in her limbs rushed up to her cheeks. Georgie wondered if her face could burn any hotter. She broke off his mesmerizing gaze and reached down to draw another blanket around Chloe, patting the soft woolen length into place.

"As you know, my name is Colin, Baron Danvers." He bowed slightly, his strict formality truly a farce in light of the fact that he was half undressed and knew her . . . knew her so very intimately.

He paused, then glanced once again at her. "Now it's your turn."

"You already know my name."

"Yes. *Georgie*."

He needn't make it sound like a caress, she thought, wishing she had a blanket to wrap around herself and ward off even the suggestion of his touch.

His voice ran whisper soft and teased her to listen so very carefully. "There have been times when I thought

I just imagined you, that our night was nothing but a dream. I see I wasn't dreaming, Georgie." He said her name again, so intimately that it sounded like an invitation. And what his words intimated, his eyes echoed, smoldering with the same passion that had ignited between them. "Is that really your name?"

She nodded, unable to speak. Afraid she'd answer to more than just his question.

He smiled and shook his head. "If this were London, and we were meeting as I suspect we should have, meaning that we were properly introduced by mutual acquaintances, I wouldn't be left guessing the rest of your name."

Georgie smiled and ignored the pretty picture of civility he was trying to paint. She wasn't about to reveal her identity to him. Not as long as he was her guardian. And not just hers, but Kit's and Chloe's as well.

She'd fight him to her dying breath before she'd see either of them married off to suit some man's whims. Especially since he'd already considered the Earl of Harris a fine bridegroom for his wards.

The Earl of Harris, of all men!

"But we aren't in London," she told him. "So *Georgie* can suffice for now."

"*Georgie*, it is," he conceded.

Did he have to say her name like that? Especially when he was standing before her, half-naked, and whispering her name in that smoky voice that beckoned her back to their night. His tone echoed with memories of his lips teasing her ear, her neck, her . . .

Oh, now listen to her. Their night, indeed! What the devil was she thinking? It was his fault entirely—

calling it *our night* and trying to convince her that he'd been dreaming of her.

She was the one with dreams, not him. Not this Lord Danvers.

Yet it was her Colin who stood before her, a man waiting for answers.

She turned away from the hypnotic sight of him *en déshabillé* and stared out the stern windows.

"You've changed course again, Captain Danvers," she said, hoping a change of subject would throw *him* off course, praying as well that he'd do her a favor and put on some demmed clothes. "Does that mean we are headed to Naples?" She hazarded a glance over her shoulder toward him.

Thankfully, he was wrestling on a dry shirt, the white, soft fabric settling over the planes of his chest like an unfurled sail catching the breeze, filling and stretching its boundaries.

As his head poked through the opening, she thought for a moment she spied his eyes narrow at her question, his jaw set in a hard line.

What should he care where she wanted to go?

He'd made it all too clear on the beach he didn't want them here to begin with.

Whatever she saw, it passed quickly, and by the time he'd tied the strings at the neck of his shirt and looked up at her, that memorable fire had rekindled in his eyes.

But now there were doubts burning there as well.

And she had a feeling he wouldn't let anything stand in the way of his quest for answers.

"Captain Danvers?" He shook his head. "What happened to *Colin*?" His voice still held the deep timbre capable of ruffling down her spine, as it had when he'd made love to her.

She steeled her heart against such sentiments and struggled to bring to mind why she was there in the first place.

Remember, Georgie, she told herself, *Lord Harris still awaits a blushing bride back in London.*

A thought that would chill even the most ardent fever.

She took a deep breath and gathered together a defense of proper indifference. "I think it would be prudent if we made every effort to forget that we were previously acquainted, *Captain.*"

This time he ignored her deliberate refusal to use his name. "Acquainted? That's what you call what happened between us?" He laughed. "That child belies any such notion."

She sucked in a deep breath as he crossed the room to stand beside his bed. He towered over the small bundle there, and suddenly her daughter seemed so very vulnerable, so very fragile. Georgie moved closer, trying to put herself between Colin and his daughter.

Her daughter, she corrected. Not his. Never his.

"I would prefer that we leave her out of this."

He didn't bother to look up at her, his gaze locked on the child between them. "I can't do that. I won't."

Georgie's insides quaked. He wasn't supposed to care about his child. Lord Danvers probably had dozens of bastards that he held no more regard for than he did his wards.

Hopefully even less.

So she tried lying. "She isn't yours."

His gaze hardened. "Oh, she's mine."

There was no hesitation in his voice, just as she had imagined Colin would have said it. Her Colin, not her faithless guardian.

"What is her name?" he asked.

"Chloe." It was a begrudging response, but it was all she was going to give him. Besides, this meeting wasn't going at all as she'd planned. She'd spent the last few hours pacing about his cabin trying to determine what he'd say . . . and just how she'd reply. Certainly, she hadn't expected him to be bothered. She'd half predicted that he'd come bursting into his cabin and give her the choices of being set adrift; marooned on a small, barren island; or sold to the nearest passing ship headed to the East.

No, he was acting as if he cared. As if they had a second chance at . . .

Georgie dismissed that notion altogether. Like a cat with its nine lives, she'd probably used most every second chance she was due in the previous year—inheriting a modest fortune from Mrs. Taft, escaping London, taking on the weeds of a widow, and finally finding the freedom she'd always longed for.

She wouldn't risk all that by believing in the myth he now dangled before her, not for anything. Certainly not on the word of an unpredictable man.

"Chloe—?" he persisted.

Georgie balked again. What was it with this man and his insatiable need for surnames? "Just Chloe."

His hand reached out and tenderly lifted the edge of the blanket so he could see her face, and Georgie thought for a moment he was going to reach down and take her up in his arms. But to her relief, his hand finally went back to his side.

"Is she safe there on the bed?" he asked.

She would be safer far away from you, her anger and frustration wanted to cry out, but she knew that wasn't true. Any fool could see the concern in his gaze, the tenderness in his touch as he tucked the blanket back around the sleeping babe.

"Safe enough," Georgie said. "As long as she stays in the middle and the seas don't get rough." She paused and glanced again at her daughter. "A cradle would be better, for she likes to be rocked."

Colin glanced up and a kindred light burned in his eyes.

She could almost hear him say, *Thank you for telling me that.*

If she hadn't felt it before, suddenly the connection they'd found the night of Cyprian's Ball flickered to life, tugging her closer to him, tearing at her resolve to have nothing to do with Colin, Lord Danvers.

But suddenly he was Colin once again. Her Colin.

Georgie backed away from him. From the invitation to trust him, to believe in him.

She couldn't. She wouldn't. He'd been right when he'd come in and introduced himself. They didn't know each other. They were strangers. And until she knew what the measure of Lord Danvers may be, either the ogre guardian of her imagination or the Colin of her heart, she had to stand firm against the temptation he represented, the passion he made her recall.

"My daughter needs a name," he was saying. "And Danvers is hers by right."

"I think not," she shot back, a tad more hotly than was probably prudent.

His eyes widened. "And what is wrong with my name?"

Everything, she wanted to say.

Instead she told him, "I just prefer not to confuse the matter right now."

"Such as using the name *Bridwick*?" he asked.

When she didn't answer, he returned to the chair where he had left his dry breeches hanging over the back rungs. There was a deliberate teasing nonchalance about the way he'd asked his question.

Georgie wasn't fooled for a minute by his feigned indifference. He was keenly interested. From the way his sharp, telling gaze stole glances at her, to the taut line of his shoulders giving him the look of a cat about to strike.

And she had no doubt, given the opportunity, he would pounce upon any offering she let slip like an unopened gift, unwrapping all her secrets.

Well, Captain Danvers, she thought. *Not if I have anything to say about it.*

"And what happened to Mr. Bridwick?" he had the audacity to ask.

"You know as well as I, there is no Mr. Bridwick."

He nodded at her concession. "Now we're getting somewhere."

"And where exactly is that?"

"Where you stop this charade and quit pretending that we are polite strangers. It starts by you telling me the truth. All of it. Beginning with your name and ending with what the hell you were doing on that beach tonight."

"I think it was obvious what I was doing out there."

He cocked a brow.

She brushed her hands over her skirt and then crossed them over her chest. "Trying to escape a bad situation, nothing more."

His hands went to the waistband of his wet breeches. He smiled at her as he started to open them. "Madame, you seem to have a penchant for bad situations."

"I have since I met you," she muttered under her breath, as she whirled around to avoid seeing . . . well, seeing temptation.

Outside, the waves reflected the pink starting to grace the sky. It was nearly dawn. "You never did say why you've changed course again. We're sailing south by southwest, aren't we?"

She didn't even dare glance over her shoulder this time.

"Why do you ask?" Again that contrived indifference marked his question.

"Because I would like to know where you're taking us." She heard him deposit his wet breeches on the floor, the sound of the cloth once again rubbing against his skin, and then the rustle of twill as he tugged on the dry pair.

Satisfied he was decently clad, she ventured a glance over her shoulder.

He was just finishing buttoning the last tab. "I'm not sure yet. Back to London, most likely."

"*London?*" Georgie shook her head. "That will never do."

"I think I'm the judge of that," he said. "I'm still the captain of this ship."

"Why, it will take months to reach London," Georgie argued, trying to think of a hundred reasons why he had to let them go and ignoring the most compelling one: that she wanted out of his company as quickly as possible. "Besides, you haven't the room for us. I see no reason why you can't just set us ashore at the nearest port—such as Naples. It will hardly inconvenience you, and then you can be on your way to wherever you decide you are going."

"Georgie, have you forgotten that there is a war going on around you?"

No, she hadn't, but the one going on inside her heart was far more dangerous.

He continued, "Haven't you a care for yourself? For your sister or Chloe? Volturno is just the beginning now that France is under Bonaparte's control. London is the safest place for the three of you. And I mean to see you there whether you like it or not."

Georgie bristled. So this was how it was going to be. He was no different from that infernal interfering vicar in Penzance. No different from Uncle Phineas and his blustering manners.

Well, she'd had a taste of freedom and she wasn't about to fall under the domineering control of yet another intolerable man. "You can't take us where you please. You have no right."

"I may not have the right," he said, his voice holding a dangerous edge, "but someone should. Dammit, woman, you need someone to see you safe. What you need is a guardian."

Chapter 9

A guardian, indeed! The very word was the bane of Georgie's existence.

Oh, she wanted to scream in frustration that this man, of all men, would lecture her on the need for someone to safeguard her welfare.

"I don't need a guardian," she said. *I don't need any man. Especially not you.* "And what I truly don't care for is being kidnapped by some . . . some pirate."

Colin's brows rose. "A pirate? You think I'm a pirate?"

"What else am I supposed to think when I find you lurking about the Italian coastline picking up stray Englishmen."

Did he really think her so dull-witted that she'd believe his appearance was mere happenstance?

"Tell me, Captain Danvers, how was it that you so conveniently arrived in Volturno tonight?"

His mouth set in a hard line and Georgie knew she was on to something.

Good. She was turning the tide on him. He didn't want to discuss his reasons for being in Volturno any more than she wanted to hand him a calling card.

"I say, it really was coincidental that you were on that beach exactly when Mr. Pymm needed rescuing," she said, pacing around the table, her fingers trailing over his open logbook. She hoped to catch an entry as to their coordinates and course, but before she could spy anything in his scrawling script, he reached over and slammed the volume shut.

She plucked her fingers back just in time, and glanced up at him. The challenge in his gaze reminded her of the dangerous gleam that had lit his eyes when he'd returned to save her from her trio of tormentors in London.

When he'd declared that she was his.

His no longer, she reminded herself. *Never his.*

To Colin, the woman before him was a tangle of con-tradictions, running afoul of everything he'd held in his memories from the night of the Cyprian's Ball.

How could he have forgotten her temper? Her fiery defiance? Or her inquisitive nature?

It was just that inquisitive side of her that made him wary. While he didn't record anything in his log that could be considered damning, he didn't like the way she was prying.

Asking questions about their course . . . their desti-nation . . . his role in Pymm's rescue.

They were, he knew, innocuous questions on their own, but Pymm's needling suspicions found one toehold after another in his heart as she persisted in her attempts to uncover his secrets.

He found himself wondering if perhaps Pymm had the right of it. *Could Georgie be a spy?*

Ridiculous, he told himself, endeavoring to ignore what Pymm would call irrefutable evidence and stick to what his heart was telling him.

Yet he couldn't ignore the fact that he'd held no doubts as to Lady Diana's affections for him until she'd all too happily tossed his ring back at him.

Now as he watched Georgie, he wondered if she too had given him the pretense of love that night. If he couldn't trust his own heart, how could he believe this woman who had stolen it with such audacious impunity?

If only he could dismiss that night from his mind as an aberration, a lapse in judgment, his memories faulty from the passing of time. Yet the long days and months hadn't diminished his need for her . . . and they had only made him realize the beauty and rarity of what they had shared the night of the Cyprian's Ball.

So how could that passionate interlude, the undeniable connection they shared, have been a deception?

He knew exactly what Pymm would say about such a theory, and the man's poisonous conjectures pierced yet another needle of doubt in his resolve to believe in Georgie's innocence.

"Just why were you on that beach tonight?" she persisted.

He glanced over at her. "I would think you would be satisfied enough that I was there and not be overly concerned with the reasons. I did, after all, save you from certain jeopardy . . . once again."

"Yes, thank you," she muttered. "For all my unforeseen rescues."

He smiled. "You needn't thank me for the time in London."

"Why is that?"

"Because you thanked me quite sufficiently that night," he said. "Three times, as I recall."

Her mouth opened in a wide, indignant O.

Colin ignored her outrage, turning his back to her and pacing a few steps around his table. It was a risk to leave himself vulnerable to this woman, but he wanted to evoke a response from her.

An angry Georgie meant that his impassioned Cyprian, his mischievous lover, still existed beneath her cautious indifference, her aloof reserve.

"As for my being in Volturno, it truly was coincidence," he continued saying. "I think the better question is what are *you* doing so far from London? Don't you realize the risks of dragging your sister and child into the middle of a war?"

He glanced over his shoulder and spied the dangerous, challenging light in her eyes.

The fire blazing in those dark, stormy depths sent his blood racing with memories.

Her urging him to take her. The heated frenzy that had overtaken them both. Her clamorous response.

It hadn't been an act. She hadn't been there just to spy on him or to learn of his mission.

He would prove it if he had to shake the truth out of her.

"What are you doing here, Georgie?" he asked, moving closer to her. "Tell me, tell me now. Who are you? What do you want of me?"

Without waiting for an answer, he reached out and took her into his arms.

He gave no heed to her squirming protest, to her threats of darkening his other eye, to any of her blustering and posturing.

Colin wasn't listening, for the only thing he wanted was to discover the truth.

What the hell had happened to his Georgie?

For a moment she stilled, and he glanced down into her wary gaze.

It held a warning beacon as bright as the lights off Portsmouth, but her eyes also burned with something else . . .

Desire.

That part he recognized, and it was as achingly familiar as the sight of England's verdant shores after a long voyage.

So he answered her siren song by closing his mouth over hers.

Again she struggled to protest, her fists hammering at his shoulders, her booted foot stomping about as it tried to connect with his bare toes. But as his tongue swept over her lips, enticed her to open her barred doors, her protests wavered and her defenses faltered.

Once he found his breach, saw the way clear through her stormy objections, he pressed forward without a second thought, reclaiming what she had offered so willingly that long-ago night in London.

Her mouth opened, welcoming him. Their lips melded together and her body pressed to his. The chills that had once racked him now were lost in the heat rising up from his gut, leaving him hard and fevered.

Swept aside in this fervent, boiling tide of emotion

were any thought of his mission, Pymm's innuendos about her loyalties, the memories that had left so many questions between them. All that was left in its wake was one thing.

His restless, unrelenting need for her.

He pulled back for only a second. He needed to hear her haunting voice. He needed her to say the words.

That she needed him as much as he wanted her.

"Oh Georgie. What do you want?"

And then he realized his mistake. Recognized that he hadn't conquered her resistance as readily as he had thought.

For yes, her eyes burned with unquestionable passion. But that passion was doused in a single moment as she caught her breath and regained her control.

"What do you want?" he repeated.

"I don't want anything from *you*." Her adamant denial took him aback, allowing her time to escape his grasp. "I just want to return to Naples."

He ignored her plea, the way her gaze beseeched him to set her free. Whatever they had rediscovered in those precious moments of their kiss was gone. Lost. Leaving Colin just as mystified by this enigmatic woman as ever.

"Why Naples, madame?" he asked, steeling his heart against her appeals.

"What difference is it to you?" When he continued to stare at her, she blustered on, filling the uneasy silence between them. "Oh, if you must know, all our belongings are there. We only planned on being in Volturno for a few days so we left the bulk of our trunks at the villa we are renting." She let out a long sigh. "Our clothes, the rest of my sister's sketchbooks and lessons, Chloe's cradle, and all her extra blankets and nappies and gowns." She tipped her head to one side. "You wouldn't happen to be smuggling any extra nappies, now would you?"

"I'm not a smuggler."

"So you say," she replied. "And if you aren't a smuggler, then I see no reason why you can't sail into Naples and deliver us back to our ordinary lives."

Ordinary! That was hardly a word he'd use to describe anything about Georgie.

As for taking her back to Naples . . . he suspected Pymm would probably prefer that they just set this trio adrift and sail for London as quickly as possible.

"Please, Captain Danvers. Let us go and forget that you found me."

Give her up? Now that he'd chanced upon her again? Give up Chloe, when he had just discovered he had a precious daughter? She truly didn't know the measure of his honor. Or his feelings for her.

"No."

"No?" she repeated. "Just like that, no?"

He nodded. "Not until you start giving me the answers I want."

"And just why should I do that?" she asked, her hands on her hips, her stance taut and fierce.

Her fire made his blood burn anew. This was his Georgie. The woman he remembered.

"If you can't be honest with me," she said, "why should I tell you anything? I don't even know who you are."

Colin stepped closer, closing the space between

them again. Close enough to smell a trace of her perfume, close enough to reach out and pluck the pins from her hair.

Temptation. The woman was blasted, passionate temptation personified.

He ignored his body's reaction and sought one from her. "You knew me well enough that night to get into my bed."

Her eyes widened again, her outrage coloring her cheeks a brilliant shade.

"How dare you!" she sputtered. "I had no choice . . . If I hadn't—" Once again her mouth snapped shut, her lips drawing a grim, resolute line across her face. When he edged nearer, she balled her fists. "Don't think about coming any closer."

Colin cocked his head and studied her. He also held his ground. He didn't relish the idea of having a matching shiner added to the first one she'd planted on his face, for it still throbbed like the devil, but he wasn't going to back down. Not now. Not when she stood so temptingly close.

"No choice?" he asked. "I beg to differ. You made every choice that night." He paused to grin. "Some that surprised even me."

He reached out to touch a wayward strand of her honeyed curls, but stopped short when she flinched.

What the devil had happened in the ensuing twelve months to change her mind so irretrievably about that night? For then there had been no hesitation between them.

"Well, I'm making a different decision now," she said, a haughty tip to her chin, an indignant uplift of her brow as frosty as any duchess.

Her outward demeanor did little to convince him of her claims, for he knew she was an accomplished actress. What chilled him was the venom and hatred behind her words—they trampled his tenuous belief that they had any chance of building a bridge of trust between them.

"I want nothing to do with you," she said, bitterly and defiantly, as if she were trying to convince more than just him. "I'd rather sleep in bilge water than ever share a bed with you again."

Colin stepped back from her. "Your kiss was enough for me. Besides, I don't remember asking you to come anywhere near my bunk." He turned on one heel and strode toward the door. "When Chloe and your sister are rested, you can move into other quarters, something more to your preference."

Before he could leave, she crossed the room, catching him by the arm. "Will you take us to Naples? Will you let us go?"

"I've already answered that," he said, plucking his sleeve free from her grasp, and shutting the door between them.

Inside, he heard her exasperated sigh and then something slamming into his table. Her fist, he surmised, when that blunt and defiant noise was followed by a healthy curse.

Yet instead of feeling victorious, he wondered at his own stubborn handling of the situation.

How did he expect her to trust him when he hauled her into his arms to steal a kiss like a thief, then ordered her about and made demands like some demented guardian in a Covent Garden tragedy?

No, if he was going to extract Georgie's secrets, he'd

need to coax them out of her, entice her with the same patience that crusty old sailor had once convinced him it would take to catch a mermaid.

All he needed was just the right bait . . .

Much to Georgie's chagrin, Colin didn't waste any time seeing them moved out of his cabin and to other, less spacious, quarters.

Georgie did her best to arrange the room to give them each a bit of space, and still be able to navigate around the water casks lashed in the corner, the bucket for their personal needs, and the basket she'd scavenged to store Chloe's dirty nappies in until she could wash them out.

What had surprised her when she'd been out locating their supplies was how well Colin ran the *Sybaris*. The crew was a diverse lot, actually reminding her of Captain Taft's own band of smugglers and sailors. But there was one distinct difference—there seemed to be an order and regulation to the ship's general organization that seemed . . . well, almost naval.

With such a well run and tidy ship, Georgie couldn't help admiring his skill as a captain. His ship was clean, his men apparently well paid and well fed, and she could see by the riggings and the care taken with the handling of the ship that Colin was a dedicated and capable captain. It warmed her heart to see the *Sybaris* under such good care, sailing as she was meant to be, and Georgie almost felt a debt of gratitude to Colin for carrying on Captain Taft's legacy.

Still, with everything so trimmed and starched, she wondered how accommodating he'd be to having nappies strung along his ship's lines? If he protested, she could offer that if anything, it would put the French ships looking for them into a quandary as to what they were signaling.

Georgie glanced down at the seam she was sewing on a new gown for Chloe, only to discover it now ran crookedly. She sighed. She'd like to think she could blame her ill-sewing on her tangled thoughts of Colin, but she'd never been very adept at the task.

"I don't know why we couldn't stay where we were," Kit complained, as she came banging through the door and then flopped down on her bunk in the tiny cabin. She tossed her sketch pad and case of charcoals and watercolors down by her feet and looked up at the ceiling. Her cheeks were flushed, and her hair all fallen out of its pins. Not surprising, since she'd been up on deck, but it gave Georgie pause.

She'd extracted a promise from Kit not to climb about the riggings. Though she had no fear for her sister's safety, she didn't want to have to explain to Colin just how it was her young sister could accomplish such a feat.

She hoped Kit's disheveled appearance was nothing more than a bit of wind damage.

After a few moments, Kit rolled over and said, "Why don't you just tell him who we are and insist he treat us better? Especially since he is our guardian."

Georgie whirled around, her finger to her lips. "Sssh! Don't you ever mention *that* while we are aboard this ship."

"Oh, really, Georgie, he doesn't seem the bad sort. Not at all like we thought. I'd say he is rather nice. He was asking me all about Chloe when I was above just now." Kit reached down and flipped open her sketch-book. "Mrs. Taft always said that a man who liked babies was one you could trust. And he seems quite interested in Chloe. I showed him my drawings of her and he thought them remarkably lifelike."

Georgie steeled her heart against Colin's intrusion into Chloe's life. Any interest, any kindness on his part had to be tempered by the fact that he was their guardian, the selfsame man who had placed a clause in her marriage papers that stated if she were unable to marry Lord Harris, Kit could stand in her place.

Rather nice, indeed!

"No more, Kit. I don't want to discuss this subject any further. Don't you remember what Captain Taft always said?"

"A ship has no secrets," Kit dutifully repeated.

"Aye, no secrets," Georgie confirmed. "If we are to hold on to ours, we must not talk about our guardian, not here. Not anywhere. Not until we're off the *Sybaris*."

Kit let out a long sigh. "That will be some time, for Raphael says we are bound for London."

"Raphael?" Georgie asked, looking up from her sewing. Her sister had hardly been out of her sight since they'd come on board and already she was on a first-name basis with one of the crew.

"Yes, Lord Danvers's brother." Kit sighed again, this time with a definite wistful air of feminine longing. "He's quite handsome, far more so than Captain Danvers. When we get to London, his brother is going to buy Raphael a commission into the army. I think he'll look splendid in a uniform and I told him thusly." She paused from her litany of gossip and sat up on her bunk. "Georgie, was that wrong to tell him that I thought him splendid on such a short acquaintance? Should I have waited?"

Her eyes glowed with the flush of something other than an hour or so of fresh air. And suddenly Georgie started to wonder if Kit's tousled looks hadn't been the result of another kind of nature.

Human nature.

She wanted to groan. All Georgie needed was her sister fancying herself in love with Lord Danvers's brother. The rogue was probably cut from the same unrestrained cloth as his rakish sibling—and if that was the case, she'd probably find that Kit had more than a broken heart to mend when they got off the *Sybaris.*

"I think it would be well if you left this Raphael to his work for the time being. You would hate to be responsible for getting him into trouble."

Kit scrambled off her bunk. "Oh, but Georgie, I promised to draw a picture of him later, when he was off duty."

Taking one look at the earnest expression on Kit's face, Georgie realized she needed to nip this in the bud as quickly as possible.

If only . . . Georgie thought for the thousandth time. If only their parents hadn't died. If only Uncle Phineas and Aunt Verena had held an iota of familial love for them. If only Kit could be dreaming about her first Season now, worrying about dresses and dances and invitations.

She certainly shouldn't have to be finding her girlish

pursuits where they may lie, especially when it appeared that right now her dreams resided with this Raphael Danvers.

Georgie knew full well that if she outright forbade it, Kit would go out of her way to see this Raphael, so "We'll see" was all she said, which seemed to satisfy Kit, who pulled out her sketch pad and charcoal and continued working on a drawing she'd been doing of Chloe.

Satisfied that Kit was engaged, Georgie decided to venture out and confront Colin.

Now, more than ever, she thought, glancing at her sister, they needed off the *Sybaris*.

Especially considering her own reaction to Colin's unexpected kiss. Her body had come traitorously to life the moment he'd swept her into his arms.

One look into his gaze and she'd known that he still wanted her.

Wanted her with the same wrenching need that filled her heart.

No, that would never do. How could she remain aboard the *Sybaris* in such close quarters with him? She certainly couldn't trust him to be civilized . . . and from the way her body still trembled at the memory of his touch, she knew she couldn't trust herself either.

"I'll be right back," she told Kit, and went out into the corridor.

The only comfort in all of this was being back on the *Sybaris*. The ship moved with a familiar roll beneath her feet, while her hand trailed along the time-worn railing running alongside the wall.

She'd gone as far as to abandon her shoes and stock-

ings, going barefoot like most of the crew, just as she
had as a child. Even her toes seemed to relish the
friendly feel of the smooth wood planking beneath
them.

How she had loved this ship as a child. Twice Captain Taft had taken them to France, much to Mrs. Taft's
chagrin. Those adventures were some of Georgie's
most treasured memories.

And of course, every time he was in port, Captain
Taft had given her free run of the ship.

She inhaled deeply, hoping to catch a faint hint of
the cargoes she remembered. Sweet rum. Thick spices.
The rich, warm odor of cognac wafting up from the il-
legal casks Captain Taft had brought from France in the
hidden hold.

Georgie grinned and wondered if Colin had found
that compartment yet, or any of the other cubbyholes
and secret cabinets for which only a smuggler would
have a use.

Padding silently down the narrow shadowed corridor, she paused before Captain Danvers's cabin, especially when she heard raised voices from within.

"Are you sure this is the safest place on the ship?"

It was Mr. Pymm speaking.

Instead of making her presence known, Georgie
paused, leaning closer to hear every word, eavesdropping shamelessly.

Truly, how many times had she chided Kit for the exact same sin? She did her best to ignore the fact that
what she was doing was wrong.

This, she decided, was a necessary evil. Mr. Pymm's
meeting on the beach with Colin hadn't been some

chance encounter as Colin insisted, and now she was going to gain the truth of the matter. So instead of knocking, she eased back into the shadows, craning her neck so she could peer through the slightly open door.

"I assure you, Mr. Pymm, your papers are more than safe here. It is where I keep all my valuables," Colin was saying, as he stood before the open panel near a bookcase that lined one wall.

So the *Sybaris* had given up that secret to her new captain. She wondered how Colin had found it, because Captain Taft had sworn it was undetectable. He'd used it to keep duplicate logbooks, cash, and jewels, as well as a spare pistol tucked away in case of an emergency.

"No one on this ship knows about this hiding spot," Colin said, "and I doubt they could figure out how to open it." He turned to Mr. Pymm and held out his hand.

Georgie stepped a little farther back into passageway. *Would you care to wager on that, Captain Danvers?*

Mr. Pymm, in his usual friendly fashion, grumbled and complained. "I daresay this appears safe, Captain. Though with *that* woman aboard there is no telling what treachery will confront us."

"I doubt our nefarious Mrs. Bridwick would be able to find this compartment," Colin told him confidently.

"Yes, if you think so, but don't be swayed by her pleasant face. Such chits use their wiles to coax astray even the staunchest hearts."

At this, Georgie smirked. So the curmudgeonly Mr. Pymm thought she had a pleasant face and possessed wiles. She rather liked the idea of herself being thought of as a dangerous siren.

However, Colin's adamant reply kept Mr. Pymm's wry praise from going to her head. "I promise you, sir, I am not susceptible to *her* charms."

I beg to differ! she restrained herself from protesting. His kiss had said something to the contrary in a thousand ways that words could never convey. Though, in truth, she had no desire for his attentions, indeed not. But still, whether she liked it or not, it stung that he would make such a claim.

Yet before she could become entirely indignant, Mr. Pymm's next remarks stopped her cold.

"Must I remind you, Captain," he was saying, "that the fate of Nelson, the fate of England resides in these papers. We must have them to London posthaste if we are to finish our work."

The fate of Nelson? Of England? Georgie's mouth went dry. So the *Sybaris* still possessed her fair share of secrets.

"Sir, I have every intention of seeing us to London without delay," Colin was saying.

London? Oh, that would never do. It would take months to get to England . . . months spent with Colin would only spell disaster for her resolve, but also for the chances of her keeping their identities a secret. She wasn't worried about herself, but Kit could become a problem, especially if she fancied herself in love . . .

Yet those weren't even her greatest fears. The more pressing problem suddenly weighing upon her shoulders was what the devil kind of havey-cavey business were Mr. Pymm and Colin about?

She certainly had a right to know, since now she, Kit, and Chloe were inextricably bound up in this nefarious pair's intrigue.

Her curiosity piqued, her imagination starting to wonder the worst, Georgie knew she couldn't stop until she learned what could possibly be in those papers that was of such dire consequence.

And there would be only one way to find out.

"Well, if you give your word these are safe," Pymm was saying, handing over a neatly tied packet of papers, watching peevishly as they were quickly stowed in the compartment.

Colin replaced the covering, which slid into place and once secured looked just like the rest of the paneling in the room. "There. Should we be boarded or inspected, no one will find them. Unless they start taking the ship apart piece by piece. Then I suggest you make short work of them."

As Pymm grumbled over that plan, Georgie edged her way back into her own cabin and closed the door behind her.

Kit started to bound up from her bunk, but Georgie put a hasty finger to her lips and silenced her sister.

Her ear pressed to the door, she listened as first Pymm ambled down the corridor, his mutterings and grumblings marking each of his passing steps. Then to her delight, she heard the ship's master call down the hatchway for Colin.

His door opened and closed, and his firm, distinct footfalls echoed down the corridor and then up the rungs of the ladder to the quarterdeck.

Georgie could have pinched herself at gaining such a good opportunity so quickly. But her elation quickly deflated when she snuck back down the hallway to Colin's door and found it locked.

For now her plans remained out of reach.

And so it seemed were his secrets. At least for the time being.

Georgie wasn't easily put off. An hour or so later, she went on deck attempting to seek out Colin, albeit under the excuse that she needed to discuss his brother's untoward attentions to Kit, as well as her desire to be returned to Naples immediately before they sailed too far west.

And at the same time, she'd put on her best manners and attempt to mend the mess she'd made of their earlier meeting. Especially since the only way to get back into his cabin was to convince him of her trustworthiness.

One thing worried her though. She found herself looking forward to finding Colin.

Captain Danvers, she muttered to herself. She must think of him as Captain Danvers, evil guardian, kidnapper, and despoiler of innocent women.

Even those thoughts did little to dispel her desire to stand in his shadow again, to feel his touch. When he'd reached out and almost touched her hair, she hadn't been able to breathe. She'd only turned from his touch out of fear.

Fear that once his fingers did find their way into the tangles of her hair, she'd be the one trapped by another one of his irresistible kisses.

Oh, she was being ridiculous. She certainly didn't harbor any feelings for the man. Certainly not Captain Danvers.

That blasted Colin was another matter.

Still, she didn't know whether to be relieved or disappointed when she discovered that he was nowhere to be seen on deck. Since she knew he wasn't in his cabin, having already checked the lock again, she beat a straight course to the ship's master's side.

"Mr. Livett," she said. "I must have a word with the captain. Do you know where he is?"

"I can't rightly say," the man mumbled, glancing left and right, anywhere but directly at her.

"You can't or you won't?" Georgie persisted. She couldn't imagine any ship's master not knowing exactly where his captain was at any given time.

"Now that's a good question, madame," he said. "One you'll have to ask the cap'n when you find him." He bobbed his cap to her and muttered a hasty "Good day to ye," before he took off and up into the rigging.

Flummoxed but not deterred, Georgie pressed on, searching the ship stem to stern. But none of the crew could tell her where their captain was hiding, nor were they all that willing to help her find him. Even the carpenter remained locked in his workshop, hammering and cursing away at some task, refusing to answer her persistent knocks at his door.

"Bother," she finally muttered and gave up. At least for the time being.

Colin Danvers couldn't elude her forever.

Chapter 10

Colin had successfully avoided Georgie for the bulk of the day. That she was seeking him out boded well for his cause . . . or he was kidding himself about her sudden attentions and she planned on tossing him overboard in a well-executed mutiny.

Knowing her, he'd wager on the latter.

But to his dismay, when he finally did venture on deck, ready to do battle with the lady, it wasn't Georgie who sought his counsel, but Mr. Pymm.

"Captain Danvers!" the indignant man called out, scurrying across the deck. "Captain, a word with you."

If only it was just a mere word, Colin thought. "Yes, Mr. Pymm?"

"I must protest. I want to lodge a most fervent protest."

Colin groaned inwardly. "What is it?"

"I'll have you know all this will be going into my full

report." He paused as if this in itself should be enough to prod Colin into action. "My full report, mind you," he said, waggling his finger under Colin's nose.

"Yes, sir. I heard you the first time. What can I do for you?"

"What can you do? What can you do, you say? I would think it is obvious."

"And that is?"

"Why, that alleged woman," he said, with a jerk of his head toward the stern. " 'Tis a crime to allow her to stroll about thusly," he complained.

Pymm had the right of it there, it was a crime. The sight of Georgie was arresting, enough to steal his speech, rob his senses.

She stood at the stern railing, her face gazing toward the eastern horizon. Her hair hung from a disheveled and windblown chignon, curls and tendrils dancing in the breeze. She wore a simple white gown that left her arms bare, exposing her neck and a fair amount of her bosom. At her feet sat a small lantern, offering a circle of light against the twilight, casting an ethereal glow about her.

But it was her expression that caught Colin's heart. Her wistful gaze stared off in the direction of the Italian coastline, toward Naples. It was as if he was tearing out her heart with each league they traveled westward, away from Italy.

Her face had worn the same expression when she'd slept in his arms that long-ago night. And it tugged at his heart now as it had then.

Tell me your secrets, he'd whispered into her ear as she'd slumbered. *Let me be your guardian.*

And as he had wanted so fervently to safeguard her

then, she now watched over their child with the same passion.

It was obvious in the way she held Chloe so protectively in her arms. He found it a touching tableau—Georgie in her Valkyrian pose, in contrast to Chloe's blissful cooing and antics. Looking at his daughter almost made Colin forget the danger swirling around them, the French hunting them, the terrible separation between him and her mother.

And yet, he could stand there all night watching Chloe's chubby hands batting at Georgie's hair. It brought a smile to his lips when his determined child finally found a fistful to wrap her fingers around and gave the strands a playful tug.

Georgie laughed and freed her imprisoned locks with a gentle motion, then tucked the tendril behind her ears. When another one fell free in the breeze, Chloe squealed with delight, her hand once again waving erratically as she tried to catch hold of it.

"Do you hear me, Captain Danvers?" Pymm was saying. "Why are you allowing her the liberty of this ship? And with a lantern, no less."

"She isn't to be allowed any light?"

Pymm shook his head. "She's probably waiting to signal her compatriots. Mark my words, the entire French navy will be breathing down our necks by first light. Meanwhile, her dwarf is most likely in my cabin searching for . . ." His voice dropped to a whisper. "Searching for certain matters."

Colin nodded in agreement, if only to humor the man.

Just then Chloe started to howl, an ear-piercing squall that made a nor'easter sound like a concerto.

"Aha!" Pymm said, pointing at the baby. "She's probably using that child to signal them as well. Such a noise could summon the dead." Pymm covered his ears and grimaced. Then in one lull of wails, his face brightened. "I have something that would silence that caterwauling, good and well. Just say the word."

Colin's hands whipped out and caught Pymm by his poorly tied and crumpled cravat, wrenching him upward until his boots dangled in the air. "You will not!"

"Aaaaah," the man gasped.

"Do you hear me?" Colin said, tugging the man up a little higher. "Harm that child and the only signal the French will be receiving is your body being shot from the nearest cannon I can load it into."

Mr. Pymm managed to nod, and a second or two later, Colin released him, dropping him on the deck with a thump.

The flustered agent immediately began straightening his collar and jacket. "Most irregular, Captain Danvers. Mark my words, this will all be going in my report."

"What report is that?" Georgie asked. She'd come up to the two men so softly that neither of them noticed her.

Pymm shot Colin an "I-told-you" sort of affronted look and then made his excuses, scurrying off, muttering something about "matters to review."

Georgie stepped out of his way. "An odd sort of gentleman, isn't he?"

"He grows on the acquaintance," Colin replied, wary of saying anything before her. But he did offer one caution. "If he offers you, your sister, or Chloe anything to eat or drink—don't touch it."

"Comforting thought," she said, casting one last glance in Pymm's direction.

"I, um—" she started to say.

"I wanted to—" he also began.

They both stumbled to a stop.

"You first," she demurred.

"No, you," he urged.

"I don't know where to begin," she said, her eyes peeking up at him from half-shuttered lashes.

A shy glance that teased him with a glimpse of her mysterious eyes. He'd been lying to Pymm earlier when he'd said he was immune to the lady's charms.

He was hardly immune; more aptly, he was infected by them.

Rocking on his heels, Colin said, "I have something for you . . . and Chloe."

"A present? For Chloe?" Was it his imagination or did her eyes flicker with a childish glee and curiosity?

"Yes, and you, I would imagine," he said, as she continued to cradle the restless babe in her arms. "Would you like to come below and see?"

She nodded, a smile on her lips.

Georgie tried to ignore the way her heart fluttered. A present? No man had ever given her a gift before.

Oh, don't be foolish, she chided herself. *He is just offering some piece of ill-gotten gain to curry your favor. To lull you into believing in him. To trust him.*

Did he really think her so shallow?

So she followed him below and down to the door of his cabin, resolved to be unmoved by his offering.

He unlocked the door to his cabin and swung it open wide.

Georgie took a tentative step inside, and then another.

"Well?" he asked.

"Well, what?"

"What do you think? I made it myself."

It was then she saw his gift.

For beneath the stern window sat a rough-hewn cradle.

Not jewels, not gems, not even gold, from this alleged pirate. From this man of ill-repute.

But to Georgie it was a gift of far more value. For it changed her view of him in an instant.

That he had thought of Chloe's comfort first, that he had made it himself, as evidenced by his bandaged and bruised fingers, wiped away everything she'd considered about her erstwhile guardian.

How could a man be so cruel and uncaring, and yet so thoughtful? This was the scourge of the Mediterranean? The traitor to England? A man who'd spent his day hammering and sawing together a cradle for his daughter.

Yet she couldn't just surrender to him because he'd chosen his gift, his peace offering so wisely. She had to consider that once she told him who she was, revealed the depth of their relationship, she was opening not only herself to exposure, but Kit as well.

The specter of Lord Harris seemed to hover between them like the heads of old on Tower Bridge—a strong warning of what was to become of those unwise enough not to heed it.

No, she needed more than this. Something that would prove his feelings, prove his honor, show the depth of his heart.

That would show he believed as well in the magic they'd found the night of the Cyprian's Ball.

She forced herself to remember who he was—the guardian who had tried to force her into an unwanted marriage. The worst sort of unscrupulous blackguard.

Yet such an assessment of his character hardly made sense in light of his thoughtful gift.

So who was Colin Danvers? Coward? Traitor? Ruthless guardian? Or a man misjudged?

After all, she had gotten most of her information about Lord Danvers from Uncle Phineas. Not exactly the most honest and trustworthy of sources, if ever there was, she had to admit.

The only thing she could be sure of was that he was the man who had stolen her heart—and of all the crimes she could tally against him, that was the worst of them.

"May I?" he asked, holding out his arms for Chloe.

She nodded, handing her daughter over to the man so very determined to be the babe's father.

"Hello there, princess," he whispered to the little bundle in his arms. Chloe gazed up at him, wide-eyed. "I have something for you."

Carefully, he settled her down into her new cradle. He'd readied it by covering the rough boards with a thick blanket and a piece of a silken coverlet that fit it perfectly—one Georgie suspected had been cut from the same rich blanket tossed haphazardly on his bed.

Chloe settled happily into the safe surroundings of her new bed, her eyes growing drowsy as it rocked to and fro with the gentle movements of the ship.

"Thank you, Captain Danvers," Georgie managed to whisper.

"You're welcome." He smiled down at Chloe, before his gaze returned to Georgie. "And I thought we settled that you would call me Colin."

She didn't reply. To call him Colin would be to admit that she had been terribly wrong about him. "I think not."

He turned to her and shot her a look of lengthy regard. She felt as if he were trying to discover the same truths about her.

And she wasn't so far from the mark.

Colin could see that his gift had shaken her out of some measure of her indifference, and now he was determined more than ever to uncover the truth about Georgie. "Why did you leave that morning without saying good-bye?"

His question took her aback. Her mouth opened to answer, then shut again, before, he suspected, the truth slipped out.

She reached down and fussed at Chloe's blankets. When finally she found the words to answer, all she said was, "I would rather not discuss it."

Oh, she was doing a fair job of feigning indifference, but he could see her breathing growing erratic, her movements a little too distracted.

He came around the edge of the desk. "I searched for you, right up until I had to sail."

Her head tipped up immediately. *You did?* her soulful gaze seemed to ask. But instead, she said, "I can't see why you bothered."

Those eyes, those dark, impossible eyes glanced away, for they were the way to Georgie's heart. They held the truth that she refused to admit.

God help me, he thought, as he continued to stalk her,

slowly, mindfully, unwilling to move too quickly and frighten her away as he'd done before. All he knew was that he wanted to prove that her indifference was just an act and that the night they had shared was anything but . . .

She skittered a few steps back, until she bumped into his chair, a massive, leather-bound behemoth that had belonged to the previous owner. She started to topple backward, so he rushed in and caught her.

As he brought her to her feet, he glanced down at her bare toes and smiled.

"I thought you said it was your shoes that were the source of your problems staying righted," he said. "I might be so bold as to suggest that it is your feet that are perhaps the problem."

She struggled out of his grasp, and once she did find her footing, she straightened and smoothed her hands over her skirt, in a vain attempt to appear in control.

But he knew better. When he'd held her, even for that mere second, he'd felt her heart racing, seen the way her pulse fluttered beneath her fair skin. And when he'd kissed her earlier . . . there was no denying her passionate, albeit brief, response.

Her brows furrowed and her mouth set in a determined line. "I think it would be prudent if we made every effort to forget our previous encounter, Captain." She put her hands on his shoulders and pushed him back away from her, putting a respectable distance between the two of them. And once that was done, she folded her hands over her chest.

Pregnancy and motherhood had added a lushness to her figure. Her hips were rounder, her face softened. Her breasts were now full and heavy where they had once needed padding and a French corset to hold up her bodice. But having a child obviously hadn't soothed her fierce nature, her damnable independence.

"Forget?" He closed the distance between them once again. He moved so close their bodies were almost touching, almost united. "I haven't forgotten one moment of that night. I'd be willing to wager that you haven't either." He took a step toward her. "So I'll ask you again to call me Colin."

She shook her head.

"Then whisper it." He didn't care how she said it, just so he heard it.

That memory, of her crying out his name, had haunted him.

Late at night, while standing on deck when the entire world slept, and the *Sybaris* swayed and rocked gently in the sleepy waters of the Mediterranean, he swore he could hear her voice come whispering over the waves, teasing him as it drifted aloft, rising through the lines and sheets overhead and back into the stars and darkness from whence it had come.

How he needed her to say his name. Just as Ulysses had longed to hear the sirens sing.

"Colin," he repeated. "Say my name."

"Leave me be," she whispered. "It was wrong then. It is wrong now."

Standing within inches of her, he reached out and stroked her cheek, trying to draw her face upward, so he could look into her eyes.

So he could know the truth of it.

"It wasn't wrong that night. I was there to rescue you . . ."

And you were there to rescue me . . .

He took her into his arms, and this time her struggles felt more tentative, which he took as the best sign of all.

"Release me at once," she stammered. "It's obviously time for us to come up with rules as to how we are to conduct ourselves. And then—"

"Then nothing," he told her. "Consider this our first rule."

With one arm wound around her waist, he pulled her up against him. His other hand caught her chin and tipped it so she looked directly at him.

And then he saw it. The dark fires he remembered from that night, burning low and hot in her smoky gaze. The blaze there told him more than if she had outright declared her feelings for him.

It begged him to kiss her.

And so he did.

Georgie had come into Colin's cabin ready to wage her own form of warfare, but she'd lost before she'd even had a chance to choose sides.

And now without her heart to guard her, she was helpless in his arms, defenseless under his kiss, her resolve never to say his name again, never to kiss him, blasted away as if by cannon fire.

"Colin," she whispered, as his lips swooped down to conquer hers.

The memory of his kiss had haunted her through countless nights, the deep timbre of his voice calling for her to return to him.

He'd tried to find her. He hadn't forgotten her.

At least that's what he claimed, her reluctance grumbled, battling with her heart's easy willingness to believe in him, believe in them. Oh how she longed to

believe him . . . And as his lips closed over hers and his
hunger swept her along on that now all too familiar
riptide of passion, Georgie could almost believe anything he said.

His kiss called to her and her body awakened, impatient to greet him. Her mouth yielded to his lips, throwing open the gates of her resistance to surrender
willingly to him. His tongue met hers, not in combat,
not to conquer, but to embrace her.

His hand released her chin to find its way to her hair.
He groaned as his fingers tangled with the pins holding her riotous curls in place. Once again, he plucked at
them, setting her tendrils free and sending her pins
tumbling to the floor.

"I've dreamt of doing this," he confessed. "The silk
of your hair, the scent of your perfume."

"I've had my share of dreams as well," she confessed.

His grin was pure triumph. "What has Queen Mab
brought to your nights, my mysterious lady?"

"Your kiss, your voice," she whispered, her fingers
reaching up to touch his lips. "I've heard you call to me
in the night."

"What did I say?"

"Nothing a lady would repeat," she told him.

"But she dreams of such things?"

Georgie shrugged. "I'm not always a lady."

"And for that, I'm eternally grateful."

They both laughed, and he pulled her close once
again, his lips seeking hers, sealing the uneasy truce
growing between them.

As his kiss deepened and intensified, there came a
great banging at the door.

"Cap'n! Cap'n! You're needed in the galley."

Colin groaned. "What is it, Mr. Livett?"

"It's the lad again. He's gone and bedeviled the last of the chickens, and Cook is in a regular state. Says he's gonna put the little rotter in an early grave, cap'n's brother or not." Even through the heavy door, they could hear Livett muttering Rafe's name, his complaints clear evidence he shared the cook's opinion.

"I'm going to set that scamp adrift," Colin muttered.

"I also wanted to talk to you about him," Georgie confessed. "I believe he's been kissing my sister."

Colin waved off her complaint. "You've only been on board since last night. Not even Rafe is that fast. Besides, he's only twelve."

"He's your brother," she commented wryly.

He shook his head. "Half-brother," he corrected.

"Apparently he inherited the incorrigible half," she teased, tipping up on her toes and kissing him again.

"Cap'n, if you please?" Livett practically begged.

"Mmm," Colin whispered in her ear. "I'll be gone only as long as it takes to drown him. In the meantime, don't disappear on me."

"Where would I go?"

As he opened the door, Livett hit him with a litany of grievances about Rafe's newest mishaps. The barrage of complaints continued as the two men made their way forward toward the galley.

And just like that, Georgie found herself alone in Colin's cabin.

Alone. Handed the opportunity to discover the truth about this enigmatic man.

She glanced over her shoulder at the open door. There was no one in the hallway beyond, but to be sure, she tiptoed over to the door and pushed it almost closed.

Taking a deep breath, she glanced about the room, realizing it was much the same austere cabin as it had been in Captain Taft's day. The only real decoration, left over from the original Spanish owner, was the intricately carved wainscoting which ran around the room. With her fingers trailing over the design, she counted off the flowers until she'd come to the eighth one from the stern window, then felt along the underside for the latch.

She'd done this countless times as a child, just for the fun of it, but this time her hand shook so that she missed the barely discernible latch. On her second attempt, her fingers found the indentation she sought, and she pressed it.

Before her eyes, the compartment sprung open. She stole another hasty glance back at the door, holding her breath as she listened for any sound of Colin's return.

She shouldn't be doing this. It was wrong. She should trust him. Believe her heart. Didn't she always tell Kit that if you were honest, you would be rewarded?

But the truth is right before your eyes, a wicked, taunting voice whispered in her ear. *Go ahead, this may well be your only chance.*

Satisfied Colin was well occupied with his wayward brother, she stuffed her hand inside the secret opening.

The first thing she bumped into was a bundle wrapped in a piece of silk. She started to push it aside, when something about it stopped her—for she could swear her fingers were trailing over the hard edge of a shoe heel.

A shoe? Why would Colin keep a shoe in a safe?

Gooseflesh rippled up her arms.

He hadn't . . . no, he couldn't have . . .

I searched for you, he'd claimed.

With trembling fingers, she pulled the bundle out and laid it on the table, staring but for a moment at it before untying the cords binding the silken bundle together.

When she saw what was inside, she gasped.

Her missing shoes. Both of them. The one she'd lost at Bridwick House. And the one that she'd lost in the alley.

The gooseflesh now covered both her arms, sending tingles of shock and amazement down her spine.

He'd gone back the next day and retrieved her missing shoe. Which meant . . . he had searched for her.

Her fingers traced over the intricate embroidery, the silk laces, now the tangible proof of his affections, of his heart.

Captain Colin Danvers wasn't just nice, as Kit had proclaimed. He was an incurable romantic.

A man who'd search through a refuse-strewn alleyway to find a missing shoe surely wouldn't consign his ward to a wretched marriage . . . he couldn't be a heartless rake. A traitor to her father's trust.

Trust him, her heart urged her. *Trust him with the truth.*

Georgie took a deep breath and glanced back at the opening in the wall. She should stow the shoes back in and follow her instincts. Trust him and toss her doubts overboard.

Wrapping the shoes once again in the length of silk, she hastily returned them to their hiding spot.

She glanced back at the door again. While finding her shoes proved one theory about Colin, there still remained one other outstanding issue.

The fate of England. Of Nelson. The dire words stirred something inside her. A distant memory. A call to action.

Georgie's lips pursed. Lady Hamilton had been extraordinarily kind to them in Naples. And she knew only too well the lady's affections for Lord Nelson. If something happened to his lordship and Georgie could have prevented it, she would never forgive herself. Not to mention what the loss of such a great man would mean to England.

Her hand pressed forward into the opening, bypassing her shoes until her fingers closed over the bundle of papers Mr. Pymm had entrusted to Colin's care.

The fate of England . . . the fate of England. The words urged her onward.

Letting out the breath she felt as if she'd been holding since Colin had left, she brought the papers out and stared down at them.

I shouldn't be doing this, she thought, fingering the string tying the bundle together. Then she thought of Kit and Chloe, trapped in the midst of all this intrigue. For their sakes she had every right to know what Colin and Pymm intended for the *Sybaris*.

Satisfied with that reasoning, she plucked the knotted cord open and started sorting through the papers.

So lost in thought as she tried to uncover the answers she hoped would eliminate all her doubts, she didn't hear the door swing open.

"Find what you were looking for?"

In many ways she had, for now she knew that Colin Danvers wasn't the monster she suspected, but from the terrible look on his face she realized she had in the process lost his trust and faith.

And more importantly, his love.

Chapter 11

Georgie found herself immediately placed under arrest. The dark fury of betrayal in Colin's eyes had been enough to silence her, especially when Mr. Pymm had come clamoring out of his cabin, delighted that Colin had "finally come to his senses and found her out."

"Found me out of what?" she demanded.

"Oh, she's a choice one," Mr. Pymm said to Colin, rubbing his hands in glee.

"A choice what?" she asked.

"As if you don't know," the odious little man interjected before Colin could answer.

When he was about to toss her into her cabin, she clung to his arm. "What is the meaning of this? I wasn't doing anything wrong—other than trying to determine what danger you've placed my sister and child in."

Colin said nothing.

"Nothing more than spying for the French, you vile girl," Pymm said over his shoulder.

"Spying for the French? Are you mad?" She looked again to Colin. "You don't think I'm a spy, do you?"

The look on his face told the entire story.

What a muddle she'd wrought of everything.

"I could get the entire story from her, if you would like," Mr. Pymm offered, his beady eyes sparkling with glee.

"Oh, do be quiet or I'll close that foul mouth of yours myself," she told him, her fist waving in warning under his nose.

Mr. Pymm bounded back, his nose twitching like a cornered rabbit.

"You'll be given a fair trial in London," Colin said. "I promise you that."

"London?" she asked again, this time fear replacing her anger. "No, I think not. Return us to Naples. Lady Hamilton and even Lord Nelson will vouchsafe my honor. I am no spy."

"Naples, she says. What, so you can carry out your vile plans?" Pymm mocked.

"Colin, please," she begged.

He shook his head. "London it is."

"Put me ashore in Bonaparte's lap if you must. I will prove my innocence."

"Oh, that would be convenient for you," Mr. Pymm said. "As if you haven't been trying all along to have your French friends come to your aid."

Georgie was growing quickly short of temper with the man. "I've done nothing but try to protect myself."

"Well, a court will decide that," Colin said, before closing the door in her face. He ordered one of the men to stand guard and then she heard his footsteps retreat to the sanctuary of his own cabin.

A few minutes later the door opened, and for a wild moment Georgie thought it was Colin returning to discuss the matter, but it was only Mr. Livett bringing in Chloe's cradle.

It was with a bitter heart that Georgie laid her daughter down inside the gift that had swept aside her own doubts about the man she loved.

The rest of the night, Georgie paced the space between the two bunks.

If only Colin believed her. If only he trusted her.

With each step, she knew she was only ignoring the obvious.

If only she *had believed in him.*

Exhausted, she lay down, her hand on Chloe's cradle, a constant reminder of what she had lost.

Oh, what was she to do? How would she ever convince him that she wasn't a spy?

She closed her eyes and wept silent tears. And in her misery, she fell into a deep sleep. For once her dreams didn't haunt her, for how could they compare to the horrible mess of her life?

Yet if her situation had seemed dire in the darkness of night, dawn brought a new disaster.

Georgie caught herself just before she tumbled out of her bunk, the *Sybaris* leaning hard to larboard, the ship's timbers straining and creaking as it raced to cut through the waves at a dizzying speed. Overhead and in the corridors, she heard the crew scrambling about, as if they were racing against the devil.

She climbed out of her bunk and up to the porthole.

Closing in on their position was a sloop. Hardly a problem enough for such a drastic course change, but she soon realized the little ship wasn't alone, for when she glanced ahead, there was another speeding toward them like a crafty little hawk.

Georgie swallowed. One sloop with only twenty-four guns was one thing, but a second would present a problem even to the larger and better armed *Sybaris*. If Colin was half the captain she suspected him of being, he'd have no difficulty dispensing both ships before they brought too much harm to bear.

Still, there was something in the pitch of the ship and the frantic tattoo of footsteps above deck that made her suspect something more was amiss.

She glanced over at the bunk opposite hers, where Kit was softly snoring. In her cradle, Chloe slept nestled in her blankets.

Quickly and quietly, she dressed. Cautiously opening her door, she found that the guard stationed there had left his post, so she made her way up onto the deck without being stopped.

As she climbed up the ladder to the rear deck she spied Colin standing beside the wheel, his legs set apart, his arms across his chest. He wore dark breeches and a white shirt, his unruly dark hair tied back in a queue. He'd tucked two pistols into his belt, and strapped on a sword as well.

He stole her very breath, her fears having found a champion to chase them away.

Beside him, Mr. Pymm buzzed like a fly. "You must flee," he complained. "We cannot be captured."

"Don't you think that's what I've been trying to do since dawn? But we may not have a choice," he warned. "Like I said, be prepared to do what we discussed. If they board us, you'll have no other option."

"Board us?" Mr. Pymm squeaked. "I would hope you have no intentions of letting them get that close."

"I'd prefer not to," Colin said, his gaze taking in the sails overhead. "But the wind is dying and they've still got the advantage."

Board them? Capture? Why would he even be considering giving up the *Sybaris* to a mere pair of sloops? Georgie scrambled up on the quarterdeck, only to discover the true reason for Colin's gloomy prediction.

They were about to be cut off.

She'd seen the two smaller ships from the porthole, but what she hadn't seen was the ship-of-the-line bearing down on them. Her gun ports were open and at the ready, and she had every inch of sail stretched and filled, making good use of the last vestiges of the morning breeze. With the advantage of the wind, the French ships were drawing their net closed tight.

Oh the devil with it all, when she'd told Colin yesterday that she hadn't cared if they were put ashore in Bonaparte's lap, she'd been lying. Uncle Phineas's and Lord Danvers's machinations were one thing, but dealing with the French was an entirely different matter.

And though her mother had been French-born, as had Mrs. Taft, they'd been raised in a France that no longer existed. Georgie had heard her fair share of stories since the Revolution from frightened émigrés about French atrocities. The passing regimes over the years had wiped away the veneer of civility that had once held the country together.

"But we must get to London, sir," Pymm was complaining, as if his tea had just been brought to him cold.

"The Foreign Office is going to find it most inconvenient if we are delayed, not to mention how annoyed they will be if I am captured."

"Someone get him out of my way," Colin said, sweeping past the man and climbing up on the railing to gain a better look at their position.

Livett elbowed Mr. Pymm aside and handed Colin a spyglass.

Georgie crossed the deck, her hands gripping the railing as she got a full view of the desperate situation before them. "Can't you slip through? Make a run for it?"

Colin glanced down from his survey, his annoyance at Pymm growing to outrage at the sight of her.

"What are you doing up here?" he barked. "I gave orders for you not to leave your quarters."

"You also gave orders for all hands," she shot back. "And if you think I am going to sit below and wait to be blown to kingdom come by those dogs, you're wrong. I can help. I know how to rig sails. I can carry powder. Just let me."

His gaze narrowed. "I think you've helped enough. Besides, I thought you would be thrilled to see your friends coming to your rescue."

Georgie's hands balled into tight fists at her sides. "I am not a French agent, you mutton-headed—"

She never finished her curse, for just then the great ship sent forth a volley, her cannons roaring to life, sending one ball after another ripping through the shrouds.

Colin finished her curse for her, then hopped down from the railing and paced to the middle of the quarterdeck.

"Mr. Livett," he shouted, "get the men ready. I intend to blast these devils to hell."

"You can't fight them," Georgie said. "They've got you outgunned." She glanced over her shoulder at the sloops now taking up flanking positions fore and astern. "They've got you surrounded."

"Madame, get below. This is the last time I'll tell you." He turned his back to her, dismissing her as he had Pymm.

"I will not. Not until you come to your senses. Have you forgotten your daughter is aboard?"

Colin stiffened. As he slowly swung around, his gaze bore into her, hard and glittering. "Suddenly this morning she's my daughter? How convenient." He strode past her and began shouting more orders.

Georgie sped after him. "Don't be such a lobcock. Of course she's your daughter, just look at her." She caught him by the shoulder and spun him around. "If it were just me aboard, I'd tell you to send them to the bottom, but there are Kit and Chloe to think of. I won't have them hurt, or worse." She took another glance at the ship-of-the-line now looming darkly toward their position. She swallowed and took another deep breath. "If we are captured, I can't believe they'd harm a babe or a young girl."

"I fear your trust is sadly misplaced, *that* is exactly why I must fight." He offered her the spyglass. "Take a look for yourself. 'Tis the *Gallia*. I know her captain. Bertrand. Perhaps you know him?"

She shot him a withering glance. Why did he persist in assuming she was a spy?

Well, because he caught you snooping like one, she told herself.

Colin said, "Just thought I'd ask. You could say I met the *Gallia*'s captain when he commanded the *Taursus*. Most likely he volunteered to come after me just to return the favor."

She tipped the glass to her eye and surveyed the ship. "What favor was that?"

"The last time I saw Captain Bertrand, I'd just put a broadside into the *Taursus*'s waterline and she was sinking fast."

"You do have a way of making friends," Georgie muttered. She glanced back at the French ship, their need for revenge blazing in every inch of sail they had unfurled to catch the *Sybaris*. "Perhaps he's forgotten," she offered, taking one last peek through the spyglass, hoping to catch a glance of this Captain Bertrand and take a measure of the man for herself. But the French decks were in the same flurry of activity as those behind her and it was hard to discern her captain amidst the numerous men in bright blue uniforms.

Colin snorted. "I doubt that. You never forget the bastard who shoots your ship out from beneath you."

Despite the morning sun beating down on the deck, a cold chill ran down Georgie's arms. "And now he has the opportunity to return the favor."

He shook his head. "Not quite. He'll want the *Sybaris* as a prize to replace the ship he lost. And he'll haul me into the most wretched, dirty hole of a port he can find so I can rot out the rest of the war in some French cell. Or he'll just save himself the trouble and hang me for piracy outright."

"Or spying," Georgie muttered, not realizing just how loud she had said it.

Colin smirked. "Thank you for reminding me. Perhaps you can start keeping a list for him, so as to make my trial that much quicker. Besides, I don't know him well enough to know what he would do with your sister . . . or Chloe. And for that fact alone, I cannot risk letting him take the ship."

Georgie noticed that he hadn't mentioned her welfare in his list of concerns, but before she could thank him for his lack of consideration, the French fired a second round.

This time a ball hit the front of the ship, tearing through the decking and sending up a shower of debris.

"Captain Danvers!" Pymm came scurrying back up from behind a water barrel where he'd taken refuge. "They are getting closer by the minute. Will you please do something?"

"If you don't quit complaining, I'll send you over there to deal with them. Serve Bertrand right to have to listen to you nattering on," Colin said, as he stomped forward, shouting orders as he went.

"I protest—" Mr. Pymm began.

"Mr. Livett!" roared Colin, stopping the other man's complaint. "Get these people below or throw them overboard." Mr. Livett looked ready to choose the latter, so Georgie scrambled across the deck to the companionway. Mr. Pymm darted after her, hard on her heels.

Just then another cannonball exploded, sending her sprawling forward. She landed with a hard thump, the air knocked from her lungs. For a while all she could do was lie on the deck, gasping like a freshly caught mackerel. Breathing was made all that much more difficult because something or someone had landed atop her, pinning her down. She struggled to roll over and when she glanced over her shoulder, she discovered Mr. Pymm's unconscious form pinning her in place. A gash on his forehead bled profusely, soaking her dress so badly that it was hard to tell that she wasn't hurt.

At least she didn't think she was hurt, other than the burning in her lungs as she struggled to fill them again.

Colin was at her side in a heartbeat. He gently brushed aside the tangle of curls covering her face. "Are you injured?" The anger and sarcasm of his earlier expressions were gone, care lacing his words.

She tried to speak, but still couldn't catch her breath, so she shook her head. Colin rolled the prone man free of her legs, and Georgie pulled herself up to her knees, crawling to Pymm's side. She placed her hand on his chest, which rose and fell under her touch. Then he stirred slightly.

"He's alive," she managed to gasp, glancing up at Colin. "Go. Do what you must. I'll see to him."

Colin nodded and shouted for Rafe. "Help her get Mr. Pymm below and then stay there."

Rafe started to protest, but his brother shot him a glance so angry and hot, not even the rebellious lad dared utter another word.

With the boy's help, Georgie managed to get Pymm below. Kit stood in the corridor with a wailing Chloe in her arms.

"What's happened, Georgie?" she asked.

Taking Chloe up into her arms, she settled her daughter down with a quick hug and a kiss on the forehead. "The French have attacked us. Get back in the cabin."

Kit's nose pinched in dismay. "But it smells awful in there. Chloe just filled her nappy. And the basket of dirty ones is nearly full."

"I don't care if the entire room is filled with dirty nappies, just get in there." Then all of a sudden it hit Georgie. *Dirty nappies.*

They were the solution to everything. At least for the moment. Her head turned in the direction of Colin's cabin, and to her delight, it appeared the guard he'd posted there had decided to join the fight above.

"Just bear with it," Georgie told Kit as she handed Chloe back to her, and began herding them all into their cabin. "Besides, Rafe is going to stay with you."

At this, Kit brightened, just as Georgie surmised she would. Her lovesick sister happily tripped back inside, now oblivious to the cannon fire overhead or the thought that any moment might be their last.

Rafe, on the other hand, appeared less than thrilled with the prospect of spending his first battle in a room with an overflowing basket of dirty nappies, though the knowing wink Kit cast in his direction quelled most of his reluctance.

They laid Mr. Pymm out on Georgie's bunk. "Do you think you can clean up that gash on his head?"

Kit nodded. "I'll use my extra petticoat."

Georgie smiled at the idea of Mr. Pymm waking up to find his head bound in ladies' undergarments. As her sister and Rafe set to work on the unconscious man, she kissed Chloe once more and then was down the hall and into Colin's cabin.

She only hoped this time he wouldn't kill her for what she was about to do.

* * *

It had been a trap from the start. Somehow the French had been following him since he'd gone to Volturno to pick up Pymm and, he'd wager, since his meeting with Nelson in Naples. And he could only guess who was responsible for that . . .

Georgie. His bitterness rose like gall around his heart. In his desire to see what he wanted in her, he'd endangered his mission, his crew, and the *Sybaris*.

Pymm had probably been right last night. She had been on deck signaling her compatriots.

The *Gallia*'s cannons let loose another disastrous volley, bringing Colin's attention back to the matter at hand. He knew Bertrand was only toying with him, shooting out his foremast, tearing apart his lines with round after round of shot, crippling him one bit at a time until now the *Sybaris* was nothing more than an easy prize.

The *Gallia* began to turn and Colin knew she was drawing closer to board them.

He had two choices: fight to the last man and go down with his ship, or surrender and barter to save the lives of his crew.

If he chose to give up, that would buy him enough time to get down to his cabin and destroy Pymm's documents.

Then at least the French wouldn't have any tangible evidence with which to damn his entire crew, other than the traitorous testimony of their beautiful and enticing agent.

And in the back of his mind, he couldn't forget the other reasons to stand down.

Kit and Chloe.

As for Georgie, he cared less if she ended up at the bottom of the sea.

But the others, especially Chloe, were innocent of Georgie's deceptions, of her duplicitous nature. And while he may not trust Bertand, he wouldn't sacrifice her sister or his child just to see Georgie gain the retribution she deserved. He had to believe that if anything was true about Georgie, she'd safeguard Kit and Chloe to her last breath.

"Strike the colors, Mr. Livett," Colin called out.

"What?" Mr. Livett asked, staring at him open-mouthed.

"You heard me. Strike the colors. Surrender the ship before we lose any more lives."

Mr. Livett nodded and passed on his orders.

As the *Sybaris's* flag fell, the French cheered and jeered their victory. He could hear Bertrand's nasal shouts, giving the orders to start boarding and secure his prize.

Colin ignored their jibes. He'd never lost a ship before, and he still didn't consider the *Sybaris* lost. He'd find a way to regain command, but for now he made a hasty course through the wreckage strewn over the deck and down the companionway to his cabin.

His mind raced with ideas as to where to hide the damning documents so they still might have a chance to reach London, but he couldn't think of anywhere the French wouldn't be willing to look. Since Georgie knew about the secret compartment and how to open it, there wasn't anywhere safe for them.

His only choice was to reduce them to ashes before Bertrand arrived aboard.

His cabin was in disarray, one of the windows in the rear shattered, and his possessions scattered about. Ignoring the mess, he went straight to the panel and opened it.

But when he stuck his hand in, his fingers found nothing. Not the packet of papers, not even the silk-wrapped bundle he'd held on to for foolish, sentimental reasons that now seemed to mock his judgment even further.

For once again, she'd gotten the better of him.

Georgie. Damn her traitorous hide.

He'd have her neck before he'd let her give Pymm's hard-won secrets to the French.

But as he whirled around, ready to confront her, he found himself staring down the muzzle of a pistol held by a French officer. Behind him stood two more men, large brutes who looked capable of tearing a man limb from limb.

"Captain Danvers, I presume?" asked the man with the pistol. "I am Capitaine Charles-Augustin Bertrand. I believe we have met before."

Colin nodded in greeting. "Yes, as I remember the last time I saw you, you were up to your fancy ass in seawater. Imagine my surprise when I discovered they'd given you another command to lose."

"Ah, but I haven't lost today."

"Not yet, you haven't," Colin told him.

The Frenchman's smile faded to something akin to outrage, until he spied the open compartment behind Colin. "What have we here?"

He came around and peered inside. "Empty. Now where could those documents you are carrying be?"

"What documents?" Colin asked. He leaned over

Bertrand's shoulder and peered into the empty compartment. "I don't see any documents."

Bertrand glared at him, and then nodded to his two henchmen. "It appears we have much to discuss, Captain Danvers. Is it not so?" He stepped aside to allow the deadly-looking pair to begin his unholy revenge.

Colin knew only pain. His ears rang and his head throbbed. He thought his arm might be broken, his ribs were surely cracked in several places, and still they beat him. And every so often Bertrand would ask him where the papers were and Colin would reply, "What papers?" and the beating would continue.

Then out of the blackness and roar of pain he heard her.

That sweet voice that rained down on his ears like a balm of honey and spring flowers.

"Capitaine! Oh, please have mercy," Georgie was saying. "You cannot kill this man; it would be unfair."

She was begging for his life? And in French, no less. Perfect French. Why that should surprise him, he couldn't fathom.

"I would ask that you not harm him any further," she continued to plead.

Bertrand's tone was cultured and smooth, with a touch of arrogance. "Madame, who are you?"

Colin answered for her. "A traitorous bitch!"

For that, he received another kick in the ribs.

"Capitaine, I would prefer to speak to you alone," she said. "Away from *that man!*"

He just bet she did. She probably had his papers sitting on a golden salver in her room just waiting to be served.

Glancing up out of his one eye that would open, he could see she wore the gown she'd had on last night, the one that had set his blood afire. Her blond hair, the silken curls he loved to touch, were dressed perfectly in long ringlets and held up in a white ribbon, and as a final adornment to her perfectly feminine costume, she held Chloe to her low-cut bosom.

She looked as innocent as the Madonna, but as far as he was concerned the resemblance ended there. Colin knew only too well that Georgie and her Gorgon curls put her more akin to Medusa.

"Madame, I would ask again, who are you?"

"I am a citizen of France, and I beg your protection from that animal, that fiend." She drew Chloe closer to her breast, shielding the child from witnessing the sight before her. "In truth, I am Madame Saint-Antoine, the widow of General Bonaparte's Assistant Surveyor of Antiquities in Egypt." Georgie raised a lacy bit of cloth to dab at her eyes at the mention of this newest fictitious dead husband. "But more importantly, I have information dire to the welfare of France."

"I should have thrown you overboard, you lying—" Colin didn't have the opportunity to finish, for Bertrand nodded to one of his assistants and the man leveled another kick into Colin's already throbbing ribs.

"Is that really necessary?" she asked. "I would have him live long enough so that General Bonaparte can mete out a punishment fitting his numerous crimes." She held out a piece of paper. "I have a full accounting, to be presented as soon as possible to the nearest magistrate."

Bertrand took the paper, glanced at it, and sighed. Even to Colin's limited perspective, it was apparent he was growing weary of Georgie's theatrics. "This hardly explains why the First Consul would want this man."

"The First Consul? My Napoleon has been promoted?" Georgie smiled and then nodded. "Of course he has. He has great plans for France."

"Yes, madame," Bertrand replied, his boot tapping against the wood-planked floor. "But you haven't answered my question. Why would Bonaparte want this man?"

Georgie's eyes widened. "Isn't it obvious?"

"*Non*. Not to me." Bertrand looked about to agree with Colin's earlier suggestion and toss Georgie overboard.

She sighed and edged closer to him. "For one thing, this English dog kidnapped me, my maid, and my child from the transport ship *mon cher* general sent to Alexandria to bring me home."

"The First Consul sent a ship to Egypt for *you*?" The disbelief in the man's words echoed through the room. "Why would he do that?"

Undaunted, Georgie leaned even closer, this time her voice dropping to a whisper. "That's why it is imperative that we speak in private, Capitaine. It is such a delicate matter that I would not like to bandy it about in front of just anyone." She glanced over at Colin, her nose pinched in dismay.

But Bertrand was done with pleasantries. "Out with it, madame. Why would the First Consul send a ship to a British-controlled port for you, the widow of his assistant surveyor?"

Georgie blushed. Actually turned a bright shade of pink. The woman was beyond incorrigible.

Colin almost felt a surge of pride at her consummate skills of deception. At least he wasn't the only fool being taken in by her pretty glances and pleas for help.

She smoothed a hand over Chloe's dark hair. "You see, after my husband died of a fever, the general took a great interest in my welfare. As it was a difficult time for him, with all the rumors circulating about his wife, well . . . well . . . he sought my companionship."

"That's all? You were the general's lover?" Bertrand laughed heartily and loudly, his great belly shaking over his belt. "And you would have me believe he went to such great lengths to bring a former paramour home? Madame, really, that is unbelievable."

Georgie drew herself up, and Colin didn't miss the aristocratic tip of her nose or the outraged flare of her nostrils.

He considered warning Bertrand about her right hook, but decided to let the bandy-legged Frenchman find out about that for himself.

"He may no longer seek my company, Capitaine," Georgie was saying, her words as aloof as if she were a queen. "But I assure you, he is very interested in the welfare of his son." She thrust out Chloe so the squirmy child was right under the man's nose.

Capitaine Bertrand sputtered for a moment. "His what?"

Georgie drew Chloe back to her breast. "His son. This child is the acknowledged issue of Napoleon Bonaparte, and now that you have rescued us, Capitaine, I am sure you will be forever in the general's indebtedness."

Colin could only stare at her as if she had lost her mind. The bastard son of Napoleon? Only a fool would believe such a claim. Notwithstanding the small detail that the child she held was a girl.

But it seemed Georgie knew the measure of the man before her. And for whatever reasons, she'd found her cat's-paw.

For Bertrand sucked in a deep breath, and eyed the child as if he'd been handed Midas's treasure.

Georgie continued to do her best to hold her horror in check at the sight of Colin.

Dear God! He looked as if he had been beaten within an inch of his life.

"The First Consul's child?" the French captain repeated.

"*Oui*," she said, beaming down at Chloe, not sparing a glance in Colin's direction. "The finest son a man could ever ask for." She was counting on the fact that Capitaine Bertrand didn't appear the type to want to change a nappy, for that would surely unravel the dangerous web of lies she was spinning to save all their lives. "And now, Capitaine, you are our dearest salvation."

He bowed slightly at her pretty words of praise. "Madame Saint-Antoine, isn't it?"

She nodded.

"Yes, well, Madame Saint-Antoine, it would be my deepest honor to see you safely to the shores of our beloved country."

"And mine as well, *mon cher capitaine*," she told him, sparing a glance at Colin. "Mine as well."

Chapter 12

"Take him away. Put him in with the rest of his crew," Capitaine Bertrand ordered, waving his hand over Colin's beaten form.

The henchmen dragged him away and Georgie could only pray that there was a real surgeon amongst Colin's crew who could tend to his injuries. If not, she'd find a way to see that he got the medical attention he so obviously needed.

Mr. Pymm's purported medical prowess she discounted as a complete fraud.

"Madame Saint-Antoine, I would invite you to move over to my ship, but I fear my best accommodations were destroyed in the exchange with that devilish man." He glanced around the wreckage of Colin's cabin and sighed. "I myself am moving over here to the *Sybaris* to personally oversee her delivery to the authorities in Toulon. If you could bear a few more weeks aboard this ship, I will see that you are treated with every accord." He held out his arm to escort her out of the cabin.

Georgie pasted on her prettiest smile and placed her hand on his sleeve, allowing him to lead her next door to her cabin. He opened the door for her with the gallantry and smooth finesse of a courtier.

So courtly manners hadn't died with the Revolution, she thought, considering that perhaps Colin had been wrong in his assessment of his adversary. But when she glanced up at Bertrand and found him surveying her cleavage, a hungry light in his eyes, she quickly shifted Chloe so the baby covered her from his wolfish gaze.

Chloe, unhappy at the sudden jostling, let out a wail of dismay.

The *capitaine* jumped back, eyeing the child's ear-piercing laments with obvious distaste.

"Perhaps we can—" he tried to say, his words drowned out by Chloe's ever-increasing screams.

"Oh dear," Georgie shouted over Chloe's head. "This could go on for hours. If you'll excuse me."

The *capitaine* bowed and took his leave with what Georgie would have guessed was relief at not having to endure much more of the babe's squalling—son of the First Consul or not.

She backed into her cabin and closed the door, throwing the latch to bolt them in. She sat down on her bunk, opened her bodice, and gave Chloe a breast to suckle. The babe grinned and happily settled in for her late breakfast.

Kit eased off from the cask where, in her guise as Georgie's maid, she'd sat darning a stocking. "What happened?" she asked, the garment tossed aside and quickly forgotten.

Georgie put her finger to her lips. "They believed me," she whispered. She glanced around. "Where's Rafe?"

At this Kit positively beamed. "Do you remember the hold Captain Taft used for brandy? The one that the excise men never found?"

She nodded.

"I put him in it," Kit said. "And you'll never believe this—there are still brandy casks in there. When Captain Taft's cargo was sold off, they forgot about his brandy hold."

"Perhaps we'll drink a toast to all this business when we get the *Sybaris* freed," Georgie said.

"How are we going to do that?" she asked. "I overheard two of the French officers talking and they said they were going to tear the ship apart beam by beam until they found what they wanted."

"I don't know," she admitted. "But we'll find a way. We must, for all our sakes."

Though Colin thought of her as a faithless traitor and he might never again regard her with anything but contempt, she would not stop until she'd found a way to free him and his crew. He'd risked his own safety twice to rescue her, so if anything, she owed him some portion of that in return.

Snuggling Chloe closer, Georgie glanced out the porthole. *Toulon.* It wasn't that far away, which gave her little time not only to come up with a plan, but to execute it as well.

For the moment the *Sybaris* arrived at that French port, her lies would unravel and then, she suspected, there wouldn't be a hope or a prayer for any of them.

* * *

That evening, Capitaine Bertrand knocked on their door and invited Georgie to join him for dinner.

She had little choice but to say yes. She could hardly count on Chloe to set up a fuss every time the man came by.

He took her by the arm and led her on deck, where a dining table, complete with white linen and silver settings, had been set up. Candles flickered from a heavy candelabra, while the plate appeared to be rimmed in gold. A basket of fruit and cheese sat to one side, and from somewhere the delicious odor of fresh-baked bread wafted enticingly.

The night was clear and warm, and apart from the wreckage and damage of the *Sybaris* around them, it held all the evidence of an elegant and formal repast. "We would dine in the captain's quarters, but we are still searching the room for contraband." He glanced at her, as if he thought she might have something to add on that point.

"You'll have to excuse my ignorance on these matters, Capitaine Bertrand, but wouldn't they be carrying such things in the hold?"

He laughed. "Yes, if it were, say, brandy or Holland laces, but Capitaine Danvers is more than just a smuggler. I believe he is a spy."

At this Georgie laughed.

"What does the lady find so amusing?" This question came from a stranger who stepped out of the shadows of the ravaged deck.

The unspoken authority of this man was unquestionable—from the way Bertrand immediately began bowing and scraping, to the way his deep, imposing voice sent shivers down Georgie's spine.

"Ah, monsieur, there you are," Bertrand said, rising from his low bow. "I was starting to wonder if you were going to offer us the privilege of your company." He turned to Georgie. "Our guest prefers the shadows, for he lives in fear of being discovered." Bertrand waved his hand over the feast. "Come now, Mandeville, this is a loyal lady, you have nothing to fear from her company. Except perhaps falling in love with her fair beauty."

Georgie ignored Bertrand's thick flattery; it was as oily as the man was loathsome, and instead she concentrated her attention on this newcomer in their midst.

"You set a tempting repast, Capitaine," Mandeville said, sliding toward the table in a sleek, dark movement. "But the company you have discovered is the true *pièce de résistance.*"

Cloaked at first in darkness, he came looming out of the shadows, a great cape over his shoulders and a black patch over his eye. Mandeville could have been the devil himself. His tricorne hat sat low on his brow, obscuring his features, while the rest of his black clothes aided in his ability to meld into the night.

But what frightened Georgie the most was that she found something oddly familiar about him, something about his voice, perhaps the superior set of his shoulders, that jolted her with awareness.

And when he took her hand and placed a cold kiss on the tip of her fingers, that awareness filled her with an icy fear.

"Have we met, madame?" he asked, releasing her hand and tipping his head to gain a better view of her.

There were lines about the one dark eye she could see, and his face was weathered. From his voice, Georgie had thought him younger, but now looking at him, she gauged him to be much older. Perhaps even as old as Uncle Phineas, though in far better figure.

"I was about to ask the same thing," she said, taking her seat and trying to pull from her jumbled memories where she could have seen him before.

He shook his head. "I don't believe we have, for I would have remembered you. I never forget a face."

The deadly finality of his words set Georgie's heart racing.

Bertrand took his seat and waved his napkin at the young boy standing off to one side. The lad jumped forward and began pouring wine. "Madame Saint-Antoine, allow me to introduce Monsieur Mandeville. He has joined us from the—"

"Tut, tut, Capitaine Bertrand," Mandeville said. "The lady cares not for our business. Tonight we dine as friends. Does that not sound pleasant, madame?"

"Yes, quite so," Georgie replied, wishing they could indeed discuss business. She needed to know how far the French would go to find the information Colin carried and who this dangerous man to her left could be. "I only hope your business here will not delay us in reaching France."

"No, madame. For I depart on the morrow to continue my own affairs."

I depart on the morrow . . .

Georgie's hand faltered as she reached for her wineglass and splashed some of the contents onto the table. She stuttered an apology and said, "I fear I will never manage dining aboard a ship."

Both men laughed and accepted her apology and explanation.

I depart on the morrow . . .

Why did those words set her hands trembling, while her heart went still? She could swear she'd heard them before, spoken by this very man. But that couldn't be.

Capitaine Bertrand poured her another glass. "You were laughing before, Madame Saint-Antoine, at my assertion that the *Sybaris* is a spy ship."

"Actually I was amused at the idea of her captain being intelligent enough to be a spy. I fear he is a rather stupid, ignorant man. Hardly smart enough to fool anyone."

Mandeville had started cutting into his meal but stopped, his knife poised in his hand. "Why do you say that?"

"His manners, his way of speaking. Why, his French is atrocious. He is no spy. Just an opportunist."

The *capitaine* tore a piece a bread from the fragrant loaf. "Those kinds often make the best spies. But I fear your sex is often deceived in these matters."

Mandeville leaned over his plate. "Perhaps you are wrong, *mon capitaine*. The lady has had a unique opportunity to observe our adversary, intimately."

"Hardly intimate," Georgie protested, doing her best to sound appropriately indignant.

"My apologies," Mandeville offered. "But your proximity to the man may be able to give us some clues as to what we seek."

"I've gone to great lengths to avoid the man, monsieur." *How much, you'd never guess*, she wanted to add, but instead said, "I doubt I could be of any help."

"Oh, but you can. Say, to begin with, how long have you been on this ship?"

Georgie put her finger to her lips. "Hmm. I fear it has been at least two months. I've begged and begged him to ransom us or set us free in a decent port, but he has refused, instead sailing from one wretched place to another, taking on the poorest of cargoes."

"Any passengers?" Mandeville asked ever-so-casually as he took a bite of meat. "A man perhaps, in the last few days. He would have been taken on very late at night. An Englishman."

Something about the way he spoke niggled at Georgie's ear. He spoke perfect French. Too perfect. Not with the languid, natural inflection of a native, but like someone who had been taught the language. Mrs. Taft had done her best to make sure both her and Kit's French sounded as if they had been born at Louis's court.

This Mandeville spoke it like a well-educated Englishman.

Her gaze sprung up. *A traitor.* A spy for the French. Mr. Pymm had accused her of being one, but Georgie saw now that whomever Colin was looking for, she'd wager this was the man. Now all she had to do was find a way to tell Colin that his enemy was close at hand.

"Anyone unusual come aboard?" he prompted further.

"Passengers?" she managed to stutter, then shook her head. "*Non.* None. I would have remembered a new face, for it would have been a welcome sight. Even an English one," she said, not daring to glance in his direction, for now she understood only too well the dangerous game Mandeville played.

He was looking for Mr. Pymm and his papers. She suddenly realized that whatever business Colin was in, the stakes were far higher than even she had suspected. For Mr. Pymm's papers must be far more valuable than she'd first thought if the French would go to such great lengths to retrieve them, and Colin would risk so much to see them taken to London.

Now the task of seeing them safe rested on her shoulders.

"A stranger amongst the crew, perhaps?" Mandeville was asking.

"Did you say a stranger?" she replied, coming out of her musings. His question gave Georgie an idea. "I can't say for certain, but if you would like me to view the men you have in the hold, I would happily point out anyone whom I don't recognize."

"An excellent suggestion, madame," Bertrand said.

"Anything for France, *mon capitaine*," she murmured. "Anything at all."

After dinner, Bertrand ordered the prisoners mustered, and the entire crew of the *Sybaris* was brought up from the hold.

To her chagrin, Mandeville slipped back into the shadows, so he was well concealed but still able to observe the proceedings. She had hoped that Colin or Pymm would be able to see the man for himself, recognize him, and give her some idea how to stop him.

Yet as she watched the crew file up, some of them bandaged, others being prodded along by their French captors, her fears shifted.

There was no sign of Mr. Pymm or Colin.

Could Colin have died? It was a thought that nearly wrenched her heart in two. No, it couldn't be so. He'd been beaten, yes, but Colin was strong; his formidable will would keep him alive. It had to.

Georgie knew one thing for certain in those horrible moments waiting to catch a glimpse of Colin, whatever he'd done or had failed to do as her guardian, she no longer cared. It was only Colin who mattered. The man who had rescued her, the man who had claimed his daughter with such devoted strength.

The man she'd fallen in love with that passionate night in London.

Then as the last of the men were being brought up, Georgie spotted him at the end of the line. Her heart started to beat anew, while at the same time she found herself fighting back tears. She did her best to hide her alarm by picking at the leftovers on her plate and ignoring the sight that struck her with horror.

Colin struggled along, held up by his ship's master, Mr. Livett, and on the other side by Mr. Pymm.

Pymm still had Kit's petticoat bandage around his head, and thankfully appeared no worse for his injuries. Georgie might not care for the man, but she hardly wished him ill.

As for Colin, she shuddered inwardly. She wondered how he was even able to stand upright, so pale and battered did he appear.

"Do you see anyone who might have been brought aboard recently, madame?" Capitaine Bertrand asked. "Someone you don't recall being here during your capture?"

She made a great show of walking along the line of

men, examining each one, until she got down to Colin, Pymm, and Mr. Livett, where she paused. She couldn't help herself, for when Colin looked up at her with the one eye that would open, the anger and hatred shining there made her falter.

Bertrand spotted her hesitancy and waddled his way up to the trio. He reached out with the baton he carried and prodded Livett in the gut. "Who are you?"

"Livett, the ship's master," he answered, shifting his weight to keep Colin upright.

The *capitaine* turned to her, seeking confirmation.

Georgie nodded.

He stepped past Colin's wilting form and studied Mr. Pymm. "And you?" he demanded, prodding him in the same manner.

"Phillips, monsieur," he said. "The ship's surgeon."

Colin glared at Georgie, daring her to contradict their story.

When Bertrand turned his gaze back to her, she nodded once again. "*Oui*. Monsieur Phillips has been most kind. He helped me when my son took a fever a few weeks ago."

This time she stared at Colin, where all she saw was a flicker of suspicion. That, she hoped, was a good sign. That he had his doubt about her supposed guilt.

"And I would be most willing to help madame at any time," Pymm said, with a short bow.

She turned to Bertrand. "I am sorry, but there is no one here who hasn't been aboard since my ship was captured."

Bertrand shrugged and ordered the guards to return the prisoners to the hold. He lumbered over to the table and picked up the decanter that the serving lad had brought up, and sniffed it.

"Well, this will have to do," he said, holding out his glass for the boy to pour a measure. "It is my greatest hope that our new First Consul will be able to see the better vineyards put back into production. Good cognac is impossible to find."

When the decks had been cleared, Mandeville stepped from his hiding place. "Madame, you never did say, what ship were you on? And what happened to it?"

Bertrand offered Mandeville a glass.

The man shook his head, his attention focused on Georgie.

The intensity of his gaze frightened her, and she knew that she was being tested. So she made her response as glib as possible. "The *Médée*," she told him. "Her captain was a man by the name of Dubois." It was a common enough surname that perhaps it would satisfy Mandeville.

"I've met him," the pompously idiotic Bertrand claimed, as he reached for the decanter and refilled his glass. "Never thought much of him, though. Too inclined to panic."

"And what happened to the ship?" Mandeville asked.

"The poor *Médée*?" Georgie said, also shaking her head at Bertrand's offer of cognac. "After Captain Danvers and his crew pillaged the cargo and whatever wasn't nailed down, they set the crew adrift and sank the ship." She shook her head and sighed. "I believe that man enjoys sinking ships."

At this Bertrand coughed and wheezed over his glass.

To her relief, Mandeville seemed satisfied with her answers.

A midshipman stepped forward and whispered to Capitaine Bertrand.

"Harrumph," the man snorted. "They've finished with Danvers's cabin. There isn't anything there."

Mandeville muttered a curse under his breath, before he turned to Georgie. "Which cabins belonged to the ship's master and the surgeon?"

She told him, and the young officer was dispatched accordingly.

Mandeville paced a few steps about the deck, then he stopped. Staring out into the black, moonless night, he asked, "Madame Saint-Antoine, would you mind if we searched your cabin?"

His tone was casual, but Georgie felt the probing test behind his request.

Damn the man, did he trust no one?

"Is that necessary?" she asked, deciding to take a different approach rather than one of complete and utter compliance. "I don't see how anything could have been hidden in my cabin without my knowledge."

"Your maid perhaps?"

Georgie laughed. "My maid? She wouldn't help the English. She has been absolutely terrified the entire time we've been aboard." She shook her head. "The ignorant girl believes all Englishmen have tails—like the devil."

Bertrand laughed, but she noted that Mandeville didn't share in their humor.

"What are you searching for?" she asked. "Perhaps I can help."

"That is none of your concern," Mandeville said.

"If your men are going to be pilfering through my small clothes and personal items, I believe that gives me the right."

"Ha, ha," Bertrand laughed. "The lady has you there, Mandeville."

"We won't bother your personal garments," the aloof man said. "We're looking for a secret compartment, an empty spot in the walls where papers or a logbook could have been concealed."

"How very unscrupulous this all sounds." Georgie sighed. "If you think there is something to find, please do search my room, though I doubt you will discover much. With the possible exception of dirty nappies," she said with a laugh.

"Rafe?" Kit whispered when she came up on deck. "Rafe? Where are you?" She snuggled Chloe in her arms and did her best to play her role of nursemaid, all the while wondering where the devil Rafe Danvers had gotten himself off to. She'd checked the brandy hold first thing, but he wasn't there.

When Georgie, the French captain, and the stranger in the black cloak had returned to their cabin, Georgie had handed her Chloe and suggested she go on deck to get some air while the gentlemen searched their cabin.

She knew what Georgie meant—that if the papers Georgie had stolen where discovered, she, Rafe, and Chloe were to take a longboat and attempt to flee. But she could hardly leave without Rafe. Oh, where the devil was he?

"Rafe?" she whispered again, wandering along the line of boats secured to the deck.

"Kit?" came the response. "Is it safe to come out?"

Glancing around the sparsely manned ship, she said, "Yes. Just stay in the shadows."

She sat down on a barrel and settled Chloe into a coil of rope. Making a great show of opening up her sketch pad, she acted as if she were doing nothing more than finishing a drawing in the light of the lamp hanging nearby. "Is the boat ready?" she whispered.

He nodded. "I cut all the lines down to the last threads. We can drop this one into the water at a moment's notice," he said, patting the boat beside him.

Kit glanced over toward the hatch that led down to the cabins. "We may need to."

"Why? What's happening?" he asked.

"They're searching our cabin."

There was a long sigh from the darkness. "Will they find Colin's papers?"

Kit shook her head, making a few touches of her charcoal to the paper. "I doubt it." Then she leaned forward. "You should have stayed in the locker where you were stowed. If Georgie found out you were lurking about and likely to get caught, she'd be vexed beyond words."

Rafe edged out of his hiding spot. "I'm not about to leave the business of rescuing this ship to a pair of women."

She suppressed a smile at his masculine outburst. She and Georgie were quite capable of taking on the French, but it was nice to have a would-be hero about.

Especially such a handsome one.

He was pacing back and forth in the tiny space that concealed him from sight. "I should be doing something."

"You are," Kit told him. "Posing for me." She held up her pad for him to see the likeness she'd drawn.

"Hey, that's quite fine," he said. "You're talented."

Kit shrugged, but inside she warmed to his compliment. "I have others," she told him, flipping through the pad and holding up some of her favorite ones.

Rafe came even closer, edging out of his hiding spot, near enough that Kit could feel his breath on the back of her neck.

For all her recent adventures and travels, as well as growing up rather wild in Penzance, Kit felt her life had missed only one thing—romance. Now Rafe Danvers offered a dangerous glimpse into that world.

His hand reached over her shoulder to point at a drawing she'd done recently of Georgie. "That looks exactly like your sister. Why, with that drawing, I'd have known her right off." His hand dropped to her shoulder, and he gave her a gentle squeeze.

Kit smiled. She'd thought it a fine likeness as well, but it was nice to hear him say so. But far better than his praise, though, was the fact that he was touching her, and her heart hammered with a secret joy.

Oh, if only she had the courage to look over her shoulder, she knew she would be face-to-face with him, close enough, perhaps, to gain a kiss . . .

As if she dared! Of course she did. Her head turned and she found him gazing down at her, a heated warmth burning in his dark eyes. He must have seen the acquiescence she knew shone in her eyes, for it took him only a second to place his lips on hers. Tenderly, tentatively, and slowly.

Kit thought she was being carried to heaven.

But her first kiss turned out to be far too brief. Across the deck, voices caught their attention and broke them apart. Rafe dove for the shadows and Kit scrambled to right herself, dropping her sketchbook in the process.

"Kathleen?" Georgie called out. "Kathleen? Where are you?" Beside Georgie stood the French captain and the mysterious stranger.

Kit caught up Chloe and scrambled forward, leaving Rafe in his hiding spot. "Here, madame." Her precious sketchbook forgotten, she raced across the deck to her sister's side.

"Ah, there she is," Georgie said to the *capitaine*. "Now if you gentlemen will excuse me, I am going to retire. It has been a long day for all of us." She curtsied. "And again my deepest thanks for rescuing us from that English dog." She swept regally toward the ladder that led below. "Come, Kathleen."

And as Kit came past the man Georgie had called Mandeville, she stumbled. He reached out and caught her, his grip deadly firm.

"Easy, mademoiselle," he told her. "You carry a precious bundle."

"*Oui*, monsieur," she murmured as she glanced up at him. In that second she gained all that she needed.

A look at the man's face. Enough to commit it to memory. And the first chance she got, she'd consign that memory to paper.

Paper . . . Oh no, her sketchbook!

Kit glanced back to the shadows where it most likely lay. She couldn't go back now without attracting attention to Rafe's hiding spot, so she knew she'd have to come back for it later or, even worse, wait until morning to retrieve it.

She resigned her fears to the fact that it wasn't as if anyone would care a whit about her scribblings.

Except perhaps for Rafe. And he thought her quite talented. Kit sighed and followed her sister below. She only hoped he thought her kisses were just as extraordinary.

Colin sat propped up near the door to the hold. Though his body ached with a thousand different pains, his greatest problems lay not in his savaged ribs or battered face—but with his errant and lost brother, and one woman.

Georgie.

What was she up to? He'd spent the last few hours trying to decide her guilt and kept coming up with more questions than answers. She could have easily betrayed them in the hours since his surrender, but by all accounts, she hadn't.

He knew that for a fact; from the pounding and tapping going on about the *Sybaris*, the French were still looking for Pymm's documents.

Papers no doubt in her possession.

And when asked to lie about Pymm's position on the ship, she'd even added credence to their story that he was their surgeon by saying he'd treated her child.

None of it made sense. For if Georgie was a French agent, she would have handed over those precious papers and been gone from the wreckage of the *Sybaris* in a heartbeat.

And yet she was still here. Could he be wrong about her?

He shook his aching head.

"Colin? Colin? Are you in there?" a voice whispered through the grating in the door.

He sat up, struggling to gain his feet. "Rafe?" he said softly in return, quietly enough so as not to wake the guard sleeping at his post.

Relief washed over him. That had been his other fear. His brother hadn't been with the men gathered and brought to the hold, so that could only mean . . . Colin hadn't even wanted to consider that his youngest brother had been counted amongst the lost. Now his voice cheered Colin to his very bones. "You scamp. Where the devil have you been hiding?"

"In a secret hold, with a bunch of brandy."

"Brandy?" Livett piped up. "We've got a secret stash of brandy? Cap'n, you've been holding out on me!"

"Never mind the brandy, Livett," Colin told him. He peered through the grate. "How did you find this hiding place?"

"Georgie had Kit take me there when the French started boarding—so I wouldn't be caught."

"Kit?"

"Georgie's sister," Rafe said. "Her real name's Kathleen, Kathleen Escott. But she goes by Kit. She's fourteen." He waggled his brows.

Colin wanted to groan. It was bad enough his brother craved adventure, but now he was also discovering women. "And does she know you're only twelve?"

Rafe shook his head and grinned. "I told her I was fifteen."

"When I get out of here, I'll make sure she finds out the truth," Colin said. He should have listened to

Georgie and nipped this budding romance off earlier.

He should have listened to Georgie.

Now that was irony if ever there was. A few hours earlier he would have wagered the *Sybaris* that she was a French spy, and now she'd risked her life to save his brother.

For the life of him, he didn't know what to think.

One thing that gave him some comfort was that Georgie had no better luck seeing his brother toe the mark than he did. What the devil was Rafe thinking roaming about the ship with the French in control of it?

"Why aren't you still hiding?" Colin glanced over at the sleeping guard. "If they catch you now, be assured they won't be inclined to toss you in here with us. They'll most likely just shoot you and throw you overboard."

Rafe frowned. "But they haven't caught me yet." He puffed up his chest. "I'd think you'd be glad to have me out here. I've come to rescue you."

Colin was hardly impressed. "How do you propose to do that?"

Rafe looked around.

"The lock on the door is secure," Colin told him. "Not even Pymm can pick it."

"I could break the door in with an ax," Rafe offered.

Colin nodded toward the sleeping guard. "Don't you think that might wake him up?"

Rafe frowned again, this time more in vexation at having run out of ideas. "I suppose you're just going to have to wait for Georgie." He looked altogether de-feated at having to leave their rescue to a girl.

Colin offered some consolation. "I doubt Georgie will meet with much more success."

Rafe shook his head. "Kit says she'll get you out of

here in no time. Just from how well they know their way around the ship, it seems to me that if there's a chance of driving the French off the *Sybaris*, they'll see to it."

"Why do you think they know the *Sybaris* so well?" he asked, having had the same suspicions on several occasions that this wasn't the sisters' first time aboard his ship.

"The lady who fostered them was Mrs. Taft, old Captain Taft's wife. I guess he owned this tub before you did."

Colin refrained from correcting his landlubber brother that the *Sybaris* was no tub but a fine vessel, for his revelation explained how Georgie had known about the hidden compartment in his cabin.

"Mrs. Taft took the Escotts in after their parents died and—" Rafe was saying.

Pymm pivoted up from the floor where he'd been half asleep. He elbowed past Colin and stuck his nose out the grate. "Escott? Did you say Escott, lad?"

The guard shifted position, and they all froze. Then the man starting snoring again, first ever so softly, then in earnest.

Pymm took a deep breath and repeated his question, this time quietly. "Did you say Escott?"

"Aye. Georgiana and Kathleen Escott."

Pymm stepped back from the doorway, his face white, his body trembling. "Escott. It cannot be true. It just cannot be." He staggered back, shaking his head. "Escott! How could I have not known?" He went back to the window and stuck his hand through, catching Rafe by the collar. "Tell me! What has she got planned?"

Before the boy had a chance to answer, Colin grabbed Pymm by the shoulder and shook him free from Rafe. "What, Pymm? Who the devil are they? French agents?"

"French? Bah! They're *Escotts*," he said with such reverence that Colin would have thought he was discussing royalty. "I knew there was something about them. I should have recognized them . . . I'm surprised the older one doesn't remember me. Ah, but it was dark that night and long ago." Pymm shook his head. "Georgiana and Kathleen Escott! Oh, I almost pity our friends above."

Georgiana and Kathleen Escott. Colin repeated the names, something about them tauntingly familiar.

"I've heard those names before, but I can't place them. Who are they?"

"They are the daughters of the best agents the Foreign Office ever had. Your father and Franklin Escott were good friends. I'm surprised you don't know the name. I believe your father had the guardianship of the girls after their parents' death."

Guardianship! Now Colin knew with certainty where he had heard those names. The betrothal papers he'd signed in London.

Pymm, in the meantime, had sunk back against the wall. "It was all my fault, you know."

"What was?" Colin asked, still reeling from the revelation that Georgie was his ward. His responsibility. His obviously *failed* responsibility.

"Their deaths. Franklin's and Brigitte's. Murders most foul. And at Mandeville's hands."

Mandeville. Colin was growing to hate that name with the same vehemence Pymm held for it.

"Mandeville?" Rafe whispered. "Why, that's the name

of the man who came aboard from one of those sloops a few hours ago."

Pymm's eyes bulged. "Mandeville? Here? Aboard this ship?" He turned to Rafe. "Warn the sisters. At once. If he recognizes them, he'll kill them without a second thought."

"Why would Mandeville want them?" Colin asked.

"Whatever story she's told them, it obviously isn't that she's the daughter of one of the best agents the British Foreign Office ever produced." Pymm's eyes narrowed to a dangerous gleam. "Yes, I'd bet my best informant's gold tooth that if she's her father's daughter, or even her mother's, she'll have spun a most convincing tale, one credible enough for even Mandeville." He paused for a second. "But, he's clever, and he's thorough. Whether or not he doubts her story, he's still likely to place her. For though he doesn't know it, Mandeville's left only one witness behind in his career. The night he murdered their parents."

Colin knew exactly who he meant. *Georgie.*

And what cut at his honor, buried his heart in grief, was the realization that as her guardian, he, who should be safeguarding her from harm, was helpless to save her.

"Thank you, madame," Capitaine Bertrand said as he and Mandeville left Georgie at her room. Mandeville stalked down the corridor toward Colin's cabin, while Bertrand hesitated a moment. He bowed low over her hand and said, "I hope you won't feel the need to report the inconvenience of our search to the First Consul."

"Of course not," she said with a slight nod of understanding. Actually, if she ever got Bonaparte's ear, she'd probably tell the leader of France what a horse's ass he had in this ridiculous coxcomb of a captain.

"Bertrand!" Mandeville said impatiently. "We've business to finish."

"I bid you good night," the *capitaine* said to Georgie before he hurried along.

The pair disappeared into Colin's cabin and the door closed with a hard thud.

She closed her door as well. "Hen-hearted old lout," she muttered, wiping off the hand Bertrand had kissed.

Kit was busy putting their meager belongings back in order. "Do you think they'll return?"

Georgie shook her head and pushed off the door, pacing about the narrow confines of their room, pausing beside the cradle where Chloe slept soundly. "No. Though I'd give my best garters to know what they are discussing in there." She looked longingly in the direction of Colin's cabin. "But it would be demmed hard to explain what I was doing lurking about the corridor if I were caught eavesdropping."

At this Kit glanced up, that only too familiar look of mischief on her face. "You know we could do it without getting caught."

Choosing once again to ignore the impropriety of her sister's knowledge on the subject, she asked, "How?"

"I can show you," Kit said, excitement lacing her words.

She shook her head. "Oh no, you don't. You have to stay here with Chloe."

Kit folded her hands over her chest. "Fine, I'll tell

you. But I'd like to protest the fact that just because you are older, you get all the exciting tasks."

Georgie took a glance at her sister's flushed cheeks and mussed hair and added, "I would venture you've had enough excitement for one night."

Kit stuck her nose in the air. "I know not of what you speak."

"I just bet you don't," Georgie said back as she gathered up her cloak and wrapped it around herself. "Now tell me how this is done."

Outwardly miffed, Kit still shared her secret. "If you sit in the far corner of the storeroom directly below the captain's cabin, you can hear just about everything said in there."

"I won't ask how you know that," Georgie said, finishing tying her cloak about her shoulders. "In the meantime, stay in here. And absolutely no visitors."

Kit blushed deeply, telling Georgie only too plainly that her sister had already considered that possibility.

Outside their cabin, the ship was devoid of activity. With the entire crew locked below and a skeleton crew from the *Gallia* manning her, the *Sybaris* felt uncharacteristically quiet.

It unnerved Georgie to be taking this risk, but she knew the only way she could help Colin, and perhaps even regain his trust, was to learn everything she could about this Mandeville.

She made her way without incident to the storeroom and found the extra key that Captain Taft had kept well hidden hanging on a bent nail in one of the beams overhead. After unlocking the door, Georgie lit her lamp and made her way to the corner Kit had described.

Almost immediately she heard Bertrand and Mandeville deep in conversation above her.

"Verify her story immediately when you get to shore," Mandeville was saying.

"And if it isn't true?" Bertrand asked.

"Get rid of her, the maid, and the brat."

The deadly calm of his statement sent Georgie shivering, wrapping her cloak around her shoulders as if to ward off his evil intent.

"I don't trust that woman, Bertrand," Mandeville was saying. "There is something familiar about her, something I cannot place, and that makes me uneasy, for I never leave witnesses. Never." There was a pause, one meant obviously as a warning for Bertrand and his blundering ways.

"Of course, monsieur. Of course," the *capitaine* blustered on.

"Yes, see that it is so," Mandeville replied. "Since the documents have not been found, I must return to London in all haste to finish my business. Do not fail me on this end of the matter, Bertrand. Discover who the lady is, and if she isn't this surveyor's widow, as she says she is, eliminate her. The fate of France rests with you."

"It is in good hands, monsieur," Bertrand said. "I will not fail you. Anything for France. We both serve the same aims, is it not so?"

Georgie didn't miss the overly ingratiating tone of the *capitaine*'s words, or the rapidity with which he rushed to assure this mysterious and dangerous man.

"See that we do," Mandeville said, before his firm booted steps crossed the room.

Georgie heard the door open, then close, and Mandeville was gone, leaving her in silence and the echoes of words that rattled at her memories.

Never leave witnesses.

Mandeville crossed the deck of the *Sybaris* furious that the inept Bertrand had blundered the capture of Danvers's ship. The idiot had taken too long to board her, and now there could well be consequences to pay. Not that Mandeville had any intentions of allowing himself to become the debtor in this mishap.

Yet the dangerous shift of this mission had only made his blood burn all that much hotter. He'd come this close to ruin only once before and he'd outwitted his adversary. He'd do it again.

Still, he was loath to leave without those damning papers. Oh, they were aboard this ship, or they had been. Whatever the case, he'd run out of time. In his experience, documents were either readily available or hidden so well that no amount of searching would uncover them. It seemed this was going to be a case of the latter. And as long as the *Sybaris* was held by the French, her secrets would remain lost within her beams and planks—as good a place as any for them.

And then there was the mystery of Madame Saint-Antoine. While she was a charming enough lady, he suspected her story was as much a farce as Bertrand's claims of great daring. He didn't like leaving her behind, but he could hardly afford the time to take her into a French port himself and wait out verification of her story.

Regretfully, he'd once again have to rely on Bertrand. At this Mandeville shuddered.

One of his men stepped forward. "Back to your ship, my lord?"

"Yes. And be quick about it."

As the others started readying the longboat, Mandeville paced about the deck, lost in thought, until his boot stubbed into something. When he glanced down, he spied a notebook of some sort.

Curious, he picked it up and flipped it open, hoping to discover some piece of the *Sybaris*'s mystery, only to find Madame Saint-Antoine's lovely face staring up at him.

Just a sketchbook, he mused, leafing through the drawings of ruins and churches and other sites. Well done, he thought. Obviously created by someone with a deft hand. One in particular caught his eye, for it was a remarkably detailed likeness of Madame Saint-Antoine.

One, he realized, that might come in handy later on.

He ripped the page out of the book and carefully stowed it inside his cloak. As for the notebook, he tossed it overboard, since it was of no further use to him.

And as he was rowed back over to his vessel, he pulled the drawing out of his pocket and studied it over and over again.

Her face seemed so familiar, but for the life of him he could not place the chit. It was as if the past was reaching out to taunt him, to tell him that he was making a critical error.

But how could that be? he mused. He never left witnesses.

For some time Georgie dared not move from her hiding spot, hugging her knees to her chest, letting the words swirl about her in a hypnotic blur.

Never leave witnesses. Never leave witnesses.

The words, like the first dangerous whispers of wind before a thunderous gale, whirled about her in a dizzy blur. Then suddenly her years of nightmares merged into the single memory—one she'd never before been able to piece together—the past and the present merging out of the darkness in blinding clarity.

She sat bolt upright, her heart hammering in her chest.

Dear God, she did know Mandeville.

And she knew now why she should be afraid. So very afraid.

Chapter 13

Standring Abbey
Devon, England
1788

"**B**rigitte, I must go to her." Franklin Escott's voice rose through the house. "She is expecting me tonight. I will hear no further arguments on the matter."

"But Pymm's letter says to wait for him to arrive." Her mother's stubborn voice challenged her father's firm authority. "He warns you not to confront—" she started to say before her husband cut her off.

"Pymm is too cautious by half. And if I don't go tonight, her ladyship will be found out. And then there will be no sparing her life."

Georgie sat perched on the stairs outside the library, listening to the rare sound of her parents arguing. Despite the fact that they spoke in hushed tones, the urgency and desperation in their voices had broken the peaceful night and brought her creeping from her bed to investigate.

She shouldn't be eavesdropping, but she couldn't help herself. It was unlikely she'd be caught, for all the servants had all been given the night off; this she had learned earlier from listening to their nurse, Ninny, and the cook talking. And Ninny was the last one to discover her missing for she was snoring away in her narrow bed, while little Kathleen slept soundly in her trundle nearby.

So there was no chance of Georgie being caught, unless her parents suddenly came out, but from the sound of their voices, their discussion had their attention focused completely on each other.

"Franklin, this could be a trap. Pymm says that his lordship has grown suspicious of late. If he discovers his wife is going to betray him—and with your help, no less—there will be no stopping him from destroying her, the evidence we have sought for so long, and you as well."

"Brigitte, you worry needlessly. You know I am a far better shot than that man. I proved that when he and I fought over your hand."

Papa had fought a duel for Mama? Georgie hugged her knees tightly to her chest, her heart hammering with pride. Mama needn't worry so. Besides being the finest shot, Papa was also an excellent swordsman. No one could defeat him. No one.

Yet Mama's tone sent a frisson of worry through Georgie's convictions.

"Franklin, that duel was fifteen years ago. Neither of

you are callow youths any longer, playing at fool's games. The stakes are so much higher now."

"And that, my dearest love, is why I must go tonight. The stakes *are* too high. Not just for her ladyship, but for *England*."

It was the way Papa said it, *England*, that sent another proud thrill through Georgie.

Her father's voice softened. "Brigitte, if you had married that man, it would be you risking everything tonight. It would be you walking away from your child, risking your life to do what you know is right." There was a moment of silence, then Papa spoke again. "Don't give me that look, my dearest stubborn Gigi, you know you would be doing the same thing. And you know that is why I must go and help her."

"Then let me come along with you," her mother argued. "Her ladyship may need a sympathetic ear, another woman to lend her support."

At this, her father laughed. "You aren't fooling me in the least. I can see it from here. Your face is flushed, your heart is hammering with anticipation."

"I think it is quite unfair that I had to retire from the Foreign Office service after the girls were born."

Again her father laughed. "If only you *would* retire. No, my love, I need you here. To wait for Pymm."

Her mother sighed.

"What would you have me do?" her father asked. "Wake Ninny and ask her to remain vigilant for an agent of the Foreign Office?"

Both her parents laughed at this.

Georgie considered getting up and telling her parents that she would wait for this Mr. Pymm, that she could be entrusted with such an important task. But she knew if they discovered her awake and out of bed, not to mention eavesdropping, she'd likely spend all of the next day sequestered in the nursery practicing her stitchery.

She shuddered at the very thought.

"Take the lamp with you," her mother was saying. "There is no moon out tonight. And it is cold, so please button up your cloak."

"Stop fussing," her father said in a voice that Georgie loved, for it was warm and reassuring. "I have to go no further than the hunting lodge and back. I'll return soon enough."

Georgie shrank into the shadows, thinking her father would leave from the front door, but instead she heard the library window squeak open, and her mother chiding him not to tear his breeches on the roses below.

What could be so important that her father had to leave the house in the middle of the night, through the library window, no less?

Georgie knew there was only one way to find out.

Follow him.

Mama might have to stay home and wait for this Mr. Pymm, but Georgie wasn't under any such admonishment.

She quietly dashed up the stairs, sneaking back into her room and snatching up her boots from underneath her bed and her cloak from where it hung on the peg by the door.

Tugging on her boots, she glanced once more at Ninny to make sure the lady still slept. Her cap had tipped over one eye, and she was snoring heavily.

Ninny wouldn't awaken until the old red rooster started crowing at dawn.

Georgie wrapped her cloak around her shoulders and went down to the kitchen. There near the door hung several small lanterns. She wasn't allowed to use them, but since she was already going to be punished if she was caught, she might as well break all the rules.

She lit one from the embers in the fireplace and went out into the night.

This wasn't the first time she'd been out at night, for Papa often brought her outside to teach her about the stars, but this was the first time she'd been out alone.

It was an entirely different world without Papa's strong hand clasping hers.

Swallowing back her fears, Georgie made her way across the stable yard toward the path that led to the hunting lodge.

The house they lived in had once been an abbey. On the border of the property sat an old house, formerly reserved for guests to the cloistered world of Standring Abbey. Now it was merely called the hunting lodge, though as far as Georgie knew, no one hunted for anything there—except for the occasional rabbits who got into the garden.

Taking a deep breath, Georgie trudged down the path, her little lamp casting a swaying circle of light as she trod along. She moved silently, just as Papa had taught her. What had seemed like fun games, how to creep up on someone without being seen or heard, how to write a letter with ink that couldn't be seen until a candle was run under it, and other clandestine adventures that her mother sorely disapproved of, suddenly seemed to have been more than just games.

No, it was as if Papa had been preparing her for just this moment.

Up ahead, she spied the lights of the lodge burning like a beacon, illuminating the path ahead.

Not quite sure what she was going to find, she made her way to the hollow of a great oak that grew at the edge of the trees that encircled and hid the lodge in their green embrace.

She blew out the candle inside her lamp and settled in to watch.

Her father paced on the steps, beneath the heavy wooden lintel and timbers that made up the house.

He glanced down at his pocket watch, and then out into the darkness again.

Then she heard the rustle of leaves, the crackle of sticks being broken by frantic and hurried footsteps. And then out of the darkness rushed a lady.

Her hood had fallen away, and Georgie took a deep breath.

The lady was gorgeous.

Her dark hair was piled high on her head in a delicate array. Her features were soft and sweet. But it was her face that struck Georgie.

It was obvious that she was terrified. Wide-eyed with it. Whatever danger Mama had worried about seemed to enfold this mysterious lady like a shroud.

"I've done it," she said breathlessly. "I did as you instructed. I got the papers," she said in a rush. She hurried into Papa's arms and began to sob. "I have done this terrible thing. Oh mercy, what is to become of me?" The lady began to weep, slumping against Papa, her small frame heaving up and down as she began to cry in earnest.

"There now, my lady. You must remain strong," he said. "I'll take you up to the house. A carriage will be there to take you to London, and then on to your new life."

The lady laughed bitterly. "My new life! What life can I expect? My husband will be hanged for treason, and I will be disgraced. I won't be welcomed anywhere, certainly not in Society."

"I will see to it that your bravery and duty to the King are not forgotten."

"No, my dearest wife, your deeds this night will not be forgotten," said a man who stepped out from the shadows of the forest. He stood almost as tall as her father, and wore a black cloak that swirled about him like ravens' wings. She couldn't see much of his face, except his mouth, which was drawn in an ugly line.

Almost a smile, but not quite.

To Georgie's horror, he held a pistol pointed at Papa and the lady.

"So I was right. It is you," Papa said.

The man nodded. "I see I arrived just in time," he said, stepping a little closer. "A few minutes more and you might have done something foolish, Mary. Like give Escott those papers so he could prove to his superiors in the Foreign Office that I am Mandeville." He held out his hand. "Give them to me and go home. And we will never speak of this again."

The lady shook her head, edging closer to Papa. "So you can kill me without any witnesses?" she said. "Never."

"Who said I intend to wait until we go home?" Mandeville raised his arm, pistol in hand, and fired a shot at the lady. Her mouth opened in shock, her eyes widened, her hand going for a moment to the stain now spilling over her bodice before she crumpled to the ground.

Her lifeless eyes stared directly at Georgie's hiding spot.

Georgie stuffed her fist into her mouth to keep from crying out. *No. No. No. This couldn't be happening.* The lady was dead.

Papa dropped to the lady's side and held her hand in his. "You've murdered your wife!"

"Disloyal whore," Mandeville sneered. "She stopped being my wife the moment she stole from me. Betrayed my trust."

"Don't you mean when you betrayed her? Lured her into a lie of a marriage? Good God, man, why did you wed her when you knew what it would mean?" her father asked, rising slowly and menacingly from the ground, a good head taller than Mandeville.

Georgie thought for a moment her father would triumph over this evil man. Her Papa, who always knew right from wrong, who always knew the correct answer to difficult questions, he would stop this ghastly nightmare.

But to Georgie's dismay, the scene before her only worsened.

Mandeville pulled out a second pistol and aimed it at her father. "As I told my wife, I don't intend to leave witnesses, Escott," he said. "The Mandeville legend has survived in my family for the last one hundred years by ensuring that there are never any witnesses. My sincerest apologies." With that, he fired another shot.

Papa fell beside the body of Mandeville's errant wife.

With quiet efficiency, the man searched the pair until he found the packet of letters his wife carried.

"So you thought you could steal these from my desk and I wouldn't notice? Bah!" he said to his wife's still form. "These shall never see the light of day."

The silence around the hunting lodge was broken by the sound of feet running down the path from the house. Mandeville rose from the carnage of his wrath, his eyes narrowed, his body taut as he awaited his next prey.

"Franklin? Franklin, where are you?"

Georgie nearly bolted from her hiding spot at the sound of her mother's voice, but fear held her in place.

No, Mama, Georgie tried to cry out, terror strangling her throat. *No!*

Her mother burst into the clearing, her red hair falling out of its usually perfect chignon. She came to a stumbling halt, her gaze wild as she took in the atrocities before her.

"Non! Non!" she cried out, reverting to her native French. Her keening wail tore at Georgie's heart, pulling her from her hiding place, but suddenly the dark ominous man who had called himself Mandeville stepped forward.

Georgie shrank back at his menacing presence.

"Brigitte! Brigitte!" he said, pulling her from the tangle of bodies.

"Non! Non!" her mother continued to wail. Then as if her mother sensed the darkness around her, she stiffened and pushed away from Mandeville.

When he tried to hold her still, she fought him in a wild rage. "Murderer! Murderer! Murderer!" she cried.

"Brigitte, my Brigitte, it is not what is seems. He drew on me. They were lovers," he lied.

She yanked herself free from his grasp. "And your wife? How did she die?" Brigitte shook her head. "I know the truth. You are a traitor, and a murderer."

Mandeville shook his head. "No! It doesn't have to be that way." He held out his hand to her. "Come with me, Brigitte. We will go to France. You and I. I depart on the morrow, as it is. We'd have money, position, and you would have the chateau you always wanted. Just forget this night, and come with me."

Georgie held her breath as her mother stared first down at the body of her husband, then at that of Mandeville's wife.

Her mother said nothing, just flew at the man, tearing and pulling at him like an animal gone mad. "Never. Never would I go with you, you lying monster."

"So be it," he pronounced with a devilish air of finality. He swept her aside, flinging her body against the stone porch of the hunting lodge.

There was a sickening crack and then Georgie watched her mother fall limp and still to the ground.

She closed her eyes tight, hoping that when she opened them, she would find herself back in the nursery and all of this was nothing but a bad dream that Ninny would chase away with a posset of warm milk.

Please be a bad dream, she prayed over and over, until she thought she could hear the crackle of the fireplace and dear Ninny's snoring.

But the fire she heard wasn't coming from the great

stone hearth in the nursery, but a much larger blaze. And when she opened her eyes, she discovered the hunting lodge was on fire. The horrible man was just tossing his wife's body inside, before the flames drove him back.

Georgie couldn't see her father's or mother's body, but guessed that he'd already consigned them to the flames.

"Mother?" came a voice over the carnage. "Mother? Father?"

Into the clearing came a young man, a few years older than Georgie. He carried a lantern much like the one she had purloined. "Father? Did you find Mother?"

"What are you doing here?" Mandeville barked. "I told you to stay home."

"But I saw Mother leaving, and then heard you call for your horse—" he started to say.

Mandeville sent a shattering blow across the boy's mouth, sending him reeling to the ground. "Never mention that woman. Ever."

The boy glanced up and at the fire, and must have seen what had become of her. "Mother," he sobbed, his hand reaching out toward the flames.

"Didn't you hear me?" his father said, hauling him up to his feet. "Never say her name again. She betrayed me. Betrayed us."

The boy's lip quivered, his eyes never leaving the flames.

"Do you hear me?" Mandeville continued to rant. "She chose Escott over her family. She betrayed us."

The boy shook his head.

His father caught him by the shoulders, turning him

from the fire. "One day you will be the Mandeville. Then you will understand. We cannot let anyone betray us. And to remain safe we never leave witnesses. They must be dealt with so, or else all we hold dear is lost."

He prodded the boy toward his skittish horse, and then mounted. Holding out his hand to his son, he said, "Come away, Byron. You must now learn what it is to be the heir to a legacy."

The lad spared one last glance at the fire, and then took the proffered hand. He pulled himself up and onto the horse's rump, his hands clinging to the back of the saddle, and the pair rode away.

The entire hunting lodge was now engulfed in flames. Georgie crawled from her hiding spot, moving ever closer to the blaze. "Mama," she managed to whisper. "Papa."

Suddenly there was a hand on her shoulder and she twisted around.

Another stranger stood before her, holding a lantern. "What happened here? Where are your parents, child? Where are the papers?"

No witnesses. No witnesses. The words ran a chilling warning through her heart. She could only manage to shake her head at him.

His hand reached for her again. "Tell me what happened. Did you see anyone?"

"No," she managed to whisper, sure if she told the truth that evil, horrible man, the very devil himself, would swoop back out of the darkness from which he'd come and take her away. "I didn't see anything," she sobbed.

Meanwhile, the man rushed up toward the house,

his hand shielding his face as he tried to go inside, to see if he could save anyone.

But the heat and flames forced him back and he sank to the ground beside her.

"I'm too late," he said, pounding his fists into the turf. "Damn him. Damn that Mandeville to hell. He'll pay for this. If it takes me the rest of my life, he'll pay."

The Sybaris
1800

Georgie leaned over and blew out the flickering light in her lamp. She shivered in the damp air of the hold, shivered at the memories that now lived anew in her mind.

She remembered. She remembered every bit of it. How had she forgotten for all those years? How had her fears kept the memories trapped away for so long? Now that she did remember, it was as if a great weight lifted from her heart. It buoyed her strength, her will, her resolve.

Shaking off the worst of the images, she considered what she must do now.

This was no longer just Colin's battle. It was hers. And while he may be fighting it to save a nation, her reasons went far deeper.

She would wage this war to regain her soul.

Chapter 14

Just before dawn, Georgie realized Mandeville's sloop was gone, as was the other vessel, leaving only the *Gallia* and the *Sybaris* sailing side by side.

She had spent the night pacing her cabin, trying to come up with a plan to subdue the French crew, but had discarded one idea after another.

As the sun started to spill over the horizon, Kit rolled over in her bunk. "Are you still awake?"

"Yes." Georgie couldn't stop Mandeville's words from echoing in her ears.

No witnesses, Bertrand. No witnesses.

They didn't have long before they'd reach port, and then all would be lost. Not to mention that with every moment, Mandeville was sailing closer and closer to London and back to his nefarious plans.

"If you don't get some sleep, you'll end up with one of your megrims. And from the shadows under your eyes, you'll be in for a time of it." Kit pulled her blanket back over her head.

Her sister was right. That was all she needed. One of her megrims. And she doubted either ship carried any willow bark with which to relieve her misery.

Certainly, there was nothing worse than one of her wretched megrims.

Wretched megrims . . .

Suddenly Georgie's skin tingled with gooseflesh. "Kit! That's a perfect idea. A bad case of the megrims."

Her sister peeked out from beneath the gray woolen coverlet. "You intend to give the French a headache?"

"In a manner of speaking," she said, settling down on the bunk beside her sister and whispering the beginnings of her plan into Kit's eager ear.

The hatchway above opened and let in a flood of sunlight, blinding Colin. His one open eye blinked, while the other just throbbed with pain.

He also had a devil of a headache, his ribs ached, but he consoled himself that nothing seemed to be broken. He'd mend with time—that is, if he had any left. With Mandeville aboard, there was little hope for any of them.

Even that hadn't kept him from spending the entire night considering Pymm's revelations about Georgie's identity.

So much of it made sense now—why she wouldn't tell him her identity, her adventurous spirit, but it also left a spate of questions. Why was she so afraid of him? Why had she fled her betrothal to Lord Harris? Obviously the union hadn't been the love match his solicitor had assured him both parties found it to be.

Perhaps Pymm knew a thing or two about Lord Harris.

But before Colin got a chance to ask him, the ladder creaked and groaned as a guard lumbered down it, grumbling about the foul smell of the hold and how he was missing his morning repast.

"Do you think they're finally going to get around to feeding us?" Livett asked, rising up from the floor and coming to stand by Colin's side.

"One can hope," he offered, though he doubted that Bertrand would waste the *Sybaris*'s plentiful stores on a captured crew.

If they were lucky, they'd probably get the *Gallia*'s weevil-laden fare. And though it wasn't the most appetizing thought, food was food. If he was going to regain his strength, he needed to eat—there were Georgie and Kit and Chloe, as well as his troublesome brother, to see to safety.

And Mandeville to stop.

Then he'd make good on his promise to Bertrand and see the *Gallia* burned to the waterline.

How he was going to find a way out of his current predicament and do all that was an entirely different matter.

The guard stood at the bottom of the ladder, while Bertrand struggled down to the lower deck.

"This can hardly mean breakfast," Livett muttered, turning away from the door.

At that point, Colin was no longer thinking of his empty stomach, but of the third person venturing down the ladder.

The slight ankles and trim calves could belong to only one person.

Georgie.

His heart thrilled at the sight of her. She was safe and sound. At least so far.

Bertrand held out his hand as she neared the final step and she took it, offering him that smile of hers that was guaranteed to melt even the stoniest of hearts.

"Thank you, Capitaine," she murmured. "You are being most indulgent." She allowed him to hold her hand for a little longer than was necessary, and as Colin watched the other man drool and gape over her, he vowed to sink every ship that Bertrand ever gained.

"*Oui*, of course," the old fool stammered. "Any accommodations, madame, to see you in good spirits." He huffed a bit more before he turned to the cell. "The surgeon? Where is the surgeon?"

Colin held out his arm to block Pymm's path. "What do you want with him?"

Bertrand's gaze narrowed. "None of your affair, Danvers. Stand back or I'll have Brun bring that man out over your corpse."

Colin stood his ground. "What do you want with Mr. Phillips?"

Bertrand began to bluster and posture some more, but Georgie intervened.

"I have need of Mr. Phillips's services."

What the devil was she up to now? Crazy, headstrong Georgie had some wild plan in the works, and Colin was sensible enough to fear for all their lives based on those suspicions. Her foray into the dangerous world of the Cyprian's Ball was enough evidence for him to know she wouldn't stop at anything once she'd set her mind to a plot.

He eyed her from head to toe. "You look well enough to me."

"What is troubling the lady is none of your concern," Bertrand said. He turned to Brun. "Get the surgeon out and then watch to see that he doesn't harm Madame Saint-Antoine."

Bertrand bowed once again over Georgie's hand. "When you are less troubled, perhaps you will be able to dine with me again."

"It would be my pleasure," she said in her best purr.

The *capitaine* climbed up the ladder, making every effort to look the ready gallant, which was made all the more difficult when his belly barely fit through the hatchway.

"Please, Captain Danvers," Georgie said. "If you could but spare me a moment of Mr. Phillips's services, I assure you your kindness will be repaid in full." Her gaze begged him to trust her just one more time.

What choice did he have with Brun standing at the ready, looking only too willing to add a few more lumps. So Colin backed away from the door.

After Pymm was hauled out of the cell and the door locked once again, Brun lounged against the wall.

Georgie looked from the brutish man to Pymm and then back to Brun. "Monsieur, if you would be so kind as to allow me some privacy with the doctor?"

The oaf frowned. "I was told to stay."

"Yes, but my troubles are of a female nature, and it would greatly embarrass me to have to share them in front a man."

Female troubles? Colin wanted to tell Brun he was looking at feminine trouble personified.

When her persistent guard still didn't move,

Georgie added, "In anticipation that this may take some time, and since I would hate for you to miss a meal, I went to the trouble of asking my maid to bring you a tray."

As if on cue, Kit stuck her head through the hatch-way and waved a small loaf of fresh bread, as if she were trying to coax a rat from its hiding spot.

The man's gaze roamed from the fragrant loaf back to Pymm, obviously assessing the danger presented by the older man.

When even the offer of a good meal failed to prod him up the ladder, Georgie launched into a litany of fe-male problems, a descriptive list of ailments that was enough to send any man running for cover.

Colin's only consolation was that his crew spoke lit-tle to no French. It spared them a medical history that had even the jaded and worldly Mr. Pymm turning the shade of a well-cooked lobster.

When she started into her monthly complaints, Brun had heard enough to ignore Bertrand's orders. He mur-mured a hasty, "I'll be right back," before launching himself up the ladder.

"Oh, gracious," Georgie said. "I thought he'd never leave. I was running out of maladies."

"God in heaven, madame," Pymm sputtered. "Have you no decency? I beg you, spare me any more details of your disorders, for I fear I will be ill."

"Some ship's surgeon you make," she told him. "That is if you actually do have any medical training."

"None you want to rely on," Colin told her. "Now get on with it. You've gone to great lengths to get down here, what are you up to? I won't have you—"

"Captain Danvers, do shut up. I don't think you are

in any position to complain," she said. "But if you must know, I am here to rescue you."

Colin threw up his hands. "You? Rescue us?" So his worst fears were about to be realized. "You know most of the money being wagered by the crew is on you being the reason we are in this mess. So please don't do anything that will only jeopardize our already tenuous position."

Georgie stalked up to the door. "Is that what you still think? Well, let me tell you, I'm not a spy. I'm no agent of the French."

He couldn't help himself. He grinned at her outburst, her fiery temper, her vehemence. Damn, he loved this unmanageable woman.

He loved her. The idea sent shivers down his limbs. And what a darned foolish time to admit it.

"I know," he said. It was all he could say.

Still, even that admission took her by surprise. "What did you say?"

"I said I know you aren't a French spy, *Miss Escott.*"

She backed a few steps away from the door. He could see her mind whirling with the likely means as to how he'd discovered her identity. And she came to the correct one. "Rafe."

"Yes. Rafe. Apparently he's been stealing more than just kisses from your impressionable sister." He pushed his hand through the opening in the grille separating them. "Georgie, whatever you have planned, don't do this. Save yourself. Save Chloe."

She reached out and tentatively touched the tips of his fingers, as if she were afraid to connect with him any further. "Why did you save my slippers?"

"That hardly matters now."

"It matters to me," she whispered, closing her hand over his.

The warmth of her fingers spread through him like a soothing balm. Here was his strength, his resolve. It lay in this woman. But he couldn't let her do this—whatever it was—he wouldn't see her come to any further harm.

He'd already done enough.

"Georgie, this is no game. This is not some London ballroom in which to caper about. There is no rescue coming. You must do whatever you can to safeguard yourself, your sister, and our daughter."

She pulled her hand away from his, her mouth setting in a stubborn line. "I can't do that. Not now."

Damn her obstinate hide, he thought, his fingers winding around the iron bars. He shook the door, wishing for the strength of a hundred men to pull the accursed thing open and throttle her. But since the door held against his anger, he said instead, "As your guardian, I am ordering you to—"

"My guardian? Bah!" Her hands went to her hips. "For that alone, I should see your sorry neck stretched by the French. Trying to marry me off to the likes of Lord Harris. *Lord Harris!*"

She said it as if she hadn't wanted to be married to the man.

"I was told—" he started to say in his defense.

"You were told?" She stomped forward, her nose nearly pressed to the grille. "Did you think to ask me?"

Colin flinched, and for the first time in the past day felt thankful for the steel bars and sturdy locks that held her at bay. Especially since he had no excuses for the way he'd blundered his responsibilities.

"I didn't think so. Men!" she said. "You're all the

same." She frowned at him. "I don't know why I'm even bothering to help you out of this mess."

Then he saw it. That flicker of light in her eyes he remembered from their night in London. An ember he knew was capable of burning into a passionate fire.

For all his mistakes, she still cared.

"Why are you here?" he asked, looking for confirmation.

"Oh, don't be such a nit," she told him. "If you have to ask, then you wouldn't understand." Again the light flared to life, and she looked about to confess so much more, but she closed her mouth and turned away from him.

Colin did understand, too well. And that only made him fear for her safety all that much more.

She had turned to Mr. Pymm, who was still red-faced and blustering from her recitation of female disorders. "Sir, do you have any more of that powder that you gave the widow back in Volturno? The one that made her sleep?"

He shook his head. "Not enough to handle your vast complaints, madame."

She waved aside his response. "No. No. Not for me. For the crew. For the French."

"Madame, I hardly see how the French can be complaining of . . ." Then he faltered to a halt.

Whatever she was about, Pymm obviously understood, for his eyes sparkled with such dark intent, Colin wondered if he shouldn't warn Bertrand.

Then the wily agent started shaking his head. "Not enough for the entire crew. And without enough, it would be a dangerous proposition."

Georgie took a deep breath, her hand tugging at her chin. "Then how do I prepare more?"

At this, Pymm balked. "I couldn't. I can't. 'Tis a family recipe. On my mother's sainted soul, I promised never to share it."

Colin coughed. "You old fraud," he said to Pymm. "I have it on good authority that your mother is alive and well and making a fortune selling patent potions in Edinburgh."

Pymm's lips pursed in vexation at being caught. "The recipe is very delicate. I would be compromising a long-held family secret—"

"Stow it," Georgie said. "You once said that if I ever needed anything, all I had to do was ask. Any favor."

"I never—"

Georgie cocked a brow at the man. The tip of her chin and the level stare she shot at Pymm was enough to pin the man in place.

"What I meant at the time—"

"Uh-hmm." She continued to stare at him, unflinching and unblinking.

"But my dear woman, what you ask is impossible," Pymm told her, fidgeting in his tracks. "If my mother ever found out that I'd revealed her most revered potion, I cannot vouch for your welfare."

She closed her eyes and looked to be counting to ten. When her lashes fluttered open, she held out her hand. "The formula, sir."

"It's not something I have in writing. Why, it is far too dangerous to commit to paper. For if it were to fall into the wrong hands—"

"Sir, stop stalling. The potion, or I'll go on deck and toss your precious papers overboard."

"My papers!" he squawked. His voice then dropped several octaves. "You have them?"

"Of course I do." She tapped her foot. "Now a fair trade sir, your life and papers for the potion."

Pymm looked caught between the devil and a rock.

"Georgie, get rid of those papers at once," Colin told her. "If you're caught with them . . ."

She waved her hand at him. "They're safe. Believe me, no one is going to look where I have hidden them." She glanced back at Pymm. "Well?"

He took a deep breath. "Your word, madame, on your parents' souls, that you will never divulge what I am about to tell you."

She nodded and leaned forward. Pymm cupped his hand and began whispering into her ear. After a few minutes of quiet conferring, they stepped apart and shook hands.

"The amounts are very delicate," Pymm warned her. "And don't overmix it, for it has been known to have explosive properties."

Colin groaned. Georgie and explosives? He might as well start bracing for the impact.

"Now if I put it in brandy—" she started to ask.

"*Brandy*?" Pymm shook his head. "It will make it very volatile. And I can't guarantee how it will react when mixed with an intoxicant. It could have disastrous results."

"Sounds like a terrible waste of good brandy," Livett muttered.

Colin put his head against the bars. "Georgie, I wish you would reconsider."

"I cannot. Not now." She moved closer. "Mandeville was aboard. Last night."

"Yes, I know. Rafe told me. That's why you can't do this. If he suspects you of anything—anything at all— you won't be safe."

"He's no longer aboard. He left before dawn."

Colin let out a sigh of relief. With only Bertrand lurking about, Georgie stood a good chance of going undiscovered. Still, to have had the man so close and not be able to apprehend him cut Colin to the core. Perhaps there was still a chance. "Did you learn where he was headed?"

She nodded. "London." Her gaze bore into his. "You must stop him, Colin. You must. And every minute you are locked inside this cell is that much further he will gain on us. So you see, there is no other way."

He knew she was right. But God have mercy on all of them if she failed.

It took Georgie and Kit most of the day to gather the necessary ingredients to concoct Pymm's potion. She'd even had Bertrand send over to the *Gallia* for some of the items—with a shy smile and invitation that these would most assuredly put her in the mood to dine with him.

As Kit gave their potion one last stir, Georgie took a sniff of the sweet-smelling brew and sighed.

"Do you think it will work?" Kit asked, peering into the pot.

"I hope so," Georgie said. She only hoped she had remembered the proportions correctly from Pymm's dashed-off recital. He had cautioned that an ill-made batch could have disastrous results. Instead of putting the men to sleep, it would just loosen their inhibitions.

Leaving her and Kit alone on a ship full of randy sailors.

"Put a little more of that in," Georgie said, pointing at the saltpeter.

Kit appeared skeptical, but added a hefty spoonful. And then after a nod from Georgie, added another.

They poured the mixture carefully into a leather wineskin, mindful not to spill any on their clothes.

That had been Pymm's other caution. To keep it away from their clothing. He had muttered something about it being able to eat through wool serge on a warm day.

Georgie slipped from their room and down into the hold without being seen. That was the advantage of having the ship staffed by a partial crew from the *Gallia*. There were few hands lolling about.

She followed the corridor to what seemed to be a dead end. The wood curved upward as if she'd reached the bow, but actually the ship had been built with this false wall, to make it appear that way. She tapped along the wall until she came to the latch hidden in a beam. Opening the small door, she slipped inside.

The secret hold was narrow, and a small lantern burned from a hook in the ceiling. "Rafe? Rafe, are you in here?" She held her tin lamp aloft.

"I'm here," he said, rising up from between two small casks. "I was starting to think you'd forgotten me." He glanced over her shoulder. "Is Kit with you?'

Georgie smiled inwardly. "No, she's with Chloe."

He shrugged. "She said she was going to draw my picture so I could send it to my mother."

She reached over and ruffled his hair. "And she will. Once we get the *Sybaris* back. Now, let's get to it."

They set to work unsealing the casks one by one and pouring a measure of Pymm's potion into each. Rafe then tapped the corks back in and rewaxed their seals.

When they had finished the last one, Rafe grinned. "Makes one thirsty, eh? Care to have a glass?" he joked.

"Not for a king's ransom," she said.

Then down the corridor they heard the echo of footsteps coming in their direction.

Georgie nodded to Rafe, who ducked to the far end of the compartment and wedged his lithe body between the stacks.

"What have we here?" called out Capitaine Bertrand. "Come out, you scalawag. I'll have no thievery on my vessels."

Georgie took a deep breath and poked her head out the door. "Oh dear, Capitaine, you've caught me."

"Madame Saint-Antoine?" he said. "What are you doing in there? One of my men above deck heard voices coming from down here and reported it. I thought I had thieves breaking into the stores again."

Georgie noted the "again" part. She didn't doubt that foolish and vain Capitaine Bertrand was robbed blind by his duplicitous crew. He reminded her of Aunt Verena.

Stepping out of the doorway, she crooked her finger at him. "Come see what I've discovered." She swung the door closed, and his eyes widened at the ingenious and seamless way it fit into the rest of the wall.

"I knew you were searching for something, and once my megrim cleared away this afternoon, I recalled a conversation I'd overheard between two of the *Sybaris*'s crew when I was first aboard. They were discussing some secret stores and the fine brandy held within." She reached over and unlatched the door and opened it once again. "I came down here to see if I could find it and surprise you by discovering whatever it is you seek. But alas, there are only these casks of cognac within."

"Cognac?" Bertrand asked, peering into the hold. *"Sacré mère*! That cask is from the Marquis de Villier's private vintage. Why, it hasn't been made since before . . . before . . ." He glanced over his shoulder and lowered his voice. "Since before the Revolution."

"Is that good?" Georgie asked, knowing full well the rarefied liquor was worth a fortune.

Captain Taft had always smuggled the best.

"It isn't just good, *ma cherie*, it is excellent." He stepped further into the room, clucking his tongue as he examined the various labels.

"When I discovered these casks, I thought I might present them to you and your crew as a token of my appreciation for rescuing me. It was my hope that perhaps I could offer a toast around this ship and the *Gallia*." She smiled again.

Bertrand frowned. "Such fine cognac to be wasted on common sailors? I hardly think so."

Georgie ground her teeth together to keep from telling the parsimonious old goat that if he shared a bit more freely with his men perhaps they wouldn't feel inclined to steal from him.

Besides, what had happened to the revolutionary spirit of "Liberty, Equality, and Fraternity"?

"Perhaps this once you could make an exception," she suggested. "Sadly, I think a few of the casks have broken seals, and I fear their contents may have soured a little. Mayhap we could offer those to your men?"

At this, he nodded in agreement. "A perfect solution. I doubt any of them would know the difference."

At this she laughed and patted him on the arm. "Then please order some of your men to fetch this on deck and we can start our celebration immediately."

Bertrand nodded to one of the sailors behind him, and the man went to call for more assistance. As the word spread, it seemed every sailor wanted to help retrieve the hidden bounty.

At Georgie's insistence, two casks were rowed over to the *Gallia*. If anything, she knew the officers would imbibe, and once they passed out, it was only a matter of time before the other cask would get passed around by the crew.

She only needed the *Gallia* short-handed, so that once she had Colin and his men free, they could easily escape the much larger warship.

Bertrand took center stage atop the quarterdeck, the French crew gathered below.

The men came around, cups in hand, and Georgie only too happily filled their glasses, careful not to spill any of the liquor on her clothes.

Once all the men had their measure, Bertrand raised his mug. "As your *capitaine*, I would like to offer a toast of appreciation for your courage and strength in helping overcome the notorious pirate Danvers. I hereby offer this cask to you, my loyal men, as a way of saying thank you."

Georgie noticed that he'd seemed to have forgotten that she'd been the one to find the cognac and that it had been at her insistence that the crew received any of the precious vintage.

No matter, she thought. He'd be more than happy to

give her the credit and blame in the morning, when he awoke without the *Sybaris* under his control.

As the men began to drink, someone started playing a small pipe. Soon they were dancing together and the celebration was well underway.

Georgie had known that things might get out of hand, so she'd had Kit and Chloe, along with Rafe, bar themselves in their cabin. Kit had even managed to steal a pistol and shot, which Georgie had given to the young lad.

She didn't bother to ask her sister how she'd managed her latest felonious exploit.

"Do you know how to use this?" Georgie had asked Rafe.

"Aye, ma'am," he'd said, taking the gun and tucking it into his belt like a pirate. "I won't let any harm come to Kit or my niece."

So he knew about Chloe as well. Perhaps that was for the best.

Kit sighed and gazed with open longing at her beloved champion. So much so, that when it came time for Georgie to close the door on the trio, she wondered if Rafe might have to defend himself against a worse foe.

Her amorous fourteen-year-old sister.

Now she was wishing she'd had enough sense to lock herself away as well, for the festivities were quickly turning into a lewd display. Some of the men, the smaller and skinnier fellows, were already starting to doze off, but the larger fellows, like Brun and, worse, Bertrand, were eyeing her as if she might suddenly turn into a willing doxy.

*If they don't have enough of the potion, it could become an
ugly situation for you, Miss Escott,* Pymm had said. *It will
only unhinge their inhibitions, and for men who have been at
sea for some time . . .*

"Madame Saint-Antoine," Bertrand called out, waving at her by wiggling his fingers and waggling his
bushy brows. He sidled up to her, his belly swaying to
and fro. "This is the finest vintage I have ever had the
pleasure of partaking in." He took her fingers and
brought them to his fleshy lips. "At least up until I met
you."

Georgie smiled, while doing her best to hold back
the urge to be sick.

"I have a cabin below," he was saying, the thick
scent of cognac washing over her. "I think we would be
much more comfortable down there." The brows wiggled again, like two lap dogs competing for attention.

Pulling her hand free, she did her best to wipe the
back of it nonchalantly on her skirt. "Oh, not before another round, *mon capitaine*," she told him, ladling out
another measure for him, and offering to pour another
cup for those still standing.

Dear Lord, the man had already downed four mugs full,
she thought as she topped off his next one. How much
more was it going to take?

One of the bolder members of the crew came
strolling forward, obviously having forgotten rank and
any regard for discipline. "Come and dance. You're a
hot, sweet thing and wasted on the likes of that
blowhard." He nodded toward Bertrand, who was just
finishing his mug and wobbling like a ninepin.

"Go along, *ma chère* Georgiana," he murmured. "I'm

going to have one more . . ." Bertrand finished his sentence by toppling over backward.

The remaining crew roared with raucous laughter.

One of them went over and gave the captain a hearty kick to make sure that he was good and passed out. Then like a pack of dogs they all turned and cast hungry looks at Georgie.

Her breath caught in her throat.

Think, Georgie, think, she told herself. "Wouldn't you like some more?" she asked, holding out the ladle. Brun swiped it out of her hand and kept stalking forward. "I suppose not," she muttered, finding herself backed up against the deck railing. "I fear the British were right. That is rather too potent for a man to imbibe too much."

"Bah!" he spat, hurling a large wad onto the deck. "The British and their beer. What do they know of a good drink . . . or good sport?"

"Indeed," she said. Once again, she nodded toward the cask. "So you men could finish off that cask and still offer a woman what she wants. I would *enjoy* seeing that." It was Georgie's turn to waggle, batting her lashes at Brun.

He nodded at her challenge and hoisted the last cask up on his shoulder. "Drink up, *mes amis*. The honor of France is at stake." He plucked the cork out with his horse-sized teeth and spit it to one side. Then he tipped the cask over and let the amber liquor churn down his throat.

When he started to choke, he passed it to the next man, and so it went around the circle until not a drop remained.

And still they stood.

Four men with the look of the devil in their eyes and not a shard of decency amongst them.

"Come along, little pigeon," Brun said. "We've done our part of the bargain."

"Yeah, the bargain," one of them said, before he toppled over.

His companions laughed and called him names, until one more of them pitched forward, landing on the deck like a fallen oak.

Two down, two to go, Georgie thought. But these two looked as if they had been tossing back buckets of chamomile tea, not twenty-year-old cognac.

Brun held out his open hand to his companion. *Dice.* He was going to dice for her. The other fellow nodded and swiped the pair from Brun's palm and threw them onto the deck. He leaned over to spy what he'd thrown and fell on top of them.

All she could do was shake her head in dismay, in fear, in abject terror, and wish with all her heart that she'd put in the measure of nightshade that Pymm had advised her to use, and just outright poisoned the entire lot of them.

But her conscience hadn't allowed her to commit wholesale murder. Not that her lofty ethics would save her now.

"What the—" Brun said, trying to pick up his leaden feet. He shook his head like a sleepy dog, while his entire frame lolled from one side to the other.

Georgie held her breath as Brun wobbled.

He glanced over at the empty cask, then back at her. A final blaze of light flared in his dull-eyed gaze. He knew. He knew what she'd done. In his murderous realization he took two faltering steps toward her. He opened his mouth to cry out, but his tongue was too thick and fuzzy to make anything other than an unearthly growl.

As the last discordant notes wrenched from his foul throat, he fell to the ground in defeat.

Georgie let out a great sigh of relief. "Wretched lout," she muttered as she walked over to him and gave him a swift kick in the ribs. "This is for beating Colin," she told him. "And this is for what you were thinking about doing to me."

Shuddering, she retreated to Bertrand's slumbering form. The man snored so loudly, she feared the watch on the *Gallia* would hear it and mistake it for a warning bell.

Her nose pinched in dismay, she searched his fleshy form until she found the ring of keys that he had shown her earlier, now buried deep in his jacket. Grimacing as she pulled the chain out of his sweaty pocket, she walked across the deck as if nothing were amiss.

The last thing she wanted to do was to alert the *Gallia* crew that anything was wrong.

But once she got to the gangway, she was down the ladder in a flash. The guard was snoring away at his post, an empty wineskin beside him, so she raced past him to the doorway. Catching up the lantern, she held it to the opening in the door.

"Colin! Colin, I have the keys," she called out.

Colin rose stiffly from the floor. Pymm was right behind him, as were Livett and the rest of the crew.

"Dammit, Georgie, I told you not to do this. From the sounds up there I thought . . . I feared . . ." He let out a sigh of relief and reached out to touch her hair, her cheek. "If you ever disobey me like that, I'll—"

She dangled the keys just out of his reach. "Do you want out of there or not?"

Colin's brow furrowed. "Why, you—"

"Tut, tut, tut," she muttered, taking a step back from the cell.

He mumbled something under his breath, but when he next spoke aloud it was in a different vein. "Do you know how worried I was? Georgie, my foolish, head-strong Georgie! Did you not see the trouble you were courting? I tried to live without you once. I don't think I could do it again. Not now," he told her, reaching out one more time.

It was all she needed to hear. Georgie stepped into his touch and let him kiss her brow, her lips, while she fumbled with the keys to set him free.

"The crew is unconscious, but I don't know the con-dition of the *Gallia*'s men. I convinced Bertrand to send over two casks. I tried to get him to send three, but the greedy fool refused." Georgie didn't tell Colin that that extra cask had probably saved her from Brun's un-wanted attentions.

Instead, she continued her description of what awaited them above deck. When she finished, Colin nodded.

He gave his orders rapidly. The *Sybaris*'s crew moved stealthily about the decks, gathering up their fallen enemies and loading them into three of the ship's longboats. Quickly and quietly, they lowered the boats from the side of the ship opposite to the *Gallia*, so their work went unseen.

Then every man took his position, aloft and on the decks, awaiting the signal. And when Colin gave it, they doused every light on the ship, cloaking the frigate in darkness. They changed course and moved away from the *Gallia*.

There were cries from the other ship, but obviously no one among the officers was sensible enough to give the orders to send up signal lights or to alter course.

Meanwhile, unbeknownst to the *Gallia*, their captain and a good portion of their crew drifted farther and farther away.

"Will they survive?" she asked.

"Aye. I told Livett to spare a compass and see them provisioned with enough water. If they start rowing in the morning they should see land in a day or two." Colin shrugged. "If they don't get picked up before that."

"Captain Bertrand is going to be angry when he awakens," Georgie said, as they watched the longboats disappear into the night.

"I would think he would be relieved," Colin replied, pushing back from the deck and turning to take her in his arms.

"And why is that?" she asked.

"The *Gallia* is still afloat. I promised him if I got the chance I would see her burned to the waterline."

Georgie shot him a sideways glance. "You wouldn't have done that, would you?"

Colin looked back across the waves at the ever-growing distant lights of the *Gallia*. "No," he said. "No, never. That would hardly have been fair."

Somehow, Georgie didn't quite believe him.

Chapter 15

By later that evening, Colin stood on the quarter-deck surveying the ongoing repairs to the *Sybaris*. Damaged as the ship was, he pushed the available sail they had, using every bit of the wind he could find, for each fathom they moved forward brought them that much closer to seeing Nelson safe. It would take days before the *Sybaris* was sailing as she was meant to, hell-bent and flying over the waves, but in the meantime, all he could do was pray that what wind he could catch was enough.

Over on one side of the deck, Georgie and Kit were settled in repairing lines and ropes. Beside them, Chloe was happily tucked in her cradle, playing with a small toy horse Livett had carved for her.

He hadn't really had a chance yet to thank Georgie for rescuing them, since their first task had been to put as much distance between themselves and the *Gallia* as possible, before the French crew regained consciousness.

After they had set Bertrand and his crew adrift, Georgie had escorted him down to her cabin, with Mr. Pymm in tow, and returned the packet of documents to them.

Her undetectable hiding spot? Chloe's dirty nappy bucket.

There, tucked in amidst the stained and smelly cloths, had sat the destiny of England, Nelson's very life.

Colin had to wonder if Mr. Pymm would be putting *that* bit of information in his full report.

As he walked over toward Georgie and Kit, he found himself feeling a bit uneasy. Whatever was wrong with him?

Oh, he knew. He'd admitted he was in love with Georgie during the long night he'd worried about her fate at Mandeville's hands. To be honest, he'd fancied himself in love with her since the Cyprian's Ball.

But in truth, now he knew the measure of the living and breathing woman before him, not just the mysterious and intoxicating Cyprian who'd stolen his heart that long-ago night.

His dreams of a quiet respectful wife, a cozy hearth, and years of domestic bliss had been blasted away in the past twenty-four hours. Now he knew what he truly wanted—a partner, someone whose heart thrummed to the same salt-soaked rhythm that claimed his.

Glancing across the deck, he could only hope and pray that Georgie shared those selfsame dreams.

Her bold, inviting smile offered him hope that she did. And her eyes, those dark, mysterious eyes he adored so much, called to him like the sirens of old, leaving him crazy with want, full of wishful thinking.

As he followed that tangible thread that tied their hearts together, making his way slowly across the deck, a new purpose filled his stride.

Yet for the life of him, he couldn't think of what to say to her . . . where to begin.

When he had treated her so poorly, when he had doubted her so completely . . . how did he start over?

He supposed it was akin to repairing a ship, one line at a time, one beam after another, until there was nothing left to do but unfurl all the sails and hope like hell it held together.

"Has either of you taken a break?" he asked.

Georgie shook her head. "There isn't that much more to do."

He had to admire her tenacity, for there was enough to keep the two of them busy for a week.

Kit, however, did not share her sister's dedication. She frowned at the large pile of ropes and lines, and then cast an annoyed look toward her sister. She was more than ready to call it a day.

"Those can wait until tomorrow," he told Georgie.

"Oh yes," Kit said, setting aside her work without hesitation. "I want to go look for my sketchbook. I lost it last night."

"I'll ask the crew and see if anyone has seen it," he offered.

Kit beamed. "Thank you, Captain Danvers." She glanced around the deck. "By the way, where is your brother? I haven't seen him."

"He's been assigned below. He's skimming out the waste in the bilge."

Kit's nose wrinkled in disgust. "Why, he'll smell like a—"

"Yes, it's my hope that a day or so below will help curb his tendency toward telling untruths."

"Untruths?" she asked, her attention now all his.

"Yes, at his age, he should know better than to go about lying to ladies."

Her eyes narrowed. "What lies would those be, Captain?"

Colin shrugged. He hated to hurt the girl or even embarrass her, but he suspected once she knew the truth, she'd be put out enough never to want to speak to Rafe again. Or at least for as long as the rest of their voyage.

He leaned forward and whispered into her ear.

As he suspected, his revelation as to Rafe's real age worked. Kit Escott might not look like her sister, but she shared her sister's fiery temperament.

"He's twelve?" she burst out, rising to her feet, her hands balled into fists.

Colin nodded.

"But he told me he was—" Her mouth snapped shut, her pert mouth drawn in a thin, cold line. "Are you positive? Twelve?"

He nodded again.

"Oh! I never!" she sputtered. "And he never will again, mind you." She stomped off toward the ladder, a woman vexed.

Georgie rose to her feet, watching her sister depart. "I couldn't have done it better myself."

"Do you think I hurt her feelings?"

She shook her head. "Oh, I think that was inevitable. But you've given her something to be indignant about, which in itself ought to soothe over her embarrassment. But I wouldn't want to be in your brother's shoes if he decides to venture into her path in the next few hours. You're likely to have to fetch him out of the water."

"It wouldn't be the first time," Colin told her.

They both laughed, and their shared good humor gave him the measure of hope, the prod to take that last hazardous step across the chasm and reach out to her.

"Georgie, I am so sorry. I've failed you in so many ways," he said.

She shook her head. "I haven't been much better."

"No," he told her, the depth of his regrets filling his words. "I failed you when I signed those betrothal papers. Pymm nearly had a fit of apoplexy when I asked him what sort of man he found Lord Harris to be. He's so furious over my mishandling of your betrothal that I doubt he'll ever forgive me—nor can I expect you, the most grievously injured person in all this debacle, to pardon my inexcusable indifference on the matter." He paused for a second. "Georgie, if I had known, I would never have allowed such a match, never have signed the betrothal agreement."

She started to say something, but stopped.

"I know, I know," he said. "I should have met you beforehand to see that you were indeed happy with the match, or at the very least I should have read the betrothal papers."

Her eyes widened, in what he guessed was a mixture of outrage and horror.

"You have every right to be furious, but in my defense, I was in a hurry. I was on my way to be—" He stopped short of telling her he'd been on his way to his own wedding. That could wait for another time. "My mind was on other matters. My father wasn't very good at managing his estates or his legal affairs. When he died, I inherited more than just a title; there was a rat's nest of paperwork."

She didn't look all that appeased by his explanation . . . well, his excuses.

"I know, I should have straightened out the tangle and paid more attention to what I was signing. But my solicitor assured me that your match to Lord Harris was a love match—"

"A what?" she burst out. "I'd have rather been married to a—"

"Yes, I'm well aware of that now. But given that Harris was willing to forfeit your dowry to your uncle for the privilege of your hand, I assumed he was in love with you."

Georgie's gaze swung up. "Say that again. My dowry? What dowry?"

"Your dowry. Whatever was left of your father's fortune at the time you married was to go into your and Kit's dowries. Now granted there wasn't much left given the lavish lifestyle you and Kit were raised in, but—"

She held up her hands. "Stop right there. You are jesting, aren't you? My father had no fortune, and as for lavish, I am frightened to think of what you might regard as frugal if you think the life we've lived has been lavish."

Now it was Colin's turn to shake his head. "You have me at a loss. I saw the bills submitted by your uncle. Tutors, milliners, stationery, gowns . . . *shoes,*" he said with a grin. "I'm no judge of lady's shoes, but that pair of yours is expensive—you can't argue that."

"Those shoes were borrowed. Or rather inherited. From Mrs. Taft."

"Then where did all the money go?" Colin wondered aloud.

"Uncle Phineas," he heard Georgie say in a low menacing tone that made him fear for the other man's life. "Why, that scurvy, no account, baseborn son of a—"

"Uh, uh, uh—" Colin warned. "Not in front of Chloe." He pointed at their daughter's crib.

Georgie bit back the rest of her curse. After she took a deep breath, she continued, but in no less restrained a fashion. "When I get back to London, I'm going to—"

"You mean *we*," Colin said. "We're going to get to the bottom of this. I suspect that your uncle and my solicitor conspired together."

"Perhaps I should inform my guardian," she teased. "I hear he is a ruthless fellow."

"Hardly ruthless when it comes to you. More like helpless." He held out his hand. "I think it is about time we were introduced. Truly and completely."

She started to hold out hers, but stopped. When he looked down to see why, he realized her hands were coated in tar from the ropes. They were probably blistered and sore as well. Hardly the silken, delicate fingers of a lady, but to him they led to heaven.

Ever so gently, he reached out and took her hand in his. "My name is Colin, Baron Danvers, of late Captain Danvers of the *Sybaris*, at your loyal and dedicated service, ma'am." He bowed low over her hand, and brought her fingertips to his lips.

One of the sailors above hooted and whistled, and soon most of the men were cheering and adding their own cries of appreciation for the lady who had saved their lives.

Georgie glanced above, her cheeks pink at the praise being showered down upon her.

Or was it Colin's attentions that were bringing such a pretty blush to her features? He hoped it was the latter.

"I am pleased to make your acquaintance, my lord. My name is Miss Georgiana Escott." She paused for a second. "Though it is rather sad to have to go back to being just Miss Escott."

"Why is that?" he asked.

"I was rather fond of being a widow."

"Ah yes, the poor Mr. Bridwick. Whatever did happen to him?" Colin teased.

"A fever," Georgie said, taking a step toward the rail, looking out over the waves and striking a melodramatic pose worthy of the best Covent Garden thespian. "It was rather heart-wrenching for a man so young to die so suddenly. We'd only been married a short time."

"A very short time, I gather," he muttered.

She shot him a sidelong glance. "Jealous?" A smile played on her lips.

"Extremely," he told her, drawing her into his arms. He ignored the rising cheers of his men and pulled her closer. "But rest assured, there will only be one man in your life from here on out. Besides, you won't be Miss Escott for long. Once we get to London, as your guardian, my first bit of business will be to see that you make another name change. To Lady Danvers."

"Is that an order?"

"No, a promise."

"Good," she said, tipping her chin up so her lips were just a hairsbreadth from his. "See that you keep it. I may even like marriage this time around."

With that, she pressed her lips to his. Her mouth opened, inviting him to venture forth, offering him her forgiveness, her understanding, her faith in him.

Colin didn't hesitate, swooping forward to claim her gift.

She moaned, soft and welcoming as his tongue sallied to meet hers. Her body melding to his, ever so willingly . . .

He would never let her go. Never again would he fail her. For if he lived to be a thousand years old, he wouldn't forget the feeling of triumph, of completeness at having Georgie in his arms again.

Then through the roar of his awakened blood, of his growing passions, he realized his entire crew was witness to their kiss.

Cheers and cries of encouragement surrounded them.

He broke away from her and immediately spied the dangerous gleam in Georgie's eyes at his abrupt departure. But then the din from his men must have registered for her as well, because she glanced up and around and acknowledged the noisy calls of approval with a whispered, "Oh my."

"I fear there are no secrets on a ship," he told her.

"So I've been told." She glanced around, her mouth pursed, her brow furrowed. "What if I were to take Chloe below. I'm sure it's time for her to go to bed." She sighed. "It's too bad I'm not the least bit sleepy." She slanted a glance at him.

"I could carry her cradle down for you." Then he grinned. "And I fear I'm not the least bit sleepy either."

Georgie leaned forward and whispered, "So I hoped."

* * *

When she'd dressed for the Cyprian's Ball, Georgie had felt more than a little bit of trepidation. Now she was terrified.

She'd gone to the galley and borrowed a chunk of lye soap from the cook. The gregarious Scot had also given her a small bucket of sand and water, so she could get the tar off her hands and face. Then in a gesture of true appreciation, he'd dug around in his stores and brought out a small jar of violet-scented lotion.

" 'Tis for my Lizzy back home," he'd confided. "But I think you'll be needin' it afore she does, lass."

She'd pulled out her only decent dress, the white muslin, and smoothed it out as best she could before she donned it. As a final touch, she unwrapped Mrs. Taft's shoes and tucked her feet inside them.

From the corner of her bunk, Kit let out a snort as Georgie smoothed and prodded her unruly hair for the hundredth time, as if she could poke it into some semblance of order. "It's not like he cares what you look like, nor are you likely to stay in that gown for very long."

"Kathleen Escott! What a scandalous thing to say," Georgie scolded, though she could hardly fault her sister for her astute insight. "I'm just having a late supper with Captain Danvers." She hastily went back to attempting to tame her hair.

"Supper. Is that what you call it?" Kit rolled on her back and snorted again. "I won't wait up for you."

"Call for me if Chloe awakens," Georgie said, blowing a kiss toward her slumbering daughter and one for her sister.

Just as Georgie started out of the cabin, she bumped into Rafe.

There was no doubt that he'd been wading in bilge water all day, for he stank to high heaven. But obviously the budding Lothario didn't realize his own odorous disadvantage—or that his brother had spilled the soup to Kit about his true age.

"Good evening, Miss Escott," he said as smoothly as if he were entering a Regent Street address and this was an afternoon social call.

"I wouldn't recommend seeing Kit tonight," Georgie warned him. "She's a little put out."

Just then Kit stuck her nose out the door, and her face turned a livid shade of red. She caught Rafe by the ear and yanked him into the cabin. Then the door shut with a decided slam and her sister started giving the boy a wigging he wasn't likely to forget anytime soon.

Georgie smiled and continued down the hall, fairly confident this would be the last time Raphael Danvers came calling on Kit.

Glancing down the corridor toward Colin's cabin, Georgie felt a thrill of anticipation run through her. With each step she took, her earlier fears fell to the wayside, as her heart beat in a wild tattoo.

Colin. She'd found her knight errant again. That he was Lord Danvers no longer mattered. She could well imagine that Uncle Phineas had brokered her marriage to Lord Harris. For if there was money at the root of all this, then there was no doubt in Georgie's mind who had his greedy fingers well dipped into the coffers.

She shook her head. Her father had left them a fortune. She and Kit had once been heiresses.

Woe be it to Uncle Phineas when they got back to London. She had no doubts that Colin would see the situation rectified, but she wasn't going to let her uncle escape a bit of her own retribution. Then she'd wash her hands of her faithless relations and be done with them forever.

According to Colin, there was enough money left from their father's estate, combined with what Mrs. Taft had left them, for Kit to have a decent dowry. And that, in Georgie's mind, was all that mattered.

For she had all the riches she needed right here in the simple fact that Colin loved her—with or without her share of the Escott fortune. It mattered naught to him, only that they be together for the rest of their lives.

He utterly and completely loved her.

Georgie grinned to herself at the miracle of it.

Why, she'd often fancied that he'd fallen in love with her the night of the Cyprian's Ball. Goodness knows, he'd stolen her heart in those few hours together.

Now it was time to see if that night was nothing more than a fanciful memory or if they could find a lifetime of magic.

She lightly rapped on the door. It slid open immediately, as if he had been awaiting her just as anxiously on the other side.

Colin swept into a low bow to welcome her. "Will you come in?"

She nodded and stepped across the threshold, feeling as if she'd left the rest of the world behind in the corridor.

Colin had dressed in the same coat and breeches he'd worn at the Cyprian's Ball. Though his cravat wasn't tied with the talented touch of a London valet, there was a reckless, rakish twist to it that lent him a devil-may-care quality. He'd also shaved, evidenced by his smooth jaw and the nick on one side.

She surmised that he must have spent the rest of his time cleaning his wrecked quarters, because they were once again tidy. The only sign of the French ship's damage was the boarded-over stern window. He'd opened the remaining window, allowing the gentle breeze of the Mediterranean to drift into the room, filling it with the fresh tang of the sea. In the distance, the moon rose, offering a single, shimmering track of light across the dark, restless waves.

Candles burned throughout the room, their flickering flames lending a final touch of magic to their evening.

"Your cook outdid himself," Georgie said as she walked around the laden table. There was a thick soup, a fragrant ham, fresh bread, two different puddings, an apple tart and a plate of cheeses. "I'm starting to think you are a pirate to have such fine fare."

"If you still think I'm the scourge of the Seven Seas, I hate to disappoint you." He took a deep breath and then stared her straight in the eye. "What I am about to tell you cannot leave this cabin."

Georgie swallowed and nodded. And when he continued, she learned the true story of Captain Danvers, his court-martial and how he'd come to gain the *Sybaris*. "That still doesn't explain the pirate fare," she teased, casting another glance at the laden table, while her mind digested the truth of the matter. Colin was a spy for Nelson . . . and England. And by the same token, now she was as well . . . whether he liked it or not.

"Men who are well fed and treated justly stay loyal." Colin paused. "Please don't feel too special, everyone is eating this tonight," he confessed.

She laughed, then suddenly she grew serious. "I have one other question that has bothered me all this time."

"Yes," he said, his tone suggesting that he feared she was going to expect him to reveal some deep dark secret.

Georgie grinned at him. "Those officers, the ones at the Cyprian's Ball, why did they call you Romulus? Have you an empire hidden away somewhere?" Though light in tone, she seemed to understand the depth of his relationship with Brummit, Paskims, and Hinchcliffe.

"Ah, Romulus and Remus. That is a long story."

Georgie picked up an apple from the tray and took a bite out of it. She held out the rest of the fruit and said, "Do we have the time?"

Colin reached over and plucked the tempting piece from her hand. "Now that I think about it, it is really rather brief. I was a midshipman with them. On the *Titus*. Hinchcliffe and I were infamous for trying to outdo each other; we both wanted so desperately to be promoted and gain our own commands. And so we gained the nicknames Romulus and Remus for our bickering and rivalries." He paused, and Georgie could tell he was reliving some private nightmare.

"And then something happened," she said softly.

He nodded. "Yes. In the West Indies. We were in a skirmish, and Hinchcliffe panicked. Anyone might have—but he nearly cost us the ship."

"And you reported what happened," Georgie said.

"I had no choice. There was an inquiry. I had to tell the truth."

"And he never forgave you."

Colin nodded. "Especially after I gained my command shortly thereafter."

"You do have a way of making enemies, don't you?" She paused for a second. "I suppose you would like to hear why I was at the Cyprian's Ball that night."

He shook his head. "I've got a pretty good idea why you were there."

Georgie cringed. "It was the only way I could avoid my betrothal. If I hadn't found you, and we hadn't—" She blushed at the flood of memories from that wonderful, passionate night.

"Yes, if we hadn't, you would be Lady Harris right now." It was Colin's turn to cringe. "Oh Georgie, I'm so sorry I drove you to such desperate lengths," he said, before his mouth curved with wolfish delight. "But I can't say that I'm all that remorseful that I helped you out of your dilemma."

They both laughed.

Georgie reached out and touched his sleeve. "Thank you for being so honest."

"I hope we both can be from now on. No more secrets, Georgie. I want nothing to stand between us."

"I'd like that as well," she managed to whisper. "No more lies, no more secrets."

Colin stepped forward and drew her tenderly into his arms. "I love you, Georgie. I love you with all my heart."

"You're not saying that just because I rescued you, are you?" she teased, reaching up with her hand to cradle his battered face. How she ached at the sight of the damage Bertrand's evil pair had wrought, but it pained her even more to know that his right eye was of her own doing.

He must have seen the regret in her eyes. "I'll heal. I can't say the same for my pride, but the bruises will fade."

"I suspect your pride will regain its former stature. Besides, I love you not just for your handsome face." She stood up on her toes and started to kiss him, and when she teetered on her shoes, he pulled her closer and steadied her.

"I think you wear these shoes on purpose," he said.

She grinned. "They do have a way of bringing us together." As her body pressed against his, all her memories of their night together came rushing forward.

Could it possibly be like that again? she wondered.

When he kissed her, she had her answer. Oh, it could. And mayhap even better.

"What about dinner?" she managed to ask. She wasn't hungry—at least not for food, but she wanted to know that he burned for her as she did for him.

"Later," he told her. "Much later." He swept her up into his arms and they tumbled into his bed, Georgie laughing in triumph, Colin groaning in misery when she landed on his ribs.

"How hurt are you?" she asked, sitting up and taking a quick study of the pained expression he was doing his utmost to hide.

"I'm well enough," he told her, casting her a sly wink before leaning over to kiss her. "I've waited over a year to find you, and I'm not going to let some banged-up ribs stop me."

Georgie pushed him down on the bed and started

unwinding his cravat. With that untied, she pulled and yanked his shirt over his head.

"Anxious, are we?" he asked, his hands twining around her waist, tugging her atop him.

She stared down at his now bared chest, her mouth falling open. "My goodness, you look like you've been run over by a coach-and-four."

His chest was a cacophony of colors, his right side badly bruised, while his left was only slightly discolored.

"Turn this ship around," she demanded.

"Whatever for?"

"If you don't intend to burn the *Gallia*, I do," she sputtered. "That bastard will pay for this. Why, I'll—"

"You'll do nothing tonight, my little vixen, but love me." He reached up and began plucking the pins from her hair.

With each one that came free, he sighed and growled, while Georgie relished the feel of having her hair tumble down.

And once he had loosened all of it, he wove his hands within the silken array and pulled her face down to his. "Love me, Georgie. Love me with all your heart."

His words mesmerized her, leaving her only too willing to do as he bid.

Closing the inches between them, Georgie pressed her lips to his. His mouth welcomed hers, and with a hunger that belied a need for food or sustenance, he kissed her deeply and impatiently. His hands left her hair, brushing it out of his way, as his fingers pulled at her bodice, edging it down over her shoulders.

He rolled them onto their sides, so their bodies touched in so many places—her breasts pressed to his chest, their hips moving together, their legs twining them together.

His mouth moved from her lips to nibble at her neck, to taste her bared shoulder, to nuzzle down to her breasts and suckle there.

"Having a child has only made you that much more beautiful," he murmured.

She sighed and arched back, reveling in his compliment and his touch. "Tell me more."

His fingers toyed again with her breasts, sending ribbons of desire coiling through her limbs, while his lips covered hers again, kissing her with a hunger that left her breathless.

The only thing she wanted now was for him to love her, thoroughly and completely.

"I seem to recall you liked this," he said, stripping off her gown and kissing her bared skin. When he realized she hadn't worn anything beneath her muslin, he laughed. "Presumptuous, aren't we?"

"Tired of waiting," she said, reaching out to pluck impatiently at the buttons on his breeches. When she had them open, she tugged and pulled them off, only to find that he too had forgone unnecessary clothes.

"And you call me presumptuous?" she teased, her hands closing over his manhood, welcoming the feel of his hardness beneath her touch.

He groaned at her eager strokes. "You've a wicked way about you, Mrs. Bridwick." His hand stroked her thigh, teasing her legs apart, kindling a fire of passion.

"I had a very good teacher," she said back. Her hips began to move on their own, following the beckoning touch of his fingers.

When she thought she wouldn't last another second under his lavish attentions, she caught him by the hips and rolled him on his back. Before he could even utter a word, she moved over and atop him, covering his hardness, taking it inside her, and letting the motion of the ship, of their passion, be her guide.

But the gentle seas outside were no match for the raging storm inside Georgie. She wanted a hurricane, a furious tempest to carry them along. Rocking back and forth, she carried them both along, riding the wild waves that were casting them to and fro.

Colin shared Georgie's wild urgency. He could almost hear the roar of the waves and howl of the wind, as she rode ahead of the storm. His own body trembled, every bit of it alive and tensed and ready. He wanted to breathe, but couldn't. He wanted to cry out, but couldn't, too intent was he on holding on to her hips, guiding her and urging her on, as they tumbled together into this glorious mayhem of their own making.

And then she found her release, her body shuddering, wrapping around him even tighter in a cataclysm of waves. Her lashes fluttered and then closed, while a wide smile spread across her face.

His own came only seconds later, the warmth spreading quickly from his body to hers, and leaving him spent and sated.

He wound his arms around her and pulled her down into his embrace, cradling her close to his body, enjoying the sound of her heart pounding in her chest, listening to her once again find her breath.

Kissing her lightly across her lips, her nose, the top

of her head, he murmured words and secrets that he'd wished he'd said that long-ago night. And holding her tight, he knew this time, he wouldn't wake up alone.

Georgie loved him, and was his for all eternity.

That they were surrounded by an entire sea helped matters considerably.

His little Cyprian could only flee to one place . . . back into his arms.

And nothing would ever part them again.

Chapter 16

Georgie's bliss ended several months later on the morning they were sailing up the Thames toward London.

She had been digging through Colin's trunk in a fit of domesticity, looking for any of his town clothes that needed a press or mending.

Not that she was a dab hand with a needle and thread, or an iron for that matter, but she felt the urge to make the attempt.

Digging around in the bottom of the battered sea chest, she found a piece of paper that whisked away every dream, every cherished moment she'd spent over the last three months in Colin's arms.

As she looked down at the sheet, she could only gasp.

A Special License to Marry is hereby granted to Colin, Lord Danvers, to wed . . .

She read it twice, then a third time searching for the name of his intended, but for some reason the bride wasn't named. Not that it mattered to Georgie, for the truth was there before her eyes: Colin had meant to wed another.

And it was dated the day of the Cyprian's Ball. The day they met.

She dug around a little more in the sea chest and found a miniature wrapped in a small silk pouch. It slipped into her hand, the cool silver frame chilling her to her very soul.

The face looking up at her was everything an elegant miss should be, delicate and demure. Whoever she was, the lady was a beauty, fair of feature, her blond hair framing her face in an array of perfect curls. Bright blue eyes stared out from beneath perfectly curled dark lashes, while her smile was both wistful and modest. A pearl necklace decorated her throat, while her dress bespoke rich style and infallible good taste.

Georgie knew immediately she was looking at the woman who was meant to be the next Lady Danvers.

Suddenly so many things fell together . . . the flowered boudoir at Bridwick House . . . the absence of servants . . . his reluctance to bed her at first . . . something one of the trio of officers had said. Hinchcliffe, she believed it was.

Perhaps I'll start calling on Lady Diana. I hear she's no longer engaged . . .

She had wondered who the lady was that night when she'd heard the name. Now she guessed she knew. And as she turned the miniature over, there lay her answer.

Lady Diana Fordham, 1798.

Georgie swallowed back a throatful of fear and anger.

Colin had been betrothed. He might well still be, for all she knew.

No more secrets, he'd said.

"No more secrets, my dead Aunt Sarah," she muttered. "We'll see about this."

She marched up the ladders and onto the quarterdeck. They were already well into the pool, the London cityscape passing by in all her glory of grime, haze, and hum of activity.

"There you are," Colin called out. "What have you been about? Nothing that should be keeping you from this."

He grinned and wrapped his arm around her, pulling her to his side.

They were moving closer to a slip now and there was a crowd of people at the dock, even a carriage or two nearby.

Possibly even this Lady Diana, Georgie thought. At that, she shook off his unwelcome touch and took a couple of prudent steps away from him.

Colin shot her a sidelong glance. "Whatever is the matter?" But before she could answer, something across the deck caught his eye and distracted him. He strode over to the railing, shouting orders, and even lending a hand, until everything was back in the meticulous order he expected aboard the *Sybaris*.

Too bad he didn't apply the same painstaking regard to his personal life, Georgie fumed.

He came back alongside her, grinning. "Now what has you in a state? And don't try to deny it; I can see you are vexed. Is it that nonsense about you staying at

Lady Finch's again? I'd have you in Bridwick House tonight, but there will be questions enough until I can get our marriage in order—"

"Would that be before or after you inform your betrothed that you've changed your mind?"

"My what—" he stammered.

"Your betrothed. Lady Diana? Obviously, somewhere between the Straits of Gibraltar and the Italian coastline you seem to have forgotten her." She held up the special license in one hand and the miniature in the other. "Do these help?"

Colin felt his heart sink. "Georgie, I can explain," he began. "Yes, I was betrothed to that lady, but she cried off."

"When?"

He cringed. Oh dammit. He'd meant to tell her about Lady Diana for the past three months, but there had never seemed a good time. And now . . .

"Are you certain she cried off, Captain Danvers?" Georgie was asking from her spot near the railing.

"Of course I'm certain," he told her. "She told me she never wanted to see me again."

Georgie had straightened and was staring down at the dock as the *Sybaris* moved into the slip. She glanced back over her shoulder at him and said, "Then you had best remind her, for she is here to greet you."

"What?" Colin crossed the deck in a flash, his hands grabbing at the rail as he nearly went over the side.

There indeed on the wharf stood Lady Diana, flanked by her father, the Earl of Lamden, and Colin's grandfather, the Duke of Setchfield. Behind this trio stood Temple, leaning negligently against their grandfather's well-appointed and polished carriage.

Colin couldn't believe his eyes. Lady Diana was shocking enough. But his grandfather? Temple had told him that the duke had ordered Colin banned from the Setchfield estates, his name stricken from the family annals after word of his court-martial had spread like wildfire through the London *ton*.

And now here the old codger was in all his regal glory, along with Lamden and Diana, like a happy wedding party.

What rattled Colin to his very core was the sight of his grandfather . . . smiling. The Duke of Setchfield smiling?

This did not bode well.

After a nudge from her father, Lady Diana began waving a handkerchief at Colin, albeit with little enthusiasm.

"Harrumph," Georgie snorted, turning on one heel and stomping across the quarterdeck. The crew scuttled out of her path, for now having sailed with the lady for several months, they knew well enough to steer clear of her when her face set like granite and her shoulders straightened with taut and unerring resolve.

Colin went after her, amidst more than a few muttered "a braver man than I" comments from his men. "Georgie, hold up there. Stop right this minute. This isn't what it seems."

"That your beloved and legally betrothed is standing on the docks, happy and ready to wed you at a moment's notice?" Georgie glanced back at his welcoming party and frowned. "I can see how I was confused. Now if you will excuse me, I must finish my packing."

"Cap'n?" Mr. Livett called out.

"Not now," he said.

"But I fear you must," Mr. Livett said, casting a speculative glance at Georgie's retreating figure, but not venturing any closer. "It's the excise man and the harbormaster to see you."

Colin muttered a curse under his breath and went over to the railing to meet with the dockside officials. Every once in a while he glanced over to see his grandfather beaming up at him with pride, while the Earl of Lamden looked more pleased than if he'd just been given the keys to the Treasury.

By the time he'd finished with the harbor officials, he turned around to find Georgie, Kit, and Chloe disembarking, along with Mr. Pymm.

"Georgie," he called out. "Where the devil are you going?"

"I don't think that is a matter of your concern any longer," she said, with all the wounded air of a martyr.

"Like hell it isn't. I'm going to marry you, not her. The minute I get this straightened out."

"Are you going to toss her over to wed me?" Georgie shook her head. "And when you tire of me, then what?"

"Don't be ridiculous," he told her, trying to catch her by the arm, but she shook him free.

Turning to face him, she glared at him. "Tell me this, Captain Danvers. Are you still legally betrothed to that woman?"

Colin took a deep breath. "Well, yes, in a manner of speaking, but—"

Georgie held up her hands to stave off any further explanations. "That is all I need to know. Good day to you, sir. And good-bye." With that, she went stomping up the dock, past his grandfather, Lady Diana, and the earl, without a second glance at any of them.

As she marched by Temple, his errant cousin did a double take, first at Colin then at Chloe, who was now wailing unhappily in her mother's arms, and finally his glance fell back on Georgie. His eyes narrowed, then his mouth fell open in shock.

Meanwhile, Georgie had hustled Mr. Pymm and her sister into a carriage and was instructing the coachman which bags were hers and where she wanted to be taken.

"Georgie!" Colin started after her but found his path blocked by his grandfather.

"My dear boy," the duke said, not about to surrender his position or be passed by. "Nelson feared you lost, and so did I. But now here you are, well and hearty. I can't tell you, my boy, how relieved I was when the Admiralty's messenger arrived not an hour ago with a note saying that your ship was coming into the pool. And see here, I've mended things with the earl and his lovely daughter, your dear betrothed." The crotchety old man grinned widely and Colin thought it might be the first time in his life the duke had dared turn his mouth in that direction.

Meanwhile, Temple ambled up and held out his hand. "That isn't the one from the—"

"Yes, it is, if you must know," Colin said. "Go after her. See that she reaches her lodgings safely."

"Certainly," Temple said. "But I expect a full accounting."

Colin cocked a brow at his cousin.

The man just laughed. "Never mind. I'll get the real

story from Pymm. He's always a stickler for details. Full reports and all." With a jaunty bow to his grandfather and the earl, and a tip of his hat and a scandalous wink at Lady Diana, he ambled toward the carriage, greeting Pymm in great style and insisting on accompanying his party into town.

Georgie shot Colin one more bereaved and piqued glance before she accepted Temple's assistance up into the carriage. Temple joined the party, and the crowded hackney rolled away from the docks.

"Grandfather," Colin said, "what is the meaning of all this?"

The duke lowered his usually booming voice to a dense whisper. "Lord Nelson wrote a confidential letter to me and one to the earl explaining the reasons behind your court-martial. Upon his word, I realized that you were acting with all the honor I'd expect of my grandson, and Lamden here is of the same mind. Your wedding can continue as planned." He clapped Colin on the back and turned to Lady Diana. "He's speechless, my girl. I told you he would be."

The Duke of Setchfield's carriage wasn't the only one waiting for the arrival of the *Sybaris*. For just up from the wharf sat a plain, nondescript hackney. The curtains were parted only slightly, but it offered the occupant an excellent view of Captain Danvers's homecoming.

"Damn Bertrand's idiotic hide," Mandeville muttered. "He let Danvers escape. I should have done away with the man when I had the chance."

Then as a woman came down the gangway, he nearly came out of his seat. Hardly the prisoner as she had claimed, Madame Saint-Antoine—if that was her name—appeared right at home on the London dock. And with her was the ship's surgeon, Phillips.

"Pymm," he whispered. "It must be."

"Who is it?" Mandeville's companion asked, straining to catch sight of their quarry.

"Pymm. I don't know why I didn't recognize him before, but I would never have thought the Foreign Office would send *him* out into the field after all these years." Mandeville sat back in his seat. "I assume he'll be off to Lord Sutton with my documents. Sutton is the best cryptographer they have. No matter. By the time they determine what we are about, the deed will be done." He rapped on the top of the carriage and instructed the driver to follow the other hackney at a discreet distance.

"And what about the woman?" the man beside him asked. "Isn't she the one in your drawing?"

Mandeville smiled and pulled the sheet out of his coat pocket. "So you noticed her as well. Good eye. And yes, she is. We'll have to eliminate her. Remember our family motto."

"No witnesses, Father. No witnesses," the man said, looking down at the picture of the lady once again, and wondering where he had seen her before.

Not that it really mattered. It wouldn't be long before she was dead.

Georgie and Kit went immediately to Lady Finch's town house in Mayfair. After writing their long-time family friend from Italy, Georgie had received a pointed letter from her, advising her that when she and her sister returned to London they were to take shelter at the Finch residence there. Mrs. Delaney, the house-keeper, had been advised to keep rooms at the ready for them, and Lady Finch's Aunt Estes was available as a chaperone.

Georgie wondered at the need for a chaperone, but Lady Finch was not one to overlook propriety, even for a ruined young lady with a child in tow.

Within hours of their arrival, Aunt Estes made her appearance, bags in hand. Yet after the lady had settled in for a cup of tea and a "chat," Georgie didn't mind her presence in the least. The affable old lady was only too thrilled to have new ears to delight with her vast repertoire of gossip, though she was hard of hearing and tended to shout her news with little thought of discretion.

As for Mr. Pymm and Lord Templeton, they had asked permission to use Lady Finch's library as a meeting place. Apparently the pair were well acquainted, and Georgie suspected that for all Temple's exaggerated manners and foppish antics, he was no fool.

Not if Pymm considered him invaluable to his efforts to stop Mandeville.

The two had summoned Lord Sutton to join them and the three had remained closeted away for hours, long into the evening. Messengers had come and gone at a furious pace, and Georgie knew they were trying to locate Lord Nelson, who had arrived in England a few days earlier. She only hoped they were able to warn him about the suspected plans before it was too late.

Outside of this hubbub of activity, Georgie found herself in the parlor overlooking the street. She paced about the room, half listening to Aunt Estes's chatter and pausing at the window each time she passed it, hoping to spy just one more visitor to the Finch house.

But the street remained empty.

Damn Colin's hide, she fumed for the hundredth time. Why hadn't he told her the truth?

In the corner, Kit sat happily ensconced on a stool with a brace of candles glowing at her side. In her lap was a brand-new sketchbook that the housekeeper had managed to find for her. After months without one, she was drawing furiously as if to make up for lost time. She'd never been able to find her other one, and Georgie suspected it had blown overboard.

The door opened and Mrs. Delaney brought in a tray laden with food. Behind her a maid and footman carried in additional provisions, including a full tea service. "I thought you might prefer to eat up here rather than all fancy-like at the table."

"Thank you," Georgie said. She didn't feel the least bit hungry, but imagined everyone else might not be so affected. "Have you taken in a tray for the gentlemen?" she asked, though she had no doubt the efficient housekeeper had seen to them as well.

"No need," called out Temple from the doorway. "We've come to join you."

Georgie made the introductions for Aunt Estes, who seemed to know everyone but Mr. Pymm. The talk started out inconsequential, but eventually the men fell into a debate as to how to proceed on their search for Mandeville.

"If only you could give me a better description of the man," Pymm said to Georgie.

She held up her hands. "I've done the best I can.

He's about average height. I think his hair was dark, but I couldn't be sure, as I only saw him in the vague light on deck and down below." She sighed. "I'm not very good at describing people—that's Kit's expertise, not mine."

Until now, Kit hadn't said much, between bites of cheese and a few sips of tea. She had been working frantically at her sketchbook. But now she paused and held up the drawing she'd been working on. "Did he look like this?"

Georgie grinned at her sister's deft drawing. "Exactly. That's him. How did you know?"

"When I bumped into him on the ship. I saw his face. I knew it would be important and wanted to get it down on paper, but I lost my sketchbook. I didn't want to say anything until I was sure I could capture what I remembered."

Georgie caught up the pad and stared down at it. "Oh, you've got the right of it. 'Tis perfect, Kit." She held the drawing up for Pymm, Temple, and Lord Sutton. "This is your man, gentlemen. Find him and you'll have found Mandeville."

The three men stared at the drawing, but from the blank expressions on their faces, none of them recognized the visage.

That is, until Aunt Estes glanced up from the evening paper. She'd been buried in the gossip column and had turned down Mrs. Delaney's repast until she'd determined who the "Lady S" mentioned there might be. "Who is this you are looking for?" She adjusted her spectacles and peered at the drawing. "Whatever do you want with Lord Cunningham?"

The room fell silent.

"You know who this is, madame?" Temple asked.

"Of course. That's Lord Cunningham. Though I daresay, that's a very flattering rendition. And while I haven't seen him in ages, I would know him anywhere. Oh my, there was a delicious scandal about his wife about a dozen or so years ago. She was having an affair with their neighbor, and her paramour's wife shot them *flagrante delicto* and then killed herself in the process of burning down their meeting spot. A hunting lodge or some other thing that bordered the two properties."

Georgie glanced at Mr. Pymm and he looked at her. "Mandeville," they both said.

"Oh no, that isn't right," Aunt Estes said. She tapped her chin and then smiled. "The family name isn't Mandeville, but—"

And when she said the name, suddenly all the pieces fell together.

Mr. Pymm nodded to Lord Sutton, who was already out the door calling for another messenger.

"What are they about?" Aunt Estes asked Georgie. "I can't hear a word they're saying."

Georgie leaned toward the lady's ear. "They are going to go find Lord Cunningham."

Aunt Estes leaned back in her chair. "They needn't go to such bother." She pointed at her paper. "It says right here that he is one of the guests at a dinner honoring Lord Nelson this evening at—"

Pymm was across the room and had the paper in hand before the lady could say another word.

"Lord Botham's residence. Tonight. A dinner to honor Nelson." He glanced up from the paper. "He'll do it tonight. Especially if he's heard that the *Sybaris* is returned." He plucked out his pocket watch and frowned. "We haven't much time. The guests are probably already arriving."

"I'm going with you," Georgie told Pymm. "And I'll brook no arguments."

Temple started to open his mouth, but Pymm held up his hand. "I wouldn't suggest it. She has a wicked right hook."

Temple grinned. "Yes, I believe I remember seeing a demonstration of that."

Pymm paused for moment. "It says here that the other guests will include Lord Danvers and his betrothed, Lady Diana Fordham. You won't make a scene if we should run into them, will you?"

"This is for England, sir," she told him. "Whatever happened between Lord Danvers and myself is of no consequence."

Kit rolled her gaze skyward, while Temple put his hand over his mouth to cover a suspicious fit of coughing.

"Truly, I don't care a whit about him," Georgie declared, though the idea of seeing Colin with his betrothed pained her more than she'd ever admit. "The only thing that matters is that we stop Mandeville."

"Who's this Mandeville? And what is he about?" Aunt Estes asked, as the men started grabbing up their coats and hats, and Georgie rushed from the room to catch up her cloak.

Kit rose from her seat, her eyes burning with excitement. "Mandeville is Lord Cunningham, and he means to murder Lord Nelson. Mr. Pymm and Georgie intend to stop him."

"What? Murder? And your sister is going along with these gentlemen? I say not," Aunt Estes declared.

Georgie had already donned her cloak and was tying on her hat. "I'm doing this to save England, to save Lord Nelson. And never you fear, I'll be safe, milady, with these gentlemen."

"England and Lord Nelson are no concern of mine. 'Tis your reputation. Whatever are you thinking, going out with these gentlemen unescorted?"

Colin stood in the long receiving line at Lord Botham's house, Lady Diana on his arm.

He'd only conceded to attend this dinner because Lord Nelson was the honored guest and it seemed the most expedient way to get to see the admiral and warn him as to what was afoot. The moment the *Sybaris* had been spotted, his grandfather had conveyed a request to Lady Botham to include his grandson and betrothed in the party. Since the duke was never naysayed, Colin's invitation was assured.

Pymm had sent word that they were working on the translation, and would dispatch anything they discovered the moment Lord Sutton managed to break the code.

The cagey agent hadn't included any information about Georgie.

Colin had spent most of the afternoon arguing with his grandfather over his betrothal, having informed the duke that he had no intention of marrying Lady Diana, that he'd fallen in love with another.

His grandfather wouldn't hear a word of it, and when Lamden and Lady Diana arrived to accompany them to the dinner for Nelson, Colin had promised his grandfather to at least see this evening through before he made any decisions.

But in truth, Colin was only putting his best face forward to humor his elderly grandfather, and gain this opportunity to have a heart-to-heart with Lady Diana. He'd already decided to inform her of his intentions to cry off the first private moment they got.

However, privacy was in short supply at Lord Botham's crowded house. The place was a complete crush, and Lord Nelson had yet to arrive.

It was as good a time as any, Colin mused.

"Lady Diana," he said. "Would you mind if we found someplace a little quieter and had a word in private?"

Her eyes lit up, and Colin felt the weight of guilt pull him under. He could only hope she hadn't had a change of heart in the ensuing months and wanted him to honor their previous engagement. Telling her the truth, that he loved another, wasn't going to be easy. No more easy than trying to get back into Georgie's good graces, he mused.

They worked their way through the crowd and out a side door. After a short trip down the hall, they ducked into a small parlor. Discreetly, Colin glanced back, realized no one was watching them, and closed the door.

When he turned to Lady Diana, she had already set down her reticule and was toying with her fan.

"Lady Diana, I want to say something—"

She held up her delicate lace and ivory fan and said, "Please don't embarrass us both by renewing your addresses. If you think that I am going to marry you, now or ever, Lord Danvers, I'm afraid you are quite mistaken."

* * *

ONE NIGHT OF PASSION 365

Georgie, Pymm, Temple, and Lord Sutton abandoned their carriage a few blocks away from Lord Botham's and started weaving their way through the traffic on foot.

Aunt Estes had nearly thrown herself in front of the door to keep Georgie from leaving unchaperoned, but finally they had convinced the lady of the gravity of the situation and the extenuating circumstances that precluded social niceties.

And though she'd agreed, she claimed that calamity was sure to follow a young lady as headstrong as Georgie.

"And you only met her today?" Temple had the audacity to ask Georgie as they dashed down the front steps to his waiting carriage. "You've made quite an impression already."

"Miss Escott has that way about her," Pymm added, as Temple's driver, Elton, snapped the reins and sent the horses bolting forward.

Georgie ignored them both. She was far too excited and impatient to care what anyone thought. They were going to capture Mandeville and save Lord Nelson.

Finally her parents' deaths would be avenged. And in the process, England's greatest hero would be saved.

And perhaps . . . she might even see Colin.

Oh bother, she told herself, as Elton sped the carriage through the streets, careening around one corner, then another. Some spy she made when all she could think about was her faithless lover. And when they got out of Lord Templeton's carriage into the choked streets, Georgie could think of nothing but of a similar night scene with Colin holding her hand.

As they approached the house, Georgie heard a distant voice calling out her name.

"Georgiana? Is that you, you troublesome chit? Come back here right this minute."

She glanced back down the street, and there across the way, coming up the sidewalk at a furious pace, were Uncle Phineas and Aunt Verena. Her uncle was waving his walking stick like a maniac possessed, while Aunt Verena went from fluttering her handkerchief to dabbing her eyes with the lacy cloth.

She turned from the frightening thought of a possible reunion with her relations to the trouble Temple was having gaining entrance for them to Lord Botham's. Apparently any number of the *ton* had been crashing parties that Nelson was rumored to be attending, just for the opportunity to say they had met England's newest hero, so Botham's servants had been instructed to be vigilant against the uninvited.

And the majordomo was taking his job very seriously.

"My good man," Pymm ranted, " 'tis a matter of life and death. Do you hear me? Death!"

The man shot Pymm a look of pure dismay and closed the door in their faces.

"This way," Temple said, dodging back through the crowd outside and down the block. Lord Sutton declared he would wait out front for the authorities and in case Mandeville had yet to arrive.

"Oh, where do you think you are going, miss?" Uncle Phineas called out, from where he was trapped in the middle of the street between two carriages. "You won't escape your responsibilities to your family, you selfish girl!"

"What is all that about?" Temple asked, glancing

over his shoulder as Uncle Phineas railed on and on at the driver to move his confounded conveyance out of their way.

"I haven't the vaguest notion," Georgie said. "This night seems to be bringing out all types."

They came to a garden wall and a locked door, but it was no match for Temple, who pulled a long narrow piece of metal out of his boot and started toying with the lock.

Georgie stared wide-eyed at the man's skill, for in less than a few seconds the door swung open.

Temple shrugged and they made their way through the garden and slipped into the ballroom. No one noticed their arrival, as all eyes were on the arched doorway beyond, where Nelson was making his entrance.

"At least he's still alive," Pymm muttered. "Now to find Mandeville." He turned to Georgie. "Do you see him?"

She shook her head. "I can't see a thing over all these people."

Temple pulled a chair out of an alcove and pushed it next to her. "I don't care how it looks. Get up on this and give us a good survey of the room."

Georgie scrambled up and looked around. With all the feathers and hats and bewigged gentlemen, it was hard to tell one person from another, but suddenly, she saw him.

Mandeville. Otherwise known to the *ton* as Lord Cunningham.

"He's over there," she said to Temple. "To the right of Nelson." She glanced again, and realized the man had two glasses of wine, and that he was heading straight for the admiral. Something about the color of the wine and the way he smiled as he carefully carried the glasses sent a cold shiver through Georgie's heart. "Oh dear. I believe he means to poison Nelson. Do stop him. Stop him now."

Temple and Pymm shoved and pushed their way through the crowd. A great commotion followed in their wake, and both Nelson and Mandeville looked up to see what the disturbance coming in their direction was about. In that moment, Mandeville spied Georgie on her perch, and his cold smile changed to one of fury. He turned to flee, but it was too late.

Pymm caught the evil man by one arm, while Temple seized the other. The murderous glasses of wine crashed to the floor. They wrestled with Mandeville for a few more seconds before Temple succeeded in knocking him unconscious with a tremendous blow.

Georgie watched as Pymm knelt down and dipped his finger into the spilled wine. He placed a tiny drop on his tongue and shivered. When he looked in her direction, he nodded.

The wine had indeed contained poison.

As Temple and Pymm carried Mandeville out of the room, Georgie started to climb down from the chair, fully intending to join her friends, but a rough hand caught her and pulled her down the rest of the way.

"Be quiet and do exactly as I say," a man told her.

She was going to protest despite his threats, but felt the cold, hard muzzle of a pistol being jabbed into her ribs. She glanced up at her captor and said, "Commander Hinchcliffe. Why am I not surprised."

"None of your saucy tongue, whore," he told her, dragging her along the side of the room. "Your friends have my father, and now I have you."

* * *

Colin and Lady Diana's tête-à-tête was interrupted by the arrival of Pymm, Temple, and Lord Nelson dragging an unconscious man into the study.

"Well, this is cozy," Temple said, as the twosome sprang up from the couch. "Here we are saving the world and you two are off giving the cats of this city more scandal to lap at."

" 'Tis hardly that," Lady Diana said. "Your cousin and I were reaching an understanding."

Colin nodded. "We don't love each other, and we certainly don't want to get married."

"And while you two were coming to that inevitable realization, your Georgie, Pymm, and I were doing the hard work." Temple nodded at Mandeville, whom Nelson and Pymm were binding to a chair with a drapery cord. "May I introduce Mandeville?"

"Georgie?" Colin asked. "Georgie is here?"

Temple glanced up at the ceiling. "Yes, you lovelorn fool. She's in the ballroom, but be forewarned, she's in a rare mood."

"I expected as much." Colin turned to Lady Diana. "Let me take you back to your father, so I can—"

"—get married to the right lady," Lady Diana said, smiling at him.

They started for the door, but it opened on its own. Out in the hallway, there echoed a ruckus from down near the front door, but that was nothing in comparison to the sight barreling into the study in a wild flurry of muslin. To his amazement and delight, Georgie stumbled forth.

Colin was about to catch her, when he realized she wasn't alone.

"Hinchcliffe?" he said, as he saw his old friend, and now nemesis, had a hold of Georgie's arm and a pistol pointed at her head.

"Ah, Romulus," Hinchcliffe said. "I should have known you wouldn't be too far away from your bitch."

Georgie struggled and twisted at Hinchcliffe's grasp, but he held her tight.

"Tell her to remain still, Romulus, or I'll kill her right now." Hinchcliffe's eyes were wild, unfocused, his mouth tight and deadly.

"Georgie, do as he says," Colin pleaded.

She frowned, but at least she stilled. Then she caught sight of Lady Diana behind him. Her face pinked in outrage, but luckily for all of them she held her tongue.

"Let her go, Remus," Colin said. "She has nothing to do with the business between us."

"*Au contraire,*" the man said. "She has everything to do with it. She is the one who betrayed my father." He nodded over at Mandeville. "And I intend to see she pays. Pays for what her father did to my mother by joining her murderous parents in hell."

"Mandeville and Hinchcliffe?" Colin said, glancing over at Pymm, who nodded in confirmation.

"Yes, my father. He raised me to follow in his footsteps as his father did before him, and as every Hinchcliffe son has done for five generations—serve the glory of France."

From over in the chair, Mandeville stirred. His head lolled from side to side, and then his eyes opened and focused on the scene before him.

A sly, wolfish smile turned his lips.

"Untie him," Hinchcliffe said. "Untie him now!"

Pymm shook his head. "No."

Georgie's mouth opened to the size of a platter.

"I'll kill her," Hinchcliffe said. "I'll kill her right before your eyes."

"Just like your father did to your mother," Georgie shot over her shoulder at him.

Hinchcliffe's eyes narrowed.

"Yes. You heard me," she said. "Your father murdered your mother. I saw it all. He killed her for running away with evidence that he was a spy. And then he shot my father and killed my mother when she happened along."

"She's lying," Mandeville cried out. "She couldn't have been there. I was—"

"Alone?" Georgie spat back at the older man. "Hardly. I was hidden inside the hollow of an oak tree. I saw everything. You shot your wife without blinking an eye." She turned to Hinchcliffe. "He killed your mother; it was not my father. He lied to you when you arrived. You were carrying a small tin lantern. When you tried to go toward the fire, your father stopped you, and when you protested, he struck you. Across the face. I was there." Defiant and glorious, Georgie's words rang with a truth that tore through the room like a hurricane.

Colin could see the doubts rising in Hinchcliffe's eyes, the uncertainty in his wild gaze. And now all Colin needed was for him to become just a little more distracted, and he'd have an opportunity.

And suddenly he had it.

Outside the room, the disturbance in the hallway grew louder and more boisterous.

"I tell you, my niece is in there, and I mean to see her now!"

The door came banging open, bouncing into Hinch-cliffe and sending him stumbling forward.

Colin lunged into the fray and pulled Georgie out of Hinchcliffe's grasp even as the pistol fired.

He and Georgie toppled to the floor. For one horrible second, Colin feared that she'd been shot. His love, his life, the only woman he wanted to marry.

"Georgie, Georgie, my dearest girl, are you hurt?" he said, his hands roaming over her body, turning her to and fro, searching for any sign of blood.

"I'm fine, Colin," she said.

They stared at each other, and Colin had never seen a sight more blessed than her angry dark gaze.

"Now unhand me, you wretched scoundrel."

"Never," he told her, and pressed his lips to hers in a hard, demanding kiss. At first she fought him, but slowly and eventually, she gave in, surrendering herself to him.

When they came up for air, they found Hinchcliffe sobbing at the foot of the chair that held his now dead father.

The bullet meant for Georgie had pierced Mande-ville's heart.

And from the doorway, Uncle Phineas stood gaping at the chaos he'd wrought.

"Dammit, gel, what is it with you and sailors?" he said.

Epilogue

The Sybaris
1814

"**G**eorgie! Dammit, where are you?" Colin thundered, striding up and down the decks of the *Sybaris*. He turned to his ship's master, Mr. Livett. "I know she's here. I just know it. I caught her eavesdropping when Temple called last night with Pymm. I'd bet my last inch of sail she's aboard."

"The men have searched everywhere, Cap'n. All her usual spots and some I wouldn't put past her," Livett said, with the resigned nature of a man defeated. "Perhaps her ladyship decided to leave you be this mission."

Colin snorted. "And you searched *all* the holds?"

Livett nodded.

Colin glanced at the river flowing around them. If they didn't leave now, they'd lose the advantage of the tide. He had no choice but to sail.

And so he gave the orders, looking again toward the docks where his wife should be standing waving her farewells. Instead there were only a few hands and the regular riffraff one found around the London waterways.

The *Sybaris* slid into the river, her sails catching the wind, her sleek lines riding the tide, and moving with an eager elegance out of the pool.

For the rest of the day, Colin held his breath, waiting for his wife to come popping out of some hidey-hole or another, but Georgie was nowhere to be seen.

Perhaps he had indeed outfoxed his wife and sailed before she'd been able to sneak aboard.

Not that he liked sailing without her, for he cherished having her at his side. She understood his love of the sea, it was one of the many things they shared. But this trip was different. There were rumors afloat that Napoleon, safely held on Elba, was planning to flee. The *Sybaris* was being sent to keep a watchful eye on Bonaparte and report anything irregular back to London.

And if need be, to stop the wily Corsican from making good on his vow to return to France.

Once they had cleared the river and started into the Channel, Colin finally breathed a sigh of relief, and with the sun well set, decided to head to his bed for some much-needed rest.

His cabin was dark when he entered, but he hardly needed a lamp. He knew every inch of it by heart, pulling off his boots, his breeches, and his shirt en route to his bed and a well-deserved respite. But on his final step, he stumbled, tripping over something. He felt around until his hands came upon the culprit.

A lady's shoe.

"Georgie!" he said, getting into his bed, his hands wrapping around the naked and glorious body of his wife. "How the devil—"

"Sssh!" she whispered, her lips meeting his in a kiss meant to silence his protests. "I thought you'd never give up looking for me and come to bed."

Oh, he knew her tricks. After all these years of marriage, he knew his Georgie girl only too well. But he had to admire her tenacity. And her resourcefulness. They were just two of the myriad things he loved most about her.

And so he gave in to what she offered, making love to her, reveling in the joy he found each time he held her in his arms.

As the dawn started to come across the horizon, spilling its soft light into Colin's quarters, he awakened to find Georgie standing before the open stern window, gazing out at the sea she loved so very much.

He'd been a fool to think he could ever keep her at home. Keep her free from the danger in which his work for the Admiralty and the Foreign Office so often placed him.

"How did you do it?" he asked, rising from their bed and pulling on his breeches before he joined her at the window, stepping carefully over the shoes she'd left discarded in the middle of the room.

Her own personal calling card, those shoes.

Her blond hair fell in an unruly tangle, ruffled by the salty breeze. He reached out and tucked a strand up into the hasty collection of pins she'd used to capture her curls.

"So how did you get aboard?" he asked again.

She turned and grinned at him. "If I told you, that would ruin the surprise of it."

"I'm going to stop sailing on the *Sybaris* and start using the *Gallia* for these missions." He'd captured the *Gallia* years earlier from its inept captain, Bertrand, and placed the ship-of-the-line into the service of his own private fleet of spy ships.

"Then I'd commandeer the *Sybaris* and come after you," she said.

"You would." He kissed her deeply and thoroughly. "And I'd do the same thing I've done every day since the first night I met you, my dearest Cyprian."

"What is that?" she murmured, laying her head on his chest.

"Surrender."

Author's Note

While I know of no French plot to assassinate Lord Nelson, he was eventually killed by a French sharpshooter at the Battle of Trafalgar. His death was a tremendous loss to England, and to his ladylove and mistress, Emma, Lady Hamilton.

I have strived to use as much accuracy aboard the *Sybaris* as possible, and would like to thank naval expert and author Ron Wanttaja for his unstinting assistance. If you would like to learn more about this time period, visit his website at *http://www.wanttaja.com*.

I hope you've enjoyed *One Night of Passion*. Watch for Temple's outrageous adventures, coming next year.

All my best wishes,

Elizabeth Boyle